# Nearly Departed

## by

## Suzanne Rossi

**Nearly Departed**

Cover Art by *Tamra Westberry*

The Wild Rose Press
PO Box 708
Adams Basin, NY 14410-0706
Visit us at www.thewildrosepress.com

Publishing History
First Faery Rose Edition, 2010
Print ISBN 1-60154-867-2

Published in the United States of America

**"Are you aware romance novels accounted** for over fifty-three percent of all mass published paperbacks sold last year, and almost forty percent of all books?"

He cleared his throat. "Really?"

"Yes, really. If a man wants to understand a woman, he should read a romance. They have wonderful insight into how we think and what we feel."

"I don't think any book ever published can do that. Men are simple. We have simple tastes and don't beat around the bush. Women, on the other hand, think too much. There is no way a man can ever understand a woman."

Boy, his ex-wife must have been a pip.

Max looked at his watch, and then finished his beer. "I've got to get back. I feel more like a referee today than a boss. Had a couple of guys call and quit this morning."

He helped me pack everything and carried it back the way we'd come. Instead of entering the house through the back, we strolled around to the veranda, mounting the steps to the door. He set the bag down, and lightly grasped my shoulders.

"Thank you for a wonderful lunch, Cybil. You know, you're quite a girl." He leaned down and gave me a brief but hard kiss, and then disappeared inside.

When he left, I placed my hand against the wall until my legs stopped shaking. Deep breaths helped also. Finally, I picked up the bag of leftovers and walked inside.

In spite of his commitment problems and lack of understanding about my career, Max Maitland was the man for me. Now, how the hell did I convince him?

## Praise for *NEARLY DEPARTED*

*NEARLY DEPARTED* finaled
in the following 2006 contests:

Indiana Romance Writers Golden Opportunity,
Lowcountry Romance Writers Jasmine Contest,
and
River City Romance Writers Duel On The Delta.

# Dedication

I love ghost stories. Always have. I think I lived in a haunted house in Rockford, Illinois. Strange noises and my shih-tzu barking at nothing on the staircase made me wonder enough to do research. Ten years later, the research paid off.

*Nearly Departed* was born after a couple of martinis made me play the "what if" game. Cybil evolved quickly. Max soon followed. I love both characters, but it's the ghosts who hold my heart. I wish they lived with me.

So this is for my otherworld companions, Ruth, the Colonel, Hester, Antoine, and Zoë. May you all exist somewhere other than in my imagination.

And I must thank my wonderful husband, Bruce, who while sometimes exasperated still understands.

Also a big thank you to my editor, Sarah Hansen, who helped me weed out the bad and re-write the good.

Thanks to all.

## Chapter One

*Lord Edgeware stood over his vanquished opponent, the barrel of his dueling pistol just inches from the man's forehead. The Duke of Wakefield glared with hate-filled eyes.*

*"Now I have you, Duke. Sign this confession telling how you disgraced my family or die!"*

*"No!" a voice screamed from across the room. The duchess flew to her husband's side. "I beg of you, no!"*

*"M'lady, remove yourself. I have no quarrel with you," he said in a chivalrous tone.*

*"Lord Edgeware, it is my fault. I told the lie," the lady swore, hands clutched against her breast.*

*"Madam, there has been bad blood between our families for generations. Now, step aside while I..."*

The doorbell rang.

I leaned back and shifted my gaze from the computer screen to the ceiling. Why is it every time I'm in a pivotal passage, I get interrupted?

A glance at the clock had me shaking my head. Nine-thirty in the morning? I was tempted to ignore it, but whoever was there leaned on the bell again— longer this time. Heaving an irritated sigh, I rose and stomped to open the door.

It was Martha Stewart.

"Oh, hello, Mother." I inhaled a deep breath and automatically avoided making eye contact.

"Cybil, are you going to let me in or leave me standing on the doorstep like the Fuller Brush man?"

My mother grew up in Memphis during the fifties and can remember when salesmen came door-

1

to-door. She often makes references to long-forgotten cultural phenomena during casual conversation.

I stepped back, muttering, "Sorry. Why are you here so early?" Mother pops in whenever she feels like it.

She looked me over from head to foot, disappointment in her eyes. "Aren't you ready yet?"

"Ready for what?"

"To go shopping, of course. I called and reminded you yesterday. Don't you ever listen?"

Mother lives for two purposes in life: to control her family and to shop.

"Why do I need to go shopping?"

She sighed and got that martyred expression on her face. "Your cousin Jody is graduating from junior high school tomorrow, and of course, you're going to want to wear something new. Now hurry. We're already behind schedule."

Mother lives and dies by schedules. She makes lists for everything and expects everyone else to do the same.

"Mother, I'm not going."

"Don't be silly. Of course you are."

Did I mention my mother and I don't have the coziest of relationships? She intimidates the crap out of me. Always has and always will. I've never won an argument with her.

I attempted to stand my ground. "I can't. I'm too busy. I have to get the rewrites finished on my manuscript. I'm two weeks late. My editor is screaming. The Lord Edgeware series is doing well, and she wants this book. Besides, it's not like Jody is *real* family."

I wanted to bite my tongue. Mother's straight spine stiffened.

"How can you say that? Jody's been a member of this family ever since her mother married your second cousin, Albert. That makes her kin. You can write your little book when we get back. I talked to Aunt Violet last night. She said Sally Dodd's brother is in town and will attend."

Ah, now I got the drift. This had nothing to do with extended family, but with my unwed status. For Mother, this was subtle.

"Mother, why should I care who attends this shindig?"

The martyred look deepened. "Cybil, I know you make some money from your writing—it's a nice little hobby—but you are thirty years old and still unmarried. People talk. Nothing would give me greater pleasure than to have you settled down and raising a family."

Mother never acknowledges that my writing is important or a career. And when she says, "settled down," she means living close to her so she can meddle. We'd had this conversation before—many times. The beginnings of a headache tapped in my temple.

"I don't care what other people think."

"Well, you should." She smoothed an already smooth strand of hair. "It's bad enough I have to keep dodging questions about your brother."

"Mother, Daryl is gay. Accept it."

"Nonsense. He's just going through a phase."

Mother refuses to face reality about things she doesn't understand or can't control. To the family, she refers to his partner, Steve, as "Daryl's friend," but to acquaintances, "Steve" becomes "Stephanie." She delicately wiped a tear from her eye with a lacy handkerchief. No tissues for Lilith Austin. I caved, just like always. We'd both known I would.

"All right. I was in the middle of a scene. Give me a couple of minutes to finish, and then we'll go shopping."

"And lunch. I told Penelope and Francine we'd meet them at Rosie's Tea Room."

Swell. Just what I needed—my two older sisters yammering in my ear about my perceived shortcomings.

Mother sat on the sofa while I returned to the office. She always got her way by refusing to take no for an answer. She'd long ago perfected the art of manipulation and used guilt to keep us kids in line.

I plunked my fanny in front of the computer and reread what I'd written, then hit the delete key.

Garbage. Total garbage. The noose of mother-love tightened around my neck. If I didn't want to become a Germantown housewife concerned only with soccer games, gymnastics classes, and trying to keep one step ahead of my friends when it came to ostentation, I had to do something drastic, and soon.

****

"Cybil, you are driving me nuts!"

I shot a glance at Julie Aldridge, my best friend since grade school, and heard the frustration in her raised voice.

Julie is one of those people who are frighteningly efficient at everything. She has no problem multitasking and juggling several projects at the same time. I wish I could hate her. Julie is also the hottest real estate agent in Memphis, which is why I now sat in her Lexus.

"I'm driving you nuts? How?"

"Two months ago, you called and begged me to find a house far enough away from your mother so she couldn't just pop in on you. That ruled out Germantown, Cordova, and Collierville."

"Of course. I timed the distance from her house to those cities. The longest drive took only twenty minutes."

"First, you wanted to locate downtown on either the riverfront or Mud Island, so we looked at condos and villas. You couldn't decide. Then, you thought perhaps a little house in Midtown near your brother would do, and we scoured the area. You changed your mind. We ended up back downtown in the old warehouse district inspecting lofts. Now we are in Mississippi, and I'm not sure what we're looking for. Cybil, for God's sake, make up your mind."

I didn't blame Julie for her outburst. As usual, I had gone into this house-hunting thing with no clear idea of what I wanted or where to go. Although, regarding the latter, I harbored a feeling my best buddy had a suggestion.

I'd called Julie the day after the graduation fiasco. I'd left after an hour, much to my mother's displeasure. I felt guilty for a week.

"I'm looking for a place that's *me*. When I find it, it'll talk to me."

"There is no such thing. Houses are property—investments. As much as I'd like to make a sale, I have to think you'd be better off in your apartment."

"But my mother will continue to harass me."

"Then tell her to stop. You're a grown woman. Start acting like it. Quit being a wimp."

"I am not a wimp!"

"You're a doormat. You allow your mother and sisters to walk all over you."

"That's not true." Of course it was true. I just didn't like hearing it.

"Last spring, while you were meeting with your editor in New York, your mother came into your home and totally redecorated. You thanked her even though you hated it. Now, *that* is being a doormat."

*Zing*—the arrow found its mark. I prefer the sleek lines of metro contemporary or whatever it's called. I returned after a week to a house filled with country kitsch, florals, and plush sofas and chairs. I hate it.

"Julie, what could I say? It was a birthday gift. I was raised to never say anything negative about a gift. I couldn't hurt Mother's feelings. It would have been rude."

"It was rude of her to just come into your house and change things without your permission. Good grief, you call her Martha Stewart behind her back."

"Well, she looks like Martha Stewart."

"Your mother is a Martha Stewart clone. I've never seen such a devoted fan in my life."

She was right. Mother looked, decorated, and cooked just like Martha. I squirmed, trying to practice family loyalty.

"Our family holidays could step right off the pages of *Martha Stewart Living.*"

Everything my mother did was Martha Stewart perfect. It was a gift, and she was good at it.

"Cybil, your mother wrote a letter to the mayor of New York, protesting when the woman was sentenced to prison. That's obsessive."

"She was upset."

Julie shot me a glance. "Oh, Cybil, I'm sorry. I didn't mean to criticize. You get enough of that. I just keep hoping someday you'll grow a backbone." She slammed on the brakes, stopping in the middle of the road. "Where the hell are we?"

Julie, lost? Miss Perfect? I could sling a few arrows of my own. "I have no idea. You're driving."

I looked around and had to admit, I had no clue where we were either. The paved road stretched in front of us. For miles in every direction, I saw nothing but cotton fields and the occasional clump of trees indicating a house. The car's air conditioner blasted in my face, but outside, shimmering heat waves rose, and then hovered over the fields and asphalt.

"I think you should have turned left instead of going straight back at the last four-way stop."

Julie drove on. "I'll turn around in the next driveway."

Less than a mile later, the opportunity

presented itself. She pulled into a weed-choked drive. Two dilapidated brick pillars sat on either side about thirty feet off the road. A cement sign implanted in the bricks read "Shady Oaks." Attached to each pillar was a gate, the kind that meets in the middle. The hinges of one gate had rusted through and that half had fallen into the driveway. The other hung by a thread, sagging. The next strong wind would do it in.

Julie started to back out when I yelled, "Stop!"

She jammed on the brakes again. "What?"

"Look," I said, pointing to the base of one of the pillars. There, poking through the weeds stood an old, rusting For Sale sign.

"Cybil, no." She spoke in a voice usually reserved for her dogs.

I dug in my purse for a pen and the little notebook I always carry. Who knows when a writer's muse will show up? I scribbled the faded phone number in it.

"Come on," I wheedled. "Just drive over the gate on the ground. It won't hurt to take a look. Shady Oaks—doesn't that sound peaceful?"

"It sounds like a rest home, which I seriously believe you need."

"Are you or are you not my real estate agent? And as such, aren't you supposed to show me houses? Well, I want to see this house." If I planned to quit being a wimp and a doormat, I might as well start now.

With ill-concealed exasperation, Julie drove over the fallen gate and up the barely discernable path. Years ago, it must have curved gracefully among sheltering trees and beautiful shrubs. Now, it twisted through a jungle of overgrown vegetation, including kudzu, a fast-growing vine that can cover a small child in a matter of hours.

Then rounding the last bend, we drove into what

was left of the yard. I never noticed. The house rose majestically before me. I'd found what I sought.

"Holy shit!" Julie exclaimed.

I didn't blame her. The place looked like something out of *Gone With the Wind* after Sherman marched through. Over the years, the painted brick had faded and peeled off in places, giving the house a blotchy appearance. A porch—no, a veranda—stretched across the front supported by four huge columns. The floor sagged, but the roof shading it seemed straight enough. The name Shady Oaks came from four magnificent live oaks shading the immense side yard with huge hundred-and-fifty-year-old branches.

I got out of the car and tripped over a shutter lying in the grass. I looked up. Only one shutter remained attached, hanging drunkenly from an upper story window.

"Cybil, be careful," Julie warned from behind me. "This place looks like it could disintegrate at any moment. Don't go any farther."

I ignored her and mounted the steps. The veranda floor gave under my weight. I didn't expect the house to be unlocked, but placed my hand on the doorknob anyway, turned it, and pushed. The hinges broke. The door crashed into the foyer, stilling the chirping insects and sending birds into frantic flight.

"Oh, my God. Cybil, let's get out of here. It's dangerous."

No way. The house owned me now. The foyer ran from front to back. Through the broken panes of the French doors at the rear, I saw a patio or terrace. I wrinkled my nose at the smell of musty mold and dust, and then promptly sneezed.

I investigated the ground floor, my imagination taking off. In my mind's eye, I pictured ladies in hoop skirts and gallant gentlemen having tea, presenting musicales, while damning all Yankees to hell and beyond.

Julie flatly refused to go upstairs, but I had no qualms. I counted seven bedrooms and one bath, which looked to have last been remodeled sometime in 1960.

I came back down and announced, "I'll take it."

Julie's jaw dropped to her knees, and she forgot everything she'd ever learned at real estate school.

"Cybil! You're crazy. You can't do this. It's insane."

She grabbed my shoulders and shook. How about that? I, Cybil Austin, had managed to unglue the most efficient, put-together woman in Memphis, Tennessee.

"Julie, I know it's in bad shape, but I can't help it. The house talks to me." I handed her the phone number. "Be a dear and call. Find out how much they're asking and negotiate. I'll be in the drawing room."

I heard Julie talking with someone, but didn't pay much attention. I was too busy mentally arranging furniture, fantasizing about parties and where I'd put the Christmas tree.

Then it hit me. *Oh, God, what will Mother say?*

****

I fingered the business card in my hand and read the inscription again: *C. Maxwell Maitland, General Contractor, Renovations and Repairs.* He'd come highly recommended by the local real estate agent.

"What does the 'C' stand for?"

"Doesn't matter. Everyone calls me Max." I looked up into Max Maitland's smiling brown eyes and knew I could trust him, in spite of the funky little flutter in the pit of my stomach. I couldn't tell if it was nerves about what I'd undertaken or the sexy aura the man exuded.

"Well, Mr. Maitland, what's the bad news?"

"Max," he said, shaking his head. "You need to replace the roof. It's over forty years old and leaking. Thank goodness there's not too much damage yet. It has to be fixed. The good news is I saw no big holes or evidence of critters taking up residence."

"Lack of critters is good. What do you suggest?"

"Shingles would be the cheapest, but there are a lot of new materials on the market you might want to explore. A metal roof would last damn near forever. You'd pay for it, though. They're not cheap."

"How long do shingles last?"

"A good quality shingle should last twenty years."

"Mr. Maitland, I'm on a budget and twenty years sounds like a long time. I'd better go with shingles."

"No problem. I can have a crew out here on Monday morning. And it's Max. My father is Mr. Maitland."

My heart did a stutter step and my stomach fluttered again when he smiled. "Wow, Monday? That's only four days. What about the building permits and such? I haven't even applied for one yet."

"I'll take care of everything. I can run into Cherokee, take Billy Bob Benson to lunch, and have the permits by late afternoon."

"That soon?"

"I grew up with Billy Bob. He does double duty as head of the building department and county commissioner. There's not much call for a building department, so the paperwork doesn't take long."

I had to forget about the bureaucracies of Memphis. I was in rural Mississippi where they did things differently. Besides, the thought of confronting county officials scared the crap out of me.

"Thank you, Mr. Maitland. I'd appreciate that.

What about the rest of the house?"

"Max," he said again, and then proceeded to give me a rundown on the repairs needed. "All you need to occupy the house is a working bathroom and kitchen. We can start on the kitchen while doing the roof. Keep the bath upstairs for the very last. By then the master bath will be done. From the looks of your kitchen, I'd say you can move in about three weeks from now. We'll still be working, but you'll have appliances and can dodge the mess. Then, we'll get to tearing down some of the walls and expanding a couple of rooms."

Three weeks. Holy shit. This meant I had to tell my mother what I'd done. I'd kept the house a secret since signing the papers. This was my first step toward independence. I inhaled deeply. *You can do it.*

"Thank you, Mr.—ah, Max. I'll leave my house in your capable hands."

"You won't regret it, Miss Austin. It'll be nice to have the old LaForge place looking like it used to." He gazed around the foyer as though remembering.

"Are you familiar with the house?"

"Only from a distance. My father and grandfather worked on projects here from time to time. I heard it used to be quite a showplace."

He left. I strolled back into the house and sat on the lower step of the staircase, my chin in my hands, wondering if maybe I hadn't been a bit impulsive.

Julie told me the real estate agent, a Mr. Toombs, damn near had a heart attack when she called. He must have kept an aspirin bottle handy because he recovered quickly, and rushed out to Shady Oaks, the contract clutched in his hand. I'd let him and Julie negotiate while I wandered about, daydreaming.

They hammered out a price that sounded only a tick under the national debt. Julie insisted it was fair, so I signed on the dotted line and became a homeowner.

Shady Oaks came with a hundred acres of very rich soil just made for growing cotton. The previous owner died five years before and her heirs rented the acreage out to local farmers. The relatives paid Mr. Toombs to keep an eye on the house—an eye that had seen less and less as the years passed. I would continue leasing the land and use the money to pay an outrageous mortgage. My books sold well, but I had most of my savings earmarked for the good-looking Mr. C. Maxwell Maitland.

I sighed and walked out to my car, mentally preparing how I'd tell my family I would soon move to Cherokee, Mississippi—a little over an hour south of Memphis and my mother.

****

Ruth LaForge sat in her favorite rocking chair in the back parlor of Shady Oaks, knitting needles in hand, counting stitches. "Let's see, knit two, purl two, slip two stitches; yes, I think that's right," she murmured.

She dropped the tangle of wool in her lap and sighed. This Cybil person represented the first serious threat to their existence (or non-existence, she was never sure which) since the other ghosts had elected her caretaker of the house. She'd been forced to sadly watch as the years of neglect had taken a toll on Shady Oaks. In a way, Ruth was rather glad someone had plans to fix it up. But renovations posed a problem. The thought of leaving the grand house she'd called home for so long in both life and death... Well, she just didn't want to think about it. She picked up the needles and resumed knitting.

A little *pop*, like that of a champagne cork leaving the bottle, interrupted her thoughts. She looked up to see Antoine materializing.

"Antoine, how nice to see you. It's been a while."

"Why did you call me, Ruth? I was sleeping."

Before she could answer, another *pop* produced another apparition. Zoë drifted over to the sofa and lounged languidly in the corner.

"Sorry to interrupt, Zoë. I know how much you like your peace and quiet. I'm glad you came so quickly."

Zoë smiled and stifled a yawn with the back of her hand. "So, what's this all about?"

"I'm afraid trouble's brewing."

Antoine made a face. "What trouble? Have you called Hester and the Colonel?"

"No, not yet. You know how upset the Colonel gets when we interrupt his naps or battles, and Hester hates to come out of her wall. She has it to herself and wants to keep it that way."

"I can't imagine anyone wanting to share with Hester," Antoine murmured. "Why have you called us?"

"Let's see, have I got this right? Knit two, purl one or is it purl two?" Ruth muttered. She always had trouble remembering. She hadn't seen the pattern in almost sixty years.

"Ruth, put the knitting down," Zoë said. "What kind of trouble?"

Ruth looked at what was supposed to be a sweater and sighed. No matter how much she knitted, the garment never changed. It must have something to do with being dead. She rested the needles in her lap again.

"The house has been sold."

"What?" Antoine yelped.

As usual, Zoë responded with an intelligent answer. "To whom?"

"Well, from what I could overhear, the woman's name is Cybil, and I'm afraid she has plans for renovations."

"Renovations? As in knocking down walls and such?" Antoine asked.

"Precisely."

"That could be a problem." Zoë's perpetually bored look changed to one of concern.

"Ruth, you've done an excellent job keeping watch on the house, but if walls are gutted, not even you will be able to contain the others," Antoine said with a frown.

"I know. What should we do? Any ideas?" Ruth looked from one to the other.

"Why do anything?" Zoë replied, stirring herself enough to lean forward. "Cousin Germania renovated. The results weren't too bad."

"Excellent idea." Antoine applauded. "I seem to remember Hester saying the house has gone through several changes over the years, and most of us weren't disturbed."

"As long as they keep things simple, I don't think we need to worry." Zoë shrugged. "I suggest we take a wait-and-see attitude."

"Yes, I guess that makes the most sense for the time being." Ruth picked up her knitting again.

"Perfect," Zoë replied. "Now, are we finished? I'd like to go back to sleep."

"Knit two, purl two, slip two—what? Oh, yes. If the two of you are in agreement, I think we should give the new owner a chance. I'll keep my eyes open."

The ghosts shimmered, and then popped out of view. Ruth sat in the old back parlor by herself, thinking and rocking. She hoped Zoë was right and she wouldn't have to call in Hester or the Colonel.

She picked up her knitting again with a sigh. "Now, where was I? Oh, yes, knit two, purl two, slip two stitches..."

Chapter Two

I walked into the side yard of Shady Oaks admiring the accomplishments of the lawn service. They had beaten back the kudzu—it's never really defeated—and the scrubby bushes had disappeared. The grass would take a while to grow in, but it looked better than a few weeks ago.

A sudden noise distracted me. A ladder, one of those extension thingies, stood propped against the side of the house. I walked over and looked up as Max descended. I was about to say hello when my voice caught in my throat.

Coming down the ladder was the best denim-clad rear end I'd seen in forever. My mouth went dry. I gazed in awe as each step down the rungs shifted both the denim and those buns of steel. The lower he got, the closer the view. If I didn't move his derriere would soon be, literally, in my face. I backed up several paces for a wider, more Cinemascopic look.

He still hadn't seen me, a good thing since there was no way hell I could have answered even a simple greeting. Taking several steps back, I sighed like a lovesick teenager.

Something struck the backs of my calves. I let out a startled cry and windmilled my arms furiously, but to no avail. I tumbled before landing flat on my back. My head whacked the ground, and I saw stars. At the same time, the air rushed out of my lungs. I lay like a grounded fish desperately searching for oxygen.

"Miss Austin, are you all right?" Max leaned

over, holding out his hand.

I took it, and he hauled me upright.

"Oh-h-h," I muttered while the world spun. I assumed my dizzy state resulted from the knock on the head and not his hand holding mine.

"Here, sit down."

I sat on whatever I'd fallen over, while he crouched in front of me. "Shall I call a doctor?" His worried face swam into focus.

I drew in a breath. The merry-go-round effect stopped. The tips of my ears burned, a sure indication of embarrassment. My face usually followed suit.

"N—no, I'm fine. I just didn't watch where I was going." I couldn't very well tell him what I *had* been watching. My gaze shifted downward. I sat on a roll of roofing paper, the culprit that had nailed my legs.

"You gotta be careful around construction sites. Are you sure you're not hurt?"

I looked into those concerned brown eyes. My heart did a little flip-flop. I refocused my attention to very broad shoulders. I hadn't noticed how well-built he was before. My interest had been on the house and his suggestions. His T-shirt fit as snugly as his jeans. I glanced at his biceps, wanting to wrap my fingers around the bulges and squeeze. As a lady, I ran out of places to look. My mouth was no longer dry. I salivated, proving Dr. Pavlov's theory.

"Positive." I looked at his chest again. Bad move. I tried his face. He had a little cleft in his chin. Kind of a Michael Douglas thing. I took a deep breath and changed the subject. "How...how's the roof coming?"

"Fine. We should be done by Friday. Then we can tackle the kitchen."

A loud noise from the other side of the house, like a tree crashing to the ground, caused me to jump.

"What was that?"

"Oh, we have to remove the old shingles. You've got four layers up there and the rafters won't hold any more. Don't worry. I included the removal in my quote."

I rose a little too quickly and swayed. To my horror, I swayed in his direction. His hands came up to catch my shoulders and mine found those bunching biceps. Oh, sweet Jesus, like rocks!

"Hey, are you sure you're okay?"

*Get a hold of yourself, dummy.*

"Yes, I'm fine. I just feel a little foolish, that's all." No shit. I gulped and tried to ignore all the warmth that wasn't embarrassment gushing through me. I cleared my throat. "You...you say you're about to start on the kitchen?"

"Yeah, next week. I'm glad you came down today. I was going to call later. I need some decisions regarding appliances, flooring, cabinets, and paint — things of that sort. There's not much left to demo in there and you're not too far away from your move-in date. As long as you have a stove, a fridge, and a sink, you can set up housekeeping. We'll work around you."

I followed him back to his pickup where he removed several large sample books and chucked them into my car.

"Start with the appliances. Just decide what you want over the weekend and let me know. Then, do the flooring and the cabinets. The rest can follow later. We'll have you up and running in no time."

Over the weekend? With my decision-making prowess? Did he know what he was asking? "And when do you think I can move in?"

"I'd say a week from Friday. That'll give you Saturday and Sunday to get settled."

Ten days? Damn! Ten stinking days? I still hadn't told my mother. My mental fingers reached for the panic button. Maybe I could call her after I moved in. No, that would piss her off. Of course, this whole house thing was going to do that. If I wanted to achieve non-wimp status, I'd have to knuckle down and spill my guts. The few left, anyway.

A car swept up the driveway and stopped behind mine. It was Julie. I brought my mind out of panic mode long enough to remember why I'd asked her to meet me today: to inspect the progress. I looked at the roof, pleased to see the front portion finished. Already Shady Oaks had shed some of its shabby appearance.

Julie got out of her car, letting her gaze travel over the house and yard. As usual, she was perfectly put together. In spite of the drive down, her cornflower blue suit showed nary a wrinkle, and a white headband secured her auburn hair, not one of which was out of place. I marveled at her ability to negotiate my gravel driveway in four-inch heels. I'd have broken an ankle.

"I see some improvement. At least that damned kudzu is gone. In another couple of years, the house would have disappeared," she said, joining Max and me near the front steps.

Max laughed and extended his hand. "You certainly know your kudzu. Hi, I'm Max Maitland, Miss Austin's general contractor."

"I'm Julie Aldridge, the idiot who helped Cybil buy this place." She threw me a glance that said I had a lot of questions to answer regarding my contractor. I doubted any concerned his professional qualifications. I pretended to inspect the finished portion of the roof.

"So, Mr. Maitland, how is the work coming along?"

"It's Max. So far, so good. I'll start the kitchen next week."

"Isn't it exciting, Julie?" A crash from the side yard signaled more shingles had hit the ground.

"They have to take off the old roof," I explained, eager to expound on my newfound renovation knowledge.

"Of course. You get too many layers built up and the rafters can't support them," Julie replied. She smiled at Max. "My husband and I have renovated a couple of houses over the years. We buy, fix them up, and then sell."

"That can be a very profitable venture if you get in the right neighborhood." Another crash echoed across the lawn. "I'd better get back to work. It was nice meeting you, Mrs. Aldridge. Hope to see you soon."

Max nodded and walked away. Happily married or not, Julie watched that fine rear end disappear around the corner of the house. So did I.

"Come on in, Julie. There hasn't been a whole lot done with the inside, but someone managed to swoop most of the crud out."

"I'm more interested with what's outside. Do tell, girl. What is the lowdown on Mr. Tall, Dark, and Handsome, Max Maitland?"

"He's my contractor."

"He's your *gorgeous* contractor. Is he married?"

I stopped dead in my tracks, realizing I had no idea. Oh, swell. I could be getting all hot and bothered over a married man.

"I really don't know."

"Well, find out, silly. If he isn't, then being out here in the boonies won't be so bad. Use your head. See to it the renovations take for-*ever*." She drawled the last word and rolled her eyes.

I laughed. This was the Julie of our high school and Ole Miss years.

"So, what did your mother have to say about all this?"

I'd go to the ends of the earth to avoid answering that question. I practically pushed her up the steps and into the house.

"Come look at the drawing room. Isn't it huge? The fireplace alone must be close to ten feet wide."

"You'll need it come winter. The wind will roar through those big windows and French doors. Ask Max about finding someone to sweep the chimney. How many fireplaces does this place have?"

"Five downstairs and one in the big bedroom upstairs. I guess whoever slept in the other rooms just froze in cold weather. Max thinks the kitchen has one, too. When the house was built, the kitchen would have been a separate building so the cooking fires wouldn't heat up the house in the summer. Somewhere along the line the breezeway and kitchen were combined."

"What did your mother say?"

"Speaking of the master bedroom, you've got to see it." I grabbed her hand and dragged her to the staircase. "These treads are mahogany. Can you believe that? The LaForge family spared no expense when it came to building the joint." I tugged her upstairs and into the room I would claim. "Look at this! Isn't it something?"

Even Julie looked impressed. This room required little renovation. Close to thirty feet long, it would serve the lady of the plantation very well. A fireplace graced the outer wall near the far end of the room and the four huge windows (two in front and two on the side) allowed light to stream in.

"Max says we can convert the old nursery into a master bath and walk-in closet. The other bathroom is right next door. We can just hook into existing plumbing."

I proceeded to show her the rest of the bedrooms, giving a running commentary the whole time.

"Of course, most of the bedrooms are on the small side, but Max thinks we can knock down a wall or two and reduce the number from seven to four. And the farthest one back is right over the kitchen, so we can convert to another bath. I'm excited."

"It sounds like Max has made quite an impression on you," she murmured.

"Well, of course. He's my contractor. I listen when he's talking. You never know when I might use the information in one of my books."

"You write historicals, dear. Your heroes and heroines are aristocrats who wouldn't begin to know how to roof a house."

Back downstairs, Julie pulled me around by the arm and said, "You haven't told her yet, have you?"

I looked at the peeling wallpaper in the foyer. "Her who?"

"Cybil!"

I gave up pretending not to know what she was talking about. "Oh, all right. No, I haven't."

"Oh, Cybil, why not? It's a done deal and there's nothing your mother can do about it."

"Wanna bet? She can hammer at me until I just give up. She's relentless. I figure the farther away I am, the less she can ball-peen me to death."

"Ball-peen?"

"It's a metal worker's hammer. I came across it once during research." My mind often retains useless bits of information.

Julie rolled her eyes again and heaved a sigh. "When are you moving in?"

"Max says I'll have a working kitchen in ten days. That's a week from Friday."

"Cybil, just tell her. I swear sometimes I don't understand you."

I sighed. "Sometimes, I don't understand myself either. In my mind, I'm brave and refuse to let her run my life. Then she shows up on my doorstep, and I cave in."

"Cybil, you aren't a coward. You just take the easiest way out. Look at the heroines in your novels. They're strong, assertive women who put their lives on the line for the hero. Deep down inside, you have guts—right there."

She made a fist and gently pushed it against my stomach. Julie was dead-on. My heroines always represented the woman I wanted to be.

"You may be right. All I know is I can't take much more."

"Your mother doesn't own you, but she keeps trying. Look at Daryl. He came out of the closet, and all the ranting and raving, all the manipulation in the world, didn't change a thing." Julie looked up at the house. "You know, at first I thought this was a crazy idea, but now, I think it's the first sensible decision you've made in a long time. And you did it in an instant. No dithering. You go girl!" She leaned down and kissed me on the cheek. "Now, go tell her, and get it over with."

She was right, of course. The longer I delayed, the angrier Mother would get. I sucked up my courage and made a decision. I'd tell her tonight. Let her rant and rave. I would be the rock of Gibraltar.

****

It didn't take long for the rock of Gibraltar to tumble. In fact, I managed to dynamite the damned thing. It had been a week since I'd sworn to be strong and I still hadn't told Mother.

I'm a whiz at procrastination, especially if I have to do something nasty. I started by telling myself it was too late in the day to have a knockdown dragout fight with Mother. I'm a morning person. I'd be stronger then.

Besides, she was still miffed about Jody's party. At the following Sunday dinner (attendance mandatory) she invited the son of a former neighbor to join us and made sure I sat next to him. The next day, she had knocked on my door at ten in the morning, gushing on all eight cylinders about wonderful Granville, interrupting Lord Edgeware again in the bargain.

She sat on the edge of the floral sofa and adjusted the vase on the coffee table one inch to the left before launching into her catechism after a brief hello.

"I noticed you and Granville spent a lot of time on the patio together after dinner. What did you two talk about?"

"Nothing important."

"Oh, don't be coy. I'm your mother, you can tell me."

"I mean it. *We* didn't talk about anything. Granville talked. He couldn't shut up. I politely listened for almost an hour about how he's going to make a bundle as a doctor."

Mother tweaked the flowers in the vase and patted her hair. "Well, it's the truth."

"Mother, he was the most egotistical blowhard I've ever come across."

"But he's a doctor! I'll bet he makes house calls."

Oops, another fifties thing. I'd never known a doctor to make a house call.

She left, once again disappointed in me. On the days she dropped by while I was in Cherokee, I answered her question as to my whereabouts with one word: research. Since Mother didn't understand my career, I could spin a tale regarding libraries and historical societies.

So, I continued to rationalize and put off calling, deciding to look at the books Max had lent me instead.

Who would have thought so many refrigerator choices existed? They came in every conceivable size and color with some possessing the ability to do everything except tap dance across the kitchen floor.

I was thoroughly intimidated. When my confusion hit overload, I called my brother, which meant I had to tell him what I'd done. But unlike the rest of my family, Daryl and his partner supported my career. He and Steve read my novels, giving excellent feedback. They've evolved into critique partners.

"Cybil, you're joking!"

"Nope. I did it. I bought a house out in the boonies in Cherokee, Mississippi. Daryl, you're gonna love it." I gave him a detailed description of the house and my trials and tribulations with renovations.

"And you're moving when?"

"A week from Friday."

"Have you contacted a moving company and begun packing?" I had to admit I hadn't. "Look, don't worry. Steve and I will help. We'll also corral a couple of friends to come along. I'll call the rental agency tomorrow and reserve a truck. You don't have that much stuff. One trip should do it. What did Mother say?"

My silence spoke volumes.

"You haven't told her yet, right?"

"Not yet. I figure the less time she has to digest the news, the less time she'll have to be devious and manipulative."

"Want me to be there when you do?"

Of course I did, but stuck to my guns. "No, thanks, Daryl. If I'm going to grow a backbone, I have to do it alone. You managed to tell her you were gay."

"Honey, I had no choice. She practically had me walking down the aisle with Jessica Hardy. Maybe that's your out. Tell her you're gay."

I laughed and sputtered into the phone, "I want to get her off my back, not kill her. Now, what can you tell me about refrigerators?"

Daryl guided me through the various models. I

finally decided on the sleek, modern lines of a stainless steel side-by-side. I love those ice and water dispensers.

When it came to cabinets, I was on my own.

I had taken charge! I called Max and gave him the information, then spent the rest of the evening looking at flooring and paint samples.

That was a week ago. During that span I had called Max four times with a different choice. Honest to God, every time I looked at those books, I changed my mind. Yesterday, I had been in Cherokee with yet another revision whereupon Max had confiscated the books.

"Cybil, please, no more changes."

We had gotten beyond "Miss Austin" and I had checked out the ring finger on his left hand. No ring and no pale band to indicate he'd removed one recently. Of course, not all men wore wedding rings, but it was a start.

"If you want to move into a house with appliances, I have to order them today."

He brushed a lock of dark brown hair off his forehead. It promptly fell back giving him an endearing little boy appearance.

"Well, I like them all. I just can't make up my mind." So much for taking charge.

"Your cabinets are dark cherry with black trim. Very modern. I suggest the stainless appliances and go with a floor that matches the rest of the house. It's light oak and will be a nice contrast."

In his own way, he intimidated me as much as my mother. However, the stainless had been my first choice. I needed to trust my own judgment.

"Okay, I guess that's the best idea. You're right, the stainless and cherry will look great together."

When I returned home, I called Mother and asked her over for tea and muffins the following afternoon. She accepted, but I could hear the puzzlement in her voice. She knew something was up.

I smoothed the skirt of my dress as I awaited her arrival. I wore a dress she had given me last Christmas. That alone should make her suspicious. It was a frilly design in lavender. I hate the color purple. I'd stuffed the offensive thing into the back of my closet and forgotten about it.

The doorbell rang and my nerves jumped into high panic mode. I lifted my chin. *You can do it.* I repeated the phrase until opening the door.

Mother breezed in, and then turned to stare. "My goodness, don't you look nice. Isn't that the dress I gave you for Christmas? Oh, honey, it just looks wonderful on you. We must do something with your hair next. Maybe go a little more blonde and cut it like mine."

Mother ran out of breath and stopped chattering. When she did, she must have realized my sudden metamorphosis into a minor-league Lilith was out of character. A funny look came over her face.

"Why are you wearing a dress?"

"I have the teapot on the table and some wonderful muffins. I got them at that new bakery on Poplar just west of Kirby."

"A real hostess would have made them."

I ignored the criticism and led her into the dining room, offering her a seat like any well-bred Southern matron. She didn't buy it.

"Cybil, what's going on?" Sitting down, she drew in a sudden breath and placed a hand over her heart. "It's about a man. Have you found someone? Who? Do I know him? Who's his family?"

I poured the tea and set the muffins on the table. "No, Mother, this isn't about a man. It's about a house."

There! I'd said it. Straight out and to the point.

A little rush of pride tripped through me.

She looked at me blankly for a moment. "A house? What house?" Mother took a sip of tea and nibbled a muffin.

"My house. I've bought a house."

She choked, and then gulped tea to wash down the muffin. "A house! Where? When? Why didn't you ask me for help?"

The light of battle formed in her eyes. A frown marred her smooth, Botoxed forehead. Even those paralyzed muscles couldn't overcome her anger.

"Actually, I bought it about a month ago. I'm moving in on Friday." I picked up my cup with shaking fingers and sipped, concentrating on the liquid. It was safer than looking at her.

"And you're just now telling me?" Her voice took on a deceptive, sweet tone, but a lifetime of living with Mother told me the storm was about to break. She set her cup down in the saucer with a hard little click.

"Well, I've been busy. It's an older house and needs some renovation."

"Oh, Cybil, for Pete's sake! You've gone off and bought somebody else's problem. You have no sense whatsoever. Where is this place?"

"Cherokee, Mississippi."

"Are you nuts? That's in the middle of nowhere! If you had to have a house, why not buy one in Germantown or Cordova? At least it would be close to your family. I worry about you. You're thirty years old, unmarried, and go off and do stupid things like buying rundown houses. Cybil, I will not accept this. Get the loan cancelled. I'll help you find a decent house near me. You need watching."

We argued for the next thirty minutes. I told her a bit about the house, but she remained unimpressed.

"You've chosen appliances, floors, *and* kitchen

cabinets? Oh, no. You have no taste whatsoever. And what about this contractor? He's probably giving you a load of crap about repairs to pad his bill. You have no experience with mortgages, insurance, or taxes. You'll never afford it."

"I'll learn. Part of Grandfather Austin's inheritance made the down payment and is helping pay for the renovation. My books do quite well, and I'm leasing the acreage to local farmers. I don't imagine the cost of living in Cherokee is very high."

I couldn't believe I'd held out this long. From the look on her face, Mother couldn't either. I hadn't caved or shriveled, but dug in my heels. I liked it.

Mother switched tactics. She pulled out her handkerchief and dabbed her eyes. "Cybil, I want what's best for you and, sweetie, this is a terrible mistake. I love you so much. You're my favorite child, you know."

I refrained from rolling my eyes. This was Mother at her most manipulative, guilt-lashing best. I'd heard her say the same thing to each of my sisters while browbeating them. I knew it was a stinking lie. For the first time I didn't feel guilt, but anger.

"Oh, Mother, please! That is such a crock and you know it. I'm not your favorite child any more than Steve is your companion of choice for Daryl."

She shot me a furious glance, but tried again. "But darling, suppose I can't get a hold of your sisters and I'm having a heart attack or something."

"Call 9-1-1."

Mother stopped dabbing her dry eyes and stiffened her spine. Glaring at me, she rose, whirled, and headed for the front door.

"Mark my words, Cybil. You will fall behind with the payments, your contractor will bilk you, and the house will look like garbage because you have no decorating sense."

On that exit line, she left.

I sagged and staggered on shaking knees over to the sofa, then plopped down. I'd done it! I'd defied my mother, but at a cost. Her barbs regarding taste and decorating hit home. Indecision trampled over me like a herd of elephants. I reached for my cell and called Max.

"Max, about those appliances. Maybe I should go with the white after all. I don't want to..."

"No, Cybil. I've already ordered everything. Relax, the house is going to look great," he said, his tone a mixture of frustration and exaggerated patience. I had the feeling he'd like to hang up on me.

I really didn't blame him.

****

Ruth hovered a foot above the floor, wincing when a workman yanked another piece of plaster from the kitchen wall.

"Oh, dear. This is not good. He's close to the Colonel," she murmured to herself.

Sure enough, a few minutes later a large slab came down. The Colonel drifted out and stood in front of her.

"Ruth, what's going on? I was off fighting the Yankees when suddenly my wall disappeared."

Ruth sighed. The Colonel often fought the Yankees.

"Bad news, I'm afraid. The house has been sold. The new owner is renovating."

"Impossible. Why would Germania sell?"

"Germania died five years ago. Don't you remember? That's when the rest of you elected me caretaker."

The Colonel harrumphed and looked around. "Have you talked to the others?"

"Just Antoine and Zoë. I haven't disturbed Hester yet. We decided to wait and see what was done. I'm sorry you were bothered, but I believe I told you taking up residence in the kitchen could be an iffy proposition. Kitchens and bathrooms are always remodeled first."

"No one wants to live in a bathroom," he grumbled. "I suppose I can find another place to stay. How about the dining room?"

"You'd be sharing a space with Cousin Jonah. He snores," Ruth warned.

"The back parlor?"

"I believe there's a nice, cozy spot still available on the west wall. Why don't you try that? Go back to your Yankees. If there's any change, I'll let you know."

The Colonel drifted through the wall. She hoped he found comfort in his new surroundings. The poor man never chose the correct space and usually ended up moving every twenty years or so.

Another large hunk of plaster hit the floor. Dust billowed like a summer cloud.

"Oh, dear, this is turning into a disaster. I may have to call Hester."

And that, Ruth knew, was tantamount to declaring war.

## Chapter Three

I'm not sure how long I sat and stared at nothing after talking to Max. My elation at standing up to my mother rapidly gave way to guilt. I should have expected it. A lifetime of habit is hard to break overnight. I reached for the phone to call and apologize when my eyes fell on the hated floral print sofa, then shifted to probe every corner of the living room.

My hand fell to my lap. Why should I have to accept furniture and decorating I loathed? So what if Mother hated my tastes? She didn't have to live with them. I did. And I loved sleek, modern lines.

Her voice still echoed, and I had no intention of staring at a bunch of flowered chintz the rest of the day. I rose, stomped into the kitchen, snatched my purse from the table, my car keys off the counter, and fled, frilly lavender dress and all.

Evolution caught up with me and I did what every female does in a time of crisis. I shopped. I ignored the usual feminine happy places, hitting furniture stores instead.

I inspected, rejected, and refused to settle for anything less than what I wanted, making decisions with authority. I informed sales people when and where I wanted things delivered, staring them down if they dared to suggest another time. The pod people had arrived and replaced the old Cybil.

I celebrated my accomplishments by consuming a huge dinner complete with three margaritas at El Porton, then threw caution and good sense to the wind by driving home, somehow making it through

Germantown without seeing a cop. I wasn't drunk, but I wasn't legal either.

At home, a glass of wine gave a nice polish to the margarita glow. I sat staring at a painting on the wall and wondered what Max was doing. Was he alone like me? Or did he have an active social life, and by social I meant females. Someone that good-looking was probably knee deep in women throwing themselves at his feet. Maybe I should be one of them. It was something to consider. A little light flirting couldn't hurt.

I went to bed happy in the knowledge I had taken control of another chunk of my life even though my credit cards now sizzled. I yawned, settling deeper into my pillow. So what? Lord Edgeware would have to work harder.

**\*\*\*\***

I was packing up the last of the kitchen when my phone rang. The caller ID verified it was not my mother or either of my sisters. Mother decided to punish me with the silent treatment. I hadn't heard from her in two days, but that didn't prevent her minions from harassing me.

Penelope called twice to say I was evil and a bad daughter for disrespecting my mother. According to her, Mother was broken-hearted by my callous behavior. I kept my composure. I didn't argue, but neither did I defend myself. I finally just hung up on her.

Francine took a different tack. She wailed and moaned that I would never find a suitable husband down in the "wilds of Mississippi" and did I want to be an old maid? I told her I was gay. She hadn't called back.

No, this call mercifully did not involve family, but my agent, Carol.

"Cybil, darling, you are a genius or maybe I am, I can't tell."

Carol always spoke this way—drama queen with no apologies. As a former actress, her personality worked wonders with everybody. She could sell wine to a teetotaler.

"Why am I—or you—a genius?" I held the phone between my shoulder and ear as I packed another glass.

"Because I just sold *The Devil and the Princess*, that's why." Her voice oozed triumph.

Great. Maybe the advance would ease my credit card pain. I'd written *The Devil and the Princess* a couple of years ago between Lord Edgeware books, but hadn't gotten around to sending it to Carol until recently. To tell the truth, I didn't think it was all that good.

"That's terrific. Who bought it?"

"Lion Press, of course, but..."

I stopped packing. But? This didn't sound good. "Buts" always meant problems.

"But?" I asked, hoping the answer wouldn't be massive revisions due within the next three days or something.

"Genevieve Holcombe loves your voice and wants to sign you to a five book deal."

Holy cow! My heart did handsprings, and I gulped a shout of triumph. *You're an author. Be cool.*

"That's every author's dream. What's the problem?"

"She thinks Lord Edgeware has run its course as a series. She suggests wrapping it up in one last book. He and Katrina should solve all problems with his inheritance and get married, happily ever after, yadda, yadda."

I straightened from bending over the half-packed box. Finish with Lord Edgeware? He'd become a friend, almost a surrogate lover, over the years. He represented my career comfort zone. I couldn't jettison him like yesterday's news. Could I even write about anyone else? I clung to him as a desperate woman would a favorite pair of shoes.

"But Carol, Lord Edgeware has a lot of fans. They visit my Web site and blog. I think she's wrong."

"Don't panic, Cybil. You're a terrific writer and won't have any problems with new material. The deal could be quite lucrative."

She named a figure that had me gasping. Credit card balance bye-bye with a lot left over for the house. But at the expense of an old and profitable friend? Indecision gripped me.

As though reading my mind, Carol said, "Look, think it over for a couple of days. Get back to me on Monday."

"A couple of days? I'm in the middle of moving. I've just bought and am renovating an old house down in Mississippi. I won't have time to think."

"Of course you will. What better incentive to take the deal than having a mortgage and a bunch of bills to pay? Oops, I've got to go. I'll talk to you on Monday."

She hung up, leaving me with a churning stomach and a profound sense of loss.

****

After Carol's call, I forced myself to focus on the move and spent the entire night getting ready. I finished taping the last box just as Daryl and Steve drove up.

Groggy without sleep, I answered the door and inhaled the wonderful smell of fresh, hot coffee. I forced my eyes open further.

"God bless you," I croaked, snatching the steaming cup from Daryl's hand.

"Thought you might need that. Did you get everything packed?"

"Just finished. How long do you think it'll take?" I swilled the strong brew and savored the smooth

French vanilla creamer, ignoring the scalding heat.

"To load, drive down, and then unload, maybe four or five hours."

"Hey, Cybil, how're you doing?"

"Steve! I haven't seen you in ages. You look great."

I gave my brother's partner a huge hug. I was genuinely fond of him and since he made Daryl happy, he climbed to the top of my favorite people list. I'd too often seen Daryl unhappy.

I adore my younger brother. Even as a kid, he'd slide in under Mother's radar and get into the worst scrapes, usually taking me with him. I'd feel guilty for having upset Mother. Daryl never did. Somehow, she never got to him the way she did the rest of us.

He and Steve complemented each other. Daryl stood about six feet tall, and had inherited Mother's blond hair and blue eyes. Those eyes, along with his ability to always look innocent even with his hand in the cookie jar, had bamboozled more than one parent or teacher. Dimples melted a lot of hardnosed female authority figures. He also had a body most women drooled over. Sorry, girls.

Steve Bacardi was the exact opposite. His dark good looks and hair-trigger temper spoke volumes about his Latin heritage. He had won my undying devotion the first time I met him when we both ordered anchovies on pizza.

They had just entered the apartment when two pickups arrived, and another three guys walked up.

"Sis, I'd like you to meet Gary, Fred, and Mike, our Wednesday night poker buddies. Guys, this is my sister, Cybil."

The five of them immediately let me know my presence was unnecessary. They had the loading down to a science and after I made several aborted attempts at helping, Daryl said in an exasperated voice, "Sis, you're in the way. If you want to be useful, go get us something from Wendy's or Burger King."

"I am not some useless female at your beck and call to serve food," I said in an injured tone.

I went to Wendy's anyway and delivered as requested. They gobbled the burgers and fries. I sulked before making the brilliant decision to head on down to the house where I could make sure Max's men and the movers wouldn't stumble all over each other. Besides, I looked forward to seeing Max again. This might be a good time to do the flirting thing. I'd have practiced on one of Daryl's friends, but if my brother caught me, I'd be the brunt of jokes for weeks to come. *Not that I'm out of practice.* Before I could leave, Julie arrived, dressed in jeans and an old T-shirt.

"Hey, Julie. Do us a favor and get Cybil out of here," my brother called out.

Julie laughed. "Daryl, honey, I haven't seen you in the longest. How you doin'?"

"We'd move a lot faster without a certain author interfering. Food notwithstanding, she's trying to help. Take her down to the house and do whatever it is women do when they move."

I glared at my brother and his grinning companions as they shoveled in the last of the fries.

"Daryl Austin, I don't care if you are gay, you're still a male chauvinist pig!"

Trying to maintain my dignity, I turned and marched to my car, followed by a chuckling Julie.

****

I pulled up in front of the house, marveling at the progress. The roof was finished and someone had begun scraping the peeling paint off the wooden portions of the house. I still wasn't sure what I wanted to do with the bricks. Sandblasting would cost a fortune. Oh, well. Tara had been whitewashed brick, and if it was good enough for Scarlett, who was I to argue?

White with pretty green shutters sounded nice. Or maybe cranberry red. No, black. Or maybe I'd paint the house cream with white trim. I saw major indecision ahead.

It took a few moments to realize Max's truck was the only one parked in the yard.

"Did you check him out?" Julie asked.

"What? Check who?"

"Max, you goose! Is he married?"

"Oh, I don't think so. He's not wearing a ring and there's no ring mark on his finger."

"Doesn't mean a damned thing."

We exited the car. The porch floor no longer bent under our weight. The men had temporarily braced it and would work on it at a later date. The front door hinges had been replaced. The solid oak panel opened smoothly.

As soon as we entered, I heard the sound of hammering from the rear of the house. Eager to see the progress in the kitchen I almost ran, then skidded to a halt and stared in disbelief.

The room looked like a bomb had exploded. Debris from wall demolition dotted the floor and a large portion of the ceiling had disappeared. Appalled, I gazed upon the chaos thinking, *how the hell am I supposed to cook in this mess?* Then I remembered I didn't cook.

The cabinets stood in cartons in the middle of the floor. A base unit with a sink had been installed, but that was it. The refrigerator sat off to the side, humming along, indicating it worked. A stove was ensconced along a wall. I assumed someone had plugged it in.

Max had set a piece of plywood on two sawhorses using it as a table. He bent over it now, hammer in hand, reading blueprints, giving Julie and me a great view of that fantastic rear end.

I elbowed her, my eyes raking up and down his lower half before saying, "Max, what on earth is going on? I thought you said I'd have a kitchen. My brother and his friends will be here in a couple of hours." I looked around in dismay. "Somehow, I don't think all of this is going to miraculously get done by then."

Max straightened and turned to face me with a look of exasperation. I was on the receiving end of a lot of that today.

"The appliances arrived this morning. If I remember right, you called *how* many times to change your mind about what to order?"

Heat flooded my face and Julie snickered.

"We stopped work for today. I wasn't sure when you'd be down and didn't want to get in the way."

"Holy cow! What a fireplace!" Julie exclaimed.

I swiveled my head to the left. A huge fireplace had materialized on the far wall. I immediately envisioned a cozy seating area or the perfect place for a kitchen table.

"Yep. Broke through late yesterday. I knew there had to be one somewhere. I suggest putting a couple of French doors on either side of it and extending the patio. It'll look terrific."

"It's wonderful. What happened to the ceiling?" I turned my gaze up to inspect the damage.

"More bad news. A leak years ago softened the plaster. We removed a chunk from the wall and dislodged a good piece of the ceiling. It can be fixed, but it'll take a little longer. At least the appliances work. I'll leave the sawhorses and plywood up so you can use them."

Julie eyed him. "Well, I think you've done a great job. You must be handy to have around the house. I'll bet your wife counts her blessings every night."

I groaned. How could she? She wasn't even

being subtle. I wanted to drop through the floor.

Max grinned. "I may be handy, but I don't have a wife to count anything, including how many beers I have. Been there, done that, still paying the tab. A wife is not on my agenda."

My heart dropped to my toes. Swell, an ex-wife loomed on the horizon. Men never quite got over an ex.

"Goodness, that sounds bitter. Was she a bitch?"

"Only while I was married to her."

Julie batted her eyes, a half-smile curving her lips. "Well, I just bet the right woman can change your mind."

Married or not, Julie could still flirt with the best of them. I half expected her to say, "I do declare," like any Southern belle.

"I'm too busy to even think about marriage. It's one of those things better avoided."

"Come on, Julie, let's go tidy up a few other rooms and let Max get back to work."

Tugging her away, I glanced over my shoulder as he bent over the improvised table again. God, it was criminal.

"See? All you had to do was ask," Julie hissed in my ear.

"He has an ex-wife."

"So what?"

"You heard him. He has no interest in marriage."

"Oh, nonsense. They all say that. It's your job to change his mind."

I saw her point and cast another glance through the doorway.

She sneaked a peek also. "Whew-ee! Girl, that is one prime ass. If I wasn't happily married..."

"Remember you are. Besides, I saw him first. Come on," I said, pulling her into the drawing room.

We spent the next couple of hours sweeping and

washing windows in the rooms where I planned on putting furniture. I also told her about Mother's reaction and my shopping expedition.

"Good for you! It's about time you asserted yourself."

Daryl and the guys showed up with the van as we finished the last window. Max came out to help, and while I directed what went where, Julie opened boxes. Max had not been idle. During our cleaning, he'd mounted several shelves by the sink and shoved another cabinet base unit next to the stove.

"You'll still have to wash the dishes and glasses off before you use them, but at least your pots and pans will be handy," Max said, heaving a partial sheet of plywood on top of the cabinet.

Daryl was in the room at the time of that last statement and laughed. "My sister consorting with pots and pans? She can't boil water."

"It was my way at getting back at Martha," I snapped. Honestly, brothers!

"Martha?" Max had a quizzical expression on his face.

"Never mind. Daryl, shouldn't you be hefting another box or something?"

Most of the cartons had been off-loaded, and when Steve and Gary lugged in the sofa, I pointed to the back parlor. I'd had the old, mice-ridden sofa and chairs hauled to the dump, but kept an antique rocker. I don't know why, but it belonged in the house. Call it an overactive imagination, but I could have sworn it had seen recent use.

"Stuff it in there," I told them. "Don't bother to arrange anything. I'll get to it later. Oh, and the bed goes in the room second on the left from the top of the stairs. Follow me. I'll show you."

A few minutes later, a delivery truck pulled up out front. Excited, I scampered down the steps. *My* furniture had arrived.

An hour later the deliverymen left. I stood in the drawing room, my arms linked with Daryl and Julie.

"I love it!"

"Sis, it's you."

"Daryl's right," Julie declared. "Although I still can't figure out why someone who loves the no-frills simplicity of modern bought an antebellum house."

I shrugged. "If personal taste ruled my life, I wouldn't write historicals. I have no explanation."

I gazed at the new drawing room.

Two black leather sofas sporting chrome trim flanked the enormous fireplace. A couple of matching chairs faced it, and in the middle stood a five-foot square glass-and-chrome coffee table. I hate end tables. As far as I'm concerned they're just another place to clutter, so I opted for two floor lamps with long arching arms, one beside each sofa, as my main light source. A smaller torchiere lamp sat behind the chairs. I'd get around to an area rug after refinishing the floor.

I glanced at the chandelier centered over the table and decided that with new globes, the whole room would be an eclectic blend of old versus new.

Mother would have a cat.

"You know, this shouldn't work, but somehow it does," Max said from behind us.

"You took the words right out of my mouth," Daryl replied. He squeezed my arm. "Cybil, I think you're going to be happy here. Don't let *anyone* talk you into leaving."

"Don't worry, I won't."

In spite of the rubble in the kitchen and the chaos to come, I experienced a sense of belonging. This was my home. Before I could get sloppy and sentimental, I turned to the others.

"Okay, dinner's on me. Max, is there someplace we can go for burgers and beer in town?"

"The Cherokee Café is strictly a greasy spoon of

last resort, but the Paisano Pizza Palace is pretty good."

The thought of eating pizza and swilling beer with Max lifted my spirits. Not that they needed any more elevation. Today had been a turning point in my life. Nothing could bring me down. Except Mother showing up, of course. But the likelihood of that happening was about the same as the Second Coming occurring on my front lawn.

****

We invaded the Pizza Palace like Visigoths—or hungry people who had spent the day moving boxes and furniture. Julie and I rode with Max in his pickup. After dinner, she'd catch a ride back to Memphis with Daryl.

I practically elbowed Julie out of the way to sit in the middle. I felt like a high school kid again and ignored Julie's amused snort. The truck was roomier than I expected, but Max filled his section of the front seat. Every time our arms touched, I reveled in the fire racing through my arm at the point of contact. And when his thigh brushed mine...well, let's just say I did more than burn. I almost suggested driving seventy-five miles to Memphis just to prolong the experience.

In the restaurant, I sat next to Steve so we could share the joy of anchovies. Everyone shunned us as heretics even though pepperoni, mushrooms, and loads of cheese were visible.

I was across from Max and covertly watched him to my heart's content.

The waitress brought our five pizzas (even for a Friday night, we had to be a bonanza for the Palace) and set them among the nearly-empty five beer pitchers. Max ordered another round. It was a free-for-all with everyone grabbing at the same time. Steve and I each bit into a slice of salty, anchovy-laden pizza. He grinned. I turned my attention to

Max and stopped chewing.

He used his tongue to wrap up a long string of mozzarella. I almost quit breathing. Fascinated, I gazed as his tongue circled the cheese before the slender thread finally broke, and he popped it into his mouth.

I'm a writer and have a vivid imagination. It now kicked into high gear. I visualized that tongue doing wonderful things to all kinds of places on my body. When he sucked an oozing of sauce from his finger, I damn near rose out of my chair to tackle him. I wanted him sucking more than his fingers and would love to return the favor.

A sharp kick to my ankle from Julie brought me back to earth. I tore my eyes and imagination away from Max and saw my best friend trying not to choke on her pizza as she smothered a laugh. The tips of my ears burned. If Daryl noticed the telltale signs of embarrassment, he wouldn't smother any noises. I'd never hear the end of it. What are brothers for if not to humiliate older sisters?

I resumed chewing. Conversation had flowed all the while I'd lived in Never-Never-Land.

The object of my fantasies finished his tongue exercises and said with a smile, "I hope you like Cherokee. It's not a bad little town. The people are friendly and willing to help if you need it. In fact, I bet tomorrow morning, half the female population will show up with casseroles, cakes, pies, and anything else they can think of."

"Along with their curiosities," Julie added.

"No doubt about that. They'll want to know all about the newest Cherokee resident and what she's doing with the house. Suellen Wiggins, the worst gossip in town, will probably lead the parade. She can talk for a solid thirty minutes and not say a damned thing."

"I'll buy earplugs," I said.

"She's also the president of the First Baptist's Ladies Auxiliary. She'll pressure you to join, so be warned."

"I'm Presbyterian," I told him.

"They'll be right behind her."

The party broke up shortly afterward. I paid the bill, and then joined everyone on the sidewalk. Julie hugged me, whispering in my ear, "Sweetie, if you get the opportunity, feel free to go ahead and do everything I wouldn't!"

I laughed and hugged her back. "Don't be silly. Thanks for your help. I'll be in touch."

I waved as they pulled away, and then slid into Max's pickup. This time I had to sit on the passenger's side, but my mind remembered all the marvelous contact from the ride into town.

Back at the house, he exited the truck with me. "I'll check through the place. You're kind of isolated out here and some of those doors are flimsy."

"Be my guest. I feel safe. I know this sounds goofy, but I think the house will protect me."

He didn't say anything, just raised his eyebrows and proceeded to look through all the rooms.

While he was gone, I inspected my face in an old mirror hanging in the foyer. Could he find me attractive? I was one of those "between" people. My shoulder length hair wasn't quite brown, but neither was it blonde. My eyes hovered between blue and gray. I conceded I had nice cheekbones, but felt my nose was a bit too long and my chin a tad too strong. I straightened my spine to show off my five-foot five-inch height. My figure wasn't bad, but nothing to rave about either. I slumped. I was just so *average*.

Max returned and I walked him to the door.

In the entryway, he turned, placed his hands on my shoulders and looked into my eyes. My heart missed a beat, and then pounded like a drum. Suddenly the night resembled a sauna. My ears buzzed. I prayed that if I fainted, I would do so gracefully at his feet á la Lady Katrina, my heroine and alter ego.

"Please don't think me forward, but welcome to Cherokee." He kissed me briefly on each cheek, smiled, and walked down the steps. "I'll see you tomorrow."

"Th—th—thanks," I stammered. My knees wobbled. "To—tomorrow." I waved a limp hand as he drove away.

As a welcome, it sure beat the hell out of a casserole. Too keyed up to go to bed right away, I walked around the house making future renovation plans. Most of the downstairs rooms had fireplaces. They also had ugly wallpaper, but I'd deal with that later.

I yawned and finally mounted the stairs, then stopped in the master bedroom doorway to admire my new bedroom furniture. Satisfied, I unearthed the linens I'd bought and laundered before moving, and made the king-sized platform bed.

I brushed my teeth, donned my pajamas, then slid between the crisp white sheets and pulled up the black comforter. It was summer and I'd end up baking by morning, but didn't care. Turning out the light, I stared into the darkness, totally happy for the first time in a long while.

****

"Well, she's here," Antoine said, gazing at Cybil's sleeping form.

"She seems nice. I watched today as they moved her in. She has some lovely furniture in the back parlor. I wonder if she'd mind us using it once in a while," Ruth commented.

"How would she know?" Zoë asked. "I like her bed. It's huge."

"Yes, but the style is strange."

Antoine shrugged. "Ruth, *your* furniture looked

45

strange to me. It's another era."

"I like the clean, crisp lines," Zoë stated.

"So, what do we do now, Ruth?"

"Our work is just beginning. Keep your eyes open and hope the kitchen is all they remodel. Where's the Colonel?" she asked.

"Off fighting the Yankees, of course," Antoine answered with another shrug. "If things reach a crisis, he'll show up. What about Hester? Have you contacted her?"

"No, not yet. She won't be happy that I've left her to last, but we don't need abrasive comments at the moment. If I wake her, she'll have plenty of them, I'm sure."

"All we can do is wait and see," Zoë said, yawning. "I suggest we call it a night and get some rest like Cybil."

"Very well. You two go back. I think I'll watch a little while longer."

Zoë and Antoine popped out of sight. Ruth didn't have the heart to remind Zoë ghosts were in eternal sleep. They had no use for any of the earthly pleasures anymore. Ruth sighed. She really did miss apple pie.

Cybil muttered in her sleep and turned onto her side. A nice girl, she decided. And pretty, too. But why would she buy a dilapidated old plantation house in a backwater town like Cherokee? She'd sensed Cybil's happiness and suspected the young lady had experienced little of that in her life.

"I wonder why," Ruth murmured. Now, she not only watched over Shady Oaks, but its new owner as well.

Chapter Four

I stood with the instruction booklet to my new Perfect Coffee Coffeemaker in one hand and glared at the monster machine in front of me. When it comes to anything mechanical, I am a total and complete dunce. I admit it and offer no excuses. My DVD recorder flashes a series of little dashes where the time should be, and I continue to wear an analog watch. It came as no surprise when I had trouble with Perfect Coffee.

I'd found the machine sitting on the plywood counter in the kitchen this morning with a note attached. *Happy new home! Plug it in and read the instructions. I have faith in you. Daryl.*

Bully for him. I'd managed to set the clock—after three attempts—but the delayed brewing just didn't seem to work right. Maybe I had a defective coffeemaker.

"While on the clock mode, press delay button," I read out loud. Okay, check. I'm pressing the delay button.

"Now, press and hold down hour and minute buttons to set time." How many fingers does it take to do all this? I pressed and held. The numbers whizzed by until settling on six A.M.

"Press delay brew and you're set!" I pressed. The screen went blank.

I tried not to cry. I wanted my eight-year-old coffeepot that cost me nine dollars at a discount store. The only mechanics involved filling it with water, scooping the coffee into the little basket, and setting it on the stove. I couldn't find it and wondered if Daryl or Julie had thrown it out. If I didn't get caffeine soon, I'd turn into a serial killer. I tried again with the same results.

"Oh, damn!" I threw the instruction book on the board.

"Having a problem?" Max asked from the doorway.

I whirled, my heart kicking into a thumping hard pump and my face hot. The heart thing was due to remembering Max's welcome to the neighborhood the night before. The facial heat was embarrassment that he'd caught me unable to do the simplest of tasks.

"I don't relate well to mechanical things," I mumbled.

"No problem. Let me help. What are you trying to do?"

I told him and within thirty seconds he'd read the instructions and had the timer set. I hoped Cherokee, Mississippi, possessed a reliable power source.

"There, you're good to go. Wait here. I'll be right back." He left and returned a few seconds later with a couple of grocery bags. "I stopped by the store. I figured you might not have thought to stock anything in the fridge. Yesterday was kind of hectic."

I assumed he was being kind. It sounded better than, "You are such a doofus you can't remember anything."

"Thanks. How much do I owe you?"

He shot me a sidelong glance and a killer smile, making my knees only a tad weak. "Don't worry. I haven't had breakfast yet. Why don't you make the coffee and start the bacon? I have to get some things out of my truck and call a couple of contractors."

He walked out before I could protest. Oh, well. I did occasionally make toast. What could be so hard about bacon and eggs?

I located a frying pan and having no idea how big an appetite Max possessed, dumped one of the packages of bacon into it before cranking the burner up to high. I put away the rest of the groceries, and then looked down at myself. I needed to get dressed in something a bit nicer than a fraying terry cloth robe and old rubber beach thongs.

I dashed upstairs, washed my face, brushed my teeth, changed into a pair of cut-off jeans, and a tank top. Twisting in front of my mirror, I decided I looked damned good. The cut-offs were short enough to give me modified Daisy Duke ass and legs, while the tank clung in all the right spots. I dawdled a few minutes longer messing with my hair before running down into the foyer. I struck a pose in the doorway. Max was next to his truck on the phone walking back and forth. He waved and returned to his conversation. Men! Maybe I was out of practice after all.

I gathered my deflated ego, turned, and started down the hall toward the kitchen when I noticed a strange smell. A second later gray smoke wafted in my direction. Oh, shit! The bacon! I'd forgotten all about it. I hit the panic button.

"Help! Fire!" I screamed, racing for the scene of certain destruction.

Coughing and gagging, I saw through smoke burned eyes flames shooting from the frying pan. I had no idea what to do. I snatched a hot pad from the counter, and grabbed the handle, ready to sling the whole mess into the sink when I heard a shout followed by footsteps behind me. The stove, the pan, and I were hit with a blast of white foam.

"Put the pan down, Cybil," Max ordered.

I blindly set it on the stove and wiped the sticky stuff out of my eyes. Max stood in front of me with a small fire extinguisher.

"Are you all right? My God, what happened?" he asked, turning off the burner.

"I forgot about the bacon."

I was now grateful for the concealing foam. The heat frying my face had nothing to do with bacon. I had to be blushing like a halogen taillight. How humiliating. I may not know how to cook, but I swear to God, I'd never set anything on fire before. Unless you count the time a bagel got stuck in the toaster and that wasn't my fault. I had no idea the damned thing wouldn't pop up.

I looked at the stove and saw it, too, covered in foam. Then I looked at Max trying to suppress a grin. I wanted to die on the spot.

"I know your brother said you couldn't cook, but I thought he was kidding."

"No, he wasn't joking, but I've never done this before. I just forgot."

No way would I confess my absentmindedness was because I primped to impress him. Fire extinguisher foam did nothing to make me look sexy or attractive.

"At least no cabinets got scorched. Why don't you go shower and change while I clean up and make breakfast?" Max said, grabbing the pan from the stove and heading out the back door.

Sounded like a plan to me. I left still feeling like a first class idiot—which I was.

Twenty minutes later, I walked back into the kitchen and inhaled the appetizing aromas of freshly brewed coffee and non-burning bacon. Max had cleaned the stove and most of the foam from the wall. He smiled as I entered, removing the perfectly fried strips from the pan to drain on a paper towel.

"Why don't you get the silverware and set us up in the dining room? Scrambled okay with you?"

"That's fine." He expertly cracked three eggs into a bowl along with a touch of milk and whipped them into froth with a fork.

I found the silverware in the drawer of the cabinet next to the stove and hurried into the dining room. I set two places, and then sat down. Helping in the kitchen seemed out of the question. I'd changed into another pair of cut-offs and a T-shirt. My attempt to attract Max had failed miserably. He probably wouldn't notice if I stripped naked.

The object of my fantasies entered carrying two plates filled with bacon and fluffy eggs. "How do you take your coffee?" he asked, setting one in front of me.

I jumped up. "I can get it."

"Relax. I'll get it. Cream? Sugar?"

I understood. Keep Cybil out of the kitchen. I sighed in defeat. "Both."

He grinned. "Coming up. All this excellent service should be worth a big tip." He left and returned a minute later with two cups of coffee. I noticed he took his black.

I bit off a chunk of bacon. Perfect. Not too crisp and not too soft. Then I shoveled in a mouthful of the eggs. These, too, were done to perfection. Needless to say, the coffee was perfect. It was so Martha. Inadequacy dumped over me like a cold shower. I hoped Mother never heard about this. Maybe I should try to explain.

"I want to thank you for coming to the rescue. I'm not normally this pitiful. I can't believe I almost burned the house down. Did I do much damage?"

Max laughed, but it wasn't offensive. "No. It was just a little grease fire. I could see you were about to dump it into the sink. Bad move with grease. Next time smother the flames. Keep the lid handy, slap it on, and remove the pan from the heat. And never turn a burner on high unless you're boiling water."

Next time? "Apparently, I can't do that either," I replied ruefully. I was still embarrassed. It would be a long time before I saw the humor of the situation.

"From what Daryl told me last night, you have two older sisters. How come you never learned to cook?"

I ate and drank some more before answering. "Defiance."

"Defiance? Of whom?"

"My mother." Maybe if I ate fast enough, I wouldn't have to bring her into the conversation.

"A little friction, huh? I take it you don't get along. Who's the Martha you mentioned yesterday?"

"Look, it's a long story and I'd really rather not go into it right now. I don't need my mother's ghost hovering over me."

Max gulped some of his coffee. "I'm sorry. I didn't realize she had died. Was it recent?"

"Oh, no, she's not dead. Lilith Austin died a long time ago, but my mother is still alive."

"Who's Lilith Austin?" He had a confused expression on his face.

"My mother."

People in the South are used to dealing with eccentrics—all those cousins marrying years ago and what—so I wasn't surprised when Max just stared at me. If he'd been less well brought up, he'd have moved his chair several feet farther away. Right now, I guessed he was trying to figure out a way to break the renovation contract. Between the fire and this conversation, he had to be convinced I'd just escaped from the nearest asylum. I finished eating and hoped I looked normal.

"You know, at some later date, I'd like to hear more about your family, especially your mother."

If Mother ever forgave me and showed up while he was here, he could see for himself with no explanation needed.

"In the meantime, may I make a suggestion?"

"Yes, of course." *Like flame retardant wall*

*coverings in the kitchen or an automatic sprinkler system?*

"I know you can hit the bowl with cereal and milk, and I'm sure you can also slap some meat between two pieces of bread, but for a real dinner, why not hire a cook?"

The thought had never occurred to me. From what I'd seen, Cherokee didn't offer a whole lot of dining possibilities. In Memphis, a two-minute drive had several good restaurants available.

"A cook? That's a wonderful idea. Where would I find one? Know anybody?"

"As a matter of fact, I do. Her name is Lavinia Rogers. She often helps out when people are in the hospital or something. Let me give her a call."

While Max made his call, I washed the dishes. The smoke and most of the smell had dissipated. He returned as I finished.

"Vinnie said she'd be here at one to interview you."

"Interview me? Doesn't it work the other way around?"

"Not with Vinnie. If she doesn't like you, she won't work. Suellen Wiggins can't hire her for any amount of money. Vinnie's got the tongue of a snake and calls it being blunt. Most other people call it being rude, which probably explains why she's fifty and never been married. Don't worry. You'll do just fine."

His cell rang and he left the room to answer. My watch read ten o'clock and so far today, I'd made an idiot of myself on several occasions, set fire to the kitchen, and now would be interviewed by a prospective employee. It didn't get any crazier than this. Maybe there was something in the water.

\*\*\*\*

I believe job interviews demand professionalism, so I dressed in a conservative navy blue skirt and white top. I even took the time to struggle into pantyhose and my dark blue flats shined with polish.

She arrived promptly at one o'clock and before I could ask her in, sailed past me.

Eyeing my furniture, her first words were, "Strange kinda couches." She fixed me with a stern glare. "You not into weird things, are you?"

Taken aback, I replied, "Excuse me?"

"Don't matter. I won't have nothin' to do with the drawing room anyways. Have a seat."

She gestured to the sofa and I sat. She plunked herself down on the chair. Lavinia Rogers stood close to six feet and could play linebacker for any NFL team. Her craggy features looked as thought they'd been carved out of solid granite. She wore a frown on compressed lips and her beady brown eyes glared at me. The interview began.

"Hear you're from Memphis."

"Yes, ma'am. Born and bred."

"Who's your kin? You got family?"

"I've got two older sisters, a younger brother, and a mother."

"How come you're not married?"

"Haven't found the right man."

"Mr. Right don't exist. I should know. What do you do for a living?"

"I'm an author."

"An author? You don't write smut, do you? Won't work for no porn queen."

I choked. While I did write love scenes, they were chaste.

"Certainly not. I write historical fiction. My stories take place in England in the eighteenth and nineteenth centuries."

Lavinia grunted. "Why'd you buy this place?"

"I liked it." Holy cow. This woman should have worked for the CIA. She could pull information out of anybody.

"Why do you need a cook?"

"Because I don't know how. I just never learned." I was completely intimidated and had the feeling I had come up lacking in her opinion.

I was wrong. She rose and said, "Okay, you're on your own tonight, but I'll be out tomorrow at three. Make sure whatever you want is thawed and ready to go. I'll cook it, but it's up to you to serve it and clean up. If you don't need me, I want twenty-four hours notice." She patted her bun of iron gray hair. "I'll come out after church on Sundays. You do go to church, don't you?"

"Oh, yes, ma'am, every Sunday," I swore, lying only a little. The fact is I rarely make it.

"I want twenty dollars a day."

Damn. That was a hundred and forty dollars a week. I had no idea if that was the going rate or not. I tried a little negotiation.

"Miss Rogers, I'm on a tight budget and that sounds awfully high—"

"My time and my expertise," she interrupted. "Course, you could just eat sandwiches or starve."

I caved, visualizing endless baloney sandwiches.

"Very well. Twenty dollars a day and twenty-four hours notice of cancellation."

She nodded, and then added, "And I won't put up with any weird goings on, is that clear? My grandmother worked here and told me all about it."

What the hell did that mean? Rather than ask, I merely nodded my head. I was afraid she'd tell me the previous owner was into Satanism or something.

Without another word, she left me sitting there and sailed out, her formidable bustline outthrust like the prow of a ship. Sitting back, I heaved a sigh of relief. And Max thought I was nuts? There *had* to be something in the water. Oh, well. At least I wouldn't starve.

\*\*\*\*

I never realized how chaotic living in a house full of workmen could be. I should have anticipated the sounds of pounding hammers and shrieking power tools would not be compatible with writing.

I tried setting up shop in the dining room. It had a huge window with a view of the oak trees and I'd hoped inspiration would come calling to thank me for such thoughtfulness.

Alas, inspiration abandoned me. The noise from the kitchen drowned out anything the muse may have said. I wrote a grand total of three pages.

The next day I camped out in the back parlor with my laptop on a flimsy card table and discovered I was no better off. The circular saw and the nail gun did me in. I stuck it out for a few hours, and then hightailed it into the drawing room, setting up my computer on the coffee table.

An hour later, my back let me know that if I didn't stop and rest, I would assume a permanent hunchbacked posture. And while it was called a laptop, I never could get comfortable balancing the silly thing on my knees. I did feel, however, that I was making better progress. By early afternoon, I had twelve pages finished.

Massaging my back, I re-read what I'd written over the past hour, until I came to this passage.

*"Katrina, my love, I assure you I have longed to make you my wife. Without your undaunted support, I would never have succeeded in tracking down the Duke of Wakefield or the duchess,"* Lord Edgeware declared.

*"Oh, my darling, how I have prayed to hear those words! I would cross any mountain, any raging river to stand by your side. I suspected the duke was merely a pawn of the duchess. Soon, you will have your good name and your inheritance restored. When, oh, when can we wed?"*

*"In a matter of weeks. I can hardly wait to make you my own. Your hair shines like spun silk, your eyes sparkle like dew on the grass, and you are such a dumbass, I can't believe it. The light switch belongs to the right of the doorway."*

What!

I read it again and slumped against the back of the sofa. What the hell? I had accidentally typed in a comment from one of the workmen. The noise was muted in this room, but evidently I'd heard enough and incorporated it into the story. I would now have to reread everything I'd written over the past two days.

I turned off the computer, unplugged it, and staggered, bent over, in search of another place to work. I had just connected things back up in the spare bedroom when Max came upstairs carrying a crowbar.

"Hi, Cybil. Am I interrupting?"

"My work? Yes. Anything else? No. It doesn't matter. I'm trying to find a quiet place to write."

"I'm sorry. I was about to start ripping up some of the old nursery in preparation for the master bath and closet."

I hit the off button. "Go ahead. This day's a bust anyway. I'll do some editing instead."

He nodded and left as my phone rang. I still hadn't heard from Mother. She must have been really upset with me, because this was the longest silent treatment I'd ever experienced. I winced when I saw the caller ID. It was my editor, Genevieve Holcombe. At the moment, I would have preferred Mother.

"Hello, Genevieve, how are you?"

"Sweetie, I'm fine. Did Carol call you?"

"Yes, and I have to apologize for not getting back with you, but I've just moved and things are chaotic."

"I understand, but I do need an answer about the book deal soon. How are you coming with the last Lord Edgeware story?"

"Slowly." That was an understatement. Any more of the hero calling the heroine a dumbass and I might never get it done.

"Well, honey, do you think you can finish up in say, oh, eight weeks? I'd really like to have it in the bag, ready to go. That way you can start on something else."

Eight weeks? Was she kidding? "Gen, I might be able to get it to you in four months. It's a madhouse around here."

"Can't you work after the workmen have gone for the day? Lots of writers do their best work at night."

"But Gen, I'm not one of them." A panicked little rush shot through me.

"Cybil, we want to wrap up Lord Edgeware. That way we can use him to promote your next book. We'd like to see something different from you. Keep it historical, of course, but maybe do a *Roots* kind of thing. You know, following several generations of the same family. Or maybe the lives and loves of people in the same town in 1890."

"But...but," I stammered. Where on earth would I find characters for something like that? It had taken me years to develop Lord Edgeware and Lady Katrina. They had been born at Ole Miss during my junior year. Oh, this couldn't be happening!

"Now, don't worry, Cybil. You'll come up with great stories. I have faith in you."

Swell. I felt comforted by the knowledge my editor and my brother had faith in me.

"Gen, I'm sorry, but I just can't..."

"Sure you can. I've already sent the contract to Carol and she'll send it on to you when she's finished reviewing it. In the meantime, you get to work on

Lord Edgeware and a proposal for the new series. Remember, eight weeks."

"Twelve," I bargained.

I heard silence for a moment followed by a small sigh. "All right, twelve weeks, but I want a good edited version on my desk by then. I've got another call coming in, honey. I'll be in touch."

Genevieve hung up and I stared into space. Twelve weeks. Three stinking months to finish with characters that were more real to me than my family? How on earth was I going to accomplish anything in this renovation hell?

As if on cue, I heard the screech of protesting nails being ripped from wood in the direction of my bedroom, the high-pitched whine of a saw from downstairs, and someone cursing outside the window.

I had only one refuge. Packing up my laptop, I scrounged every extension cord I could find and strung them together. I plugged one end into an outlet in the foyer, ran the cord out the door and across the veranda to my car. I sat in the passenger seat, connected my computer, and proceeded to write.

****

"What the hell are you doing out here?" Max asked. "It's gotta be close to a hundred and ten in the shade. Why are you sitting in the car?"

I didn't need him to tell me that. The sweat rolled off of me, plastering my tank top to my body. Moisture dripped down my cheeks and off my nose. The last two hours had been like living in hell, except hell couldn't be nearly this bad.

"It's the only place I can work and not be disturbed. My editor just gave me an impossible deadline, and I can't afford to miss it."

"Ah, geez, Cybil, I'm sorry. It's my fault for telling you to move in."

"No, it's not. I should have realized the problems, but as usual, I didn't stop to think." I wiped the perspiration from my forehead with a now-sodden napkin I'd found lurking under the seat earlier.

"Come on. Get out of there before you have heatstroke or something." He snatched the laptop from my knees and hauled me up. "Let me make it up to you. How about dinner tonight? There's a nice restaurant in Senatobia."

He gently removed a tendril of hair stuck to my face. Dinner? Alone? With Max? You betcha! Then I remembered.

"I'd love to, but Miss Rogers says I have to give her twenty-four hours notice if I cancel. If I don't, she can charge me another twenty dollars."

"Twenty dollars?"

"Yeah, she gets twenty dollars a day for making dinner and I have to make sure everything is ready to go when she gets here."

Max drew his brows together in a scowl. "Twenty dollars? The old bat! That's highway robbery."

"I kinda thought so, too, but it beat the alternative of sandwiches or starvation. Could...could I take a rain check?"

"We'll go tomorrow night. Tell that miserable witch you won't need her." He smiled and ran his knuckle down my jaw and winked. "See you in the morning."

My heart accelerated along with my breathing.

He got into his pickup and left, throwing his hand out the window in a casual wave. I stood in a daze sweating and looking like the wreck of the Titanic.

A date. I had a date with Max. A dinner date to a restaurant in Senatobia. What kind of a restaurant? Casual or formal? *Oh, get real. Formal in Senatobia?* But, I'd love to wear a nice little dress or a skirt and top to show him I could look nice. Certainly a lot nicer than in extinguisher foam. Under normal circumstances, this was the kind of thing a girl took to her mother, but for obvious reasons, I couldn't do that.

Julie. I could ask Julie for advice. No, bad idea. Julie would demand details and I didn't have any to give her, other than the fact my heart pounded like a tom-tom and my knees wobbled a little. She'd want something more substantial.

I tried to steady my jumping nerves and was mentally reviewing my entire wardrobe when I heard a car coming up the drive. It turned out to be a caravan.

The lead car stopped and a heavy-set woman wiggled out from behind the wheel. She tugged her overstretched flowered dress down her ample hips and straightened a wide-brimmed hat, then opened the back door and struggled to remove something. A passenger followed suit.

While I watched, I noticed the same maneuvers being replicated from the other three cars in line.

The woman smiled and called out, "Yoo-hoo! You must be Cybil Austin. I'm Suellen Wiggins and we want to welcome you to Cherokee. I'm also the president of the First Baptist Ladies Auxiliary and would like to extend an invitation join us."

Beaming, she and the others brought forth casseroles, pies, and other assorted dishes. Oh, my God. The church ladies had arrived.

****

Ruth sat in the back parlor, rocking fast and waiting for the others to join her. She was so agitated, she forgot all about knitting even though the unfinished sweater of almost sixty years lay in her lap.

Antoine and Zoë popped in quickly, but they had

61

to wait on the Colonel. He finally put in an appearance.

"Ruth, dear, I must protest this new spot I've chosen. The noise is most annoying and that mischievous little imp, Roland, thinks it fun to wake me. How can I fight the Yankees with that scamp around?"

"Colonel, I'm sorry for your problems, but we have larger ones looming."

"What's wrong, Ruth?" Zoë asked. "You look all flustered and out of sorts."

"I am. This has not been a good day. No, not a good day at all."

"Come on, Ruth. Calm down and tell us what's happened. I take it the renovations aren't going as we'd like," Antoine said.

"No, I'm afraid not. They're still fooling around in the kitchen, but today that young man, Max, came up into the old nursery and began to rip out some of the plaster and the baseboards."

"In the nursery, you say? Isn't that where Cousin Margaret lives? Why, I don't believe she's been disturbed in over a hundred years," the Colonel stated.

"I know. He was working very near to her."

"She came out when we elected you, but only for a moment. Maybe he won't get any closer," Zoë said.

"No, I overheard this Max telling his workmen that they could begin on a new bathroom when the kitchen was finished *and* that the other walls could be demolished soon. No, I'm afraid we have real trouble."

"Oh, dear, that will bring out Jeremy and Walter." Zoë's face wore a frown.

"Exactly!" Ruth rocked harder.

"Jeremy? Who's Jeremy? I remember Walter as being rather bad-tempered, but I don't recall Jeremy," the Colonel replied.

"Jeremy was a distant relative's little boy. He drowned in the pond out back in, let me see, 1924, I think. He was an awful child. A brat," Zoë informed him.

"So, Ruth, what do you suggest?" Antoine asked.

"Let's give it one more day. If they do any more work or release someone, I'll let you know, but be prepared. I don't think things will go well. We may be dealing with an apparition invasion that could spell disaster for us."

"Keep us up to date," Zoë said.

One by one they popped out of the room, leaving Ruth alone to rock and worry.

Chapter Five

I found myself between a rock and a hard place, betwixt and between, a fish-or-cut-bait situation—it didn't matter. Pick a cliché. I had a problem.

It was late August and I couldn't continue writing in my car. It was too damned hot. Yet the construction noise drove me from the house. I'm an early riser. I do my best work in the mornings. By mid-afternoon my mind and imagination have been drained. I need iced tea and Oprah or Judge Judy to rejuvenate. The former I can get. The latter two were still iffy what with the workmen and all.

According to Julie, I take the path of least resistance. That's what I finally decided to do. I followed Genevieve's advice and tried to write in the evening. So far, it had proven difficult. I found myself at loose ends during the day and drowsy by ten at night.

The workmen had another job today, so I took advantage of the quiet and set up my computer in the dining room where Lord Edgeware and Lady Katrina could hold court.

Inspiration poured into me, and I produced steadily all morning. Scenes flowed and dialogue sparkled. I worked through lunch and contemplated a break when my cell phone rang. It was the call I had been dreading for over a week.

"Hello, Mother."

"Don't they have phones down in Mississippi?" Mother asked in a chilly voice.

"Of course they do. I've been busy. How are things in Germantown?" I was bound and determined to be polite.

A delicate sniff sounded from her end. "Do you really care now that you've abandoned your family?"

"I have not abandoned my family. It takes a while to unpack and some things can't be unpacked until the kitchen is finished." I would *not* be intimidated.

"And you didn't have time to pick up the phone and let me know some backwoods serial killer hadn't slashed your throat?"

Uh-oh. Yellow alert. Guilt rising.

"I'm sorry you worried, Mother. You could have called."

"I do not as yet have your number," she replied in a lofty tone.

"Mother, you just called me. My phone number didn't change. I can give you my address, if you'd like."

"Of course I want your address and that phone you have is *not* a real phone. I don't understand what's happened to real telephones."

Believe it or not, my mother still has a corded Princess phone in her bedroom. If she keeps it much longer, it'll qualify as an antique.

"Get a pencil. Here's my address." I gave her the information. "Got it?"

"Yes. So, has your contractor finished the kitchen yet? I don't see why you bother. You can't cook. I just know you're going to be malnourished. I worry about you, Cybil. You need someone to look after you. I wish you'd reconsider this whole move. Sell the house and come home. There's a nice little three-two for sale down the street from me."

Mother's voice had a plaintive, pleading tone. She'd missed her calling. She should have been an actress. Bette Davis had nothing on Mother when it came to theatrics or manipulation.

"Mother, I can assure you I will not starve or

become malnourished. I hired a cook."

Silence greeted the statement. I could almost hear Mother's mind shifting into fourth gear. I held my breath, certain I'd made a major mistake.

"Well, I'd better check this out for myself. How about next Sunday? If you're going to own a home, then you should be gracious and invite your kin down to see it. We'll all come for dinner. Penelope and Francine are curious, and I'm sure you're anxious to show the place off. You were the only one of my daughters not here for Sunday dinner."

Home run! Grand slam! She'd done it. Not only did I feel guilty for missing Sunday dinner, but she also had my fist hammering the old panic button. This is why she'd called in the first place—to invite everyone down so they could criticize everything from my taste to my decisions.

"Mother, I'm not ready to entertain guests yet."

My heart and breathing rates increased. Red alert! Backbone in serious meltdown mode. Soon I'd be limp.

"Are you saying we're not welcome?" The frost turned into ice.

"Of course not. It's just..."

"Good. We'll be there after church, say about two o'clock. We can eat right away, and then discuss this venture of yours. Now, don't go to any fuss and I'll see you Sunday."

She hung up before I could argue further. I closed my phone and sat back in dismay. Don't go to any fuss? Who was she kidding? Dinner? With the entire family? I felt sick to my stomach. Miss Rogers would demand a fortune, and if I'd been living in the Taj Mahal, Mother and my sisters would find something to complain about and ridicule.

*Why do they enjoy torturing me? The bigger question is why do I allow them to do it?* I didn't want to know the answer.

The entire family. Did that include Daryl? I needed reinforcements and dialed his number.

"Daryl, help!" I cried when he answered.

"What's wrong, sis? Did the roof cave in?"

"Worse." I told him what had happened. "Has she said anything to you yet? I'm sure Penelope and Francine are in on it."

"Not a word. I haven't been to a family affair since Steve and I got together. That includes Sunday dinner."

I detected a note of hurt in his voice and my heart ached. Daryl and Steve were two of the nicest guys I knew and being cut out of the family was just plain wrong.

"Well, since this is my house, I can invite anyone I please. You and Steve are issued a formal invitation to Sunday dinner in Mississippi."

"Mother won't like it," Daryl warned.

"She invited herself, so she can live with it." Spine re-solidified. How come I wasn't this decisive and determined ten minutes ago?

"Okay, sis. We'll be there. What time?"

I told him when the others were due. "Come early. I need the moral support." He laughed as I hung up.

I sat back and stared at the computer screen, and then shut it off. Lord Edgeware and Lady Katrina would have to wait for that walk down the aisle.

****

I was sitting in a wicker chair on the veranda drinking iced tea when Max pulled up. He got out of his truck and walked, graceful as a sleek cat, up the steps.

"Hi," I greeted. "How's the other job going?"

"Almost finished. We should be back here by tomorrow morning. Sorry, but old man Jessup's roof needed repair immediately. He's almost eighty and couldn't do it himself."

"No problem. It gave me a chance to get some work done. What's up?"

"I want to take another look at the nursery, if that's okay with you."

He followed me upstairs, and paced off the master bedroom and the nursery.

"I have an idea," he said.

Watching that fine rear end walk across my floor gave me an idea, too, but I kept my mouth shut. I really had to stop these fantasies. The man already thought I was a flake. I didn't want him thinking I was a nymphomaniac in the bargain.

He pointed to the wall separating the bedroom and nursery. "Suppose we move this entire wall forward three feet. It's not load bearing and won't affect the fireplace. I can expand the new bathroom and closet. You'd have room for a Jacuzzi and one of those super showers."

A Jacuzzi? One big enough for two? I visualized Max seated next to me and could feel those whirlpool jets bubbling, throbbing, and pounding. A-h-h.

I gave myself a mental whack up alongside the head. *Cut it out, dummy.*

"What about the plumbing?" I asked.

"Shouldn't be a problem. I can run a new drain line down the outside wall and hook up to the septic system, if necessary. But first, I need to see what's behind the wall."

I trailed after him into the nursery where he grabbed a crowbar and pulled off another baseboard with a screech, tossing it into the corner.

"What about those?" I asked, pointing at two electrical outlets on the wall.

"I'll move them and rewire. It's only three feet. I'd have to do it anyway. Some of your wiring is insufficient."

He stepped back and took a giant swing at the

plaster with a sledgehammer. The wall exploded. A huge chunk fell onto the floor with a crash, filling the air with dust.

I choked and coughed, waving my hand in a futile attempt to fan the particles away.

He took a stand, ready to swing again. "Stand back."

Wham! Another chunk hit the floor. Ten minutes later I stared at a hole almost four feet square. It matched the holes in the opposite wall where the bathroom plumbing lived. Max stuck his head in.

"Cybil, hand me that flashlight, will you?" I handed it to him, and he swept the beam into the dark recess. I rubbed my arms as a shiver of cold swept over me.

*Ruth stared in consternation. Oh, no! Cousin Margaret drifted out of the hole in her wall.*

*"What is going on? I was sleeping peacefully when suddenly someone shone a light in my face. Ruth, what's happening?"*

*"Some renovations, I'm afraid."*

*"Renovations? By whom?"*

*"We have a new owner, Margaret. She has big plans for the house," Ruth explained.*

*"Well, she'd best be careful. Uncle Jedidiah lives next to me in the corner. The light disturbed him, but he went back to sleep. He doesn't like being disturbed."*

*"I know, but I can't do much about it right now. Go find yourself another resting place. I suggest the front bedroom opposite the big one."*

*Margaret drifted away and Ruth watched as Max spoke to Cybil. She strained to hear over the moans and groans of those they had semi-awakened.*

"Yep! Just as I figured. A piece of cake. This won't be any trouble at all. Tomorrow, I'll send some of the guys up here to start tearing things down. The rest can work on the kitchen wiring."

*"Oh, dear," Ruth said. This did not sound good. She would have to wake Hester and call a meeting.*

I followed Max downstairs. He washed up in the kitchen sink while I poured him a glass of iced tea.

He drank it quickly, and then glanced at his watch. "What time shall I pick you up? You did tell Vinnie you'd be out tonight, didn't you?"

"I did, and any time is fine with me. What shall I wear? How nice is this restaurant?"

"Nothing fancy. You can wear slacks and a shirt. How does six o'clock sound?"

"Fine."

I walked him out and waved as he drove away. Three hours to go and I needed every minute to look spectacular.

****

The Senatobia Inn proved to be a decent place. A converted Victorian house, it oozed charm while at the same time conveyed a casual atmosphere. My white slacks and bright green top fit in perfectly.

Being a Southern gentleman, Max held my chair and waited until I was seated before sitting down. Even in the new South, some things never changed, thank goodness.

I opened the menu and studied Max from behind it, a constant pastime with me lately. He wore a pair of khaki trousers and a kind of russet-colored polo shirt, the reddish brown doing wicked things to his eyes. I wanted to eat him up, but decided to choose from the menu instead.

A waitress came by to take our drink order. I celebrated our first date with a glass of white wine. Very genteel and acceptable in a former Victorian home. Max ordered beer.

"Do you have any suggestions?" I wasn't necessarily referring to the menu.

"The prime rib is good and you can never go

wrong with the fried chicken."

"Hm-m. The prime rib sounds like a winner, but this Italian chicken does, too."

"It is. This menu hasn't changed in five years."

"It sounds like you come often," I ventured. With other dates?

"I get out here maybe once a month or so when I'm tired of my own cooking." He laid his menu down. "Speaking of cooking, what did Vinnie have to say?"

"She wasn't thrilled. I almost told her not to come for the next few days. I have a couple of casseroles in the fridge, but when she grumbled about losing money, I didn't have the nerve. She can heat them up for me and make a salad or veggies to go along with them."

"Casseroles, huh? Suellen showed up." Max grinned.

I set my menu aside, too. "Yep. She and several other ladies in a caravan of cars. She wasn't sure how to sit on the furniture. It was kind of funny watching her get out of the chair."

He chuckled. "I can imagine. I suppose she managed to get a look at the whole house."

"Just the downstairs. I didn't offer the bedrooms for view."

The waitress brought our drinks and we ordered. Prime rib for him and Italian chicken for me.

Max picked up the conversation thread when she left. "I'm sure Suellen and her friends are speculating on what you have to hide up there."

"Maybe I'll be the mystery woman. The kitchen was a hit, by the way. Suellen was impressed with the fireplace and said she'd have to give you a call."

"Thanks for the warning." He took a long pull of beer while I sipped my wine. "Tell me about your family. Do they all live in Memphis?"

"More or less. My brother lives in Midtown. I lived in East Memphis and my mother and sisters live in Germantown."

"How many sisters do you have?"

"Two. Penelope is the oldest. She, her husband, and their three children live two streets over from Mother. Francine and her family live about a mile away."

"It sounds like a big family. I'll bet holidays are fun with everybody being so close to each other. How about your brother? Is he married?"

"Kind of." I didn't want to spring Daryl's sexual orientation on him yet. It's not the sort of thing done to a small town, obviously heterosexual, Mississippi man.

Max nodded. "I get it. He's living with someone. Another man?"

I choked on my wine. "How did you know?"

"Men can tell. Besides, I saw one of the guys give him a kiss on the cheek during a break when they moved you in."

"That would have been his partner, Steve." I placed a big gold star next to Max's name. He hadn't sounded judgmental or disapproving. "You don't seem shocked."

Max shrugged. "What people do in the privacy of their own homes is up to them. I don't have to agree with the lifestyle, but I respect the right to live it. What about the rest of your family?"

"Mother refuses to accept my brother's lifestyle and until Steve leaves, Daryl is not welcome in her house. My sisters follow Mother's lead."

"That's a shame. They seemed like nice guys."

"They are."

"How does your father feel about his son being gay?"

"Daddy died six years ago before Daryl opened the closet door. I don't think he would have cared as long as Daryl was happy. What about you? Have you always lived in Cherokee?"

"My family settled here in the 1800s. They owned a small farm north of town. The war pretty much did them in."

"Which war?"

"The War Between the States, naturally. Since then, Maitlands have done everything from owning a lumberyard to running a saloon. My grandfather got into building things after World War II. My dad took over, and I continued when he retired."

"Do you live in town?" I needed this information, in case I had to drop by one day—strictly business, of course.

"I bought a little house just east of town three years ago. It's close to my parents, but far enough away so I can live my own life. Mother didn't want to stifle me."

A mother who didn't want to stifle her child? I'd heard rumors these mothers existed, but had never met one. I suffered an instant case of mother-envy.

The waitress brought our food. I sniffed. The aroma sent my salivary glands into overdrive. I cut off a piece of Italian chicken and popped it into my mouth. Too delicious for words. For the next several minutes the conversation revolved around the meal and how it tasted.

With assurances I found the food wonderful, Max asked, "I'm curious. Why do you call your mother Martha when her name is something else?"

It wasn't something I wanted to discuss. I was having too good a time, but dodging it would only cause him to wonder about the mental health of my family.

"Look up the word 'dysfunctional' in the dictionary and you will see a family portrait. My mother lives and breathes the gospel according to Martha Stewart. She adores the woman. My brother

and I started calling her Martha as a joke. It stuck."
I gave him the *Reader's Digest* version of life with
Mother.

"God, I'm sorry I asked. So, she controls your
two sisters and you to a certain extent, but not
Daryl."

I shrugged. Wimp status lay heavily on me.

"You know, in your own way, you're striving for
independence and have been for years. It sounds like
you want to keep the peace, so you give in on the
little things, but remain strong on things that
count."

Oh, my God. His words echoed those of Julie
several weeks ago. That had to be the most
comforting, uplifting thing anyone had ever said to
me. Suddenly, I no longer felt like a wimp. *He* had
faith in me, too. I wanted to plant a big wet one
smack on his lips, but resisted the urge.

I don't remember what we chatted about on the
drive home. I savored what he'd said concerning how
strong I'd been all these years. Approval was good.

Max insisted on making sure the house was safe
before leaving. I followed him from room to room like
a lost puppy.

Desperate to prolong the evening, I asked, "How
about a nightcap?"

He smiled a slow smile and said, "Love one, but
make it iced tea."

Thank God. I didn't have anything considered
nightcap material. Vodka didn't count. To me,
nightcaps involved exotic liquor like brandy or
Drambouie.

"One iced tea coming up. Shall we sit on the
veranda?" That sounded so grand. The veranda. My
hoop skirt showed.

As he went out the front door, I practically fell
over my feet rushing to the kitchen. I slung ice into
two glasses, and then dumped in the tea. Taking a

moment to smooth my hair, I carried them out onto the veranda. God, I love that word.

We sat in wicker chairs and listened to the chirping of insects and the rustling of leaves stirring in an occasional breeze. The scent of some sweet smelling shrub hung heavy in the air. I wanted to say something witty and brilliant, but came up dry. I'm a writer and couldn't think of a thing, so I remained silent.

Max didn't, thank God. He smiled and took a long swallow of his tea before asking, "So, you're an author. What do you write? Mysteries?"

"No, romance. Historical romance to be precise."

A funny look came over his face. "Romance? You mean like lots of heavy breathing and women fainting all over the place? I thought you were a real writer."

His comment caught me in mid-swallow and I choked. Had I heard right?

"I beg your pardon, but I *am* a real author."

"I'm sorry, I didn't mean it that way," he said, backpedaling fast.

"Well, exactly how did you mean it?" I didn't care how handsome he was, no one disparaged my writing genre.

"It's just not the kind of book that appeals to me. I like man books—thrillers and mysteries. I didn't mean to be insulting."

"Well, you were. And I'd like to remind you that the greatest mystery writer of all time was Agatha Christie—a woman. Romantic elements are often found in her books."

Max gulped the rest of his tea, set the glass on the floor and shifted in his chair. I hoped he felt as embarrassed as he looked.

"You're right, of course, and I didn't mean to insinuate that women can't write what men like. It's just that romance isn't high on my list."

"Well, it should be," I snapped, draining my glass. "Romance is all about relationships. It's about men and women falling in love, losing that love, and then finding it again. And since sex is part of any normal relationship, it's often crucial to the story." Lavinia's words rumbled through my mind. "It is not pornography."

Max picked up one of my hands, cradling it between his. "Of course it isn't. Cybil, I'm sorry I made such a stupid statement."

He smiled and my indignation melted. "Okay, I guess I forgive you. But it's a sensitive subject for romance writers. It's an image we've been fighting for years."

"I guess I need more education."

"I guess you do."

Max dropped my hand and picked up his glass, rattling the ice around in the glass, then set it on the floor again.

"Would you like some more?"

"No thanks. I have to be going. Tomorrow's a busy day." He rose.

I rose with him. He paused at the top of the steps, his body silhouetted against a starlit sky. Almost in slow motion, his hands cupped my face and his head lowered, those magnificent lips stopping just inches from mine.

"I swear I have never kissed a client." He spoke in a low voice.

My insides quivered and the old Jell-O knees returned. Our little spat receded in importance. *This* counted. I felt suspended between life and death.

"Until now?" I whispered.

"Uh-huh. Until now."

Max closed the gap and the instant those lips met mine all bets were off. I was no longer suspended anywhere, but shooting toward the moon on a rocket. And by God, somebody had set me on fire. I burned from within like a Roman candle ready to explode.

Then, I was in his arms and we clung to each other like limpets. Our tongues danced and intertwined. My fingers tunneled through his hair and my heart hammered against my ribs in an effort to escape. I wasn't sure if I breathed and quite frankly, didn't care. If I died now, I'd be a happy woman.

Max lifted his head. The dim light spilling from the foyer revealed a dazed expression on his face.

"Oh, wow," he said in a hoarse voice.

"Yeah. Wow."

He stepped back and right off the porch. I'd forgotten where we were, too. Unfortunately, he still held me. We stumbled, and then tumbled down the steps where I landed on top of him, our legs tangled. I wish I could say it was graceful, but I'd be lying. We both grunted from the impact. It took several seconds for him to catch his breath. I laughed, and when he could breathe, Max joined in.

Chuckling, we unsnarled ourselves and he helped me to my feet.

"Are you all right?"

"Yes. I'm fine. For once it happened to someone else. That's usually the kind of thing I do."

With the laughter over, it dawned on me that the body I'd landed on was as hard as I imagined, and oh, Lordy, it felt s-o-o good.

"Never let it be said, I don't show a girl a good time. Leave 'em laughing, I always say. Are you sure you're all right?"

"Perfectly. How about you?" I brushed the grass and dirt from my slacks. Should I entice him back up the steps for an encore kiss?

"It's a good thing it's dark. My face is probably red as a rising sun." He dropped a kiss on my nose. "Good night, Cybil. I'll see you in the morning."

I climbed the steps, stood at the front door and waved as he tooted a farewell on his horn. I remained planted long after the glowing taillights disappeared around a bend in the drive.

I heaved a sigh and went inside. I wasn't sure, but I think I had just fallen in love.

\*\*\*\*

"Ruth, why didn't you call me sooner?" Hester demanded. "You've allowed this to go on much too long."

"Now, Hester, it isn't Ruth's fault. Renovations have taken place in the past and not bothered us," Antoine said in a soothing voice.

"Apparently, things are a bit more extensive than we first thought," Zoë added.

"Well, we can't permit any more of this. It could release some very undesirable former residents or people who think they're residents." Hester's voice had taken on an edge. "Where's the Colonel?"

"I don't know. I've called him twice," Ruth said in a worried tone. "You don't suppose something's happened to him, do you?"

"Oh, for pity's sake, Ruth. What could happen to him? He's already dead," Hester snapped. "The silly old fool is probably off playing war games. Call him again and if he doesn't come, tell him I'll do the calling."

Before Ruth could act, the Colonel appeared with a very loud *pop*. "Ruth, what's going on? I was in the middle of a tremendous battle with the Yankees."

"You're always fighting the Yankees. I suppose you were killed again, too," Hester said with a sniff.

The Colonel harrumphed and glared. "So what? I died a long time ago. Who cares how many times they kill me?"

"Dying once was quite enough for me, thank you," Hester declared.

"What's happening, Ruth? Have things taken a turn for the worse?"

"Yes, Colonel, I'm afraid they have." She brought him up to date on having to relocate Margaret. "They'll awaken Jedediah soon and Wesley won't be long after that. We need to decide on a course of action. What do we do?"

"I never liked Cousin Jedediah when he was alive. He's no nicer dead. We'll have to get rid of her, of course," Hester stated firmly."

"Yes, but how? Any ideas?" Ruth looked from one to the other, waiting.

"We'll scare her off!" the Colonel replied.

"Yes! We can materialize, jump out at her, make noise, and do everything those silly ghost stories say." Antoine clapped his hands with enthusiasm.

"Bad idea," Zoë countered, yawning. "She's liable to call in an exorcist, and then we'd all be history for real this time."

"Oh, dear," Ruth said. "I love this house. That's why I didn't pass over. I just couldn't bear to leave it."

"So, what do we do? We have to get rid of her." Hester grimaced. "I feel the same as Ruth. I was born and died here. Why should I leave now?"

"We must be subtle with this Cybil person," Zoë remarked, stretching and yawning again.

"Subtle how?" the Colonel asked.

"Well, renovations require workmen, right?" Zoë gazed at her fellow apparitions, her lips curving in a conspiratorial smile.

"Zoë, that's brilliant," Antoine said, his eyes lighting up. "We'll harass them.

"And she's hired Lavinia Rogers as a cook," Ruth supplied in a censorious voice.

"Lavinia Rogers! That nasty thief? She sometimes came to do for Germania," Hester said in outraged tones. "I won't have her in my house."

"I agree. We'll take care of her, too," Ruth replied.

"Excellent. No workmen, no demolition. Simple plans are the best. General Lee should have had a simpler plan at Gettysburg," the Colonel said. "It could work."

Ruth assumed the Colonel referred to their plans and not those of General Lee.

"Yes, I do, too. Scare the stuffing out of the workers and as for Cybil, we'll *Gaslight* her." Ruth picked up her knitting, the needles flashing in the lamplight.

"Gaslight her? What do you mean?" Antoine had a funny look on his face.

"*Gaslight* was the name of a movie in the 1940s. It starred Ingrid Bergman—a marvelous actress—and Charles Boyer. Oh, he was so charming and women swooned just watching him. I have to confess to being a little bit in love with him."

"Ruth, get on with it," Hester demanded.

"Sorry. The plot of the story was that Ingrid Bergman was rich and Charles Boyer married her for her money, then tried to drive her crazy so he could kill her. It would look like suicide and he'd get it all. At least, I think that's how it went. Maybe he was searching for something in the attic. It's been a while since I've seen it."

"Did he succeed?" Antoine asked.

"Almost."

"What did he do?" Zoë said.

Ruth could always count on Zoë to get to the nuts and bolts of a situation.

"He played tricks on her mind. If she left a book on one table, he'd move it to another. If a vase stood on the left side of the mantel, he'd switch it to the right. He'd hide her belongings, and then suddenly have the items appear again, things like that. And the gaslights would dim, and then get bright again, only he'd pretend everything was all right."

"Sounds like a total bastard," Zoë commented.

"Oh, he was. But he did it so charmingly."

"Well, I vote to begin this campaign immediately," the Colonel said. "All in favor?" Five hands rose. "Then let's get started. Antoine, you and Zoë take the workmen. Ruth and I will deal with Cybil."

"I want the cook," Hester said in a grim voice.

"She's all yours, dear. You know, it's been ages since we did anything like this. I believe the last time was when we ran off that unsuitable boy Germania's daughter wanted to marry. If I'm not mistaken, he made disparaging remarks about Shady Oaks." Ruth rose from her rocker. "I feel quite invigorated. Let the haunting begin!"

## Chapter Six

"Are you accusing me of being a thief?"

"I left *my* tool belt with *my* brand-new thirty-dollar hammer in it on this back porch day before yesterday. I come to work this morning and find it in *your* tool belt."

"Well, I'm missing a couple of screwdrivers. Any idea where they might have gone? And while we're on the subject, who the hell ripped out the work I did on the kitchen wall?"

"It wasn't me!"

I listened to the workmen arguing in the kitchen while I nursed a cup of coffee in the dining room. They'd obviously gotten up on the wrong side of the bed, too. I wasn't grumpy—just tired. I hadn't had the best of nights.

I expected an old house to make strange noises and found the creaks and groans to be comforting, like company settling in for the night.

But last night had me up wandering the hallways on more than one occasion. I hadn't been disturbed by creaks and groans. No, these noises had been more like closing doors and footsteps. Maybe it had to do with the new roof or perhaps my imagination worked overtime. In view of my experience with Max last evening, anything was possible.

And to make matters worse, the power had gone off because the damned coffeemaker clock flashed. I'd have to beg Max to reset it.

"Are you calling me a liar, too?"

"Yeah! I am!"

"Why you..."

I was about to go in and try to defuse the worsening situation when I heard a familiar voice.

"What's going on here?" Max demanded.

"He tried to steal my hammer."

"I never touched your stinkin' hammer. Where are my screwdrivers?"

"How the hell should I know?" A brief scuffle ensued.

"Break it up or you're both fired. Randy, do you have your hammer back?"

"Yeah."

"Then go on back to work. We'll find your tools, Dave. They can't have gone far. Nobody was here yesterday."

"I never moved a damned thing. I went fishing."

"I'm not a roofer either. I spent the day at home fixin' stuff my wife's been naggin' me about for weeks."

"Okay, okay. What the hell happened to the wall?" Max's voice rose.

"I don't know. It was like that when I got here."

"Randy, go upstairs and finish demolition on the wall between the master bedroom and the nursery. Dave, redo the wall in here."

I sipped my coffee and wished I had the energy to get up and see what they were talking about. I was barely awake and wondered if I could catch a few Zs in my car before it got too hot. Max walked into the room, a frown on his face.

"Cybil, were you here all day yesterday?"

"Yep. Other than dinner with you, I spent the entire day writing."

"Did you notice anything out of the ordinary or hear any strange noises?"

"Not during the day. The house creaked and groaned more than usual last night."

"Didn't you notice the work that was undone in

the kitchen?"

I yawned and gulped from my cup. "Can't say that I did, but then I didn't look either. I'm useless until after my second cup of coffee. Which reminds me, the power must have been off last night because the coffeemaker clock is flashing. Could you reset it for me?"

"Yeah, sure."

I drained the dregs, followed him back into the kitchen, and saw what he was talking about. Yesterday, the area where the refrigerator would live had been drywalled, but today the sheets sat on the floor. I stared at bare studs.

"That's funny. The clock on the stove is fine," Max commented as he reset Perfect Coffee. "Maybe it's electrical. I'll take a look."

*Antoine chuckled as he and Zoë watched. "Zoë, I think we did an excellent job. Where are the screwdrivers?"*

*"Upstairs. I put them behind the wall they tore apart. I also unplugged that coffeemaker, then plugged it back in to mess up the clock. You know, that machine is kind of nice. Wish I'd had one when I was alive. How did you get that stuff off the wall?"*

*"It wasn't easy. It took me almost the entire night. How long before the workman finds the tools you hid?"*

*"Anytime now. He should be confused and if we play our cards right, another fight will break out."*

"Is it dangerous? I mean if the electrical's screwed up, will I have to worry about fire?" I asked.

Max grinned. "Only if you cook."

"Oh, very funny." I stared into the bottom of my empty coffee cup to hide my smile. I liked being teased by Max.

"I don't know what's going on around here, but my guess is someone is playing a practical joke. I'll bet the jokester came in while we were at dinner and did all of this."

I shrugged. "It doesn't sound like a very nice thing to do. It wasn't funny. Those two were ready to fight and taking down the wall costs you time and me money. Maybe it wasn't meant as a joke. Do you have any enemies?"

Max shook his head and furrowed his brow. "Not that I know of."

"No disgruntled or fired workers?"

"I haven't had any problems with competitors or workers lately, unless you count Jason Hollis. I caught him sneaking a joint on the job and gave him the boot. I won't tolerate drugs or liquor on the worksite."

"Could he have sought revenge?" I felt like a sleuth hot on the trail of a criminal. Maybe I should try writing a mystery. How about a historical mystery?

"I doubt it. That was over four months ago, and he moved to Jackson not long after." He ran a hand over his face, and scratched his head. "When the rest of the crew gets here, I'll have a talk with them. What's on your agenda today?"

"I'll try to stay out of the way and catch up on my reading. When you guys are gone, I'll write."

Max put a finger under my chin, turned my face up and planted a very light kiss on the tip of my nose. I vibrated like a tuning fork and my heart went oopsy-daisy.

"How about you make the two of us some sandwiches for lunch. You can make sandwiches, can't you?"

"Of course I can," I declared, refusing to give in to charming smiles and mischievous eyes. Well, almost.

"Great. I know a place not far from the house that's perfect for picnics. See you at noon."

He winked and walked away while I stood there,

sighing like a teenager.

I tried to put Max out of my mind and settle into reading. It's another way of keeping up with the trends in the industry, and I had neglected doing so for several months. My stack of to-be-read books was located in one of the unused rooms downstairs. For obvious reasons, I grabbed a romance and headed for the veranda. Thinking about Max and lunch, I stopped to absently turn off a light in the drawing room. I settled in and lost myself in affairs of the heart.

I read for almost four hours. Damn, Nora Roberts wrote a good book. I wished I had a tenth of her talent and ability. Not even the workmen banging things around had distracted me.

I stretched, yawning. A nap sounded good, but lunch sounded better. I would make sandwiches to die for, add some of the goodies the church ladies had brought, and maybe a couple of bottles of beer. I couldn't burn down the kitchen doing that. Max would be so impressed, he'd fall to his knees declaring his undying love and devotion. Okay, Max was not Lord Edgeware, but he came close. I laid the book aside and entered the house.

The smell struck me first. Roses. To the best of my knowledge no rose bushes existed at Shady Oaks, yet the strong, almost cloying scent of roses surrounded me. Confused, I wondered if Max *had* become Lord Edgeware after all and done something romantic.

"Oh, for Pete's sake, get a grip," I muttered. As much as I wished, Max didn't strike me as the romantic type. His disparaging remarks last night proved it. Roses ranked high on the romance list.

Then the scent disappeared, leaving me wondering if I'd had a senior moment long before I should have. I sniffed again catching a nose full of dust for my efforts. I sneezed several times.

Definitely not romantic.

I walked past the drawing room. The lighted lamp over the sofa caught my eye. I went in to turn it off, and then stopped, my hand reaching for the switch. Hadn't I turned this off earlier or did I just think I had? I couldn't remember. I shrugged and flipped the switch. Almost immediately, it came back on. I stared and repeated my actions. So did it. Maybe Max was right and the electrical circuits were screwed up. I went around the room unplugging everything.

*"Ruth, that was wonderful," the Colonel said. "I never did understand this newfangled electric stuff. You and Zoë are the only ones who actually lived with it."*

*"I can't claim to understand how it works, either. All I know is it's better than gas. Not as smelly."*

*"It's very effective."*

"Damned old houses and electricity," I said out loud.

I paused in the doorway and looked back thinking about last night. On the edge of sleep, I'd had the strangest feeling someone tucked me in, like a mother would a child. What with everything else going on this morning, I'd forgotten about it. Odd, but that simple gesture had made me feel safe and secure.

This must be the day for strange happenings. I turned and headed for the kitchen.

*Ruth sighed. "I don't know. She didn't look scared and the noises we made last night just kept her awake. She didn't do any of the things a person who's scared would do. I even tucked the blankets around her."*

*"Ruth, we're supposed to be scaring, not coddling her," the Colonel admonished.*

*"I thought it would scare her. I don't know, but she looks kind of vulnerable."*

*"Who's this?" the Colonel demanded as a new apparition floated past.*

*"Oh, dear, it's Jedidiah. I just knew he'd be next. I'd better head him off. He looks angry."*

*Ruth drifted away to deal with the latest disturbed presence.*

\*\*\*\*

Three sandwiches lined up on the makeshift counter. I worked around the men hanging drywall and cabinets, hoping no dust had come to rest between the bread slices.

I found a small bowl of potato salad along with a container of brownies, both courtesy of a church lady. I sampled one. Not the world's greatest, but who was I to judge? My only attempt at brownies had turned out like rocks. My sisters had laughed and Martha had worn the martyred expression I hated.

Not having anything resembling a picnic basket, I settled for a brown paper grocery sack.

I wrapped two beers and a couple of bottles of water in aluminum foil, and grabbed an old blanket I'd unpacked earlier. Sitting on the front steps, I waited for Max. He pulled into the drive and exited the car. I handed him the bag.

"Do I see beer?" he asked, reading the bottle cap.

"I though you might need it."

"I'll be breaking my own rules about liquor on the jobsite, but what the hell—I'm the boss!"

Before I could answer the sound of an argument wafted down the foyer. Frowning, Max shoved the bag back into my arms and marched inside. Curious, I dumped the bag next to the blanket. What now?

"Hey, you two! What's going on?"

"I found his lousy screwdrivers, and now he's calling me a thief!"

"You had 'em hidden and just said you found them so's you wouldn't get in trouble."

The two men lunged for each other. Max stepped in and placed a hand on their chests to keep them apart. The other men gathered around.

"Goddamn it! Knock it off! I told you all earlier—no more jokes. They're not funny, and I won't put up with it. Randy, Dave, go home for the rest of the day. Cool off. And take your tool belts with you. One more incident like this and you're both fired. Is that clear?"

"Yeah," the men said together. Randy and Dave glared at each other, but left. "The rest of you take your lunch break."

With the angry look on Max's face, I reminded myself never to make him mad. I bet he'd be a mean customer in a fight.

"Sorry, Cybil. Are you ready?" The anger left his voice and his smile had me forgetting the altercation.

He led me past the giant oaks and down an overgrown pathway until we came to a small pond. The remains of an old dock, the pilings jutting up like fingers, stood on the near shore.

"What a pretty place. Do I own it?"

"You certainly do. When I was a kid, I used to trespass something fierce to come and drop a line in the water." He spread the blanket out and I sat down.

"Are there fish in it?"

"Sure are. Brim and carp for the most part. Used to be a rowboat. Guess it must have sunk."

"I'll get a new one and fix the dock. I'll bet it was also fun to sneak a swim."

He grinned. "Every opportunity I could." He bit into a sandwich and rolled his eyes. "I take back questioning your sandwich making skills. This is terrific."

"Glad to please you, sir."

Max swallowed. "You please me...very much."

My breath and my sandwich met somewhere in my throat and I coughed. Blindly, I reached for a bottle of water taking a swig. Swell. He flirted and I choked. The tips of my ears burned.

To cover my confusion, I asked, "I was surprised to find a general contractor working out of a small town like Cherokee. I expected to have to go into Senatobia or Batesville. Is there enough work to keep you busy, especially in the winter?"

"I do work all over the area and pick up crews wherever I have a job. Some guys are with me on a regular basis. I'm doing well, but not as well as I want. I want to wake up some morning and say, 'I don't feel like working today. I don't need the money.' That's all I care about."

My heart plunged down to my shoes. This didn't sound good. I threw politeness out the window and asked, "Is that why you haven't remarried?"

The instant the words left my big mouth, I wanted to drop through a hole in the ground. How stupid could I get? He shot me a sharp glance. Julie could have asked the same question and gotten away with it. Born and bred in the South, I didn't even know how to be a belle.

"Sorry, I had no business asking," I mumbled, shoving a brownie in my mouth. Instant solace.

"That's all right. It's no big secret. I haven't remarried because I don't want to. Once was enough."

"Did she break your heart?" I couldn't imagine anyone dumping Max Maitland.

"Actually, no, but she did major surgery on my bank account. Clarissa took half my assets in the divorce settlement. I've worked like a dog ever since. I'm not about to go through that again. I want to make as much money as I can, retire early, and live the good life."

My heart plummeted. "How long ago was that?"

"Four years. Nothing I did or said pleased her."

"A romance novel might have come in handy," I murmured.

He sputtered with laughter. "It may have at that. It's funny, but my mother asked about my future last week. I don't know. I'm not sure if I can handle the demands of a marriage when I haven't got as much money in the bank as I want. Suppose something happens? What if my wife got pregnant? I'll consider it when I don't have to worry about the bucks."

We ate in silence for a while as I digested this unwelcome news. Last night I'd fancied myself in love with Max and had avoided thinking about the possibility all morning. His declaration left me with a sense of loss. I wondered if he'd be making the same statement to a lady when he was fifty. I had no idea of his age, but he looked to be in his mid-thirties. As an excuse to avoid commitment, it wasn't bad.

Max opened a bottle of beer and scooped a spoonful of potato salad into his mouth. He washed it down and asked, "Okay, you're a romance writer. What kind? I know they're all different. You said something about history."

"Historical romances and adventures."

"Adventure? Does your hero brandish a sword and fight duels?"

I looked up to see if he was making fun of me, but his face looked sincere. "Of course. He's on a mission to restore his family name and fortune with the help of a wonderful woman named Lady Katrina. She loves him and is defying her family to help him in his quest."

"I see."

His voice held a note of reserve, and I wondered if he was being polite. It irked me, and I tried to explain.

"Are you aware romance novels accounted for over fifty-three percent of all mass published paperbacks sold last year, and almost forty percent of all books?"

He cleared his throat. "Really?"

"Yes, really. If a man wants to understand a woman, he should read a romance. They have wonderful insight into how we think and what we feel."

"I don't think any book ever published can do that. Men are simple. We have simple tastes and don't beat around the bush. Women, on the other hand, think too much. There is no way a man can ever understand a woman."

Boy, his ex-wife must have been a pip.

Max looked at his watch, and then finished his beer. "I've got to get back. I feel more like a referee today than a boss. Had a couple of guys call and quit this morning."

He helped me pack everything and carried it back the way we'd come. Instead of entering the house through the back, we strolled around to the veranda, mounting the steps to the door. He set the bag down, and lightly grasped my shoulders.

"Thank you for a wonderful lunch, Cybil. You know, you're quite a girl." He leaned down and gave me a brief, but hard kiss, and then disappeared inside.

When he left, I placed my hand against the wall until my legs stopped shaking. Deep breaths helped also. Finally, I picked up the bag of leftovers and walked inside.

In spite of his commitment problems and lack of understanding about my career, Max Maitland was the man for me. Now, how the hell did I convince him?

Frustrated, I did what I usually do in times of crisis—called my brother.

"Hello, sunshine. What's up?"

Without giving him a chance to get a word in, I let loose with both barrels, from Lady Katrina and Lord Edgeware to my renovation woes.

"Noises in the night? What kind of noises?" he asked.

I told him about the bumps, thumps, moans, and groans.

"Sleep I can do without, but what about my book? The characters sound like a couple of high schoolers on prom night, and my editor wants it yesterday. What am I going to do?"

"Sis, you've gone through this before. Take a deep breath and concentrate."

Never count on relatives for sympathy.

After saying goodbye, I did the only thing possible. I took his advice.

****

"Well, I'll be!" Hester declared when Cybil left the porch.

"Oh, my. I didn't think about this. Do you suppose they're in love? I didn't hear them say it," Ruth replied.

"I have no idea, but I think in this day and age, a kiss is not a declaration of love. She looked surprised."

"He had kind of a funny look on his face, too. Cybil didn't see it." Ruth sighed, folding her hands under her chin. "There's something so wonderful about first love."

"Oh, stop gushing, Ruth. We can't let this detour us from our goal. Come on. Lavinia Rogers is due soon and I can hardly wait. She'll be out the door by five o'clock."

****

*"Come on everyone, gather 'round," Antoine called. "Hester's about to begin."*

*"Are the workmen all gone?" the Colonel asked.*

93

*"They left ten minutes ago,"* Ruth answered.

*"I can hardly wait. What's up your sleeve, Hester?"* Zoë asked, a grin on her face.

They stood in a semi-circle around the stove watching as Lavinia stirred a pot of stew on the front burner. She set the spoon on the stovetop and turned to place several rolls on a baking sheet. Hester moved the spoon to the fake counter.

*"Hester, that's good,"* Antoine said.

*"I haven't even started yet."*

Lavinia turned back to turn on the oven, but stopped with her hand in midair. She gazed at the spoon, a puzzled frown on her face. She picked it up and moved it back to the stove, then poked at the touchpad and turned on the oven.

*"Ruth, what's she doing?"* Hester asked.

*"I think it's a temperature indicator. One thing turns on the oven and the other sets the temperature."*

*"Excellent. Let's give her a few more minutes."*

The cook stirred and seasoned the stew. When the oven dinged, she slid the baking sheet into the opening, then closed the door and punched in numbers on the timer.

*"Ruth, what's that she's doing now?"* Zoë wondered.

*"I think it must be the timer. How very interesting. I guess nowadays everything must be done by touching those numbers."*

Lavinia left for the back porch, which served as a pantry. Hester moved fast and held her finger down on the button, cranking up the temperature as far as it would go, and then moved the stew pot to the back burner.

*The Colonel laughed. "Hester, I'm impressed. What did you do?"*

*Ruth laughed, too. "She turned it way up. Those rolls will be burned to a crisp in a couple of minutes."*

*"I haven't had this much fun in years,"* Antoine

declared. *"She'll think she's going crazy."*

*"That's the idea,"* Hester said with a smug smile.

Lavinia returned to the kitchen with a bag of sugar and peeked through the door to the dining room. Nodding, the woman deftly slipped the bag into her huge purse.

*"Well, I never!" Ruth exclaimed.*

*"A miserable thief,"* Zoë said, indignantly. *"Get her, Hester."*

Lavinia turned to the stove and with spoon in hand stared at the moved pot. Looking over her shoulders, with a scared expression, she moved the pot onto the correct burner and stirred before opening the oven door. A cloud of smoke belched out, enveloping her head.

Coughing, she grabbed a hot pad and pulled the blackened lumps from the oven. As she dumped them into the sink, Hester opened the saltshaker and poured the contents into the stew.

*"Just watch,"* she said in a satisfied voice.

The cook marched back to the stove and returned the temperature gauge to where it belonged. Her gaze darted around the kitchen. Lavinia dipped the spoon into the stew and tasted.

Running for the sink, the woman spit out the salty concoction and rinsed her mouth. She dried her lips with the back of her hand and whirled, her head twisting from side to side, panic shining from her eyes.

*The ghosts guffawed.*

*"Now for the coup-de-grace,"* Hester crowed in a triumphant voice.

*Ever so slowly, she pushed the saltshaker across the stovetop, then picked it up and waved it under the woman's nose.*

That did it. Lavinia let out a scream, grabbed her purse, and ran.

The ghosts held their sides, rocking with

laughter.

****

I had just finished my book when Lavinia screamed. Leaping from the chair, I dashed out of the drawing room to intercept her in the foyer. She still wore her apron and had a look of abject terror on her face.

"Good grief, Miss Rogers, what's the problem?"

"I quit!" she said with a gasp. She breathed so heavily, I worried she'd pass out.

"Why? What's the matter? Did you see a mouse? I know I have some, but I can set..."

"Mice I can stand. It's the other business. I told you I wouldn't put up with any funny stuff. My grandmother worked here and told me all about it."

"What are you talking about?" Had the woman gone crazy in my kitchen?

"As if you didn't know. I worked for Germania and never had any problems, but I won't work for you!"

*"Are we going to let her get away with it?" the Colonel asked, eyeing Ruth.*

*"We can't. She's a thief," Antoine answered.*

*As usual, Zoë took matters into her own hands. "She needs to be embarrassed."*

*Stepping forward, she grabbed Lavinia's handbag from the woman's hand and upended it, spilling the contents onto the floor.*

"But why not?" I wailed. Had I done something to offend her? As Lavinia turned to leave, she fumbled and dropped her huge satchel purse, strewing stuff all over the floor, including a bag of sugar.

*"Good one, Zoë," Hester cheered. The rest applauded.*

My cook looked at the sugar, and then at me, her face beet red. Before I could question her further, she stooped and stuffed the fallen items back into her purse, grabbed the bag, shoved it into my arms, and fled out the front door, leaving me standing in total confusion, cradling five pounds of sugar like a baby.

****

Night had fallen. I was walking down the staircase when in the porch light I spied a familiar car pulling up.

I opened the door and called out, "Daryl, Steve, what are you doing here?" They each removed large duffle bags from the back seat.

"With your permission, we have decided to move in," Daryl said.

"What?"

"We each have some time on our hands and thought we'd give Max a hand. You said he's lost a couple of workers."

"We've been thinking about some renovations to our place. We'll save a lot of pesos doing it ourselves," Steve added.

"Like on-the-job training," Daryl finished.

"You're welcome, of course, but the spare room isn't made up."

"No problemo," Steve said with a grin. "We'll do it. You don't have to lift a finger. Promise."

I led them upstairs to the guest room and found the sheets in the linen closet.

"Are you guys hungry? Thirsty?"

"I could use a sandwich and a beer," my brother said.

"When you're settled in, come on down to the kitchen, such as it is." I turned to leave.

"Wait! Don't go alone," Steve yelped.

Had he gone nuts? "What?"

"I mean, I'll go with you and help."

"You don't have to do that."

Daryl waved a hand. "Go ahead. I have things covered here."

In the kitchen, we made sandwiches with Steve chattering like a chipmunk on speed. When I went into the pantry for a new jar of mayo, he followed on my heels.

"What are you doing?"

"Oh, sorry. Just getting the lay of the land. If we're gonna help, gotta to know where things are."

During the makeshift dinner, they explained how I'd inspired them to redo their house. Three beers later, they headed up the steps.

*Houseguests already.* I sighed. Oh well, at least it was Daryl and Steve, not Mother.

****

I stretched and yawned, then shut down the computer for the night not bothering to read what I'd written. My words could have been jewels or gibberish. The clock read after midnight, and I was brain-dead.

I went downstairs to make coffee for tomorrow. Max, God bless him, had not only reset the clock, but the delay brew timer as well.

*Handy with tools and understands things mechanical. Throw good looks and a body of steel along with being a fantastic kisser into the mix and he just might be damned near perfect. He still needs education in the romance department, but some things take time.*

I wondered how he and the rest of his crew would take to two gay men as their new co-workers. From our conversation the other night, I knew Max had no problem, but what about the others?

*Max will deal with it. He's laid back enough to feel secure in his own masculinity and won't let anyone harass Daryl and Steve.* Besides, my brother and his partner didn't openly advertise their sexual orientation. They were pretty laid back, too.

I still had no idea what had set Lavinia Rogers off like a rocket. After I replaced the sugar, I'd looked at the stew bubbling away on the stove and taken a cautious bite. I threw it in the garbage and wondered if the woman had planned to poison me. She'd certainly acted nuts enough. Maybe I should start getting bottled water.

The whole day had been weird. I'm not into astrology or horoscopes, but I speculated it had to be bad karma, like the planets aligning all wrong. And now I had guests. I yawned again. Tomorrow had to be better.

I made the coffee. The mail sat on the counter where I'd left it unopened. Other than my *Romance Today* magazine, the rest were bills. I'd deal with it in the morning.

I trailed upstairs, hoping for a good night's sleep.

****

The ghosts congregated in the back parlor.

"I'm concerned. She didn't act scared of anything," the Colonel complained. "Not even Lavinia's reticule falling seemed to faze her."

"Lavinia moved. I don't think Cybil noticed she hadn't dropped it," Zoë said, shaking her head.

"At least she didn't get away with the sugar," Hester said with a sniff.

"And Cybil didn't pick up on the comment about the house being haunted," Antoine stated. "Ruth, I don't think she understands."

"Well, it was only the first day. Perhaps we were too subtle. Max thinks practical jokers are responsible and Cybil is distracted by Max," Ruth commented.

"What now?" the Colonel asked.

"We up the ante, of course." Ruth smiled, and they all nodded their comprehension. It would be another busy night.

Chapter Seven

I closed the attic door for the third time that night, and then stomped back to the bedroom. I punched up my pillows and threw myself into bed. This renovation business was driving me nuts. I'd live in the house as-is.

The noises had increased and my imagination labeled old wood popping as footsteps. A loose board banging somewhere outside sounded like a door closing, and I didn't even want to get into the scraping I thought I heard cross the attic floor.

Any hope for a good night's sleep vanished. I'd slept for a total of two hours. The bedside clock proclaimed it five in the morning. The workmen would be here in a couple of hours. Might as well use the time to write a few more pages.

I set up shop on the dining room table, moving yesterday's mail to the credenza, and breathed a sigh of relief upon entering the kitchen. The coffeemaker functioned. I stared at the counter, puzzled. Something didn't look right. I shook my head. *Must have coffee first.*

Shrugging, I poured a large mug. The aroma alone helped me wake up.

In the dining room, my eyes fell on the mail I'd moved a few minutes before. That was it. The mail. I could have sworn it was next to the coffeemaker last night. Had I moved it?

I sighed, put it out of my mind, re-read the last couple of pages, and began to write.

The guys joined me a few minutes after seven. I'd just finished a chapter and we sat at the dining room table with coffee mugs.

"So, how did you two sleep?" I asked.

"Like a baby," Steve said. "How about you?"

"You didn't hear the noises?"

Daryl frowned. "What noises?"

"About two in the morning the house started with those damned noises. I'll be glad when this renovation is over," I grumbled, taking a sip.

The two men looked at each other. "Never heard a thing," Steve admitted.

Max's arrival interrupted our conversation.

"Good morning. You're certainly up and at 'em early today," Max said in a cheerful tone. "Hello, Daryl, Steve. Did you guys spend the night?"

Daryl launched into the explanation. "So, when Cybil said you were short a couple of men, we thought we'd give it a try."

"Glad to have the extra hands." He swung his gaze to me. "You look beat."

"What the hell are you doing to my house? The noises almost drove me crazy last night. I barely slept."

"Noises? What noises?"

I told him about the popping, banging, and scraping.

He raised his eyebrows and said, "I suppose the holes in the walls could magnify normal sounds. Maybe you're just hearing the wind. The construction may have redirected it."

"Yeah? Then please explain the cigar smoke," I challenged, getting up and going to the kitchen. I poured two mugs of coffee, and returned handing Max one.

"Cigar smoke?"

I hadn't meant to bring it up. It sounded too bizarre, even for me.

"Last night around two-thirty, I investigated the attic to see what was causing the scraping. When I came back downstairs, I smelled cigar smoke in the hallway."

"What scraping?" Max frowned and sipped his coffee.

"It sounded like a box being pushed across the floor. When I came back, I smelled cigar smoke."

Daryl and Steve remained silent, but exchanged curious glances. "Uh, Steve, why don't we go on into the kitchen and check out the tools?"

"Yeah, sounds like a good idea."

They finished their coffee in a couple of gulps and left.

I felt foolish. Max still frowned and had a worried expression in his eyes.

"I'll check to make sure a critter hasn't found a way in. If it has, I'll call Larry Rampling to come get it out. He's a local critter remover."

"Critter remover?"

"Raccoons mostly. They sometimes like to nest in chimneys. In the meantime, don't go up there at night. A frightened animal could attack. I can't explain the cigar smoke."

I leaned back in my chair and slowly sipped. "It could have been my imagination, I guess. I haven't been sleeping well, but it just seemed so real. It reminded me of my Grandfather Austin. He smoked cigars, much to Mother's displeasure. God, I miss him."

"Sounds like you were close," Max commented.

I heaved a sigh and nodded. "He was the greatest. My grandmother died when I was little and rather than move in with us like my mother wanted, he traveled. I don't think he liked Mother. He'd come home for Christmas, and then winter down in Florida. He was my first critique partner. I used to write short stories. Maybe it was just a grandfather being a grandfather, but he thought they were great and encouraged me to write."

"When did he pass away?"

"When I was fifteen. He sent me a letter before he died telling me to never give up my dreams of being an author. Whenever I need encouragement, I read it."

I blinked the haze of tears from my eyes. I'd dedicated my first book to him and wished with all my heart he could see Shady Oaks. He'd have loved the place. I visualized him in an old-fashioned white suit, sitting on the veranda, sipping whiskey, and swapping tall tales with anyone who would listen. It was strange, but my vision took place in another era, and I could almost hear the visitors calling him "Colonel."

*Oh, Gramps, I wish I could talk to you again. You'd tell me how to handle my life.*

I shook my head and brought myself back into the present as two workmen appeared.

"Max, whoever's messin' with us yesterday is doin' it again," one of them said.

"How so?"

"Can't find the sledgehammer or the crowbar I left on the back porch last night."

The second man confirmed it. "Not only that, but I swear some of that real nice finishing wood we were going to use in the new closet is missing, too."

Max drained his coffee and grimaced. "Just another day in paradise. I'll see you later."

I nodded, and then asked, "By the way, I need another cook. Lavinia quit yesterday. Know of anybody else?"

"Vinnie quit? Why?"

I told him of her weird behavior and comments of the day before. "I have no idea what she was talking about," I finished.

"She was stealing a bag of sugar? Miserable old bitch. Is anything else missing like money or jewelry?"

"Not to my knowledge. She never went upstairs, and I keep nothing of value in the kitchen."

Max was silent as he thought. "Let me make a few calls. I heard where Ruby Washington's oldest was looking for work. She's young and honest."

Max left and my thoughts drifted to my grandfather. I could almost hear him telling me to ignore the noise and put my nose to the grindstone.

I chuckled at the old phrase and decided to take his advice. Wandering back into the kitchen, Steve and Daryl ceased their quiet conversation and smiled. I poured another cup of coffee, marched into the dining room, and got down to it.

I'd leave them to their electric screwdrivers and nail guns. I was ready to write and would have accomplished something if my brother or his partner hadn't strolled in every half an hour to ask how I was doing.

"I'm fine, for crying out loud. Please, I'm in the middle of a love scene. Don't interrupt."

"Uh, sure, right, sorry," Steve muttered and scurried back through the door.

I raised my gaze to the ceiling. "Muse, please forgive them."

****

"Cybil, sorry to interrupt, but Carjetta Washington will come by about four this afternoon," Max said, poking his head around the door.

"Oh. Great. Thanks, Max," I murmured absently. I was in a tricky part of the plot and couldn't figure out if Lady Katrina should be the one captured and rescued by Lord Edgeware or the other way around. The feminist in me voted for the latter.

"I won't be here this afternoon. I'm having lunch in town and interviewing for a new job in Watersburg. If you need me, just give me a call on the cell."

I nodded and Max disappeared into the kitchen

as I hammered out another ten pages before stopping to re-read what I'd written. Not the best, but it would do. I stretched and massaged my lower back, pleased with the results of the morning. The workmen, including Daryl and Steve, hammered and banged upstairs. I wondered if maybe I'd gotten the hang of writing with the sounds of power tools as background music.

"Maybe there's an article for *Romance Today* in this experience," I muttered. I could write it up tonight and send it in next week.

The clock on my computer screen told me it was lunchtime. I wandered into the kitchen, pleased to see another couple of upper cabinets had been hung. Someone had framed in the new French doors on either side of the fireplace, and I assumed the men would knock down the outside bricks soon.

I rummaged in the fridge, but found little in the line of sustenance. I'd have to make a grocery run, especially if what's-her-name would take pity on me and cook dinner tonight.

*Oh, well. The muse has turned balky anyway.*

I pulled into a parking space near the local grocery store, and glanced across the street toward the café. A late lunch before shopping might be in order. The door opened and Max emerged. I raised my hand to wave and almost called out a greeting, then stopped. He wasn't alone, but with a short, trim brunette. They walked down the street a ways where he gave her a hug, got into his truck, and drove off. She sauntered on up a few parking spaces, slid into a splashy sports car, and ripped away.

Curiosity damn near killed me, but I did my shopping and drove home contemplating the mystery woman's identity. Just because he had taken me out to dinner and kissed me, didn't mean I had exclusive rights. The thought did not sit well.

At Shady Oaks, I exited the car only to be

accosted by my brother.

"Where have you been?"

"The grocery store."

"Why didn't you tell me? One of us could have gone with you."

"Why?"

"Uh, in case we wanted something special."

Not in the mood to put up with nonsense, I snapped, "You're in Cherokee, Mississippi. They don't carry anything special." I thrust the two bags into his arms. "Here. Make yourself useful."

I stomped into the dining room and plopped into a chair.

Working was out of the question. My mind conjured up all kinds of explanations for the brunette's presence, none of them pleasant from my point of view.

I was muttering to myself when Max came in. I'd been so engrossed with my thoughts, I hadn't heard him pull up.

"Talking to yourself?" he said with a grin, heading for the kitchen.

I followed. He unrolled several sheets of paper on the makeshift counter, bending over to read them.

I swallowed my irritation and enjoyed the view. "Sometimes it's the only intelligent conversation I have all day."

He straightened (damn it) and laughed. "Got any iced tea?"

I poured us each a glass. "You're back early."

"Got halfway to Watersburg when the client called and cancelled. Figured I'd come back here."

Now would be a good time to ask about the brunette, but not wanting to hear the answer, I chickened out. Instead, I probed about his family.

"You told me about your parents the other night. Do you have any brothers or sisters?"

"Yep, two sisters. Both younger. Amanda's married to a dentist in Jackson. Samantha is twenty-four and lives in Atlanta. Thinks she has the world by the tail."

I laughed. "So did I at that age. What does she do?"

"My sister is a very junior executive at an advertising firm. She has her own apartment in a good neighborhood and drives a BMW. Sammi buys her wardrobe from Bloomingdale's and eats at the finest restaurants the city has to offer. She dates, but I don't get a whole lot of information in that area."

"Sounds like your sister has expensive tastes. Maybe I should have considered a career in advertising. The pay must be terrific."

Max shrugged and drained his tea, which I refilled. "She maintains her lifestyle with a monthly stipend from brother Max."

The admission surprised me. Max hadn't struck me as the kind to tolerate supporting someone, even a relative, who lived above their means, especially since he'd intimated he was chronically underfunded.

"What happens if brother Max misses a payment?"

"Sammi is resourceful. That's why I never miss a check. I want to keep her on the straight and narrow until reality sets in."

"Reality?"

"The advertising game is unstable. One day you're on top of the heap and the next you're knocking on doors looking for a job." Max gulped his second glass of iced tea.

"Sounds like you know what you're talking about."

He waved off my efforts at another refill. "I do. Worked one summer in high school for an ad firm in

Jackson. I stayed with my aunt and uncle to see if I liked living in the big city. I didn't."

I couldn't visualize Max in a suit and tie or a corporate setting.

"What did you do? Write slogans or jingles?"

He laughed. "Honey, I was nothing more than a glorified gofer. I delivered mail, hauled presentations for the execs, primed prospective clients with coffee or martinis depending upon the time of day, and watched enough backstabbing and character assassination to know I needed to go home."

"I guess Sammi must have found your description exciting. At twenty-four, she's probably having the time of her life."

"Too good a time, which is why I send her money. I'd rather she lived off of me for a while as opposed to having some slick operator take advantage of her. She's still a small-town Mississippi girl."

"Kind of like alimony, huh?" I wanted to bite my tongue. Why had I said that?

"Exactly like that. Marriage sucks the money right out of a man. I should know, and my sister isn't bad at it either. Sammi needs to find one hell of a rich man who'll treat her like a princess and shower her with love."

"Love is the most important part."

He smiled, a soft expression creeping into his eyes. "Yeah, I guess it is. However, money doesn't hurt."

"Yes, but don't you think…"

A loud thumping from upstairs followed by angry shouts, then more clunks and clangs interspersed with muffled voices interrupted my sentence. I set my glass on the counter as Max headed for the stairs at a dead run with me close on his heels.

"What the hell is going on here?" he shouted, stepping into my half-renovated bathroom.

Two men rolled on the debris-covered floor, punching and jabbing. Max waded in to break it up, finally pulling the two combatants apart.

They glared at each other as Max demanded, "I said, what the hell is going on?"

"He's your practical joker!" the first man shouted. "I poked my head into a hole in the wall to check out some wiring and this idiot kicked me in the ass. Banged my head on a stud."

"You stupid asshole, I never did no such thing," the second man maintained. "You tripped over something and tried to blame it on me. I was checking out plumbing needs on this wall."

"Jerk!"

"Moron!"

The men lunged for each other again. Max pushed them apart. "I've had it with practical jokes. Someone's going to get hurt—or fired."

"Yeah, well, I'll save you the trouble," the first man said. "I quit. I was up here by myself yesterday, and I can tell you something ain't right about this place. I kept thinking I was bein' watched. It gave me the creeps so bad, I shivered."

"Yeah? Well, I heard weird noises in the wall earlier this morning," the second man confessed, calmer now. "Ed's right, there's something strange about this place."

"We are renovating an old house and old houses make strange noises, especially when wood that's been undisturbed for a hundred years is torn out. It has to do with stress," Max stated.

*Or mice, maybe even rats.* I shivered, wondering if he believed that or just said it for the workmen's benefit.

"Don't make no fuckin' difference. I'm outta here, too."

Max clenched the man's shirt and brought their faces close together. "Watch your language in front of the lady," he demanded with a snarl.

"Sorry, ma'am. No offense meant."

"None taken," I replied.

The first man picked up his scattered tools. "Come on, Billy Jack, let's get outta here. I hear George Rivers is hiring down Batesville way."

The two men stalked out of the room leaving Max and I standing there looking at the mess.

"Max, what's happening?" I wasn't scared, but uneasiness drifted over me.

"Just what I said. Old houses make strange noises, nothing more," he snapped, running a hand through his hair. "Damn, Jake Anderson quit, too. Claimed he was tired of the practical jokes. I needed him. When I find out who's behind this, I swear I'll kill 'em."

"What did Jake do?"

"Ceilings and drywall. He said he felt the scaffold he was using shake for no reason. I think they've all gone nuts." He checked his watch. "Aw, hell, it's almost three. I need to go scare up some more men."

I followed Max downstairs where he stopped work for the day, and then read the riot act to his workers, including Daryl and Steve, about the practical jokes.

I'd heard it before and returned to the dining room closely followed by my brother and his parnter.

"Sis, what's going on?"

I told them the gist of the incident. "Now, go back to whatever it is Max has you doing. I'm busy."

Carjetta Washington was due in another hour, but I figured I could get a couple of pages finished in the meantime.

Max and the men left. Daryl and Steve unpacked boxes in an unused room. Every few minutes one or the other would stroll past the dining room entry.

I settled down to a serious point of view from Lady Katrina. I'm glad I didn't decide to do dialogue. My concentration broke every few minutes. I had the sensation that things moved just out of my line of sight. I knew I had mice. I'd seen the evidence from time to time. Those little buggers moved fast. I hate picking things up in my peripheral vision. It makes me doubt my eyesight and gives me the creeps.

Thirty minutes later, I gave up and shut down the computer. I had written exactly two paragraphs and both sucked. Maybe I would have better luck this evening. I'd use the extra time to dress like a prospective employer.

\*\*\*\*

"How old are you, Carjetta?" I asked the girl sitting in front of me. She'd arrived at four o'clock on the dot, dressed in a simple skirt and blouse. Her long black hair hung in numerous strands of braids and her only makeup, a dark red lip gloss, complemented her chocolate brown face. She stood on the short side and definitely on the wrong side of a hundred and fifty pounds with ample booty.

On the other hand, Carjetta's butt should not concern me. As long as she could cook, I didn't care how big she let her hips grow, provided she didn't get stuck in the doorjamb.

"I'm eighteen, ma'am."

She answered in a quiet, dignified voice. Score one for Carjetta. "Did Max explain that I needed a cook?"

"Yes, ma'am. I been takin' care of my seven brothers and sisters ever since I was fifteen. Mama is housekeeper for Mrs. Hershey, so I had to do lots of cookin' at home. I can do some fancy stuff, but mostly just plain fare." She fingered the strap of a worn purse.

"I don't need anything fancy, although I will be having guests this Sunday. My family is coming down from Memphis. Will that be a problem? Working on Sunday, I mean."

Carjetta smiled for the first time and patted a gold cross at her throat. "No, ma'am. I wear my cross to ward off evil spirits. God will keep me safe. I'll bring garlic tomorrow, just in case. It's a strong mojo."

Evil spirits? Garlic? Mojo? Boy, could Max ever pick 'em. First a thieving nut case, now a voodoo princess. I thought garlic had to do with vampires. Whatever. As long as she cooked, I didn't care.

"Uh...that's fine. How does fifteen dollars a day sound to you? I'll try to give you twenty-four hours notice if I don't need you."

"That sounds fine, Miss Austin."

"Could you possibly start tonight? I have chicken breasts thawing in the fridge. My brother and a friend are staying for a couple of days."

"Oh, yes, ma'am." She beamed at me, a gold tooth flashing. "If you have some tomatoes, scallions, and mushrooms, I can make an Italian meal. I do nice salads."

I could already taste it. "That sounds wonderful, Carjetta. Now, I must warn you, the kitchen is under construction, so you may have to work around a lot of stuff, but it'll be done soon."

I rose and led her back into the kitchen showing her where everything was located, and then left her to work her magic—culinary magic, that is.

I poured a glass of white wine, grabbed a Heather Graham novel, and headed for the veranda feeling very much the lady of the manor or maybe Lady Katrina. I had a new cook. I hoped this one stayed.

\*\*\*\*

Ruth sat and rocked dejectedly. Hester, the

Colonel, Antoine, and Zoë all slumped in chairs and on the sofa in the back parlor.

"I can't see that we're making any progress," Ruth said. "Cybil isn't frightened at all."

"I thought the cigar smoke would disgust her, but she seems to have enjoyed it," the Colonel moaned.

"I overheard her telling Max it reminded her of her grandfather," Antoine said.

"I never thought haunting could be so exhausting," Zoë complained, yawning. "I could just sleep forever."

"Zoë, you do. You're dead. Remember?" Hester replied. "We all are. But I have to admit, this is sapping what little energy we have. It didn't take long to scare off Germania's daughter's suitor. We must be out of practice."

"Well, the Colonel and I didn't get into the act today until quite late, although I did move the mail last night. We spent some time earlier moving just out of sight. Did it with a workman this morning and with Cybil this afternoon." Ruth sighed and looked around the room. "You know, this is nice furniture. I wonder why she doesn't sit in here and use it."

"It's not her taste," Zoë answered. "She likes the furniture in the drawing room. I sat in one of the chairs last night. It's different, but comfortable."

"Zoë and I moved tools and wood. We hid everything in the barn. I also scared the wadding out of one of the workmen. He was standing on some kind of contraption. I shook it a little and he almost fell."

Ruth wagged her finger at Antoine. "None of that. We don't want anyone to get hurt. And it's not a barn any more. It's called a garage."

"I was told the original barn burned down in 1916. That's when my husband's father bought his first automobile. If he hadn't, I might have lived to a ripe old age," Zoë lamented.

"Does anyone want to hear what I did today?" Hester asked, a smug look on her face.

"Of course," Ruth replied.

"I worked the upstairs. When one of the men bent over to look into the wall, I kicked him in the posterior. He blamed the other workman with him and they ended up fighting. Then they quit, saying the place was haunted!"

"No!" the Colonel said with a gasp.

"Well, not exactly in those words, but close." Hester heaved a sigh. "I feel mighty successful. I also understand a new cook has been hired, a young girl who believes in evil spirits. I'll help her along in those beliefs."

"How did Max and Cybil react to the haunting suggestion?" Zoë asked.

"Max said it was hokum, someone playing a joke, but I think Cybil may have had a glimmer."

"And yet, she still doesn't appear scared. This is not a good sign," Zoë said.

"It looks like we'll have to work again tonight," the Colonel stated. "I was kind of hoping for a night off. I haven't fought the Yankees in a long time."

"You can go back to fighting the Yankees as soon as we get rid of Cybil." Ruth picked up the ever-present knitting needles from her lap. "Hester, I suggest you get started on this new cook. The rest of you think up more shenanigans for tonight."

They all drifted away, leaving Ruth to ponder the sweater that would never be finished. She tried anyway.

"Let's see. I knit two, purl two, or is it purl one? Oh, dear..."

****

I closed my book, finished the last of my wine, and then stretched like a contented cat. Rising from the chair, I entered the house, intent on refilling my glass. Tonight, I would sleep. I had a new cook and from the delicious smells wafting down the foyer, would also be well fed. Italian cooking sent my stomach straight into overeating mode.

A scream from the kitchen had the hairs on the back of my neck and arms rising to attention. I raced into the room just as Carjetta fled out the back door and across the yard, braids flapping like the wings of skinny birds.

I took off after her. I should have asked if she was afraid of mice.

"Carjetta! Wait! Don't go! What's wrong?"

The girl pounded around the side of the house, ignoring me. I increased my pace.

"Carjetta! Please," I begged at a dead run.

She hollered something over her shoulder that sounded like "evil spirits" and kept on going.

"Carjetta! I'll get mousetraps! I promise!" She never broke stride. "You can't do this to me! My mother is coming on Sunday!"

She made the driveway. I gave up halfway across the front lawn, winded. I was badly out of shape, but overweight or not, my latest cook could sure pick 'em up and lay 'em down. I'd never seen anybody move so fast.

Giving it one last try, I yelled, "But I can't cook!"

Her bobbling booty rounded the curve in the drive and disappeared from view.

****

"Good heavens, Hester. What did you do to the poor girl?" the Colonel asked.

They all stood in the kitchen awaiting Cybil's reappearance. Ruth had turned down the stove as a precaution.

"Basically, the same as with Lavinia Rogers, only this time, I sort of materialized."

"Hester, you didn't!" Ruth said, gasping. "We agreed not to do that."

"Oh, I didn't really show myself. The girl saw a column of fog in the butler's pantry doorway, that's all. After the other things, she took off like a jackrabbit."

Zoë and Antoine laughed. "Like it or not, Ruth, I think we may have to resort to partial materialization if things don't change soon," she said.

"I agree," Antoine remarked. "I think we should concentrate on the workmen by day and Cybil by night. We need more—what's it called—gaslighting."

"Okay. Tonight we'll give the noises a rest and just move things. Maybe the workers will get tired of being accused of playing practical jokes. Oh, here comes Cybil."

****

I reentered the kitchen, defeated and forlorn. Carjetta had been in my employ exactly two-and-a-half hours. I wondered if a world's record existed on how fast employers lost employees. I'd check the Guinness book tomorrow.

Walking to the stove, I looked at what should have been dinner. Could I salvage it? The frying pan held a chunky tomato sauce. I stirred it tentatively. The aroma set my mouth to watering. The browned chicken breasts lay on a paper towel next to the stove. I concluded they were supposed to cook with the sauce, but for how long? Ten minutes, twenty, an hour? I had no clue. I dropped the chicken into the sauce and slapped the lid on, then turned the timer to an hour and the burner to medium.

*"Good grief, she's going to incinerate those poor things,"* Ruth claimed. *"What kind of a mother doesn't teach her daughter how to cook even the simplest of meals?"*

I could handle a salad and would take the cheater's way out for the garlic bread—toast, then smear the bread with butter and shake on some garlic powder. I opened the refrigerator door to gather the salad makings.

*"Watch this," Antoine said with mischief in his eyes. He walked up to, and then right through Cybil.*

I gasped as the strangest sensation passed through me. I felt a sudden burst of cold, not just on my outside, but inside as well. And for an instant, I imagined I had expanded to twice my size. Then the feeling passed and I jumped back from the refrigerator, dropping the bag of lettuce and two tomatoes in the bargain.

I shivered. I'd had one helluva day. Obviously, my body, overheated from the chase with Carjetta, had a delayed reaction triggered by opening the refrigerator door. I reclaimed my dropped items and proceeded to make my salad.

*"Antoine, are you all right? You look pale," Zoë said.*

*"You mean pale for a ghost?"*

*"What on earth possessed you to do that?"*

*"Possessed. That's funny, Zoë. I wouldn't recommend it to anyone else. It's very draining," he replied.*

*"It's also ineffectual," Hester remarked. "She's going on like nothing happened."*

*Ruth fisted her hands on her hips, frustrated at their inability to scare Cybil. "Well...well...oh, damn!"*

Chapter Eight

Daryl had saved the chicken breasts from certain doom. In between chuckles, he and Steve had taken over the kitchen duties. While the guys cleaned up, I sneaked outside to sit on the veranda. The symphony of chirping insects gave me a cozy feeling. The sweet night air spelled country and the South. In just a few short weeks, I'd come to love Shady Oaks, peeling paint, ugly wallpaper, and all.

It had been a long day and I looked forward to reading in bed for an hour. Hopefully, tonight would have no noises to disturb my sleep.

I rose to reenter the house and ran smack dab into Daryl. I jumped back with a surprised cry, my hand over my heart.

"Daryl! Don't sneak up on a person like that. You scared me to death."

"Sorry. Are you all right? What are you doing?"

"I'm enjoying some quiet time and being alone. Why?"

"Oh, no reason. We just missed you and wondered where you'd gone."

"Right now, I'm going to bed." I brushed past him into the foyer and headed toward the stairs.

"But it's only nine o'clock."

"I get up early to write before the workmen arrive. I'll see you in the morning."

I settled into bed and was in the middle of a chapter when someone knocked.

"Come in."

Steve poked his head around the door. "Hi, just wanted to make sure you were all right. Do you need

118

anything?"

I looked up in exasperation. "Why wouldn't I be all right? I'm in bed. Reading."

"I...I'm sorry. I didn't mean to disturb you." He made a move to back out.

"Steve, I'm sorry. I didn't mean to bark. And, no, I don't need anything."

He smiled and shut the door. I resumed reading only to be interrupted twenty minutes later by another knock.

I sighed. "Come in."

It was Daryl this time. "Hi, sis. I wondered..."

"I'm all right, and I don't need anything," I interrupted.

"Uh, sorry. I was just going to say goodnight."

The confusion on his face made me feel like a heel. "Sorry. Didn't mean to snap. Goodnight. See you in the morning."

He shifted from foot to foot before adding, "If you hear any strange sounds, come get me. Steve and I will investigate."

"Investigate what? It's the wind and the construction."

"Yeah, well, if you're nervous, I'm just down the hall. Sleep tight."

I stared at the raised panels of the door after he left and shrugged. I tried to pick up where I'd left off, but finally closed the book and set it on the nightstand.

Turning out the light, I lay back and listened. All was quiet. I slipped out of bed, padded to the door, and opened it. Silence greeted me. I loved my brother and Steve, but they were driving me nuts.

****

"Cybil, I'd like you to meet Reba St. Clair."

I stared at Max's latest in the line of cooks and asked, "You're not afraid of mice, are you?"

The woman raised her eyebrows. "Of course not.

Mousetraps take care of that problem, and I'm not squeamish about emptying them either."

"Oh, thank God. I've got a little problem with the critters. They scared Lavinia Rogers and Carjetta Washington into screaming fits."

"Vinnie Rogers is a cantankerous old woman who should be scared of a lot of things. Rumor has it she's been holed up in her house with the vapors for the past two days," Reba stated. "Am a little surprised at Carjetta, though. I hear she once killed a rat with a shovel."

"Well, if you ladies don't need me, I think I'll get back to work," Max said, sidling toward the drawing room door. "I've got a couple of new men on the job today and want to make sure they understand what they're doing."

Reba waved him away. "Go ahead, Max. If I need a lift back to town, I'll let you know."

"Now, Ms. St. Clair..."

"It's Miss. I don't much care for the newfangled way of addressing a woman. It's either Miss or Missus."

"Uh, fine, Miss St. Clair..."

"Name's Reba. Might as well use it. Everyone else does." She settled back in one of the chairs and wiggled her hips. "Nice chairs. Don't look comfortable, but they are. Like the design, too."

I wanted to kiss her. Reba stood about an inch taller than me and had a matronly figure. Not exactly fat, but more plump-like. Her hair, an impossible color of red, told me she dyed it herself, and her sharp brown eyes didn't look like they missed much. She had a no-nonsense manner I found refreshing, unlike the rudeness of Lavinia.

"Thank you, Reba. I guess Max has told you I can't cook. I can handle breakfast and lunch, but dinner will be a problem."

Boy, was that ever an understatement. If I

didn't find a cook with staying power soon, rumors would fly I'd turned anorexic.

"How much help do you need around the house?" Reba asked, looking around the drawing room.

"The house? Well, there's not much to do. With all the construction, I ignore it."

She leaned forward and ran her finger over the coffee table, leaving a well-defined path in the dust. Okay, so I didn't keep a spotless house, but if I tried, I'd never get a word written.

"I'll take care of it. Understand you're a writer."

"Yes. I write historical romance-action stories. They are not smut," I declared.

"Never said they were. I like 'em myself. Okay, here's the deal. I will come out Monday through Friday at ten in the morning. I'll dust, sweep, vacuum, and do whatever housework there is. I'll also make you lunch and dinner. All you gotta do is write those stories. I want Saturdays off, but will come out for a couple of hours on Sunday afternoon to make a proper Sunday dinner if you want. If not, I'll make sure you have enough leftovers to tide you through the weekend. How's that sound?"

I gaped at the woman, overwhelmed. Reba sounded like a gift from God, almost too good to be true. There had to be a catch.

"How...how much is this going to cost me?"

"A hundred dollars a week. Cash. No need for the IRS to know I'm supplementing my Social Security." Reba sat back and folded her arms across her chest.

A hundred dollars! What a bargain. She would do the housework, the cooking, and be here during the day.

"I'm a bargain," she said as if reading my thoughts. "I suggest you take it. You're not likely to get anyone else to come out here."

"Why not?"

"Strange things happen around Shady Oaks. Lavinia's grandmother started the stories, although Germania LaForge lived here with a companion the last five years of her life and nobody said nothin' about any odd goings-on. Even so, you'd best face the facts. I may be your last chance."

Strange things? Like weird noises? Was she being subtle about something? What? I dismissed the implication. Max said it was just the wind, and I believed Max. Spitefulness probably ran in Lavinia's family.

"I understand your workmen have been havin' a few problems, too."

"This is an old house undergoing renovations. Max says there's a practical joker, but he thinks it'll stop now. I swear I'll take care of the mouse problem."

Reba smiled and patted my hand. "I like you, Miss Austin. You seem like a right nice lady who needs help. Shady Oaks is a lovely old house, and I approve of what you're doin'. It takes more than a little old mouse to scare me."

I melted. I liked Reba and instinct told me she was honest. I wouldn't find any sugar hidden in her purse.

"You have a deal, Reba, and please call me Cybil. I'm not a formal person." She smiled broadly and we shook hands. "At the moment, my brother and his friend are visiting and helping with the construction. Oh, by the way, my family, including my mother, is coming to dinner on Sunday."

She gave me a knowing smile. "A bit critical, is she?"

"No. A lot critical," I confessed.

"How many?"

"Including me, nine adults and at least three kids for a total of twelve."

Reba stared at me with a raised eyebrow. "Like I

said, you need help, in more ways than one. Okay, what do you want to serve?"

"I hadn't thought about it," I said.

"Go with a roast. Keep it simple."

"Okay, I'll go to the grocery store today. How big?"

"I'll take care of it. Smithson's Butcher Shop has reasonable prices. Words of advice: in a small town always try to use the local people before going to a chain. It builds good community relations."

I was touched she would advise me on the ways of small towns. I had a lot to learn. We spent the next twenty minutes menu planning, a new experience for me.

I gave Reba a tour of the house, showing her where the cleaning supplies lived, introducing her to Daryl and Steve along the way, and then returned to the dining room intending to write while she earned her hundred bucks. My eyes fell on the credenza. The candlesticks, on the right yesterday, now stood on the left, the impressions left clearly visible in the dust.

I chewed a fingernail and stared. I'd slept well last night, hearing no outlandish noises or smelling anything unusual—no roses or cigar smoke.

Troubled, I walked into the back parlor. I didn't often come in this room and couldn't remember what I'd left where. My gaze homed in on the bare mantel. Hadn't I left a picture of my father on one side and a bud vase with an artificial rose in it on the other? The picture now posed on the table behind the sofa and the vase graced an end table.

I strolled through the rest of the downstairs, saving the drawing room for last.

The sculpture on the coffee table had moved, and everything on the mantel had been rearranged. All the lights, off when I'd talked with Reba, now burned brightly. I flipped the switches. A prickling sensation skittered along my arms, raising the hairs, and I had the weird impression someone watched.

"Cybil! Cybil! Where are you? Cybil, answer me!" My brother's voice carried throughout the house.

"Oh, for Pete's sake," I muttered.

"Cybil!" This time the raised voice belonged to Steve.

"I'm in here," I shouted.

They raced through the door and into the room.

"Are you all right?" they chorused.

"What are you doing in here?" Daryl asked.

I turned, fists jammed on my hips. "I'm fine and it's my drawing room. I'm allowed to be in here. What the hell is it with you two? I can't move two feet without one of you asking if I'm all right. Quit following me around like a couple of shadows. Out of my way! I have a work to do."

They took the hint and left while I returned to the dining room. From the kitchen I overheard the guys talking in low voices. I moved to the door, eavesdropping.

"This is harder than I thought," Daryl said.

"I think we're like bulls in a china shop. It might be better if we keep an eye on her from afar. You know, stay out of sight and don't say anything when we see her."

"We should have come up with a plan for who watches over her and when. We're overlapping our duties."

"I don't believe this," I exclaimed stepping into the room. "Wanna tell me what's going on?"

Steve's face bore a dismayed expression while Daryl actually blushed.

"Sis, we were worried. You called saying something about a practical joker and hearing odd noises. It's a big house and you're alone at night. So, Steve took some time off work and we came down to check things out for ourselves. Did you hear anything last night?"

"Nothing suspicious. Just the usual. You two obviously didn't." My shoulders slumped. "I'm too old for a babysitter. Look guys, I appreciate the thought, but I'm fine."

Steve shook his head. "You're out here in the middle of nowhere in an old house with even older locks. At least, let us install a couple of deadbolts."

"If I agree, will the two of you go home and let me be?"

They exchanged glances and sighed. "I guess. But promise me you won't do something silly like go for a walk at night or sit on the front porch alone," my brother begged.

I turned my face to the ceiling and raised my hand. "I promise."

"Promise what?" Max asked entering from the back door.

I told him the situation, then wanted to smack him when he laughed.

"Go to Brewster's Hardware in town. They'll have what you need," he said.

Daryl and Steve took the advice, installed the locks, and left before noon.

I sat in front of the computer and sighed. Finally, I'd get some work done. A power saw shrieked in the kitchen. I covered my face with my hands.

Unable to work, I cornered Max in the kitchen. Those strange peripheral viewings were still with me. Practical joker or not, this nonsense was getting out of hand.

"Max, could I speak with you privately for a minute?"

He straightened from his work area. For once, I didn't notice his rear end.

"Sure, Cybil. What's up?"

We walked into the dining room. "Max, do you trust your workers?"

"Of course. I've known most of them all my life. I think the practical jokes have stopped. Nothing was missing this morning. Why?"

I told him about the way things had moved from place to place in several of the rooms, feeling foolish, once again.

"Do you think I could have a prowler? Could one of the men be coming back after I go to bed and doing this? I lock up every night, but this is a big house. Maybe someone stays hidden, plays the joke, and then leaves while I'm asleep."

I didn't like suggesting this any more than I did the thought of a stranger creeping around my house. But if I did have a prowler, I needed to know. Perhaps sending Daryl and Steve home hadn't been such a good idea.

Max frowned and knit his brow. "Cybil, I don't know what to tell you. I can't see any of them doing such a thing."

"Could someone resent me buying this place? Want me to leave?"

"People I talked to sounded pleased someone cared about Shady Oaks. You're an author and kind of a celebrity. Anyone from Memphis not want you to move?"

"Only my mother and this is not her way of doing things. She just beats on you until you give in. If she's doing this, it's the subtlest thing she's ever done. She and my whole family will be here for Sunday dinner."

This wasn't Mother's style, and I wasn't an important enough author to warrant stalking. Even though Oxford, Mississippi, wasn't too far away, I wasn't William Faulkner or John Grisham.

Max cupped my face in his hands. "Are you afraid of being alone in the house?"

Was I? Damn my brother. He'd gotten me to thinking, never a good sign. "No, not really. Could there be another entrance? One we don't know about?"

He kissed me lightly, setting my heart to beating a bit faster than normal.

"You mean like a hidden door?"

"I guess. Maybe Shady Oaks once housed escaped slaves or something."

"Not the LaForge family. They were true slave-owning Southerners. Had several family members in the Confederate army. I haven't come across anything like that."

"So, I'm just being a ninny?"

Max pulled me close and held me in a light embrace. In spite of my worries, I felt safe and secure.

"No, you're not being a ninny," he admonished. "I'm concerned, too. I still can't find some of the missing tools and Ted Connor quit today. With your brother and Steve gone, I'm really shorthanded." He looked deep into my eyes. "You know, if you're scared, I could move in—if it makes you feel better."

Make me feel better? It would probably make me feel magnificent, but Mother's face loomed in front of me.

"Thanks, but I don't think that would work. I'd hate to start out my life in Cherokee as a source of gossip, although the offer is very appealing." I ran my finger down his jaw.

He grinned again, and then proceeded to kiss the breath out of me. My heart hammered. In order to remain standing, I slid my arms around his neck and kissed him back.

Heat, warm and delicious, surged like an electrical current, but before I reached critical mass, he backed away.

My head spun and Max had a funny expression

on his face. I wanted a steady diet of Max Maitland and wondered if maybe he had the same notion about me.

His arms dropped. He smiled, and then said, "Lady, you are something else. We need to go out to dinner again. I'm tied up with business until early next week. How about then?"

I nodded, still trying to breathe.

"Are you sure you're going to be all right—at night, I mean?"

I nodded again, finally managing to speak. "I think so. I just have a case of the heebie-jeebies. I'm not normally a worry-wart or a nervous Nelly."

What was the matter with me? Since when did I string together old-fashioned clichés? Damn, they sounded like something my mother would say. Ack! No!

"Maybe I should get a gun," I said.

"Do you know how to shoot one?"

"No."

"I'd skip the gun idea. You'd probably shoot your foot off. Why don't you get a dog?"

"A dog?"

I hadn't thought of that. Mother never allowed us to have pets. She didn't want to deal with dog or cat hair and the general upkeep.

"Yeah. A dog would keep you company at night and alert you to any intruders in the house. A barking dog scares the hell out of prowlers."

"Max, that's a great idea. Any special breed?" I visualized a cute little ball of fluff curled up on my lap and sleeping at the foot of the bed.

"German shepherds, Dobermans, rottweilers are all good guard dogs. Just don't go get something like a Chihuahua or a shih-tzu. They don't scare anybody. All they do is pee when they get excited."

"All right. Do you know a good breeder nearby?"

"You don't want a puppy. Go to the pound and

get a dog that's housebroken." He dropped another kiss on my forehead. "I've got to get back to work. Lunch?"

"Yes, fine. By the way, I hired Reba."

"Good move."

He left, and I sat down to contemplate dogs. Big dogs.

****

"Well, she's noticing the moved items, but they don't seem to be scaring her," Ruth lamented to the others. "Could we be losing our touch?"

Zoë bit her lip and shrugged. "I can't believe she thinks its mice."

"Maybe she doesn't," Antoine replied. "Maybe she doesn't *want* to believe what she's seeing."

"Or what's causing it," Zoë said.

"And she has another cook," Hester stated. Even her enthusiasm had waned. She wore a dejected look on her face.

"Who?" Ruth queried.

"Someone named Reba. I don't know her."

"I suppose we continue as before?" Antoine asked.

"At least I'm more rested. We only did a few things last night," Zoë commented.

"Yes, but our time is running out. I had to relocate Uncle William, Aunt Eliza, and two cousins whose names I didn't even know, yesterday afternoon. There are entirely too many of us in the house," Ruth grumbled. "This haunting business is becoming *real* work."

"I'm tired of haunting. I want to fight the Yankees," the Colonel groused.

"Will you give the Yankees a rest? They already beat us once," Hester barked. "We have to get rid of Cybil before she opens any more walls. If we don't, we'll be sharing space with relatives and people we'd rather not."

"I heard her telling Max that her family was coming to dinner on Sunday," Zoë said slowly. "Maybe we should conserve our energy and wait until then. A family dinner complete with a haunting should scare the wits out of everyone."

"What a magnificent idea," Antoine praised. "We could do all sorts of things during a dinner."

Ruth contemplated Zoë's suggestion. "I think that might be the best idea yet. We can still do the little, annoying things overnight. That shouldn't require much energy. Then come Sunday, pull out the stops. Hester and I will see what we can do with this cook. The rest of you, go rest up for tonight."

The others popped out of sight and Ruth led the way back to the kitchen. The new cook, Reba, stood in front of the sink washing dishes.

"Okay, time to get started." Hester moved forward and used her hand to splash water out of the sink and onto the front of Reba's dress, then stood back to watch the reaction.

Reba merely grabbed a dishtowel and mopped up the moisture.

"Well! You'd think she'd notice the water suddenly looked alive," Hester claimed.

"Try something else. Just a little something to get her thinking. We can be more aggressive when she starts to cook," Ruth suggested.

Hester nodded and with a smug smile on her face, slid a glass waiting to be washed toward the sink. Reba never missed a beat. She simply picked up the glass and dunked it into the soapy water.

Hester's jaw dropped. "Merciful heavens, is she blind?"

"Saints preserve us," Ruth exclaimed. "She's...she's laughing!"

Reba finished her task, dried her hands and whirled. "Won't do you any good. I'm not a guilt-ridden thief like Lavinia Rogers or a superstitious nincompoop like Carjetta. You don't scare me. You're amateurs. Now, go about your other business. It's lunchtime and I'm making Cybil and Max sandwiches."

Stunned, Hester and Ruth looked at one another.

"Ruth, we've got big problems."

Chapter Nine

The Cherokee County Animal Shelter and Adoption Agency resembled a canine insane asylum. Listening to the incessant barking day in and day out would drive me crazy. Rick, the young man at the front desk, offered a tour of the facility, and I accepted.

"At the moment we have about two dozen dogs and three dozen cats," Rick explained, shouting over the noise. "We believe in adoption, not euthanasia. We only put down animals that come to us too sick or injured to recover and those too mean to release to a family. And we don't use any of those chambers. We have vets who volunteer their time. They're put to sleep with a drug cocktail and someone holding them as they go."

I wanted to cry at the thought of dogs and cats going to pet heaven. The eager, hopeful faces rushing to the front of the cages as I walked past made me want to take them all. And knowing my ability to make decisions, I wondered if maybe I should ask Rick to pick one.

The facility impressed me. All dogs had individual cages (he called them kennels) with a door leading to narrow runs outside. Food dishes and water bottles were attached to the cage doors. Faded rugs on the concrete floors enabled the animals to curl up and sleep in comfort.

"Our animals are spayed or neutered and given a check-up complete with all necessary shots. If we have a history on a pet, we give it to you."

"How would you get a history? Aren't they

strays?"

"Not all. Some are given up by their owners."

How could someone do that? Most people considered pets family members, although I would have no problem giving my sisters away to a good home.

We continued our stroll past the kennels. I heeded Max's warning about small dogs. Most of the dogs I saw could only be described as mixed breeds. I had no idea what to look for and threw myself on Rick's mercy.

"I'll be honest. I've never owned a dog. I live alone. That's never been a problem in the past because I lived in apartments in the city. Now, I live in the country and I'm looking for something like...well..."

"A security blanket?" Rick grinned.

"I'm a little nervous," I admitted. "A friend suggested a guard-type dog."

He led me down the aisle to the larger dogs. "This is a shepherd mix, and the one next to him has some Doberman."

They looked nice, but didn't spark much of a response. Maybe it was like the house and I needed to have one talk to me.

As we walked, I read the little cards attached to the kennel doors giving the probable breeding, age, and sex of the inmate. The lolling tongues and wagging tails begged to be chosen. We neared the end of the cages. I needed to make a decision.

The last kennel drew my attention. It contained a large, black, furry rug on the floor. Curious, I stopped in front of it. The rug bounded up with a hearty *"Woof!"* and jumped against the door. I found myself eyeball to eyeball and breathing in the doggie breath of the biggest dog I'd ever seen.

I leaped back with a yelp not unlike some of the sounds coming from behind me.

"What is that?"

Rick laughed. "He's been with us about a month. I came to work one morning and found him tied to the front door."

*"Woof!"* The concussion almost knocked me over. His coat was long and shaggy and the dog's tongue flapped from the side of his mouth like an enormous pink flag. The ears hung almost to his shoulders and the fluffy tail had lethal possibilities. It whipped from side to side with deadly force. I felt the breeze three feet away.

"Good God, what kind of a dog is he?"

"As close as we can tell, he's a cross between an Irish wolfhound and maybe a Newfoundland. We're not sure. The ears aren't from either breed, so there's probably something else thrown into the mix. The head and his size are wolfhound while the coat, tail, and body shape look Newfoundland. My guess is someone dumped him because he got too big."

"Yeah, I can see that. Does he come with a saddle?"

Rick laughed again. "He's a gentle giant—just hard to adopt. He needs space to run and lots of grooming. You can't allow the coat to tangle. Not many people want to put up with daily brushing. Wanna see him?"

Before I could stop myself, I nodded. Rick opened the kennel door and clipped a leash onto the monster's collar. He led the dog into the aisle where it promptly sat down, cocked its head to one side, and gazed at me as though to say, *You and me, babe. Right?*

Oh, hell. He talked to me. I reached out a tentative hand and patted his massive head. Encouraged by not losing a hand, I attempted a scratch behind the ears. I swear the animal grinned.

"Is he housebroken?"

"Oh, yes, and you can see, he's very well-behaved."

I stroked his neck and back. As thanks, the dog rose while licking my hand and arm with the tongue of death. I dripped dog saliva. I didn't care, wiping it off on my slacks, and checked the card on the kennel door.

"He's six to eight years old?" I'd been hoping for something a little younger.

"Uh...that's six to eight months, ma'am."

"He's still a puppy?" Okay, so I'd been hoping for something a little *older*. "You mean he's still growing?"

"It's possible, but I'd have to say he's about there."

"Does he have a name?"

"We've been calling him Dudley. Don't know why."

My scratching fingers had reached the base of his tail. My reward was another lavish dose of saliva.

"He seems to like you. Shall I wrap him up?"

"Do you also sell used cars?"

Rick and Dudley both grinned. I had no idea what I was doing, but then I hadn't with the house either. And both had talked to me. I petted Dudley's head again. Soulful eyes stared back.

"I guess I have a dog. No need to wrap, I'll just ride him home."

Rick slapped the leash in my hand. "Follow me. You can have the collar and leash. Anna will give him a final brushing while we fill out the paperwork."

I handed Dudley off to one of the attendants and followed Rick back to the office. I wondered if any of the stores in town handled dog food in bulk.

\*\*\*\*

After signing the papers, I had them hold Dudley so I could make an emergency run to a pet store for bowls, doggie toys, a bed, a new collar, grooming supplies, and food. It set me back over three hundred dollars.

I breathed a sigh of relief driving home. Dudley seemed to like the back seat of my Camry. He lay down, taking up the entire space.

Max was seated on the veranda when I pulled up. He strolled over, and then looked in the back seat.

Dudley rose poking his head out of the driver's side window. Max stared. "What the hell is that?"

"Max, meet Dudley. Dudley, Max."

Max offered a cautious hand. Dudley licked it. I got out of the car and opened the back door. My new best friend leaped out, shook, and took off to explore, sniffing every blade of grass and lifting his leg on any vertical item he found. Then he left a large deposit on the front lawn.

"Well, you're not going to have to bother with fertilizer come spring," Max drawled. "Didn't they have anything a little less enormous?"

I laughed. "I know he's big and will probably eat me out of house and home, but I just couldn't resist."

"Oh, brother. How much does he weigh?"

"I'm not sure, but the shelter gave me the name of a local vet. I made an appointment for tomorrow morning."

"Is he trained? I mean to sit, lie down, come, and things like that. If not, he's going to drag you all over on the leash or run away when loose."

"Of course he's trained," I stated, defending my dog. "The shelter employees put me through the paces before they released him. He comes."

To demonstrate, I whistled and called, "Here, Dudley. Come on, boy. Come to Mama."

The stupid mutt ignored me and continued his exploration. I tried again with the same results.

"Yeah, he's trained." Max whistled and ordered,

"Dudley, come."

Dudley responded immediately, the stinking traitor. I snapped on his leash and glared at both of the men in my life. "Is Reba still here?"

"She's in the kitchen."

"Come on, Dudley. Let's go meet Reba and see your new home."

On all fours, Dudley came up to my waist. To my relief, he behaved like a gentleman and walked serenely up the front steps. Reba met us in the foyer.

"Well, it seems you have a dog," she said in a calm voice. "I like dogs."

"Oh, I'm so glad. It gets kind of lonely out here at night. I rescued him from the animal shelter."

"Good for you, miss. May I suggest tying a clothesline to a tree and clipping him to it when he goes out at night until he learns his way around? That way he won't get lost." She petted and scratched him. His tail waved like a semaphore.

"Oh, Reba, that's a wonderful idea." She nodded and returned to the kitchen.

"I'll do it for you before I leave," Max said. "Come into the drawing room for a moment. I have a change in the bath I'd like you to okay."

*"Ruth, she has a dog!" Hester said.*

*"LaForges always had dogs at Shady Oaks," the Colonel declared. "Good idea, too. Shady Oaks needs a dog."*

*"But it's such a big dog," Zoë murmured. "Do you suppose it's vicious?"*

*"Doesn't look it," Ruth replied.*

*"Looks kind of friendly," Antoine said.*

*"We should really try to do something with this. After our experience with the cook this afternoon, I have to admit I'm confused," Hester remarked.*

*"Do you think she actually saw you?" Zoë asked.*

*"That's the feeling I had," Ruth said. "We hadn't materialized, but I'll swear she looked us straight in*

*the eyes. It was very unsettling."*

*"Well, let's not let this situation go a moment longer," Hester decided.*

*They looked at each other, then the dog, and stepped forward in unison.*

I unclipped the leash and followed Max into the room. Dudley sniffed at the furniture and I kept a close eye on him to make sure he defiled no inside vertical structures. Max picked up the plans and sat on the sofa.

"Now, if you'll look at this, you can see the wall space can be better..."

Dudley growled. My head jerked in surprise. He stood in front of the fireplace, his lips drawn back in a snarl. Then he barked. Not the friendly woof of earlier, but an honest-to-goodness don't-mess-with-me bark. Dudley growled again, but in an instant the growl turned into a whine, and finally a yelp. He cringed as though about to be beaten and dove under the coffee table, howling.

He didn't fit. The table rose a good two feet, tossing everything on it into the air. I leaped to my feet and made a grab for the sculpture before it could smash the glass. I clutched it just inches from the surface. Max made a try for the vase and missed. Luckily, it hit the floor. Unluckily, it broke, sending water and gladiolas flying all over.

Under the table, which now balanced and rocked on Dudley's back, the dog continued to cry and shiver.

"Dudley! What's wrong, boy?" I slung the sculpture on the sofa and crawled beside the poor thing.

Reba came in from the kitchen. "What's going on here?"

"Damned if I know," Max replied. "Cybil's gone and gotten herself a nutty dog."

"I don't know. All of a sudden he growled,

barked, and then acted terrified." I patted my thighs. "Here, Dudley. Come on out, boy. It's okay."

"Perfectly normal, and then scared, huh?" Reba said. She stared at the window next to the fireplace. "It sounds to me as if he saw something and was frightened. It's a new house for him. I'm sure it won't happen again."

*"Ruth, we've just been warned off scaring the dog!" Hester said. "She looked right at us again."*

*"Let's discuss this in the back parlor," Ruth said, her voice shaky.*

*"Who is this woman?" Zoë asked in a hushed tone.*

"You...you mean like a mouse?" I couldn't believe it. My dog was afraid of mice! Oh, why me?

"That's the craziest thing I've ever heard," Max said.

Reba knelt. "Come on, Dudley. Come on, boy. There's nothing to be afraid of. I promise. You won't see it again."

Max lifted the table, being careful not to dump the glass, and Dudley slunk out on his belly. He stood and stopped quivering. Shaking himself, he licked Reba's hand and my face.

"I think everything is fine now," my cook said, and rose to her feet. She returned a few minutes later and cleaned up the mess from the broken vase, while Max and I comforted Dudley. "Your dinner is almost done, Cybil. If Max is going into town, I wonder if you might drop me on the corner by the drugstore."

"Yeah, sure, no problem. Cybil, we'll go over this tomorrow morning. I'll tie the clothesline out front. The light's better and there aren't any building supplies for him to get tangled in."

"Thanks. I appreciate it."

I sneaked bits and pieces of gravy-covered noodles to Dudley during dinner daydreaming about

Max and what he was doing tonight. Was he home alone microwaving a pre-cooked meal or was he out? Did he have a date with the brunette? At her place with a home cooked meal, maybe? An unsettling dart of jealousy poked me.

*Don't go there. It'll only upset you. Perhaps I should try more flirting during the day. Bat my eyes and smile. Yeah, right. I'd look like a simpering twit.* Coquettish actions just weren't in my repertoire. I didn't have the talent.

After washing the dishes, I put Max out of my mind—well, as far out as I could, and composed another five pages of Lord Edgeware and Lady Katrina.

A little before midnight, I stood on the porch while Dudley went outside and did his business from the line Max had rigged. I placed his bed, which looked almost as big as mine, under the window. He sniffed, then with a huge doggie groan, curled up and settled in for the night. Within minutes I made another discovery. Dudley snored.

I chuckled, comforted the big lummox was only five feet away. I fluffed up my pillows and for the first time reviewed the events of earlier in the drawing room. I'd once read that animals often responded to unseen things and sometimes felt the tremors of an earthquake hours before it occurred. I really didn't think we were about to experience an earthquake—the New Madrid Fault notwithstanding.

No, Dudley had seen something, but according to the books those "somethings" only happened when involving... *Oh, don't be ridiculous. That's nonsense.* He'd seen a mouse and that was all. Tomorrow I'd go into town and buy traps.

## Chapter Ten

I paced the dining room, tweaking a fork a quarter of an inch one way and a spoon a quarter of an inch another. A minute later I'd rearrange them again. Then I wandered into the kitchen to ask Reba for the tenth time in as many minutes how things were going.

"Cybil, honey, just relax. Dinner will be served at exactly three o'clock. That gives you and your family an hour to tour the house and chat. Now, go. Get out of my kitchen."

I reentered the dining room and gazed at the place settings. My new modern dining ensemble fit well in the room. The black wood table could seat twelve, maybe fourteen with both leaves in, although it would be a tight fit. I thought everything looked fantastic. My stomach clenched. Mother would hate it.

I'd worked like a beaver to fill the china cabinet with Grandmother Austin's antique china and silver service. Both were a source of pride to me and an irritant to my sister, Penelope, who had coveted them for years. Grandfather Austin specifically left them to me in his will.

Fresh flowers in a crystal vase graced the sideboard and I carefully moved a gladiola a trifle to one side, then stepped back to scrutinize the arrangement. Did it look symmetrical? It did to my eye.

Dudley wandered into the room laid his chin on the table. "Dudley, no." I removed it before any doggie drool could spot the tablecloth.

Only in residence a couple of days, Dudley found the place to his liking. I brushed him every morning, not an easy chore, and let him have the run of the yard at noon. I used the leash for his morning walk and the clothesline for his evening business call. So far, he hadn't run off and always came back when I called. The weird behavior of the first night had not been repeated, thank God.

The other strange happenings had diminished, too. I still found things out of place, and the workmen continued to lose a few tools here and there, but if I was sleepwalking or hallucinating at least I was doing it on a lesser level.

I glanced at my watch. One o'clock. Where were Daryl and Steve? They'd promised to come early for moral support and, knowing my brother, a pep talk. I hadn't heard from him since sending him and Steve home.

Ten minutes later, they arrived, and I opened the door with a flourish.

"Welcome to Shady Oaks, gentlemen."

"Hi, sis." Daryl hugged me. "You okay? How's it going?"

"Not bad," I answered. "Everything's been quiet. Hi, Steve."

Steve also hugged me and followed Daryl through the door. "Hi, short stuff. Thanks for inviting me. Here are a couple of bottles of wine. It's Cabernet Sauvignon. I hope it goes with what we're having."

"Roast beef and this is perfect. Thanks, Steve."

I closed the door and led them into the drawing room where Dudley greeted the guys with an enthusiastic woof.

"Good God, what is that?" Daryl asked.

"My dog. Daryl, Steve, meet Dudley."

"Dog? I thought you were keeping a pony in the house," Steve teased, scratching Dudley's head.

Within minutes that silly dog had rolled over on his back while my brother and Steve scratched his belly. Dudley had an expression on his face that clearly indicated he'd just gone to doggie heaven.

I gave the guys a tour of the house renovations before everyone else showed up. The progress in the kitchen impressed them the most even though it had only been a couple of days since they'd seen it. When we finished, both gave me useful tips on decorating.

Back in the drawing room, I sat on the edge of my chair and fiddled with my skirt, my rings, and my watch until Daryl finally said, "For Pete's sake, Cybil, calm down. Mother's not going to eat you."

"I wouldn't be so sure of that," I murmured. "I haven't heard from her since she invited everybody down. She must really be pissed."

"Honcy, I haven't heard from her in three years. Does she know Steve and I are coming?"

"No. Why should I tell her that specifically? Who I invite to dinner is my business. Can you tell I'm not looking forward to this family shindig?"

"This could be a very interesting dinner," Steve said in a dry voice. "I take it that is the liquor cabinet." He pointed to a long cabinet on the front wall between the two French doors. The wine rack on top gave him the hint.

"Yes. Help yourselves. I should have suggested it. Forgive me for being a bad hostess."

"Will you stop apologizing? Steve, make my sister something. I'll have scotch on the rocks."

Steve left for the kitchen, taking the ice bucket with him. He returned and poured three stiff scotches. Scotch isn't my favorite, but I wasn't going to quibble. I sipped and the fiery liquor slid down my throat to hit my stomach, instantly calming my nerves.

I had finished my second drink and was feeling quite mellow when crunching gravel in the driveway announced my guests. I stood, smoothed my navy blue skirt, and tweaked the collar of my bright red blouse, then announced, "They're here" in much the same voice as that kid in the movie *Poltergeist*.

I took a deep breath and opened the door. They stood in front of me like a family portrait, Mother in the middle.

I put on what I hoped was a cheerful face and said, "Welcome to Shady Oaks. Please, come in."

"I do hope you're going to do something with the exterior. The house looks like it has a bad case of the measles," Mother said, firing the first salvo.

I kept my cool. "All in good time. It's not a high priority item at the moment."

Everyone trooped into the foyer. "Well, it should be. The exterior of a house is the first thing a visitor sees. As usual, you have your priorities all wrong."

I gritted my teeth. Taking her cue from Mother, Penelope chimed in, "Can't you at least have pulled down the peeling wallpaper? The hallway looks like it's shedding its skin."

I fudged the truth a little. "Actually, that's on my to-do list for next week."

My sister Penelope is thirty-five and pencil thin. She diets religiously and works out every day like a fiend. Her facial features were almost identical to Mother's and on really bad days, I have trouble telling them apart. Her husband, Tom Woodson, practices law in Germantown, DUI defense a specialty. He does brisk business. Only two of her three children were present.

"Where's Kirk?" I asked, grateful she hadn't brought the little hellion.

"With Tom's mother. I didn't want him to get hurt with all the construction materials around. I figured the place would be a mess and it is."

"I don't see how you stand being isolated out here like this," Francine said, shifting from foot to foot and shooting a glance at Mother.

I focused on my older sister. Today, she was a brunette. Francine constantly searched for herself. Her hairstyles and color changed on a regular basis, and no matter how expensive the clothing, it never quite fit. She bought what Mother and Penelope bought. At age thirty-two, she still sought constant approval from Mommy.

She'd married Brad Cummins straight out of high school. He was a developer with political aspirations. Fortunately, she'd only brought the oldest of her four children.

"Well, I think the house is wonderful," a new voice piped up from behind Mother. My Aunt Rose gave me a big smile.

I adore Aunt Rose. She's Mother's older sister. Ten years ago, her husband of thirty years up and ran off with his secretary, aged twenty-five. Before leaving, he'd managed to clean out most of the bank accounts, and while we knew the scumbag lived large somewhere in the Caribbean, no one quite knew where. As a result, the poor woman had no choice but to accept her sister's offer of refuge. Firmly under my mother's thumb, she got her jabs in wherever she could.

"Aunt Rose! I'm so glad you could come." This time, I spoke the truth.

Dudley chose this moment to make his entrance. The kids squealed, leaping back and the dog, confused by the sudden noise directed at him let out a loud woof.

"Get it away! Get it away," Penelope yelled.

"Relax, sis. He's big, but gentle," I replied, irritated at her manner.

"Are you nuts? He'll give the children asthma or something. Get him away."

"Since when do your kids have asthma?"

"Well...they could have. Just get him out of

here!"

I took poor Dudley back to the kitchen and returned to find everyone where I'd left them.

"Cybil, it's rude to just leave us standing here," Mother said. I could tell from the way her eyes moved that she couldn't wait to find fault with the rest of the house. I figured I might as well get it over with.

"Of course. Please, this way." I gestured toward the drawing room and waited. Mother and her entourage stopped dead when Daryl and Steve rose from the sofa.

"Hello, Mother. How are you?"

"Mrs. Austin, a pleasure to see you again."

Mother shot me a look clearly stating she was not happy, and my sisters grabbed their children as though to protect them from harm. Tom and Brad just looked uncomfortable.

Mother nodded in her most regal manner, but made no effort to embrace her only son. "Daryl, Steve. I didn't know you were going to be here."

"It's Cybil's way of thanking us for helping her move," my brother said.

"May I get you a drink?" Steve said in a smooth voice.

Her eyebrows rose. "Cocktails in the middle of the afternoon?"

I ignored her disdainful tone. "Well, we are celebrating my new house."

"I wouldn't mind a beer," Brad stated. "Where's the TV? The Braves are playin' a doubleheader today."

"I'm sorry, Brad, but I don't have the television hooked up yet."

"We'll all take iced tea," Mother declared.

"Cybil, you sit with your family. I'll go get it," Steve said and left, giving my arm a light squeeze.

"Sis, could I get you something?" Daryl winked.

146

"Scotch, rocks." I needed it. My family had been here ten minutes and already I felt the necessity for more strong drink.

Shocked by the presence of her son and his partner, Mother just now noticed the décor. Round two was about to begin.

"Where did you get this furniture?"

"I bought it shortly after I did the house."

"And where is the expensive furniture I gave you for your birthday? On the trash heap?"

"Of course not. It's in the back parlor. It's a very nice room. Cozy. The dining room set will go in the kitchen once it's finished."

"I see. Well, if you must reject my offerings for the most important room in the house, the least you can do is have enough seating. There's not room for all of us."

"Sure there is, Mother," my brother replied, "Three to each sofa and one in each chair. I'll stand."

Daryl handed me my drink. I bolted half of it down. Steve and Reba entered with the iced tea on trays and offered everyone not boozing a glass.

To avoid any more awkward comments, I said, "Would you like to see the rest of the house?"

Of course they did. They could hardly wait to criticize. Daryl and Steve stayed behind while I conducted the tour from hell. Nothing pleased them.

"The foyer will be too dark in the winter," Mother said.

"Yes, too dark," Francine echoed.

"Mother's furniture would look much better in the drawing room," Penelope declared when she saw the back parlor.

"Yes, much better," Francine replied.

"I'm sure the smaller rooms could be made useful, but knowing you, they won't. Go for a front parlor and a music room."

"A music room," Francine said.

Why? I didn't play any musical instruments. I nodded and made noncommittal sounds.

Mother gave grudging approval of the kitchen, but still got her licks in. "The cabinets are awful and this stainless will date things in a short time. You should have gone with a country theme."

I swore if Francine repeated the words, I'd scream.

"Yes, I like a country theme."

For some reason I resisted the urge.

Mother hated my bedroom furnishings and said the closet was too small. Francine agreed.

Penelope had remained silent for most of the tour, but I noted an expression on her face I'd never seen before—jealousy. Her eyes narrowed and her lips compressed into a thin line. If I dropped dead on the spot, she would tear everyone else limb from limb to reside here. I vowed to make a will soon.

Reba met us back in the drawing room and announced dinner.

It was three o'clock and time for round three. I led everyone into the dining room where Mother immediately moved a gladiola in the vase. Reba had already set the food out. I placed Mother at one end of the table and Tom at the other. We said grace and passed the ammunition—er, food.

"How about some wine with the beef?" Daryl asked, pouring me a glass.

"What kind is it?" Mother asked. When Daryl told her, she raised an eyebrow. "An excellent selection, Cybil. I'm surprised."

"Actually, it's a gift from Steve," I replied and enjoyed watching my mother struggle with what to say. She finally opted for polite.

Daryl filled her glass and she sipped. "Very nice."

That was the cue for the others to do the same. Now, Mother nibbled on a tiny piece of beef.

"I don't know who your cook is, but she obviously doesn't know how to cook roast beef. It should be just pink in the center. This is overdone."

"It's the way I like it, Mother."

I swallowed and hoped the food would slide down my tight throat. A small pulse throbbed in my head.

*"Heavens to Betsy, look at the expression on Cybil's face. I've never seen her so tense,"* Antoine said.

*"She does look edgy,"* Ruth replied. *"Why be edgy? This is her family. What do you think, Zoë?"*

*Zoë frowned. "I think we should have come out as soon as they all arrived. Her mother is a controlling bitch. I can feel it. She reminds me of my mother."*

"I assume you're going to do something about this horrible red wallpaper," Mother said, glancing at the wall with a shudder. "It looks like a bordello."

*"Bordello! Bordello! I'll have you know I personally picked out this wallpaper back in 1945 and it was considered extremely elegant. Who does this woman think she is?" Ruth fumed.*

*"Now calm down, Ruth. I thought it looked wonderful. This woman has no taste whatsoever,"* Hester replied in, for Hester, a soothing voice.

*"Well, I'm insulted!"*

*"Now, now, Ruth,"* the Colonel said. *"Let's hear what else they have to say."*

"What on earth prompted you to buy this rundown piece of junk in the middle of nowhere?" Penelope asked.

Her superior tone angered me. She pushed her potatoes off to the side of her plate and replaced them with an extra portion of roast beef. This must be Atkins month.

"I'm renovating the house. What did you expect to find?" I replied in a slightly belligerent tone.

149

"Don't use that voice to your sister," Mother ordered. "Quit being such a fool. Come live with me while you have the work done, turn this thing over to a competent real estate agent, and sell it. You'll make a profit, provided your contractor isn't ripping you off."

"How do you expect to find a husband out here in the sticks?" Francine said.

"Why would I want a husband?"

"Because you are thirty years old and unmarried. You need a family to be complete." She shot a hateful glance at Daryl who just grinned back.

"Oh, Francine, give it a rest. You say the same thing every time I see you."

"Brad and I have introduced you to several nice men who make good livings. You manage to sabotage all my plans to get you to the altar."

"Francine, I don't want to get to the altar. When I do, you'll be the first to know."

"For heaven's sake, leave Cybil alone," Daryl said. "She's a successful author who deserves to write in peace and quiet. This house is perfect for her."

"I agree," Aunt Rose said quietly. She'd had little to say most of the day. "Of course it looks rough now, but when it's finished, you'll have a showplace. I didn't expect anything glamorous today. After all, we did kind of invite ourselves down. We should have waited for an invitation from you. By the way, I love the roast beef. It's delicious."

Mother swelled with a deep breath and turned furious eyes on her older sister. "Shut up, Rose," she bit out angrily. "As usual, you have no idea what you're talking about. Cybil, as soon as we're finished, go pack."

"Mother, I am not going anywhere."

*"Well, of all the nerve!" Antoine sputtered.*

*"I knew it! A complete bitch, just like my*

mother," Zoë replied in a satisfied voice.

"They can't bully our resident guest. That's our job!" Hester declared.

"I thought we wanted her to be gone," the Colonel said in confusion.

"We do, but not with these people. I think it's time for a little mischief," Antoine said, pulling a feather from his pocket.

"Oh!" Francine yelped and lifted the tablecloth. "Is that nasty animal in here?"

"I don't think so," I replied also looking under the table. "Why?"

"I just felt something tickle my leg." She batted a hand at her right ear. "Have you got mosquitoes in the house?"

"Not that I know of."

Tom pawed at his nose. "I think there might be gnats. You probably have holes in your screens. They must drive you nuts at night," he said.

Francine cried out again and smoothed a hand down the back of her head. "I just felt something in my hair. Oh, there it is again. It better not be cockroaches."

"I haven't seen any, and what would a cockroach be doing in your hair?" My temper rose and at the moment, I wished they'd all take a hike.

"Well done, Antoine," Ruth laughed, her good humor restored.

"What next?" the Colonel asked.

"Watch and learn. Zoë and I thought up a few things last night. Are you ready?" Antoine looked at Zoë who smiled and nodded.

"I will not have my daughter living in a bug-infested house. Now, I want you packed and ready to come home in an hour. Is that clear?"

Six months ago, I'd have done as she said, but not any more. I stood my ground. Damn it, this was my house, and I intended to live in it.

"Mother, understand this. I am not going anywhere."

Mother stood and slapped her napkin on the table. "You are just like your father. He didn't have a sensible bone in his body either. He was all for letting you kids do whatever you wanted with no guidance at all," she declared.

"You mean, he refused to interfere in our lives," Daryl countered.

"I mean your father came from a long line of crazy people. There was never any insanity on the Hendricks side of the family."

Aunt Rose shot me a little smile. "Oh, I don't know about that, Lilith. Remember Great Uncle Reggie? He used to strip buck naked and chase chickens around the barnyard."

"He drank!" Mother yelled, losing her cool. We all stared at her while she sucked in deep cleansing breaths. "Great Uncle Reginald was not crazy, merely eccentric."

Family meltdown loomed. Reba brought in a tray and to divert everyone's attention from the subject of sanity, I said, "Dessert?"

Reba cleared the dishes and served the pie.

Mother resumed her seat, carefully placing her napkin on her lap. Reba set a slice of pecan pie in front of her. She poked at it with her fork, and then took a small bite.

"Store-bought," she stated.

Penelope nibbled at the pie, curled her lip, and pushed it away. "I never could eat store-bought pecan pie."

Mother turned her attention to her second daughter.

"Francine, I suggest you forgo the dessert. Your hips will thank you. And where did you get that dress? It looks awful on you. Give it away to the Salvation Army."

Francine stopped with her pie-laden fork halfway to her mouth. A flush darkened her face as she stammered, "Yes, of—of course. You're-you're right, Mother. As—as soon as I get home."

Part of me wanted to smack Mother for her cruelty. Because I didn't do as she wanted, Francine became a target. Before I could open my mouth in protest, Penelope chimed in with her two cents worth.

"You know, dear, if you'd exercise more all that fat and flab would firm up. Diet and exercise are the keys. Of course, nothing works if you're not dedicated. That's your biggest problem. You have no willpower. You use the least little excuse to eat a pint of Haagen-Dazs."

*Everybody* uses the least little excuse to eat a pint of Haagen-Dazs. Now, I wanted to knock her silly, too. She'd said the same kind of things to me. I felt sorry for Francine. She looked ready to cry.

"Penelope, I think we've aired enough dirty family linen in front of Daryl's friend," Mother said, nibbling in a rather disdainful manner on a small pecan. She shot another glance at her second daughter. "Francine, put your fork down. You look ridiculous holding it in midair like that."

"What?"

My sister had a dazed look on her face as if the criticism had sent her into another world. I could relate.

"Your fork, Francine. Put it down."

Before she could comply, the fork tumbled from her fingers to fall with a clatter onto the plate. The pecan pie hit the tablecloth.

"Well, really!" Mother huffed.

"How rude, Francine," Penelope said, her look mimicking Mother's stern expression.

"Oh! I'm so sorry, Cybil. I—I don't know what happened." She dabbed at the spots with her napkin.

"Don't worry about it. The tablecloth will wash."

"For Pete's sake, watch what you're doing," Mother snapped, raising her wine glass to take a ladylike sip.

I couldn't believe my eyes. The bottom of the glass tipped upward and the deep red Cabernet poured down the front of her pink suit and ruffled white blouse.

"Good grief," Penelope cried, leaping from her chair to help Mother. "Your suit will be ruined. What happened?"

"I have no idea. It was as though the glass had a mind of its own. It just suddenly...tipped. Cybil, don't just sit there. Go get some towels."

I jerked out of my stupor and ran for the kitchen. Reba looked up from loading the dishwasher as I grabbed a roll of paper towels.

"Trouble, Miss Austin?"

"I'll say. My perfect mother just dumped wine all over herself."

"How?"

"Damned if I know," I replied and took off for the dining room. But I did know. Or at least I suspected. The glass had unseen help. Okay, it sounded nuts, and I didn't really believe it—or did I?

"*Paper* towels? Really, Cybil!" Mother said in an exasperated tone. She took them anyway and tried to mop up the mess.

"They're absorbent," I defended.

"Cybil, she needs real towels. Paper shreds."

"Never mind, Penelope. The damage has already been done." Mother glared at me as if it were my fault.

I gave up, sat down, and then defiantly shoveled store-bought pecan pie into my mouth. My brothers-in-law had continued to eat uninterrupted during the ruckus, while Daryl and Steve sipped wine with bemused expressions. Not understanding the dynamics of the dinner, the kids gobbled the food, and now sat tapping their forks against the plates, bored. Would this dinner never end? What else could go wrong?

I shouldn't have asked. Penelope returned to her place and pointed a finger at me.

"This is your fault, Cybil. If you hadn't bought this dump and moved into this hick town, we would be having a sensible, decent meal at Mother's!"

*"Dump!" Hester shouted.*

*"Hick town," the Colonel grumbled.*

*"Sh-h-h," Ruth cautioned. "I don't think the fun is over yet."*

Penelope lifted her chin, folded her arms across her chest, then sat down—and missed the chair. She made a frantic grab for the edge of the table, but only succeeded in making it worse. Her high heels slipped on the hardwood floor. She slid and clutched at the tablecloth, which whipped off the table.

Daryl, Steve, and I all grabbed together to avert disaster, but were too late. Plates, pecan pie, water, and wine cascaded into the laps of everyone on the opposite side of the table with the exception of my sister. It dumped on her head.

*Ruth crowed with laughter while the Colonel harrumphed and chuckled. Hester trumpeted her mirth. Antoine and Zoë grinned at each other.*

*"Oh, that was the best," Ruth acknowledged with a gasp.*

*"Zoë, remind me never to make you angry," Hester said, still hooting.*

*"Good job, both of you," the Colonel congratulated. "The fork and wine were subtle, but this was magnificent. My hat's off to you. How can someone as nice as Cybil have such awful relatives?"*

The room erupted into bedlam. Penelope yelled and cried. Tom and Brad jumped to their feet to help her up. Mother shouted orders, and the kids (no longer bored) screamed bloody murder.

I stared in total disbelief. Not because my sister sat on her skinny rump wearing a dessert plate, pie side down, on her head like a bizarre hat, nor because half the diners looked as if they'd engaged in a food fight. Not even Dudley appearing and licking up as many remains as possible caused it.

No, my disbelief came from the fact that *I had seen the chair move!*

I gazed around the room searching every corner from floor to ceiling, then looked over my shoulders. No one was there. It didn't make any difference. *I'd seen the damned chair move!* And in spite of copious amounts of liquor, I wasn't hallucinating.

Penelope finally regained her feet. She looked like the slow dodger in a pie-throwing contest. The gooey, sticky filling clung to her hair like glue and her dress, spattered from neckline to lap, sported the remains of everything left on the table. I couldn't help it. I laughed.

"Damn it, Cybil! It's not funny!" she screamed. The dessert plate finally detached from the pie and fell back onto the table with a resounding crash.

I couldn't contain myself. I laughed harder.

"You bitch!" she shrieked, picking up the plate and throwing it at me. Luckily, it missed by a mile and shattered against the wall.

I howled, tears streaming down my cheeks. My mother quit wiping the food off her eldest daughter and turned to me, her face as blotchy as her suit.

"Cybil, this dinner is over!"

"Thank God!" I said.

"I will call you later," she declared, then whirled and stalked from the room, the others following like politicians chasing contributions.

My Aunt Rose paused. "Thank you for a lovely dinner, Cybil." She winked.

The front door slammed. I finally stopped

laughing and wiped my eyes.

Daryl, Steve, and I all looked at one another before Daryl broke the silence. "Sis, I have to thank you, too. That was the most entertaining dinner I've ever attended."

"Ditto," Steve echoed. He raised his rescued wine glass in a salute.

*"I'm exhausted," Zoë said through her laughter.*

*"Me, too," Antoine echoed. "My energy is depleted. I need to rest."*

*"I think we've done about as much as we can today," Ruth declared. "We'll haunt again tomorrow."*

*The former residents regained control and drifted toward their individual walls.*

*"I hope we can do as well," Ruth murmured.*

I pushed myself away from the demolished dinner table. "Gentlemen, will you please join me in the drawing room?"

I marched into the kitchen, snatched three glasses from a cabinet, and opened the freezer door of the fridge where I extracted a bottle of Grey Goose vodka. I rejoined my brother and his partner. It just seemed like the right thing to do.

## Chapter Eleven

I staggered into the kitchen at seven-thirty the next morning with the mother of all hangovers. I'd had no choice, the workmen arrived, and there was no way I could have survived the noise emanating from the master bath.

Daryl, Steve, and I had emptied the vodka, and then started on the scotch. I'm not sure what else passed from my liquor cabinet. Things blurred along about eight o'clock and by ten the three of us were hammered. The guys crashed to sleep it off in the spare room. I winced as I heard the sound of a power tool from upstairs. I figured they'd be up soon.

I groaned and squinted at Perfect Coffee. The carafe was full indicating somebody had taken on domestic responsibility, probably Max. I poured a mug, adding cream and sugar with a shaking hand before making my way back to the dining room. I supposed Reba must have cleaned up the mess from the day before. I made a mental note to give her a few extra bucks for her trouble.

Seated, I held my throbbing head in my hands, praying for death. God did not answer my prayers.

The back porch door slammed causing me to cover my ears and whimper. Footsteps and a ladder being dragged across the kitchen floor resonated like a buzz saw. I shuddered.

If I wanted any coffee, I understood I would have to uncover my ears, and finally had the courage to do so. I raised the cup to my lips and sipped. The strong brew mingled with the taste of old gym socks in my mouth, but I swallowed anyway.

I lifted my head at a noise from the doorway. Steve stood there braced against the doorjamb. He looked at my coffee cup and uttered, "Where?" in a hoarse whisper.

I didn't trust myself to answer. I pointed into the kitchen. He nodded and stumbled through the door, then rejoined me.

"Holy Christ, what did we do?" he asked after gulping half his cup.

"I'm not sure. I don't remember much after the scotch. What else did we drink?"

"Gin? Or maybe it was bourbon. God, I haven't been this drunk in years. I felt bad for you yesterday with that crowd. No offense, but how did nice people like you and Daryl wind up in that family?"

"No offense taken, and it really doesn't matter. I don't think any of them will ever speak to me again, which isn't a bad thing."

"Cybil, the smartest thing you ever did was to buy this house. Unfortunately, it's still too close to your family. Sell it and move a thousand miles away."

Before I could reply, Daryl slowly walked in, looked at Steve and me, and then disappeared into the kitchen. A minute later he joined us, coffee cup in hand.

"Oh, my God. What a night. I don't even remember going to bed. I thought that nail gun going off across the hall was someone trying to blow my brains out." He sipped his drink and groaned. "I wish they had."

Dudley bounded into the room with a good morning woof that had all of us shuddering and groaning.

"Geez, Dudley, not now. I'll take you out in a little while," I begged.

"No need. I already walked him," Max said. He stood in the doorway to the butler's pantry. "You

159

three look like hell. What went on here? I thought your family was coming to dinner."

I may have been hungover, but appreciated that he looked fabulous this morning. I wanted to smile, but didn't have the ability to make my facial muscles work. I opted to simply answer his question.

"I can sum it up in a few words. They did, disaster, and lots of booze after they left. I'll tell you about it later. Did you make the coffee?"

"Yeah. It's usually ready by the time I get here. I figured you'd forgotten."

"You could say that," Steve said. "Did we drink the gin first or the bourbon?"

Daryl shook his head. "We thought about the bourbon, but I don't know if we actually indulged."

Max stared at us with pity on his face. "I'll leave you guys alone. I've been there, done that. I know how you feel. Cybil, if I were you, I'd find a quiet hiding place for the rest of the day."

Sounded like good advice to me. I scratched my head. Oh, God, even my hair hurt.

The coffee helped, and the three of us spent the morning at the little pond behind the house. Daryl scrounged an old fishing pole from the garage and dropped a line in the water. Steve and I talked about the dinner and the eccentricities of families. While mine ignored Steve, his had welcomed and accepted Daryl. I wondered if they'd consider adopting me.

After lunch, I waved as the guys headed home. Much to my disappointment, Max was nowhere to be found, so I got in my car reasonably sober and in need of answers. I found the county library branch and walked up to the girl behind the desk.

"Excuse me, but do you have any genealogies or information about Cherokee residents? I just moved into Shady Oaks and am interested in the family."

"Oh, you're Miss Astin. Welcome to Cherokee."

"Austin," I corrected. "Thanks. I understand the

family's name was LaForge."

"Yes. There have been LaForges in Cherokee for over a hundred and fifty years."

"Are any of them still around..." I glanced at her nametag. "Miss Cadwallader?"

"Oh, goodness. I'm not really sure. The last resident, Miz Germania LaForge died about five or six years ago. Her son and two daughters no longer live in the area. Now, old Mrs. Perrine used to claim kinship, but some doubt that. She also claimed kinship to Nathan Bedford Forrest, the Confederate general, and to President Franklin D. Roosevelt. Personally, I wouldn't put much stock in it."

Before she could go through the entire population of Cherokee, I asked, "Is there a genealogy of the family? I'd like to know more about them."

"Well, isn't that nice? Not too many people would take the time to do that. Why don't you have a seat, and I'll go see what I can find."

I sat at a long table and pulled two bottles out of my purse—one water and the other aspirin. I figured another ten or twelve and my head might stop pounding.

The girl returned with two large books resembling the New York City Telephone Directory in her arms.

"Here you go, Miss Austin."

She set them in front of me and I read, *The Complete History of Cherokee County, Mississippi, 1812-1980.*

"Wow. That's a lot of history. Where do I start?"

"I'd start about 1840 or so. That's about when Shady Oaks was built. If you need anything else, just let me know."

She left, and I began my research. Gideon LaForge had built the house in 1842, and as I read, realized I had, indeed, bought a slice of history. The

LaForges had been fruitful and multiplied, especially after the War Between the States. In the 1890 census, I counted almost one-hundred LaForges in the county. After that the number steadily dwindled. In the last census before this published history, only ten remained. Most of them were over the age of sixty.

I took copious notes. Glancing at my watch, I decided to ask questions around town before heading home.

I stopped first at the drugstore and introduced myself to the pharmacist.

"Well, well, I'm mighty pleased to meet you, Miss Austin," he said, shaking my hand like a pump handle. "I hear tell you're doing lotsa work at Shady Oaks."

"Yes. I can hardly wait for it to be done. The house is beautiful. I've just been over at the library, trying to find out more about the LaForges."

"Nice family, nice family. Don't seem to me like any of 'em are around anymore. It's a shame how people scatter these days. My own children are in Jackson and Birmingham."

"Would you know if there's anybody I could ask?"

The man thought for a moment, and then clicked his fingers. "I've got it! You might want to try Muriel Paskins at the Elite Beauty Salon. She knows everything."

I thanked him and made my way to the Elite, but Muriel didn't know much. She directed me to Janet Bridges at the DMV. And so the ball rolled. Nobody could tell me anything until I hit pay dirt with one Eunice Ickleberry, aged ninety-one.

Her equally ancient companion showed me into a stuffy little parlor where I sat on a horsehair chair and was forced to politely sip weak tea.

"'Course I remember the LaForge family," she

said in a thin, reedy voice. "Used to go to parties at Shady Oaks when I was a young lady. They had the best cook in the county. She could bake up a storm." She eyed me with a keen look. "Hear you been having a mite of trouble with cooks lately."

"Yes. I'm afraid Miss Rogers and Miss Washington didn't work out, but I've got Reba St. Clair now and she's wonderful."

"Heard she does good work." She gave me a sly smile. "I also hear funny things be happening out there."

"Oh, there was a practical joker for a while, but that seems to have settled down."

"Uh-huh. Take my word for it. There'll always be LaForges at Shady Oaks." She cackled.

I tucked a strand of hair behind my ear, deliberately misunderstanding the old woman's sly innuendo. "Yes, I suppose so. I heard the old family cemetery is still located somewhere on the property."

I hadn't heard any such thing, but the woman talked vaguely, and I refrained from asking a direct question. I might not like the answer.

She cackled and said, "Suit yourself. Believe what you want, but you ain't foolin' me. You know what I mean."

I was afraid I did, too. We sat in silence for a couple of minutes while I sipped my tea and tried to gather my thoughts. There didn't seem to be much else to say. The companion came back into the room.

"Miss Eunice, it's time for your nap. Say good-bye to the young lady."

She was too late. While I'd been thinking, Miss Ickleberry had dropped off.

"Is she all right?"

"Oh, she's fine, don't worry none."

I rose, handing the companion the cup and saucer. "She apparently thinks..." I didn't finish. It sounded silly and I wasn't sure if I'd been interpreting the old woman's words correctly.

"Yes, I know. The rumors about strange things at Shady Oaks have been around for decades, especially after World War Two." She showed me to the front door. "You have a nice day and come again. She enjoyed the company."

I drove back to the house and ate an early dinner, then offered to drive Reba home. She declined, saying a friend would pick her up at the end of the drive.

Sitting in the drawing room, I reviewed my notes and the conversations I'd had with various residents of the town. As Dudley and I settled into bed for the night, I came to the conclusion I was not alone in this house.

I suppose the thought of ghosts should have scared the pants off me, but for some reason, it didn't. If they were trying to get rid of me, they were sadly mistaken.

*I'm not budging.*

\*\*\*\*

"This is it," Ruth declared to the others in the back parlor. "Tonight is the night we put the nails in the coffin."

"Must you use that phrase?" Hester snapped.

"Oh, sorry."

"What Ruth means is tonight we must do our best to scare her away," the Colonel said.

"I know what she meant," Hester replied.

"I'll give Cybil this, she has staying power," Zoë remarked, yawning. "She'd better go. I'm exhausted. I don't know how much more I can take."

"The Yankees will think I've surrendered."

"I'm sure the Yankees can wait for one more night," Antoine stated.

"We have to get this resolved," Ruth said. "The workers released four more of us today and an argument broke out between two of them."

"Who?" Antoine asked.

"I have no idea. I'd never seen them before. Must have died before my time."

"What will we do tonight?" Hester inquired.

The five of them put their heads together and set an agenda. The haunting had weakened them and materialization was getting harder to sustain.

"All right," Zoë said. "Let's get this done. I want to go to sleep and not wake up for another twenty years."

They drifted out of the parlor.

****

I awoke to the sound of Dudley whimpering, and then realized the bed vibrated. It took me a second to understand the latter came from Dudley also. He had plastered himself against my side, shivering. Since it was the dead of summer, I knew he couldn't be cold.

Fully awake now, I listened to the sounds of footsteps in the hallway and piano music coming from downstairs. Since I didn't own a piano, I guessed my nocturnal visitors were at it again. The lights blazed below. Moans and groans emanated from the attic. This had to be the work of more than one entity.

I'd had enough. If my mother and sisters hadn't intimidated me out of Shady Oaks certainly these spirits wouldn't either. I threw off the covers and got out of bed, ready to do battle.

The footsteps came up the stairs and halted outside my bedroom door. Dudley leaped off the bed howling, and then tried to wedge himself under it. He didn't fit. His back end stuck out like an enormous, hairy lump of coal. He looked ridiculous.

It was one thing to try and scare me, but to terrorize a helpless animal spurred me into action. I grabbed my robe and stomped down the stairs. The noises ceased immediately.

"All right!" I shouted from the foyer. "I've had it! I want all of you in the back parlor. Now!"

I didn't wait for any ghostly replies, but strode down the hall and into the well-lighted room.

I waited a few seconds, tapping my foot. "Come out and face me, you cowards!"

*"Cowards!" the Colonel said.*

*"She...she doesn't look in the least bit scared," Ruth cried, a tremor in her voice.*

I stamped my foot. "I said materialize! I know you can do it. If you don't appear by the time I count to ten, I'll call in a priest and exorcise the lot of you."

*"Oh, no!" Hester cried.*

*"She wouldn't...would she?" Zoë asked.*

*"She looks mad enough," Antoine answered with a worried look on his face.*

I waited a moment longer. "All right...one...two..." I made it to seven when an absurd little *pop* sounded behind me. I whirled and stared at an apparition of a Confederate soldier. Then, like bubbles bursting, the pops continued until I gazed at over twenty ghosts.

Stunned, I could only gape when the final five materialized in front of the others. My jaw dropped as the last one formed, and I whispered, "Grandfather?" before I realized the clothing was from another era.

An older lady glided forward a couple of feet. She stood no more than five feet tall and had white hair cut in a style of the 1950s. I took a step back when she spoke.

"You're not afraid of us, are you? Why not?"

I swallowed. "Damned if I know. Who the hell are you people...or whatever?"

"Most of us are LaForges and some of us lived long, happy lives in this house."

"Yeah, well, I'd like to live a long, happy life in the house, too, so I suggest you all leave."

A tall, dark-haired young man stepped up. Dead or not, he was good-looking.

"Please, don't make us leave. We love the house, but your renovations have destroyed some of our resting areas."

Resting areas? I had no idea what he was talking about. I should have done less research on the LaForges and more on ghosts.

"I'm sorry. I don't understand."

"Oh, dear, I'll try to explain," the woman said. "My name is Ruth Carrick LaForge. My husband and I moved into Shady Oaks in 1930. It was the Great Depression and times were hard..."

"Oh, for pity's sake, Ruth, she doesn't want a history lesson," a tall imposing woman interrupted, joining the other two. Her dress resembled those of the late nineteenth century. She wore her iron-gray hair in a bun on the top of her head with the sides pouffed out. The term Gibson girl came to mind. She also took over the conversation.

"What Ruth is trying to say is that this is the LaForge home. You're the first outsider to own it. We all live within the house in different places. Your renovations have disturbed several of us. We wanted you to go away so we can continue to live here in peace."

"You mean there are more than just what's in here still floating around?"

"I'm not sure I understand the question, my dear, but if you're asking if there are more of us as yet undisturbed, the answer is yes," the older man replied.

Being an historical novelist, I'd researched period costumes a lot and dated his from sometime just after the War Between the States. His chubby face and long white hair reminded me of Santa Claus. He was the one I'd mistaken for my Grandfather Austin.

"Well, you can't all stay here," I said. "It just won't work. I plan on doing a lot to the house and can't have ghosts running around, getting in the way. I take it you're the ones playing the jokes on everyone."

A tall, dark-haired young lady stepped forth. Her clothing and hairstyle came from the 1920s.

"We're sorry, but we didn't know what else to do. I only lived at Shady Oaks a few years, but I love the house intensely. Please, don't make us leave."

"Are you all related?" I gazed around the room. So far, none of the others had said a word.

"No. Not everyone here is a LaForge," Ruth said.

"And not every LaForge here lived in the house," the turn-of-the-century woman declared. She shot a contemptuous glance to those behind her.

"Now, wait just a minute," a young woman in a homespun dress and sunbonnet said. "I'll have you know, I died on this land before your family ever knew it existed. It was 1815 and my husband and I were on our way west when we were attacked by Indians."

"So what? That makes no difference. You are not a LaForge. We built the house," the turn-of-the-century woman stated.

"Who's that?" I asked, pointing. "How does a Native American fit into the picture?"

"Native American?" Santa said. "Oh, you mean the Indian? I have no idea. He's been around the longest, I think. We're not sure because he doesn't speak English."

I looked at Ruth LaForge. "Can you communicate with all of the ghosts?"

"Oh, yes." She shot a look at the warrior. "Well, most of them."

"Then will you please tell them they have to leave?"

"Oh, please, don't throw us out," the flapper

pleaded.

"I want everyone not named LaForge gone—now. You people died and it's time you moved on. You no longer belong in this world and certainly not at Shady Oaks."

They all stared, but none moved. I formulated a plan. I'd cut them down to a reasonable number and work from there.

A wizened little man wearing buckskin clothing laid his hand on that of the—oh, why be politically correct at a time like this—Indian.

"Don't worry. We died together. Now, we kind of take care of each other. I know a nice big hollow tree not far from where we died. We can live there."

I watched in fascination as the two of them slowly faded and disappeared, then turned to the sunbonnet lady.

"You said your husband died with you. Wouldn't you rather be with him than stuck here with all these strangers?"

"Of course, but I'm angry. We had our whole lives ahead of us!"

"The fact is you're dead. There's no reason for anger any more. Go join him. He's probably waiting for you."

She looked at the others and popped out of the parlor. I couldn't believe it. I was a travel agent for ghosts.

The soldier spoke up. "Ma'am, there's an old house on the back part of the property. Would you mind if a few of us went there? We won't bother you none."

"A house? On the property?" I hadn't seen it yet.

"Former overseer's cottage, miss," the good-looking ghost replied. "It's made of brick and is the only thing left standing from my day other than the house."

"Oh, I see. Well, yes, I guess that's all right, but

I reserve the right to fix it up, too, at a later date."

The soldier nodded agreement and five more of them disappeared. I counted seventeen left.

"The rest of us all bear the name LaForge," the Gibson girl said. "Only five of us actually lived here, not counting those undisturbed."

"Now, you listen to me, Hester. Just because I didn't live here doesn't mean I don't have fond memories of the place. It was like a second home to me," argued a woman of the same era.

"Your LaForge husband died. You remarried three times after that. You were a LaForge in name only and *that* only lasted a few years. It doesn't count."

"I think Hester's right on this one," the flapper declared. "I suggest you find a relative other than a LaForge to live with."

"Typical LaForge pride and arrogance," chimed in another woman. "I was married to Carlyle LaForge and he should have inherited Shady Oaks, not Hester."

"Hester was born and raised here. If I'm not mistaken, Carlyle was a confidence man who I'm sure now dwells in the warmer regions of eternity," Tall-Dark-and-Handsome said.

"That's an awful thing to say," a man from the back piped up. "People in glass houses shouldn't throw stones."

"What does that mean?" the one named Hester demanded.

"Gideon LaForge wasn't above bending the law."

"I'll have you know, you are talking about my grandfather," she shouted.

I stood rooted in place listening to ghosts arguing and wondered if perhaps this whole thing was a dream. Maybe I was hallucinating. God Almighty, maybe there *was* something in the water. I pinched myself hard. It hurt. Nope, no dream or hallucination. The bickering in front of me escalated.

"Take that back, you scoundrel," Lord Edgeware yelled in a furious tone.

No, not Lord Edgeware, but Santa. Oh, this bordered on the absurd. I had to do something.

"Quiet, all of you! Knock it off!" Silence descended, and I glared at the warring factions.

The Ruth ghost had a sheepish look on her face. "I'm so sorry, Cybil. We aren't like this really."

"You-you know my name?"

"Oh, yes. I knew the moment you bought the house. I listened and made reports. You see, the others elected me caretaker of Shady Oaks."

Caretaker? Elected? I shook my head. I'd deal with democracy in the hereafter later. Right now I had decisions to make.

"You—the one with the three husbands. You ceased to be a LaForge when you remarried. You'll have to leave."

"And if I don't?" she answered belligerently.

"It's called exorcism," the flapper replied, stifling a yawn with the back of her hand.

The woman glared, and then popped out of sight. Sixteen. I turned to Carlyle's wife. "If Hester was born and raised in the house built by her grandfather, then she has a greater claim. Go someplace else."

The ghost threw Hester a furious look. "You always get your way!" she snapped before disappearing. Fifteen.

I looked at the man who'd spoken up for her. "And what is your relationship?"

He drew himself up and thrust out his chin. "I am a LaForge cousin."

"Three times removed," murmured Tall-Dark-and-Handsome. "He came to the occasional barbeque or Christmas party."

I shook my head. "Goodbye." Fourteen.

And so it went. I interviewed and whittled the group down to the final five. They stood in front of me like contestants in a bizarre beauty pageant. I stared, reluctant to eliminate any of them. They stared back with varying degrees of fear in their eyes.

My attention was pulled toward the one named Ruth and I remembered several sensations from my first nights in the house.

"Did you tuck me in at night?"

"Well, yes. You had thrown off the covers and I didn't want you to catch cold."

Catch cold in the middle of summer? Maybe ghosts no longer felt the elements. I'd ask later.

"Rather strange behavior for someone who wanted to get rid of me," I commented mildly.

Ruth shrugged and smiled, then looked at the others. "And what about us? Do we have to go, too?"

Santa looked like someone had just told him he couldn't have Christmas. Hester's chin quivered. Tall-Dark-and-Handsome had a worried expression on his face. The flapper stood tense.

I should have ordered them out, but for the life of me couldn't do it. They were tied to Shady Oaks body and soul—literally. And for some obscure reason, I had the feeling I needed them as much as they needed the house. It made no sense, and I didn't have the strength to deal with it tonight.

"You did quite a dance on my family," I said in a stern tone.

"I know," the flapper replied. "I'm sorry."

I laughed at the memory of Penelope's pie-laden head. "I'm not. You can all stay, but with conditions."

Everyone heaved a collective sigh, and Santa said, "Thank you, my dear. What conditions?"

"First, all shenanigans must stop. No more hidden tools or messing with the workmen. And quit

172

moving things on me."

"Agreed," they chorused.

"Two, can you remove the rest of the, ah, people who haven't been disturbed?"

"Yes," Ruth spoke up. "I can do that. I'll deal with them when they awake. Only Margaret lived here and she doesn't like being awakened. She's very peaceful."

"In that case, she can have the attic, although I reserve the right to one day modernize that, too."

"Done. Is that all?"

"No. Three, don't harass my cook. I don't know how to cook and have no intention of starving."

"We'd like to talk to you about your latest cook sometime," Hester said.

Ruth poked her in the ribs with her elbow, and replied, "Deal."

"And four, leave my dog alone. He's big and a lummox, but gentle as a lamb. I won't have him terrorized. He doesn't understand."

"I think he's adorable," the flapper answered. "May I play with him? No scary stuff, I promise."

"You can do that?"

"Oh, yes. He'll just think of us as new people in the house."

"What's your name?" I asked. She looked to be about my age and I wondered how she'd died, but felt asking might be impolite. I wasn't sure about apparition etiquette.

She smiled. "I'm Zoë. Zoë Prentiss LaForge."

Tall-Dark-and-Handsome also smiled. "My name is Antoine LaForge, and this is Colonel George Washington LaForge. Thank you for letting us stay. We won't scare your dog anymore."

I was charmed. I bet he'd been a heartbreaker before he died. "I'm Cybil Renee Austin. The dog's name is Dudley."

"Do we have to stay hidden all the time?" Hester

inquired. "Now that the house is being changed, I'd like to see what you're doing."

I shrugged. "I don't care, but don't scare anyone. I'm sure you'll have lots of questions, and I'll try to answer them, but not tonight. I'm tired. Now, if you'll excuse me, I'll go back to bed. Since I'm still alive, I need my sleep."

The five of them laughed and drifted through the wall to Lord knew where. I trooped back upstairs.

Dudley was still half under the bed.

"Come on, boy. Come on out. They're gone now and won't scare you again."

He whined and slithered out, then licked my hand. At least he no longer shivered.

I coaxed Dudley onto his bed, and then got into my own. He turned around twice and lay down with an exhausted thump. I didn't blame him. I'd forgotten to turn off the lights, but as I watched, one by one they blinked out.

I stared at the ceiling and relived the past hour in my head wondering what Max would say if I told him. Probably what any intelligent person would say. "You're nuts!" Even Daryl would look at me with raised eyebrows and ask if I'd been drinking. The chances of me ever telling Mother about this were slim to none. I couldn't even imagine what practical Julie would say.

I yawned and rolled onto my side. Dudley snored, already in doggie dreamland. I closed my eyes and pulled the sheet up to my chin. A soft hand smoothed the covers.

"Thank you, Ruth," I whispered in a drowsy voice.

"You're welcome, Cybil."

Chapter Twelve

I floated awake; the kind of awakening that indicates a restful night. I had no recollection of having dreamed.

Heavy warmth cuddled next to me. I moved my head and got a face full of Dudley. He sprawled against my side, his head resting on the pillow. I moved to put some distance between us. He scooted along. Dudley and I needed to chat regarding sleeping space.

I got out of bed and flapped the front of my nightgown trying to cool off, and then remembered last night. I wanted to believe I dreamed after all, but knew I had stumbled upon the real thing.

"Come on, Dudley. Get up, you big ox. It's time to go out."

He rolled over onto his back, silently demanding attention in the form of a belly rub. I indulged him for a couple of minutes before renewing my request. He jumped down, stretched, yawning, and then followed me downstairs. I opened the front door. He bounded outside, did his thing, and returned, racing into the kitchen for his breakfast.

Max had already arrived for the day and was pouring a cup of coffee. He greeted Dudley and placed a bowl full of dog food on the floor. I had a superior view of his rear end. It was still downright criminal, and I shouldn't be having carnal thoughts this early in the morning. The brunette from the other day popped into my head, but I conveniently dismissed her and the little dart of jealously still lurking somewhere under my breastbone.

"Good morning," Max said over Dudley's noisy chomping. The dog scarfed down food like he'd never see another meal. "Sleep well?"

"Best night's sleep I've had in a long while." I wanted to tell him about my ghosts, but hesitated. Even though I wanted something deeper than a few kisses with him, he was the most practical, logical person I'd ever met with the exception of my brother and Julie. I'd wait until our relationship progressed further, if at all. "You seem awfully chipper yourself."

He poured me a cup and grinned. "I have reason to be. I got here about an hour ago and guess what? All the missing tools and supplies have been returned."

I accepted the coffee and muttered under my breath, "Well, I'll be damned. She meant it."

"What?"

"Oh, nothing. I guess the practical joker must have decided the jokes weren't so funny after all. Where did you find them?"

"They were all on the back porch. Did you hear anything during the night?"

Boy, did I, but it had little to do with his tools. "Not a thing. So, what's on the agenda for today?"

"We'll finish up in the kitchen. All we need is an hour or so. The breakfast area will be done in another week. The French doors haven't arrived yet and I don't want to break out the brick until they do. If you have no objections, I'll bring in the floor guy to give us an estimate on the refinishing. You do realize this is goin' to cost you."

I drained my coffee and poured another cup. "Naturally. The best always does."

"Are you sure you want to do the entire house? You could go with carpet in the bedrooms."

"Nope. The hardwood is gorgeous. I'd like to see the place looking the way Gideon LaForge built it."

Max smiled. "I had to ask and for the record, I'm glad you're doing it. Maybe the old boy is looking down on us right now and nodding in approval."

That wouldn't surprise me in the least. "How long will it take?"

"Two days for each section of the house. One to sand and sweep, another to finish. He'll most likely use a polyurethane stain. It dries fast and you can move the furniture back in a few hours."

"Dudley and I won't mind being outside for a while. I'll introduce him to the pond."

Max helped himself to more coffee, and then asked, "I take it you're feeling much better today. You and your friends looked like hell yesterday. What happened?"

I sighed and told him the story of the family dinner. By the time I'd finished, we were both laughing.

"I've heard of things like that happening on TV sitcoms," he said, chortling.

"I know. I visualized an old *I Love Lucy* rerun. I wish it had been. My mother and sisters probably won't ever speak to me again. I'm afraid, instead of being horrified about the situation, I laughed. I don't know why I was so surprised by any of it. Weird things have a way of happening to me lately. I don't know why."

"Like my grandma used to say, 'Son, if you got lemons, make lemonade.' Maybe you should write them into your books."

"I write historical romance. I don't think I could squeeze anything like what happened Sunday into a novel."

"Then try writing comedy, like *Sex and the City*. I can see you in the role of Carrie being mugged for her shoes," he replied with a twinkle in his eyes.

He reached out and tucked a strand of wayward hair behind my ear, sending a delightful shiver down my spine.

"You watch *Sex and the City?*" Somehow I just couldn't picture Max curled up on a sofa, drinking white wine, and laughing at the antics of the women in the show, which is how I watched it.

"Good Lord, no! My sisters do and whenever they come to visit they share a good laugh with each other over it. They do the same with *Desperate Housewives.*"

I breathed a sigh of relief. Max's masculinity had been preserved.

"My experiences are too hit-and-miss to sustain a chick lit novel. Guess I'll have to stick to what I know."

Max's phone rang and while he talked I finished my coffee and gazed around the kitchen. The cabinets looked sensational and the stainless appliances gleamed in the morning light. The walls had been primed and I'd finally chosen a warm yellow paint.

"That was Johnny Ray, the floor guy. He's on his way over," Max told me, hanging up.

"No problem. What else do you have planned today?"

"I'm going to rough in the closet and bath. My plumber will be here to see how much we can salvage. I assume you want new fixtures."

I had big plans for the master bath and it wouldn't be cheap.

"You betcha! I want the shower of death and everything state-of-the-art. There's a showroom in Memphis I'd like to explore. I may look at wallpaper books, too."

"Great. I also want to start demo on the areas we discussed upstairs." He finished his coffee. "I'd better get back to work. See you later."

He gave me a smile that curled my toes and warmed my insides, then left. I sighed. Dudley sat next to me, his face turned upward with his head cocked to the side as though to say, *Yeah, I like him, too.*

I laughed and stroked his head. "Between the two of us, we're quite a pair, aren't we?"

His tail thumped on the floor. Then his attention swung to the door. I turned and saw Reba standing there.

Smiling, she set her purse on the counter and also patted Dudley on the head.

"Good morning to both of you. How are you feeling today?"

"Much better than yesterday," I admitted. "What are you doing here so early?"

"Oh, I was thinking I'd make a nice meal for you tonight. Maybe Max would like to join you. I'd be willing to stay a little late to serve it."

"Reba, that's so nice of you." Where had Max found this woman? I made a mental note to ask. It also brought to mind last Sunday. "Uh, Reba, I want to apologize for my family and the mess we created. I appreciate your cleaning it up. I'm afraid I was otherwise occupied."

My cook chuckled. "Don't worry. I've cleaned up worse. I listened to the whole thing from the butler's pantry. I thought you held up very well against the onslaught."

"Well, I just want you to know I appreciate what you did and will see to it there's something extra in your pay envelope at the end of the week."

"No need, Miss Austin. Your brother was right. The entertainment value was more than worth it."

Reba's presence also brought something else to mind. "I was wondering if you could teach me how to cook? I never learned and that seems a shame now that I have this gorgeous kitchen."

"Of course I will. We can start tonight when I make dinner. How about fried chicken? Every

Southern girl worth her salt knows how to make that."

"Oh, Reba, thank you! I know a little, but not enough to actually serve it to anyone, not even Dudley."

Dudley hearing his name and being in the food room woofed and looked at his empty bowl.

I laughed. "No way, you glutton."

"I'd like to help, too," a voice said from behind me.

I whirled and stared into the blue eyes of Ruth LaForge. I'd completely forgotten about my housemates and spoke before thinking.

"Good grief, you startled me."

"I'm sorry. I didn't mean to."

Then, I remembered I wasn't alone. My head swiveled back to Reba, expecting to find her staring at me like I'd lost my marbles. To my amazement, she didn't.

"Good morning," she said over my shoulder. "It's nice to see you again."

I gasped. "You—you can see her?"

"Oh, yes. She and another lady tried to scare me off earlier in the week," Reba answered with a calm expression.

Flabbergasted, I stared. "How? I don't understand."

"Neither do I," Ruth replied. "Hester and I were astonished and suspected she knew what we'd been up to."

Reba shrugged. "You're not the first ghosts I've seen. Won't be the last either."

"But how?" I persisted.

"I just see them."

"Dudley," I gasped, thinking how terrified he must be. He sat at my feet, head cocked and gazing at Ruth. "Why isn't he afraid? Your presence sends him into shivering fits."

"Oh, he sees me now. I look just like any other living person to him. Before, he sensed us, and we tried to scare him, but last night we promised not to do that anymore."

I accepted the explanation. Why not? It made as much sense as anything else and, frankly, I didn't care as long as the poor animal refrained from diving under my coffee table and bed. Then, I remembered my manners.

"Reba St.Clair, I'd like you to meet Ruth LaForge."

The two women nodded and murmured the appropriate responses. I didn't find it at all strange to introduce a human to a ghost, nor did I feel as if I'd slipped the bounds of reality. Voices sounded in the foyer. The floor man had arrived.

"Ladies, if you'll excuse me, I have to go. I'll be back later. What time?"

"How about four o'clock? Most of the men will be finished by then. We can give you a lesson and have dinner ready by six-thirty."

I nodded and left happy as a clam. I would soon be learning culinary skills from lessons administered by my living cook and my dead housemate. And what was wrong with that?

****

Johnny Ray gave me an estimate for the floor work and for once I didn't gasp in horror. He assured me the manufactured hardwood I'd selected to replace the linoleum in the kitchen would be a match to the refinished original in the rest of the house. He penciled us onto his schedule for mid-November, and I immediately visualized Thanksgiving dinner at my house—assuming, of course, the rest of the family was speaking to me. My phone had been suspiciously quiet the last couple of days, and I figured it would remain so. This silent treatment could last a long time.

Excited about my new bathroom, I called Julie for assistance, and then drove into Memphis.

The plumbing supply showroom resembled Designer Shoe Warehouse with so many selections I naturally couldn't make up my mind. A couple of phone calls to Max nailed down the size of the Jacuzzi and shower. With Julie along, I finally made the choices, and then winced at the bill. I'd have to sell another book.

We lunched at the Peabody where I brought Julie up to date on everything. Well, almost. Some things just weren't open to discussion. I wanted to tell her about my housemates, but held my tongue.

Julie laughed at the ill-fated Sunday dinner. "Oh, God! I wish I'd been there." She wiped her eyes with her napkin. "Okay, you've given me the skinny on your house and your family. Now, how about that gorgeous contractor? Been out with him yet—and remember, you're a lousy liar."

I chuckled and told her everything from the fire to the kiss, and the tumble down the steps. I refrained from mentioning the brunette. Julie would make a sensible suggestion like asking Max who she was.

"Cybil, you need to write this down and put it in a book. It's hilarious."

"Max suggested the same thing." How could two of my favorite people be wrong?

We hugged goodbye in the parking lot with Julie promising to come down soon to see the progress. I drove back to Cherokee feeling better than I had in days and looking forward to my first cooking lesson.

****

"Now, mix the salt, pepper, and any other spices you want into the flour real good," Reba said, using her hands to demonstrate.

"But how do you know the proportions? I always under-season or over-season everything. It's never

182

right."

"Practice mostly. You can always add, but you can't subtract. And don't be afraid to get your hands into what you cook."

"Am I too late to join in?" Ruth asked, popping into sight next to us.

"Of course not. I'm just learning about seasoning. You know, Lavinia did something funny with a stew the day she ran out. It was so salty I thought she was trying to poison me."

Ruth looked embarrassed. "Oh, dear. I'm sorry, Cybil, but that was Hester and me. Lavinia had a habit of tasting as she stirred, and we thought it would scare her."

"Well, it sure worked. She flew out of here."

"The woman was a thief, pure and simple," Reba declared.

Ruth looked at Reba, a puzzled expression on her face.

"How do you know about that? Are you from around here? I don't ever remember hearing your name before," she questioned.

"Oh, I've been around for a while. Shall we continue with the lesson?"

"I just hope she doesn't start any rumors about what you guys did to her," I said.

"I don't think you'd need worry about that. She'd like to, but the fear of being uncovered as a thief will keep her mouth shut. Now, about the chicken," Reba stated, firmly shifting our attention to food.

She showed me how to dredge the pieces in the flour mixture with Ruth adding comments along the way. While the chicken cooked, we sat in the almost-finished breakfast area and drank iced tea. Well, Reba and I did. Poor Ruth had to forego this pleasure.

"I'm afraid my non-existence doesn't permit things like that." She sighed. "In a way, it's the only drawback to this whole ghost business. I do miss some of the better things in life, like coffee and apple pie."

My curiosity overrode my manners. Was there etiquette with ghosts?

"Ruth, forgive me if I'm being nosy, but why are you still here? Why are any of you still hanging around? What's your story?"

"My late husband Wilson LaForge inherited the house from Zoë's husband. They were cousins. Let's see, that was in 1930, if memory serves. The Depression was in full swing, and poor Wilson worked like a dog to keep the place afloat. I seem to remember cotton prices were down and we grew a lot of vegetables to help out with the cost of groceries. We also kept chickens."

"I can remember my Grandfather Austin talking about hard times and such. You obviously prevailed."

Ruth nodded. "Yes, hard work and determination saw to that." A far away look came to her eyes. "I fell in love with Shady Oaks the moment I laid eyes on it. Wilson was a lawyer, and we lived in Pass Christian. The day he inherited was the last day he ever practiced. Not much call for lawyering in Cherokee in those days. Besides, old Ben Rogers, Lavinia's great-uncle was already established, so Wilson became a cotton farmer."

She paused for a moment as though reminiscing and I didn't interrupt.

"Zoë's husband, Jefferson Davis LaForge, had brought the house up to date with electricity and modern plumbing in the twenties when money was abundant, so we didn't have to worry about it crumbling around our ears. Oh, Cybil, we used to invite neighbors and relatives over for potluck dinners and barbeques all the time. It was a way to socialize and get a good meal in the bargain. The place rang with laughter. It was a happy house."

I could almost hear and see it now. Children squealing with delight as they played tag on the front lawn while the adults sat under the humongous oaks or on the veranda, sipping tea and bourbon while spreading the latest gossip. I wanted that for Shady Oaks again. I wanted happy and carefree.

Ruth smiled and had a wistful look on her face. "We enjoyed over ten of the best years of our lives at Shady Oaks. When World War Two broke out, Wilson and I plunged into the effort to help. We were both older then and offered our services to the Red Cross and wherever else our experience could be used." She sighed deeply. "Wilson died in 1942. We weren't blessed with children and I dove into every war cause I could to alleviate the loss. I missed him dreadfully. We'd been married for over thirty years. He popped the question when I was sixteen. My father didn't approve and refused to give us his blessing. Wilson was ten years older than I, but we didn't care and eloped."

"How did you—I mean what caused—that is..." I stumbled and stammered. I'd never asked anyone how they'd died and wondered if I was being insensitive.

"How did I die?" Ruth smiled as if understanding my dilemma. "I developed a heart condition in 1950. My activities were curtailed and I lived here at Shady Oaks with Sarah, a wonderful companion, until 1955. One evening I was sitting in my rocking chair knitting a sweater for a niece when my heart gave out. I still knit that sweater in my spare time. Of course, it never gets finished, but it gives me something to do. I don't suppose it matters. My niece passed over a few years ago."

"So, why are you still here? I mean, don't you want to join your husband on the other side?"

"Wilson loved Shady Oaks, but always resented having to give up his career for it. He's happy where he is. On the other hand, I passionately loved this place and never wanted to leave. So I didn't."

"You said the others elected you caretaker?" I had a hard time visualizing ghostly voting rights.

"Yes. The Colonel, Hester, Antoine, and Zoë did it. We have the strongest ties to Shady Oaks. When Germania died we needed someone to stick around and keep an eye on things."

"But suppose something happened—like a fire?"

"I would have contacted the fire department immediately!"

"How?"

I glanced at Reba who smiled.

"Oh, we have our ways," Ruth said.

Apparently, there were some things I didn't need to know yet.

"Did you know the other ghosts when you lived here?"

Now that Ruth was willing to talk, my curiosity knew no bounds. Good manners be damned. I wanted to know everything she was willing to tell.

"No. I never had a hint. It wasn't until I died and settled in to my specific area that I realized I wasn't the only spirit in the house. The Colonel greeted me and over the next couple of years I met Antoine, Zoë, and Hester. We're all here because we loved Shady Oaks. Many of the others occupied space because they were confused." She shrugged. "I must admit, I was glad to see you sort them out. The more you renovate, the more entities you'll release, but don't worry, I'll send them on their way. All most of them do is sleep anyway." She leaned forward with an avid look on her face. "By the way, dear, I wanted to know what you planned to do regarding the landscaping. Cousin Germania rather let it go and after she died, her heirs weren't interested."

"I hadn't really thought about it," I confessed. "What did it look like before?"

"It was lovely. I had azaleas lining the driveway and a lot of spring bulbs in the front flower beds. In the summer, I'd plant annuals all over."

"Will you help me plan the landscaping for next spring?"

"Oh, I'd love it! I've missed gardening so much." Tears formed in her worn blue eyes.

The timer on the stove dinged and Reba, who had quietly listened to Ruth's story, rose.

"It's time to go back to school."

Max came in and sniffed. "Is that fried chicken I smell?"

"It most certainly is and Cybil helped make it."

"No kidding? And not a fire extinguisher in sight," he teased.

Heat scorched my cheeks. "I've been learning how to cook from Reba and...from Reba. I'm starting with simple recipes and working my way up. Would you like to stay for dinner? I understand mashed potatoes, gravy, corn, and a salad are also on the menu."

"I never turn down food."

He grinned and winked at me, sending my heart into a little dipsy-doodle. I wanted to be sophisticated, but damned if I didn't feel like a schoolgirl again. I looked over to where Ruth sat.

"If I were you, Cybil, I'd snatch him before the rest of the women in Cherokee wake up," she said, grinning.

I laughed. "That's what Julie said, too."

"Julie? What did she say?" Max asked.

I realized I'd goofed and spoken to Ruth. Max had no idea she was there. I'd have to get used to talking to invisible people.

"Oh, she thinks I can learn how to cook." For spur of the moment, it wasn't bad.

"Let me go home and change into clean clothes. What time is dinner being served?"

"Six-thirty, Mr. Maitland, so you'd better scoot," Reba said with a smile.

"Scooting as ordered." He winked at me again. "I'll be back in less than an hour."

My eyes followed him as he left the kitchen. Damn, he looked good. Even with the memory of the brunette still tickling my jealousy button, I appreciated what I saw and damned if I wasn't falling deeper in love.

****

Dinner was a success. The chicken was perfect and Max ate like a man on death row. Reba served and Ruth observed, making sure to stay in the background.

"I don't want to be a third wheel, dear, but I am terribly curious about how courting is done nowadays."

We had coffee on the veranda where Max slid his wicker chair next to mine and held my hand. That warm, gushy feeling poured over me.

He raised my hand to his lips. "Have I told you how much I admire you? You're doing something that few people, let alone a single woman, would attempt in restoring Shady Oaks. You have a vision and a passion for the place usually reserved for family."

"I know this sounds crazy, but the moment I saw the place, it talked to me. Not in words, but in feelings. We were meant for each other."

"That doesn't sound strange at all. Over the last few weeks, I've come to love the place, too. Every nail, every brushstroke of paint makes me proud to be a part of the renovation. You'll be happy here, Cybil. Don't ask me how I know, but I do."

He had a look in his eyes and on his face that had me thinking he might be reconsidering the remarriage thing. With me? Goose bumps popped out up and down my arms. Then the look disappeared, and I wondered if my hopes and dreams had led me to believe that's what I'd seen.

We sat silently for a few minutes finishing our coffee and I thought about Max's words. Shady Oaks talked to him, too, though in a slightly different language.

He squeezed my hand, and then said, "I talked with my folks yesterday and told them about the renovations. They'd love to meet you. Would you like to come to dinner? How about Thursday night? I'd really like you to meet my parents."

My heart tripped in my chest. In the South, meeting one's parents was the same as declaring the relationship serious—as in forever. Nervous tension gripped me and I swallowed hard. Maybe my mind wasn't playing tricks. *Maybe* Max *was* re-thinking his stance on marriage. Oh, wow. *The brunette must not matter after all.*

Trying to appear calm and cool, I replied, "I'd love to meet your folks."

He let loose a breath as though he'd been holding it in fear of a rejection.

"That's great. Suppose I pick you up around six. That way we can chat before dinner."

Chat? Uh-oh. Chat was a euphemism for catechism. I was going to be grilled like pig over a barbeque pit. With an ex-wife floating around, they probably wanted an up close and personal questioning. I gulped and hoped the smile I gave him oozed confidence. *Screw the ex. He asked me to dinner, not her.*

"That sounds lovely. I can hardly wait."

Max set his coffee cup on the porch floor and rose bringing me with him. When he pulled me into his arms, I peeked over his shoulder. Ruth watched with a look of eager anticipation on her face. I didn't want to be rude, but this was not the time for subtlety. I gave her a stern look. She got the message and blinked out of sight. Then Max's lips met mine and I forgot all about ghosts, parents, grillings, and ex-wives. There was only Max.

I slid my arms around his neck and kissed him back. Mellow warmth swam through the blood in my veins and I wanted nothing more than to take him upstairs to my bed. His hands caressed my back, and then settled on my derriere as he crushed my hips against his. His erection nestled between my legs, pressing and upping the sexual ante. I groaned and wrapped a leg around his knees.

His hand slipped between our bodies to cover my breast, the thumb rasping over the nipple. Even through my clothing, it felt like heaven. Then he pulled back. I wanted to cry with frustration.

"I'd better get out of here before this goes any further," he said in a hoarse, unsteady voice.

I wanted to scream, *Why?* but didn't.

He kissed me again, and then put more distance between us. The look in his eyes suggested maybe he was a tad overwhelmed, too. This was progress. He glanced over his shoulder as if to make sure of the porch steps' location.

"I'll see you tomorrow morning, Cybil." He ran a fingertip down my cheek. "Sleep tight."

He trotted down the steps and drove off. My blood was up and if I didn't have him soon, I'd surely die. Hot and bothered, I snatched up our cups, took them into the kitchen, and went to bed—alone, damn it.

## Chapter Thirteen

I savored my second cup of coffee of the morning, gazing at my kitchen with pride. The paint complemented the cabinets, bringing out the wood's rich, warm tones just as I'd envisioned. The sunlight blazing through the windows set the black granite countertops sparkling. It was the kind of kitchen any cook would love—even me. But what I held most dear was the fact that I'd made the decisions and stuck with them.

I'd had a restless night with dreams of Max, my mother, and the disastrous dinner intermingled—a combination of the good, the bad, and the ugly. As a result, I overslept. Max had come and gone, although he'd left a note saying the kitchen floor would be installed today.

The workmen were busy upstairs and I sat lonely, wishing I'd set the alarm clock. I missed Max. Our early morning coffee chats had become a habit I didn't want to break. Idly, I wondered what he was doing, where he was.

Max. What was I going to do? I was nuts about the guy. His kisses drove me crazy and his touch set me on fire. My ego told me I must have a similar effect on him, but whether his feelings burned as deeply as mine I couldn't gauge. He'd already warned me about his take on marriage, money, and responsibility. I suspected he was scared and used them as excuses. I had a tough row to hoe. Yet he'd invited me to dinner at his parents'.

Ruth drifted into the room, towing a sleepy apparition behind her.

"Sorry to interrupt, dear, but this is a distant cousin. He came to us after the Battle of Corinth in 1862. He died there and his last happy memory was of a Shady Oaks party before the war. I'm relocating him to the garage. He won't be any trouble."

"Uh—fine," I said. She and the cousin flowed through the wall.

I liked Ruth. She fussed a bit and sometimes seemed a little on the ditzy side, but she also loved and looked after Shady Oaks. It's a shame she never had any children. She'd have made a wonderful mother. I couldn't see her criticizing or manipulating her kids. Too bad she and Martha couldn't switch places. Of course if they did, I'd have to banish Martha to a new resting place, preferably a galaxy far, far away. I wondered if that were possible. Could ghosts go anywhere in the universe? I'd have to ask.

"Good morning, Cybil," Reba said entering the kitchen. "Oh, my, this looks even better in the sunlight. The room now has personality. When will the floors be done?"

"According to Max, sometime today. I don't know how long it'll take to install, so I guess a simple meal will be the best choice for tonight."

"Stew, I think—unsalted," Reba said with a chuckle. "I'll use the crock pot." She cocked her head and listen to the sounds of hammering from upstairs. "I'll bet they're making an awful mess. The dust will drift down, but it's useless to try and clean until they're finished. Why don't I go through some of those boxes in the other two rooms down here?"

She removed stew meat from the freezer and popped it into the microwave to defrost.

"I don't know where you'll put half the stuff in them," I said.

"I'll figure out something. What's on your agenda for today?"

Good question. I should write. The final Lord

Edgeware saga flowed nicely and if I concentrated, could finish in another two or three weeks, but today the muse wasn't with me.

"I have no idea," I answered.

"Have you been in the attic yet?"

"No. I haven't been in the basement either. Both kind of give me the willies." I remembered the attic as the source of my housemates' pranks.

Reba laughed. "There's nothing to fear, child. I noticed you don't have enough furniture to fill the house. Maybe you'll find something you can use."

She had a point. I finished my coffee and hurried upstairs, pausing before the attic door. I had only ventured partway up the other night. At the time, I'd been nervous and had shone the flashlight around quickly before retreating.

I half expected to smell cigar smoke as I mounted the steps. The only smell was the musty odor of dust, mold, and a hint of damp from a place closed for too many years.

I'd never realized the attic had windows, but it did—two large ones on either gabled end. Years of accumulated crud allowed a dim light to enter. If I ever needed to expand, this would make the perfect office or rec room. The room ran the width of the house and the steep pitch of the roof allowed an adult to stand upright with space to spare. I pictured myself writing by the windows on one end and having a study or research area on the other. At the moment, however, numerous clumps of what I assumed was furniture covered in dustsheets jammed the space.

I recklessly ripped one off and regretted my action as a cloud of dust encircled my head. I spent the next five minutes sneezing and wishing I'd worn some kind of face mask.

When the dust settled, I viewed what I'd uncovered. A dining room ensemble complete with a hutch and sideboard stood before me. I wasn't well versed in antiques, but it looked old. Even the needlepoint seats appeared in good condition.

I moved on to the next shrouded mound, this time removing the sheet with more caution and less dust. My eyes gazed upon a huge bed, an armoire, vanity table, and a tall chest of drawers—what did they call them—chiffoniers. A washstand, complete with a pitcher and basin finished the grouping.

And so it went as I continued my journey around the attic. Sofas, chairs, tables, old lamps, even a grandfather clock came to light. A few of the items had water damage from the leaky roof, but for the most part the stuff was salvageable.

Even if I didn't want to use antiques, I could sell some of them and buy what I did want. But first, I needed to know what I had. I could always call my mother. She loved this kind of thing, but would try to manipulate me into giving them to her or my sisters. No, Mother was out. Besides, I refused to be the one to break the silence.

I could call a local antique dealer, but they weren't without ulterior motives either. I'd call Daryl. He and Steve had several antique pieces in their home and of course, there was always Julie, who knew about everything.

I turned to leave when my eyes fell on a singly wrapped item leaning against the far wall. Intrigued, I removed the cloth to find layers of brown paper underneath. Bulky and heavier than I imagined, I wrestled the cumbersome five-by-four foot slab to the floor and unwrapped it.

It was a black and white portrait done in what appeared to be charcoal. The light was too dim to see clearly, but I discerned the outline of a young woman. Eager to investigate further, I dragged it to the stairs and down to the hallway.

Whoever she had been, she was lovely. Her hair

was dressed in a style of the mid-nineteenth century. An oval face with slightly slanted eyes and a half-smile gave her the look of having a secret. She wore a white dress of the era. Standing next to a pedestal, one hand rested on its top while the other casually held a rose. An ornate necklace graced her slender throat and matching earrings dangled almost to her bare shoulders. I fancied the mystery lady was about to attend a ball.

I inspected the front and back of the portrait, but found no artist's signature. If the medium used was charcoal then it needed protection. I carefully ran my fingers around the inside edges of the frame until contacting a small fragment of old glass. I'd call a framer and have it replaced. Intuitively, I knew where to hang the portrait. It could only go over the massive fireplace in the drawing room.

I got one of the workmen to carry it downstairs and prop it up on the mantel. I was right. She belonged there.

I journeyed back to the kitchen to tell Reba of my attic finds and watch as she chopped veggies for the stew while the meat browned. Pleased with my day's work so far, I wondered what to do next. I didn't think I'd spoken out loud, but Reba answered anyway.

"Why not try stripping wallpaper? It needs to be done."

Me? Strip wallpaper? I could hear my mother and sisters laughing. Well, why not, I argued. How hard could it be?

"I've never tried anything like that before."

"You can do it. Find a spray bottle and fill it with a half-and-half solution of dishwashing detergent and water. Spray it on the walls, wait a few minutes, and then strip and scrape. Are you going to hang new wallpaper?"

"Downstairs, yes, except for the drawing room. I

think I'll paint that."

"Excellent. Let me find you a bottle and you can start. I'll get the stew to cooking, and then begin on those boxes."

Reba rummaged under the sink, and reminded myself once again to thank Max for finding her. I'd love to know how to cook stew, but had more enthusiasm for my new task. She filled the bottle and handed it to me along with a wide spatula-like thing.

"Spray, wait, and use this to peel it off. But be gentle. You don't want to gouge the plaster. Which room are you going to do first?"

It was a no-brainer. The red in the dining room had to go. I like drama, but this was a little much, even for me. I visualized something in shades of green. Maybe bringing the outdoors in kind of thing. I'd look at the books Max lent me later.

Armed with my own weapons of mass destruction, including a ladder to reach the twelve-foot-high ceiling, I marched into the dining room. Another willing workman helped me move the furniture into the middle of the room. Taking a deep breath I sprayed an area three feet square and waited a couple of minutes. The seams separated and curled. I gently peeled the red away to discover—another layer of wallpaper, lavender this time. I sprayed and peeled more. Some kind of hideous flowered stuff showed up. I went through six layers before finally hitting plaster.

Okay, so it would take longer than expected. I could do it. I continued spraying and scraping, vaguely aware of the workers laying the floor in the kitchen. They glued, nailed, and tapped. The men upstairs ripped and hammered. I scraped. By using my imagination, I decided we could become a band, our various sounds the music.

A voice startled me.

"Oh, I see you're changing the wallpaper," Ruth said from over my shoulder.

It suddenly occurred to me that maybe I was removing something she'd hung. "Um—yes. I thought it was time for a change. I'm sorry. Did you hang some of this?"

"Yes. In 1945. Red was all the rage then. But don't apologize, dear. That was a long time ago. Your mother objected, and I took exception to the word *bordello*. That's when we began to play the tricks on them."

Never would I admit to Ruth that in this case I thought old Martha right. I did half expect to hear the sound of a tinny piano playing. Instead, I told her of my plans for the new color scheme.

"The outside in. What a lovely idea. I look forward to seeing it." She cocked her head. "Oh, dear. I hear another disturbed spirit calling. I'd better go." She drifted out the door and disappeared.

I worked on until almost noon when Max finally showed up.

"Holy cow!" he said, entering my little slice of renovation hell.

I looked down. I stood knee deep in a sea of soggy multi-colored paper. My feet were hidden, but the water and old glue squished inside my shoes. I'd made progress, though. I had finished one wall and was grateful the wainscoting allowed only a half-wall of paper.

"Yeah. It's a little messy. Reba told me how to do it. I expected one layer, but found six."

"That's not unusual. It was easier and cheaper to just slap the new over the old."

I put the scraper down and pushed my hair off my face. "What have you been up to all morning?"

"I had to meet with a couple of suppliers in Memphis. Have you had lunch yet?"

"No."

"Then how about we go into town and grab a bite at Rourke's? It's a little bar not far from my place."

"Sounds fabulous. Let me clean up."

With the kitchen out of commission for the moment, I ran upstairs, scrubbed the old wallpaper paste off, and changed into something a little less grubby. When I came back down, I heard Max and Reba laughing in the dining room.

I'd been so engrossed with my new project, I'd forgotten about Dudley. I had no idea where he'd been all morning, but now he stood in the middle of the sodden wallpaper. Something about the stuff must have appealed to him for the silly goof had rolled in it. He now stood woofing in delight with strips of paper stuck to his fur. He looked like a badly wrapped Christmas gift.

I joined in the laughter until realizing how hard it was going to be to get it off.

"Oh, hell, Dudley. You stupid oaf. It'll take me forever to clean you up." I tried to sound angry, but failed.

"Don't worry, Cybil. I'll take care of it," Reba said with a chuckle. "I guess he's feeling a bit left out of things." She grabbed him by the collar and led him down the hall and out the front door.

Max grabbed my hand in a similar move. I was happy as a kid on a picnic. Lunch with Max made my day.

At Rourke's, we ordered burgers and Cokes, and then discussed the house.

"So, you want to help with the renovations. Think you can handle power tools?" he teased.

"Power tools? As in one of those big, noisy saws?"

"I was thinking more along the lines of a nail gun or a power screwdriver."

I pictured Max holding a power screwdriver, the

motor whirring as the bit turned and turned, screwing and screwing. Then I visualized him with the nail gun, hammering the nail home with a single, powerful thrust. *Wow, what symbolism.*

I broke out in a sweat. Oh, my God. I was having sexual fantasies regarding Max and power tools. I grabbed my Coke, damn near draining it.

"Yoo-hoo! Cybil," he said, snapping his fingers under my nose. "Where are you?"

I jerked my attention back to the conversation. "Sorry. I was thinking about power tools and such. I guess I could learn to use the simple ones."

"Great! When you're ready, I'll show you how. A couple of lessons and you'll be nailing and screwing things in like a pro." He grinned and winked.

I almost choked on an ice cube. Oh, geez, I had to get my mind out of the gutter or I'd disgraced myself.

"Ride 'em, cowboy!" a voice yelled from the back of the bar.

"What?" I yelped. In my feeble, one track mind, it sounded as though the speaker had a direct line into my thoughts.

"Mechanical bull," Max replied amid cheers from the clientele at the bar. "Rourke has one in the back." He craned his head to get a good look. "Yep. It's Huey Dawson. He works over at the feed store and comes in every day for lunch and a quick ride. Wanna try?"

"No, thanks."

Max was the only thing I wanted to ride. If I didn't stop this line of thinking, I was going to be in serious trouble. I changed the subject and told him about my finds in the attic.

"I guess each generation of the family stuffed the old furniture up there and forgot about it. What are you going to do with it?"

"I haven't decided yet. Probably sell most of it."

Our food arrived and rather than try to make small talk, I concentrated on eating. Max did the same and thirty minutes later dropped me off at the house. I sighed watching him drive away, then turned to reenter the wonderful world of wallpaper removal.

****

I sat on my sofa in the drawing room, a Heather Graham novel open on my lap, and a glass of red wine in my hand. Reba's stew had been superb, and I was ready to relax. I'd put in a full day. A sense of accomplishment, along with the wine, gave me a mellow glow. The fact I hadn't written a single word didn't bother me at all.

After lunch, I'd turned all that unused sexual energy into stripping wallpaper and had finally been rewarded with the plaster walls. I contemplated painting them, but stuck with my original decision. Another accomplishment, I thought with pride.

The kitchen floor was finished, and I couldn't believe how great it looked. Of course, the fireplace still needed work, and the French doors had to be installed, but for all intents and purposes, it was done.

Reba made inroads into the boxes in the front room. I could now walk without tripping over something.

I'd called Daryl and Julie. Both agreed to come down on Friday to look at my attic finds. Steve suggested pizza at the Palace. Needing my anchovy fix, I seconded the proposal.

Dudley lumbered in and flopped onto the floor at my feet, yawned, then closed his eyes. Within seconds, he was snoring. Oh, well, I could have gotten a cat.

My glance strayed to the portrait on the mantel. The young woman smiled as though in approval. Whatever message she was trying to project, I agreed. The room felt good.

I had just settled back to read when a funny little *pop* brought my eyes up. Hester stood in front of the fireplace staring at the portrait. Turning, she smiled.

"I see you found Henrietta."

"Henrietta? You know the girl in the picture?"

"Yes, of course. She's my younger sister. She was eighteen when she posed for this and died shortly afterward." Hester sighed. "So young and full of life. She got all the beauty in the family, but I never begrudged her any of it. Etta pulled beaus in from all over the county. I sometimes picked off a leftover or two."

"What did she die of? Is she here?" I closed my book and curled my legs under me, then sipped some wine.

"Oh, no. She happily passed over. The poor girl never had a strong constitution. She contracted a heavy cold and died of pneumonia a few weeks later. We were all heartbroken."

"I can imagine."

Hester frowned as she stared. "That's strange. I could have sworn the portrait was done in color. Oh well, it's been a long time since I've seen it. Father consigned it to the attic after the funeral." She drifted over to the other sofa and sat down. "This looks strange, but isn't too uncomfortable. I see you've taken down the wallpaper in the dining room. About time. Don't tell Ruth, but I never liked the red."

"My lips are sealed. Which paper was your choice?"

"The green-and-white striped. My cousin's wife, Zoë's mother-in-law, chose that offensive flowered stuff, and then compounded the problem a few years after with that lavender-and-gold business. The woman had no taste."

"I have to admit that out of the six layers, yours was the best. I think I'll go with green also, although I'm sure my mother will have an opinion—assuming she ever speaks to me again," I said.

"My dear, this is your house. It's none of your mother's business. Listen to her advice, and then decorate the way you want. From what I witnessed the other day, it can't have been too much fun growing up."

"Mother likes to be in control."

"That's what Zoë said." She shot me a keen glance and leaned forward. "Don't allow anyone to rule your life, Cybil. Bullies—and that's what your mother and sisters are—will always retreat when confronted. Remember that. Be strong and your own person. Don't back down from what you believe is right. Sooner or later, your mother will see she can't control you and give up trying."

"You don't know my mother. She's like a nasty little terrier, always yipping and snapping at my heels. Max says I caved in to her on the little things, but stayed strong on the important issues—like this house."

"Listen to Max. Whatever you do, don't give up this house. Please, don't let her beat you down on that," Hester pleaded, a worried look on her face.

"Don't worry, I won't."

"Good girl. I don't mean to pry, but it seems you and Max are getting quite friendly."

"Well, yes, I'm trying."

She smiled. "My dear, Max is a treasure."

"I kind of think so, too. He's asked me to meet his parents on Thursday—dinner, no less."

Her eyes widened. "Oh, my goodness. I'd say he's interested—very interested."

"I hope so." I took another sip of wine and swirled the remainder in my glass, trying to ask about Hester's life—and death—in a tactful manner.

"Tell me about when you lived here, Hester. What was it like? When were you born?"

"I was born in 1845, the first birth in this house. My grandfather, Gideon LaForge, built it a few years earlier. My parents lived here also. They loved to entertain. I can remember being only six or seven years old and sneaking out of bed to sit on the stairs and watch. Oh, the 1850s were exciting times. My father and grandfather would gather on the veranda with other planters in the county and talk politics, often yelling about those wicked Yankees."

"I can almost picture it. The war must have been devastating."

"The war ripped apart the fabric of our lives. My grandfather went to his grave in 1866, unable to deal with having lost. My mother passed away in 1868 just a few months after we lost Henrietta. Father and I had to work hard to save Shady Oaks from those predatory carpetbaggers, but through hard work and fierce determination, we hung on."

Her words echoed Ruth's. Even now I saw the pride in Hester's eyes and hear it in her voice.

"If you don't mind me asking, how come you never married?"

"I fell in love with a wonderful man shortly after the end of the war. And he loved me. Unfortunately, my grandfather and father bitterly opposed the match."

"But why?" Having another man around to help with the work and to provide Hester with a future would be a godsend.

"My dear, he was one of *them*."

"Them? Them who?" I asked, confused.

"*Them*. He was Captain Jonathon William Ritchie with the Fifteenth Ohio."

"A Yankee? You fell in love with a Yankee?"

She nodded. "I was all set to elope. We made it as far as Carruthersburg when Daddy and a whole slew of cousins caught up to us. They'd even brought Jonathon's commanding officer. The next thing I know I was shipped off to visit Mother's sister in Mobile, dutifully chaperoned, of course, by Mother and Henrietta. When we returned several months later, Jonathon had been reassigned to one of the western forts. I never saw him again."

"That's awful! I'd have moved heaven and earth to get back to you. I'm kind of disappointed in him— no offense." I didn't want to insult Hester, but I couldn't help thinking of Lord Edgeware and Lady Katrina.

"Times were different then, and he was an honorable man. I still love him. As a result I decided to compare every man I met to Jonathon and found them all lacking. I developed a sharp tongue and drove my father crazy by refusing marriage proposals from suitors he approved."

"Kind of getting even, huh?"

"In a way, I suppose I was. He went to his reward in 1878, and I carried on here alone until my death in 1900. By the way, what year is this?"

I told her.

"Strange, but I don't feel like I've been dead for over a hundred years."

"How did you die?" It no longer seemed like a silly question to ask.

"It was the most ridiculous thing." Hester patted her hair and shook her head. "I loved going barefoot. I picked up a splinter from one of the veranda steps and the next thing I knew I had blood poisoning. I died quickly."

"I'm sorry. Why do you stay here?"

"The one constant in my life was Shady Oaks. I loved the place. I was the first to be born in it, and I just didn't want to leave. Besides"—she snorted inelegantly—"I can't think of anyone with whom I want to spend eternity. Except Jonathon, of course. I often wondered what happened to him. I suppose he married and had a family." She sighed and looked off into space, then stood blinking tears from her eyes. "I've taken up enough of your time. Remember what I said about staying strong."

Before I could respond, Hester popped out of the room the same way she'd entered. Even a ghost must want privacy.

I finished my wine, thinking about Hester and her Yankee, and then about Max and me. I tried to envision living here at Shady Oaks alone, but couldn't. I kept seeing Max by my side in the kitchen, the dining room, the drawing room—and the bedroom—with laughter echoing off the walls along with the love soaking into them. Damn it. We belonged together as much as Hester and her man. I made a promise to research Captain Jonathon William Ritchie of the Fifteenth Ohio. Maybe I could give Hester some answers.

Upstairs, I snuggled into bed, listened to Dudley snoring, and thought about Shady Oaks. With each passing day, I loved the house more and more. If I died, would I want to leave? I tried to visualize myself as a ghost, but my Presbyterian upbringing got in the way. Still, the thought intrigued me. I'd get to stay in a wonderful home, but could I stand to see someone else owning it? It wouldn't bother me if that someone else turned out to be my son or daughter. I reasoned, however, that sooner or later strangers would own it. For the first time, I understood my housemates' anxieties.

I yawned and rolled over. What a silly thing to think about. I didn't plan on dying anytime soon. And if I did, I wanted to spend eternity with Max.

Here.

In this house.

Together.

The soft touch of someone smoothing my covers

made me look up. Ruth stood next to me smiling. She then bent and patted Dudley on the head. He groaned in his sleep, thumping his tail.

Mother Ruth drifted out the door with a murmured, "Good night."

## Chapter Fourteen

Max finished his coffee and set the cup on the counter. Our morning get-togethers had resumed. A morning without Max was like a day without sunshine. Uh-oh. Was that another fifties thing again? Didn't the quote have something to do with orange juice? I shrugged. Who cared? It was the truth.

"I have to check on another job over in Senatobia, but I'll be back. Don't forget—dinner at my folks' tonight."

I hadn't forgotten. How could I with my stomach already tied up in knots over it?

"I won't. What do I wear?"

"Nothing fancy. They're just ordinary people." He leaned down and gave me a hard kiss. *Oh God, please let me impress his folks tonight.*

I waved goodbye as he walked out the back door, then poured another cup of coffee and sat at my kitchen table. The dining room had been cleared of wet wallpaper remains, but the smell of damp glue and old paper still lingered. Besides, this view pleased me.

*Rugs in front of the stove, sink, and definitely by the fireplace when it's finished, will look nice.*

My cell phone ringing interrupted the happy decorating plans. The caller ID told me it was my editor, Genevieve. Good God, what did she want at this early hour?

Genevieve had erased the word "sleep" from her vocabulary years ago. She lived on coffee, martinis, cigarettes, and the occasional salad. Time held no meaning for her either. If she had a question at one-thirty in the morning, she thought nothing of picking up the phone and calling. She did that once. I'd told her I didn't care about her business hours, but mine started when the sun came up. She'd apologized and not done it again.

I answered. The sun had risen long ago. "Good morning, Genevieve. How's New York?"

"It's freaking raining, traffic is snarled, the cabbies are rude, and work is overwhelming."

"So, what else is new? What has you calling me at seven-thirty in the morning?"

"I haven't seen your proposal yet for the new series. How close are you to getting it done?"

"I planned on doing it as soon as I finished up the last Lord Edgeware story. What's the hurry?" I didn't want to admit I hadn't a clue what to write.

"I'd like to have something in place to take to my boss by next month. When can you get Lord Edgeware's final hurrah in? We need to hurry with the revisions. The release date has been set for February fifteenth."

I sat stunned. A release date before I'd even turned it in? I didn't understand the urgency. A dart of fear stabbed my gut. "Gen, what's going on? Are you dropping me?"

She sighed. "I guess I can tell you. It'll be made public soon enough. Just promise you won't tell anyone else, including your agent."

God, they *were* going to drop me. I would have a house, huge bills, and no income. The specter of Martha Stewart danced in front of my eyes.

"Oh, Lord, what's wrong?"

"Lion Press has been bought by Oxford Publishing Company. It's a huge conglomerate. They own newspapers, magazines, along with radio and TV stations all over the country. We'll still operate under the name Lion Press, but it's practically a done deal. The announcement should be made next month sometime."

"And this affects me how?"

Conglomerates always swallowed up the little guys and Lion Press, while profitable, was small.

"They want to streamline the company, make it more manageable, so they'll be cutting back. The Regency line is being eliminated. If I can get this last book of yours in before the end of the year, you'll still get it published. They're also reviewing contracts. That's why I wanted a new proposal from you."

The Regencies gone? I couldn't believe it. I'd cut my romantic teeth on them. "What about other historicals?"

"For the time being, they're fine. The new owners are looking for material beginning in the middle of the nineteenth century through the First World War eras. They want to modernize."

"For the time being?" An icy finger of panic slid down my spine. "What other changes are they contemplating?"

"They also want to expand romantic suspense and thrillers with romantic elements. Plus, they're looking for more kick-ass heroines. Lady Katrina in the modern world would be a shoo-in."

I sat shocked, not sure what to say. Romantic suspense and thrillers? With romantic elements? I'd never attempted either. Could I portray Lady Katrina in the twenty-first century? I had no idea. What was I going to do? I needed inspiration and fast—or another publisher.

"Cybil, are you there? Hello? Cybil?"

Genevieve's voice brought me out of my daze. "Yeah, I'm here. I'm just trying to digest everything. When does all of this take place?"

"Sometime after the first of the year. That's why I'm nagging you. I want to keep you on our list. Get

Lord Edgeware in as soon as you can and e-mail me a proposal for an historical novel set in the time frame I gave you. Look, I've got to run. My other line is ringing. Remember, don't say anything."

Genevieve hung up with an audible click. I slowly folded my phone and stared across the room, seeing nothing. What the hell was I going to do? I'd been with Lion Press and Gen from the beginning of my career. I'd never written anything other than Regency romances. To suddenly switch genres seemed like an impossible task. I had no idea where to begin.

"Dudley, my career may have just gone down the toilet. My God, what am I going to do?"

Dudley lifted his head from my foot under the table and thumped his tail. He probably didn't care what I did as long as I gave him belly rubs and treats—not necessarily in that order.

I made another pot of coffee and set my laptop up on the kitchen table. I had a lot to do and not much time to do it in. I settled down and wrote.

****

All writers can relate to the desertion of the muse. It's also called writer's block. I had a serious case of it. Everything I wrote sounded like gibberish, and I visualized the sword of publishing doom hanging over my head.

I angrily held down the backspace button, erasing the last paragraph I'd written. It read as if devised in the mind of a ten-year-old. God, what else could go wrong today?

Reba had arrived a couple of hours ago and since there was no need to make dinner tonight, she'd gone directly to unpacking boxes. Now, I looked up to find her standing in the doorway.

"You have a visitor, Cybil," she said in a somber tone, the expression on her face blank.

"A visitor? I don't have time for the church

ladies, Reba. Please make my apologies and ask them to come back tomorrow afternoon for tea or something."

"It's your mother."

Oh, damn! Just what I needed. *She's probably come loaded for bear.*

It had been four days since the disastrous dinner. She must have felt a face-to-face confrontation to have its merits. The temptation to tell her to go home was strong, but I knew that would only postpone the inevitable. Besides, I didn't have the guts.

"Thank you, Reba. Where is she?"

"I asked her to wait in the drawing room."

Reba looked controlled, and I guessed Mother had been at her queen-of-the-realm best. She no doubt treated Reba like a servant, insulting her in the bargain.

I squared my shoulders and lifted my chin, then walked with a determined step down the hall to confront Mother.

"Good morning, Mother. What brings you down to Cherokee?" As if I didn't know.

"I am here to accept your apology for the unforgivable things you said and did last Sunday. I had expected you to phone, but I can see I must have failed in your upbringing. You have no manners whatsoever."

Her icy voice told me I was not forgiven for what she considered a serious breach of damned near everything. I stood my ground.

"I don't remember having said or done anything that requires an apology, Mother. I'll admit I shouldn't have laughed at Penelope, but she brought the whole thing on herself."

Mother's nostrils flared and her eyes widened. The gauntlet lay on the ground.

"Your sister was humiliated in front of the

entire family. She cried all the way home. I was made to look like a fool. My suit is ruined, and I don't appreciate your tone. You never did one thing to make us feel welcome."

"That's not true. And while we're on the subject of good manners, I'd have to say you showed a severe lack of such by inviting the entire family down for a dinner I was obviously not ready to serve."

"The food was atrocious and your cook insolent."

"I thought Reba did an excellent job considering what she had to work with as far as a kitchen was concerned. As for not being welcome, I showed you the house. After all, that's what you came to see, wasn't it?"

Her lips thinned and her spine stiffened.

"This house is a white elephant that will drag you down like an anchor to the bottom of a river. It's old, it's decrepit, it smells, and is probably ready to fall apart."

Dudley chose this moment to stroll in.

"Get that ridiculous dog out of here! Dogs do not belong in the house. He has fleas, and Lord only knows what other kind of vermin."

"Dudley does not have fleas and he's welcome in my house at any time." I patted Dudley on the head, sitting down defiantly.

Mother had not moved a millimeter. Her jaw clenched and her bosom heaved as she drew in a deep breath.

"Well, it is obvious you invite all kinds of undesirable people into your home."

"What do you mean by that?"

"You insulted me and the rest of the family by inviting Daryl's...friend. You know I don't like being in his presence, and wouldn't dream of exposing my grandchildren to such depravity. He's no good and has led Daryl astray."

I jumped to my feet. Fury ripped through me

like a tornado through a trailer park. My fingers curled into my palms and I breathed deep to keep my voice steady.

"I will invite whomever I want into my house. I like Steve. He's good for Daryl. They love each other, and if you would accept the fact Daryl is gay, you'd see it, too."

"I'll never accept anything of the sort. You have no idea the humiliation I'd feel if my friends knew about my only son's lifestyle."

"Mother, I dare say they already know. Daryl has never kept his sexual orientation a secret. Do you know how silly you sound referring to Steve as Stephanie?"

Mother gasped and clutched a hand over her chest. "Are you saying my friends are laughing at me?"

"Maybe not laughing, but they certainly must be feeling sorry for you. I know I do."

I meant what I'd said. By trying to maintain control, my mother had missed out on many opportunities to enjoy her family.

"I do not need pity! Especially from you!" Her voice had risen to a shout, but she struggled to appear unruffled. "I can see I won't get my apology. Never mind. I can deal with an ungrateful child."

Ah, the change-of-tactics time had arrived. She had tried anger, browbeating, and having me doubt my judgment. It was now guilt's turn at bat.

"Cybil, in spite of everything, I love you. I think this whole house thing is a mistake and before you sink any more of your hard-earned cash into it, I want you to come home with me. Now."

Hester appeared with a loud *pop* in the doorway. Before I could stop myself, I swiveled my head in that direction.

"Cybil, remember what we talked about last night. Be strong. Don't let her take you away from

Shady Oaks."

"Don't worry. I haven't forgotten. I am being strong. Arguing with my mother is a first for me."

"Who are you talking to?"

I whipped my head back and realized what I'd done. Mother's eyes darted about the room.

"It doesn't matter. I have no intention of leaving this house. I love it and will stay."

"Good girl. You're doing wonderfully," Hester said with a smile.

"I think so, too. I can handle this situation."

"Cybil, for the love of God, who are you talking to?"

Ruth popped up next to Hester. "Hester, I think you're distracting Cybil."

"Oh dear. I didn't think about that. Shall we materialize?"

"Good God, don't do that!" I stated.

"Don't do what? Cybil, what's going on?" Mother demanded.

I jerked my head back toward her.

She put a hand to her lips. "Oh, no. The strain of buying this dump has finally sent you over the edge. You're having mental problems, aren't you? Are you hearing voices? Are you being told to do things you know are evil? Come home with me, darling. I'll see to it you have the best psychiatrist in Memphis."

"What's a psychiatrist?" Hester whispered to Ruth.

I tried to get myself on an even keel.

"Mother, I do not need a doctor to ask me a bunch of silly questions regarding my mental status. I am not crazy," I replied, hoping the explanation helped Hester.

"But you're talking to thin air," Mother wailed.

It was at this moment Max decided to make his appearance. He strode into the room and stopped dead at the sight of two women obviously in the middle of an argument.

"Oops. Sorry. Didn't mean to interrupt."

"You're not," I said, grateful for a chance to turn the conversation away from my silly lapse in answering Hester. "Max, I'd like you to meet my mother, Lilith Austin. Mother, this is my contractor, Max Maitland."

"Mrs. Austin, it's a pleasure to meet you." Max held out his hand and smiled.

Mother presented a limp handshake and immediately withdrew her hand from his clasp.

"Mr. Maitland, tell me, how much longer is this renovation supposed to take?"

"That's hard to say, but the majority of the demolition and rebuilding should be finished by the first of the year."

Mother's cold stare should have shriveled him into a midget. Instead, Max continued smiling.

"I see. And how much of my daughter's money will it take to finish? Exactly how much has she forked over? Did you allow her to get any second bids on anything?"

I gasped. Even for my mother this was grossly insulting.

Max, God bless him, never turned a hair. The smile stayed in place, although his eyes hardened. "I rather think that's between your daughter and me, Mrs. Austin. If she wishes to share that information, that's her business."

"Mr. Maitland, I am here to look after my daughter's well-being."

"Forgive me, Mrs. Austin, but I think you're here to undermine her confidence. I discussed everything with Cybil prior to beginning, and that included prices."

Max stared her down. Mother patted her perfectly coifed hair and turned on her heel.

"You haven't heard the end of this, Cybil. I'll be

back when you are less delusional and more ready to accept reality. Good day."

I listened to her high heels tap down the hall. Then she was gone, slamming the door behind her.

"Good riddance!" Hester declared.

"Imagine suggesting you're crazy!" Ruth said.

"Holy cow! What the hell was going on here? What did she mean by delusional?" Max asked.

"The next time she comes, we'll take care of her," Hester said, lifting her chin in a combative manner.

"Oh, good grief, don't do that. I'll never be able to explain you," I replied before thinking.

Max's gaze followed mine to the doorway where Hester and Ruth stood.

"Uh, Cybil, who are you talking to and why would you have to explain me to anyone?"

Suddenly, I couldn't stand any more. I had to get out of the house. I wanted to be alone.

Whirling around, I snapped, "Go find something to do, all of you. Just leave me alone for a while."

I heard the telltale pops of Ruth and Hester obeying. I walked out the front door, and heard Max say in a puzzled voice, "All of you?"

****

I stood in front of the Maitland front porch steps and wiped my sweaty palms down the sides of my slacks. I then raised my hands to fuss with my hair, deciding to remove the large clip holding it at the nape of my neck. Dropping it in my purse, I fluffed out the tresses. Maybe I look too disheveled this way, I thought. I reached for the clip, but discovered my trembling hands had problems fastening it. I returned it to my purse and wet my desert-dry lips, trying to swallow the lump of anxiety-ridden fear forming in my throat.

Warm fingers cupped my elbow. I gasped and jumped about a foot. It was Max.

"Will you relax?" he said for what seemed like the hundredth time since he'd picked me up. "These are my parents—not the Spanish Inquisition."

The Spanish Inquisition didn't scare me half as much as saying the wrong thing to his mother. Before I could speak, however, he led me up the steps, opened the screen door, and called out, "Mom, Dad, we're here."

A small, trim woman, her salt-and-pepper hair cut stylishly short, appeared from a hallway in the back of the house. She smiled and I stared into the same warm brown eyes inherited by her son.

"Max, I'm glad you're a little early. Your father is out on the deck ready to play bartender." She laughed, extending her hand. "And you must be Cybil. I'm so happy to meet you."

I took a deep breath, lifted my chin, held out my hand, and stepped forward where I promptly tripped on the little rug in front of me. If it hadn't been for Max's quick reflexes, I'd have landed face first at her feet. As it was, I fell to one knee before being hauled up inelegantly by the arm.

"Oh, dear, are you hurt?" she exclaimed.

My ears burned, but I stammered, "N-no. I'm fine. I should have been more careful."

"I'm so sorry. I've been meaning to put a non-skid protector under this silly rug for months. Are you sure you're all right?" My hostess kicked the object of my clumsiness out of the way.

"I'm fine. It's a pleasure to meet you Mrs. Maitland." I once again extended my hand and found it clasped in a firm, but gentle grip.

Was she comparing me with her ex-daughter-in-law? Was I better looking? Did she have a curvier figure? Did she and Max's father share his opinion of her as a bitch or had they liked her? More questions swirled through my mind, but I couldn't bring myself to ask such invasive things. I tried to shift the jealousy into a box with a tight-fitting lid.

"And I'm Mae Anne. Shall we go out onto the deck? Dinner will be ready in about twenty minutes."

Max shifted his hand from my arm, sliding it around my waist, a move not lost on his mother. She smiled, then turned and led us through the kitchen from which emanated fabulous smells—garlic and oregano the primary scents—and out onto a large deck.

A tall, dark-haired man stood next to a small table laden with liquor bottles. Ice rattled in a cocktail shaker. He grinned as we walked through the door.

"About time you got here," he boomed. "I'm already one up on you."

"Two, but who's counting?" Mae Anne said.

"Dad, I'd like you to meet Cybil Austin. Cybil, this old reprobate is my father, Thomas Maitland."

He stopped shaking cocktails long enough to grasp my hand and lift it to his lips, bowing as he did so.

"Miss Austin, I can't remember when last such a vision of loveliness graced our home." He looked up with a twinkle in his eyes and winked.

"Oh, brother," Max murmured.

I could see where Max got his charm. I'm afraid I giggled, and then wondered if I sounded like a teenager.

"Please, call me Cybil, and thank you."

"I'm Tom. What can I get you to drink?"

"What is it you're shaking to death there, Dad?" Max asked, grabbing a beer out of a tub next to the table.

"Martinis, of course."

I wasn't all that fond of martinis, but didn't want to insult my host who appeared to be having a wonderful time creating them. "A martini is fine, thank you."

Tom filled a glass, plopped an olive in, and handed it to me.

"Have a seat," he said, filling two more glasses and passing one to Mae Anne. "To Cybil," he toasted.

I sipped the perfectly chilled drink, while Max steered me toward the patio seating. I sat, placing my glass on the coffee table.

"Cybil, I can't tell you how wonderful it is to have someone taking an interest in Shady Oaks," my hostess said. "It's been empty way too long. Max says there's a lot to do. Was it really such a mess?"

"Not so much a mess inside as just outdated."

"The exterior needs the most work," Max informed them. "The roof is done, but a lot of painting, landscaping, and replacement of rotten wood is still down the road."

"I remember Germania LaForge hired me about fifteen years ago to fix the veranda steps. Some visitor fell right through one, if I recall. I told her then veranda needed shoring up or a new floor. She was a stubborn old gal. Said if it held her weight, she could live with it."

We chatted in this vein for a while until I relaxed. The combination of vodka and talk about Shady Oaks lulled me into a false sense of security.

"So, Cybil, I understand you're from Memphis. Do you have family there?" Max's mother asked.

Uh-oh. Here it comes. I drained my glass and like magic Tom poured me a second.

"Yes, my mother, two older sisters, and a younger brother all live in Germantown or Midtown."

"Is that where you grew up—in Germantown? I hear it's a lovely town and a wonderful place to raise children."

"I have pleasant memories," I replied, lying only a little. "But like all places, it's growing."

We talked for several minutes about my family before she laid the big one on me.

"So, what made you buy Shady Oaks?"

"I'm a writer and wanted a quiet place to work. My apartment in East Memphis was too accessible to everyone. You know us Southerners—we just love to drop in and say hey."

"Oh, that's right. Max did say you were an author. What is it you write?"

"Mostly Regency romance." *At least for the moment.*

"Now, what exactly is that?"

"It's a time period in the late eighteenth to early nineteenth centuries."

"That sounds exciting. Please tell me about it."

I breathed easier on the safe ground of Lord Edgeware and Lady Katrina. While talking, I also sipped, a big mistake, since my overactive nerves hadn't allowed me to eat much lunch. The first buzz of lightheadedness hit me about halfway through the second drink.

I set the glass down, uncrossing my legs. I don't know how it happened, but my foot didn't clear the coffee table. I kicked it and tipped the damn thing over.

Max grabbed for his beer. It hit the deck, but didn't break. Instead, the bottle spun like a crazed second hand on steroids. Beer spewed everywhere. My glass went flying and shattered before I could catch it, as did Mae Anne's. Tom had been holding his drink, but in an effort to save the table, accidentally flung its contents all over his wife. My ears and face burned. I wanted to sink through the wooden slats into the ground below.

*Oh, God, please let me die. Take me now!*

I leapt to my feet and tried to right the table, but Max beat me to it. I gulped tears.

"I—I'm so s-sorry. I swear I don't know what

happened," I stammered.

"Oh, honey, don't worry about it. Accidents happen," Max's mother replied.

"It's my fault," Tom said, picking up the shards of broken glass. "I forgot to move the loveseat farther away from the table when I finished sweeping up earlier. Let me get you another drink."

"No, thank you," I said. More booze was the last thing I needed.

"I don't need any more either, dear," Mae Anne said to her husband. "If you'll excuse me, I'll go in and dry off. Dinner should be just about ready."

"May I help with something?" I asked politely.

"No, thank you, Cybil. Please stay and chat." She rose and entered the kitchen.

I didn't blame her for refusing my offer. She had a nice kitchen. Probably didn't want my efforts destroying it. I wondered if Max had told her about the fire.

Max escorted me into the dining room when Mae Anne announced dinner. I kept my fingers crossed that the worst of my stupidity had ended.

The meal was simple and delicious—spaghetti with meat sauce, salad, and garlic bread—one of my favorites. But any hopeful illusions about how the rest of the evening would go soon dissipated.

Trying to put my embarrassment behind me, I proceeded to do everything wrong. A large mouthful of spaghetti slipped off my fork to land on the front of my blouse before skittering on down to my lap.

I apologized.

Chianti was served and I took great pains to pace my intake. I should have been concerned with where I set the glass. I bumped the edge of my plate with the base and almost dropped it. Luckily, only a couple of drops spoiled her tablecloth.

I apologized.

I also dropped my fork on the floor. While his

mother got me another, Max gave me a strange look. My napkin then slid from my lap. I leaned over to retrieve it and on the way up whacked my head on the underside of the table, rattling the glasses and silverware.

I apologized.

I had to hand it to the Maitlands. They were gracious, waving away my apologies as unnecessary. We had iced tea in the living room, and thank God I didn't destroy anything in there. It was the only room I hadn't defiled. My offer to help clean up was once again quickly refused.

Max and I left at nine o'clock. I had failed in any effort to impress his parents. Blinking tears from my eyes, I said goodnight and headed down the front porch steps. Because of tear-impaired vision, my heel caught on one. I slipped. This time Max didn't catch me in time and my rear end landed on the porch floor.

Silence reigned. I picked myself up, brushed off the seat of my slacks, and turned to my hosts.

"Thank you for a wonderful meal. It was a pleasure meeting both of you. Please, feel free to come to Shady Oaks any time you wish. I'd love to show you around."

I didn't wait for a reply, but marched out to the truck and got in. I'd bet the ex-wife hadn't been so accident prone. *She'd* probably charmed them. We were halfway down the driveway when I burst into tears.

"Aw, Cybil, honey, don't cry," Max said in a soothing voice.

"I-I made a f-fool out of myself and—made you— look silly, too," I blubbered.

"That's not true. Mother understood that you were nervous. And nothing was a real disaster. You're exaggerating."

I wailed harder. "No, I'm not! I wanted to make

a good impression and did everything wrong."

Max reached across and opened the glove compartment, then tossed a small travel sized package of tissues in my lap. I tried to mop my cheeks, but the tears refused to quit flowing.

"Cybil, listen to me. Mom and Dad could care less about a couple of martini glasses or a few spots on the tablecloth. Come on. Dry those tears. I'll bet they both come out to see the progress on the house in a few days."

I blew my nose. "Your mother is probably saying to your father right now, 'A nice girl, but what a klutz.' I don't blame her."

Max began a running commentary on how I continued to exaggerate and how he didn't see anything so wrong with the evening. Only a man who didn't have to impress anyone could say something like that. I'd calmed down by the time we hit my driveway.

He walked me to the front door and cupped my face with his hands. "Stop worrying. I know my parents, and I can safely say they liked you. In a couple of days, you'll laugh about it."

Yeah, sure. What did he know?

He leaned down, kissing me—one of those mind-blowing, toe-curling kisses that usually wiped my brain clear of all thought. It didn't quite work this time.

"Goodnight, honey. I'll see you tomorrow."

I waved limply as he drove away, then turned and closed the door. Battling tears again, I stood for a moment in the foyer. I lost. I raced upstairs, threw myself on the bed and sobbed. My life lay in tatters.

****

Ruth and the other four ghosts hovered around Cybil's weeping, prostrated form on the bed.

"Should...should we materialize?" Ruth asked.

"No. That might embarrass her," Zoë replied.

The Colonel harrumphed. "I don't like dealing with emotional women. I wonder what happened."

"I'd say it's obvious," Hester told him. "Her big night of meeting Max's parents must have been less than successful."

"I feel rotten just standing here listening to her. Can't we do something to help?" Antoine asked.

"I think this is one time, we'll have to keep to ourselves. I don't think she'd appreciate knowing we're here," Zoë commented.

They all nodded in agreement and drifted away. Ruth was the last to leave. Looking back she murmured, "Poor baby. She tries so hard and Max is so right for her. We must do something."

Chapter Fifteen

I pounded away at the keyboard in a furious attempt to keep last night's fiasco out of my mind. Maybe Lord Edgeware and Lady Katrina's problems could be made worse than my own. I was in chapter fifteen, a key turning point, as any author will tell you.

I hadn't slept worth a damn and finally gave up trying. Instead, I got tough with the muse, demanding she appear. Knowing desperation when she heard it, she obeyed. I'd been hard at work since five o'clock, stopping only when Max arrived at seven.

Over coffee Max reassured me I had overreacted to the silly events of the night before, but my confidence level still settled somewhere between rock bottom and hell. He kissed me goodbye, promising to stop in later that afternoon. He had a couple of appointments with possible new clients in Batesville and Oxford. I wished him luck.

I squinted at the computer screen and reread the last three paragraphs, then added the final line of the chapter. A great hook, I thought. The reader would eagerly turn the page to read on.

Pleased, I stretched and sipped my fourth cup of coffee, now stone cold. I set it down. I didn't want Daryl and Julie to peel me off the ceiling when they arrived. Behind me I heard two telltale pops and swiveled to see Ruth and the Colonel, the latter holding a bouquet of flowers.

"Here, Cybil," he mumbled. "These are for you." He thrust the flowers at me.

Charmed, I accepted them, sticking my nose into their depths. The last roses of the season smelled just as sweet as the first.

"Thanks, but why are you giving me flowers?"

"We thought it would make you feel better, dear," Ruth said in her quiet manner.

"Feel better?"

The Colonel stared at the floor. "Don't like to hear women crying. Never know what to say." The poor man looked embarrassed.

"Oh. You heard me last night." In my misery, I'd forgotten my housemates would have been aware of my distress.

"Yes, I'm afraid so. We were all concerned. I know it was an important evening for you and we guessed things didn't go well. Do you want to talk about it?" Ruth asked.

Actually, I did. It was the kind of thing a girl usually discusses with her mother or best friend, but since neither was available, I figured a ghost would do. I gave them a blow-by-blow description of the dinner.

"You know, dear, I think Max may have a point. It probably wasn't as horrible as you make it out."

"A couple of accidents. Could happen to anyone," the Colonel said gruffly. "A pretty girl like you shouldn't worry about it."

"If I were you, I'd call his mother and thank her again for a lovely evening, then invite her to tea," Ruth advised.

"Yes. Excellent idea. Show her the house and praise her son to the sky. Works every time."

I wanted to hug the Colonel. "You remind me of my Grandfather Austin. He always gave me good advice and supported my writing career. You even look a bit like him. I loved him very much."

The Colonel blushed and squirmed. I stood to put the roses in water. It would give him time to compose himself. Then it dawned on me there were no rose bushes at Shady Oaks.

"Where did you get these?"

He harrumphed. "Well, to tell you the truth, we stole them."

"Stole them? From where?"

"Lavinia Rogers's garden," Ruth replied.

I laughed, found a vase, and set the bouquet on the sideboard in the dining room, then returned to the kitchen. I shut off the computer finished with Lord Edgeware for the day. I was more interested in Colonel George Washington LaForge.

I poured a glass of iced tea. "Colonel, why do you always fight the Yankees? Is that how you died?"

"No, I survived the war, but I did fight the dirty scoundrels."

"How do you fit into the Shady Oaks family?"

"Gideon LaForge was my older brother. He built Shady Oaks."

"So, that means you were...are Hester's great-uncle. Did you live here, too?"

"I lived in Holly Springs with my wife and daughter when Gideon built Shady Oaks. I'd always wanted to be a soldier, but Annabelle, my wife, objected, so I became a lawyer. In those years, times were good, and I had a thriving business. My daughter married well and lived only an hour away. Her husband was a planter and eventually got himself elected to the state legislature."

"Were you here often?"

"Yes. Gideon and his wife threw parties every few weeks. I always cleared my calendar around Christmas so we could visit longer."

I understood. Southerners of that era didn't just stay overnight. They stayed for weeks, sometimes months on end, always welcomed with open arms in the true spirit of hospitality. It was a Southern tradition that still lingered today to some degree.

The time frames had shortened and sadly, so had some of the warmth. I vowed that would never happen at Shady Oaks.

"Then the war came. Since I had quite a bit of money, I outfitted a local militia with horses and uniforms. In grateful appreciation, I was made their colonel. My son-in-law joined me as a major. We went off to fight the Yankees while my wife and daughter held down the home fronts."

His shoulders slumped and a look of sadness mingled with guilt crossed his face.

"I wasn't a very good commander. I had no experience, but I swear I tried to do the right thing. We were part of Albert Sidney Johnson's army. Saw our first real action at Shiloh. The fighting was heavy, and I ordered my men forward. They were cut to ribbons. My son-in-law died in my arms. I barely escaped with my life.

"My daughter grieved herself to death within a few months and her home, Riverside, was occupied by those blue-coated devils. When they left, they burned it to the ground."

"I'm so sorry, Colonel. But I'm sure your men didn't blame you for what happened. It was war. Even General Lee made mistakes," I said in an attempt to soothe him.

"Yes, but it doesn't lessen the guilt I've felt ever since. That's why I never moved on. I can't face my daughter, son-in-law, or Annabelle in the hereafter."

"Surely, your wife didn't blame you."

"She never knew the details of the battle—only that James had died and was followed by our only child a short time later."

"How did you come to be here—uh—afterwards?"

"When the war ended I had nothing left in Holly Springs. My wife died in 1865 just before the war ended. My house was sold for taxes to a scum-sucking carpetbagger. I had no place else to go. Hester's father, also a war veteran, offered me sanctuary. I came here to wait until I died. That happened in 1871. My heart gave out, and I died peacefully in my bed. It should have been on the battlefield. That's why I still fight. Maybe I'll win." He whispered last sentence.

I wanted to cry. Not only was he afraid to face his family and the men who'd died under his command, but he'd spent over one hundred and thirty-five years refighting Yankees in the hope of winning a battle.

I leaned forward. "I wish you could have been my grandfather. I'd have been proud of your accomplishments on the field of valor. Do you win when you fight the Yankees now?"

He wiped a tear from his eye and smiled. "Sometimes. And other times, I die a heroic death."

Another thought struck me. "You must have known about Hester and her Yankee."

"Yes, and I'm ashamed to say I agreed with her father and my brother wholeheartedly."

"What's done is done," Ruth commented. "Even in death, we are blessed with hindsight, and as much as we might wish it, we can't change the past. Come on, Colonel. I think you could use a little nap."

Ruth took the old man's arm and led him out of the room.

I blinked tears away. I had spoken the truth about wanting him for a grandfather. I loved the old codger who reminded me of a flesh and blood grandfather long since passed on. I knew it was selfish, but hoped George Washington LaForge would never cross over.

****

Daryl, Steve, and Julie arrived a little after one o'clock dressed for attic excursions and chock-full of questions.

Daryl's first words after greeting me were, "Have you heard from Mother?"

Naturally, I had to tell them the story of Mother's visit, minus my lapse with Hester and Ruth, of course.

"I'll say this, when it comes to sheer chutzpah, nobody can beat your mother," Steve said, shaking his head.

"Did she really insinuate Max was gouging you?" Julie asked with a frown.

"I'll say. It was way over the top, even for her."

"How did Max take it?" Daryl queried.

"Remarkably well, considering. That regal glare of hers never fazed him."

My brother chuckled. "Good for Max. I knew he was made of superior stuff."

"And how is Max?" Julie cooed with a glint of mischief in her eye.

"Max is fine."

"Been out on another date with him yet?"

"You're dating your contractor?" Steve asked.

"No—well, kind of—okay, yes!"

"You haven't answered my question. Uh-oh, I can tell by the look on your face, you have and that it didn't go well. Come on, Cybil. Tell Aunt Julie all about it."

The threesome stared expectantly. I broke down and told them about dinner last night still keeping the dark-haired woman at the café my secret. Jealousy is so unpleasant.

"It was worse than gruesome. I'm still humiliated."

Steve threw his arm around my shoulders, giving me a hug. "Aw, honey, it's probably not as bad as you think."

"Just because you looked like an idiot, doesn't mean you are," Daryl declared.

"Oh, thanks loads."

Julie laughed. "Quit wallowing in self-pity. Some stupid things happened, but I'm sure they don't hate you. They may think you're a little odd, but they won't hate you. If Max isn't worrying, why should you?"

Never count on friends or relatives for sympathy when you really need it. Then I had to laugh, too. Maybe it wasn't as bad as I'd made out.

"Come on, sis. Put the drama queen back in the closet. We came here to snoop in your attic."

"I don't think I'd bring up queens and closets, if I were you," Steve said with a grin.

Everyone laughed. If Steve and Daryl could laugh about queens and closets, then I shouldn't have any trouble doing the same with dinners.

Armed with a bottle of glass cleaner and a roll of paper towels, I led them upstairs to the attic. Once the windows had been scrubbed, Daryl replaced the twenty-five-watt bulb in the hanging socket with a sixty-watter.

"I'd love to slap a hundred in there, but I'm afraid I'd blow your fuses. How old is this wiring?"

"Pretty old. Max is rewiring as we tear down walls."

"Holy crap! Look at this place," Julie exclaimed.

"My God, it looks like an antique store exploded up here," Steve added.

For the next three hours, we inspected every piece of furniture and whatnot in the room.

"Oh my God, would you look at this dining ensemble," Julie said, gaping. "It's gorgeous." She turned over one of the chairs. "I'll bet the needlepoint is original."

"It is," a voice from behind me stated.

I whipped around to see my female housemates watching the proceedings. This time, I had my wits about me and didn't respond—at least not directly.

"Yes, I think it is," I said to Julie.

"Well, it's exquisite and only slightly moth-eaten. What do you want to do with it?"

"It's not my taste, so I guess maybe I'll sell it."

I glanced over my shoulder for approval and saw Hester shrug with an "it doesn't matter to me anymore" expression.

"You should be able to get a good price on the entire thing. It's not often the whole set survives. I wonder when it dates from," Julie murmured almost to herself.

"I bought it in 1885," Hester stated. "We had a great cotton crop that year."

"Uh, maybe the mid-1880s," I echoed.

"Since when do you know so much about antiques?" Daryl asked.

"I'm just guessing."

"I'd say you were pretty damned close. What's next?"

We moved on to the next grouping, one of several sets of bedroom furniture, which I had less use for than the dining room stuff. I voted to sell with Hester nodding in agreement.

"I don't know, sis. You may want to keep it. It looks to date from about the same time as the dining room furniture and while you won't be using it, you do have several unfurnished bedrooms. Keep it and let a guest sleep in a part of the house's history."

"What a lovely thought," Ruth said. "Your brother understands tradition."

"On second thought, perhaps you're right. It stays."

The afternoon wore on and so did the decision making process. I took advice from all quarters—living and dead. I hadn't had this much fun in years.

"Oh, sweet Lord in heaven, Art Deco, the modernistic style," Julie cried, uncovering yet another bedroom set. Julie loved Art Deco and had several pieces in her home.

"I bought that secondhand in 1934 from an estate sale. Got it cheap, too. Nobody thought it was anything special in those days," Ruth said.

"Art Deco is very desirable today, isn't it, Julie?"

"Are you kidding? It has quite a devoted following. Every time I see a piece I think of Ginger Rogers and Fred Astaire in *Top Hat.*"

"I remember that movie. It was so frothy and light. The two of them floated over the dance floor like feathers," Ruth sighed.

"In that case, Julie, I want you to have it. Give it a loving home."

"I can't accept this!" she said with a gasp.

"Why not? It's only a bed, dresser, and two nightstands. Take it. Consider it a bonus for finding this house."

"Are you sure?"

"Take it, Julie," Daryl urged. "Who knows when you'll come across something like this again?"

"It's yours," I insisted.

Julie smothered me in a bear hug. "Thank you, Cybil. I'll come down to pick it up next week."

A few minutes later Daryl salivated over an item.

"Wow! Steve, look at this!"

"Awesome!"

The two of them reverently inspected a stained glass floor lamp and another table-sized one. Steve lifted the shades and squinted at the underside.

"Louis Comfort Tiffany," he intoned reverently.

"Are they the real thing?" I asked.

"Cybil, they have to be," Daryl said. "Everything up here is antique in one form or another. God, these are spectacular."

"Thank you," Zoë replied. "I loved those lamps. That idiot mother-in-law of mine tossed them up here the week after I died."

"Well, Merry Christmas. They're yours."

"Cybil, you can't just give them to us. These things are worth thousands of dollars—each," Steve protested.

"And to think Jefferson's mother complained when I spent thirty-nine ninety-five on the set," Zoë mused.

"They're mine. I can give them to whomever I want, and I want you and Daryl to have them."

"Sis, I know when to shut up. Thank you."

"You're welcome, and dinner is on you tonight."

With Daryl's and Julie's organizational skills put to good use, it didn't take us long to separate things into several piles—keep, sell, giveaway, and toss. I foresaw lots of Christmas and birthday gifts in the giveaway pile, most of which consisted of collectables rather than antiques.

Tired, but happy, I led everyone downstairs to the drawing room where Steve poured drinks.

"You have a lot of nice pieces to sell," Julie said as she sipped a vodka and tonic. "I'd say that the old Visa card will be paid off next month. Who's going to handle the sale?"

"I thought I'd split it between Russ Archer in Germantown and a local woman named Joanne Hodges."

"No, dear. Not Joanne Hodges. She's not very honest and will try to hoodwink you," Ruth declared.

"Russ Archer makes sense. All those competitive Germantown and Collierville housewives will die for some of those things, especially the Lalique glassware. Russ will give you a great price because he knows he can charge the earth and they'll pay it," Julie answered.

"Well, maybe everything should go to him then."

"A very wise choice," Hester said.

"Get the most you possibly can. I'd rather someone used or displayed that Stickley desk instead of having it hidden away in an attic," Zoë added.

I was tired and had half a vodka and tonic in me. Keeping track of two conversations, simple while we'd worked, now tripped me up.

"I agree. And if you say this Joanne person is dishonest, then the Germantown man can have it all."

"I never said anyone was dishonest," Julie protested.

Uh-oh. Damn.

"Oh dear, maybe we should disappear. I don't want to make trouble for you," Hester said.

"That's not necessary. I'll be careful." Oh, shit! I'd done it again.

"What's not necessary?" Daryl asked.

Steve looked puzzled. "Careful about what?"

My mind refused to work. Heaven help me, I couldn't come up with a decent, believable response.

"Cybil, who are you talking to?" Julie demanded, looking around the room. She spotted Dudley sprawled on the hearth in front of the fireplace. "And don't tell me it's this stupid dog. He's not even awake."

I turned my gaze over to the otherworld women.

Hester shrugged. "It's up to you. I don't mind them knowing about us. I like your brother and his friends. They don't criticize."

"And they like Shady Oaks," Ruth added.

"Oh, go ahead and tell them. They'll probably think you're crazy, but it'll explain why you're talking to thin air," Zoë said.

I took a drink. "Maybe you're right. The worst they can do is think I'm nuts."

"Cybil! What's going on?" Daryl insisted, his tone more than demanding.

I turned back to them and emptied my glass.

"Okay, here it is. I'm not alone in this house. There are—other residents." I didn't want to use an offensive word for my housemates.

"What do you mean by other residents?" Julie asked.

Oh, hell. I could see political correctness had no place in this conversation either.

"I mean the house is haunted. I have ghosts."

There! I'd said it. It was out in the open. I felt as though *I'd* come out of the closet. Daryl, Steve, and Julie all gawked at me, and then looked each other.

"I don't think that went well," I said to Ruth.

"Give them a minute to absorb what you said."

Daryl cleared his throat. "Ghosts?"

Well, at least he hadn't told me I was nuts.

"Yes. There were a whole bunch of them, but we talked and I cleared most of them out. Now, I'm down to five. They're all LaForges and lived here in the past. They tried to scare me out at first, but now that I've given my word not to exorcise them, they quit doing scary things. They're quite nice. I like them."

I lifted my glass, realized it was empty, and chomped on an ice cube.

They continued to gape. Then Julie laughed. "Oh God, Cybil. You really had me going for a moment. You stinker. I sometimes forget you're a writer. What an imagination."

Steve and Daryl joined in the hilarity.

"Cybil, I never knew you had such an evil sense of humor. That was good—damned good," Steve said through chuckles.

I switched my gaze to the three apparitions. We hadn't expected this reaction.

"But it's the truth!"

"And I suppose they're here right now," Daryl said, grinning.

"Of course they are! Who do you think I was talking to? They're responsible for everything that happened at dinner last Sunday."

"Cybil, you need another drink!" Steve rose and made me one along with everyone else.

"I am not drunk nor am I hallucinating," I shouted.

"We never said you were. Oh, Cybil, honey, you're priceless." Julie laughed too hard to raise the glass to her lips.

"Give it up, Cybil. They aren't going to believe you," Zoë said sadly.

"I'd rather be thought of as nuts than laughed at!" I stated angrily.

Before anybody could answer, Reba entered the room. She glanced around and a knowing look came over her face.

"She told them about you, didn't she?" she asked Ruth.

"Yes. I'm afraid this is the result."

"I could have predicted that. Cybil, you should have eased into it carefully."

"She did rather blurt it out in a funny way," Hester told her.

"I didn't think there was anything funny about it," I stated indignantly.

Daryl was the first to stop laughing, maybe because he noticed Reba seemed to be speaking to no one somewhere over his left shoulder.

"Reba, are you saying you see ghosts, too?" he asked.

Julie and Steve laughed harder.

"You've got your cook in on the joke? God, I love it," Julie said, howling.

"It's no joke and yes, I see the ghosts very well. Three of them are standing behind the sofa."

Her calm voice and dignified manner brought the laughter to a halt.

"You're—you're serious," Steve stated.

"Absolutely."

They believed Reba but not me. I sulked and

took a long, hard swallow of vodka and tonic.

"I-I don't believe it," Julie said. She, too, took a long drink of Dutch courage.

"There's only one way to make you believe it." Reba looked at the girls, and then me. "Ruth, why don't you call the gentlemen in and make yourselves known?"

All three women gasped. "Do you think we dare?" Hester asked.

"Oh, we might as well," Zoë contended. "This way it'll prove Cybil's not crazy."

"All right." Ruth closed her eyes. The Colonel and Antoine shimmered into my vision. She told them what they wanted to do.

"Don't like this. Too many people in the know," the Colonel muttered.

"I don't know," Antoine replied. "It had to happen sooner or later. Let's do it."

Even though they had already materialized for me, I heard the usual pops followed by three separate and distinct responses.

Julie yelped, "Oh, shit!" and dropped her glass on the floor. Luckily, it didn't break.

Steve emitted a sound I could only describe as strangled and made the sign of the cross. Even lapsed Catholics turn to the familiar when facing a crisis.

Daryl simply whispered, "Oh, my God! Tell me I'm dreaming." At least, he managed to set his glass on the table.

"No, it's all very real." I felt vindicated. "Actually, the ladies have been with us all afternoon. That's how I knew things about the old furniture."

"Who-who are they?" Julie said, her voice shaking.

"Oh, forgive me. I'm not sure how to do this, so bear with me for a moment. First in line is Colonel George Washington LaForge. He looks a lot like

Grandfather Austin, doesn't he, Daryl?"

"Eh-yeah, I guess," Daryl stammered.

"Next to him is his great niece, Hester. In the middle is Zoë. Next to her is Ruth, and on the end is Antoine. They all bear the name LaForge. This is my brother Daryl, his friend Steve Bacardi, and my best friend, Julie Aldridge."

Everyone murmured, but I don't think anything specific was said. The ghosts looked uncomfortable appearing, and the living still too shocked to say much of anything.

One of those socially awkward moments when after having made introductions, no one could think of anything to say appeared. I guess the situation was a bit unorthodox. Reba came to the rescue.

"Now that they know, may I suggest that your housemates retire for a while? Materializing is very draining. It will also give your guests a chance to compose themselves." She left the room.

"Ahem—yes—yes, quite a sensible suggestion," the Colonel said. "I'll just go take a nap." He popped out of existence.

"I agree with the Colonel. Perhaps now would be a good time for Cybil and her friends to talk privately," Zoë added. She yawned. "As you can see I'm sleepy, too." She drifted out of the door and faded away, followed by the other three.

"I don't believe any of this," Steve muttered.

"Believe it. How do you think I felt? There really were a couple of dozen of them at first."

"Does mother know about this?"

"No! I did slip up when she was here yesterday and talked to Hester."

"And what about Max?" Julie asked. She bent over and retrieved her glass from the floor. "Oh dear, I've made a mess. I'm sorry, Cybil, but when they appeared, I just dropped the damned thing."

Reba reappeared with a bunch of paper towels.

"Don't worry about that, Mrs. Aldridge. I'll get it." She mopped up the mess and left, winking at me as she passed.

"Let me get you another," Steve said, taking her glass and heading for my liquor cabinet.

"Thanks. I need one."

I took a long swallow of my drink. "No, Max doesn't know and I want to keep it that way for a while. I have to think of a way to tell him without sounding, well, nuts. He already thinks I'm odd. I can just see his reaction to this kind of news."

"Yeah, I guess I can understand that," Daryl said, his voice still a bit shaky.

I understood their confusion. Fortunately, they no longer seemed scared, if indeed they ever had been. I wanted to discuss the situation, but the matter had to be put on hold when Max chose this time to arrive.

"Hello, everyone. Cybil never mentioned you'd be here today," he greeted my shell-shocked little group.

"Yeah, we came down to help go through all that old furniture upstairs," Daryl said. He was recovering the fastest.

"What did you find?"

I launched into a description of the afternoon, at least the upstairs part. By the time I'd finished the others had managed to come back onto an even keel.

"So, we were just having a drink before we took off for the Pizza Palace. Would you like to come with us?"

"I'd love it, but first I wouldn't mind a beer." Reba arrived in the doorway holding a frosty bottle. "Reba, you must have radar. Just what I needed."

I didn't think this was the time to get into Reba's rather unusual abilities.

"How did your meetings go? Max has two prospective clients on the hook," I explained to the others.

"Very well. The guy in Oxford has an old house he wants to renovate. We sign the contract next week. The man in Batesville looks hopeful, too."

"I take it most of your work centers around this area," Daryl said in what I gathered was an attempt to appear normal.

For the next few minutes, we chatted and to all intents and purposes, we must have pulled it off. If Max noticed anything stiff or stilted about the conversation, he didn't mention it.

He finished his beer and rose. "I'm starving. Shall we head for the Palace?"

Julie, Daryl, and Steve practically trampled him in their enthusiasm to get out.

"Yeah, me, too."

"Great idea. Lead the way. I love pizza."

"Boy, I can taste those anchovies now!"

Max followed them, and I followed Max, bemused by their rush to leave. I think they'd had about as much as they could stand of Shady Oaks's hospitality for one day.

****

A couple of pitchers of beer helped to relieve the remaining tension. I knew Daryl and Julie wanted more details on my housemates, but Max's presence prevented that. We were all relaxed and laughing over the descriptions of my cooking lessons.

"I think I can make fried chicken on my own and beef stew, thank you very much," I said in answer to a snotty brotherly remark from Daryl.

"Yes, but can you boil water?" he asked with a straight face.

I threw a hunk of pepperoni at him. It landed on his plate where he promptly scooped it up and popped it into his mouth.

"Did she tell you about the day she cooked me breakfast?" Max said, chuckling.

"Max! Don't you dare!"

"Do tell," Julie insisted.

Steve grinned and slid the container of extra anchovies my way. I picked one out and ate it, chasing it with a piece of crust.

"Max, I'm warning you!"

He told them anyway. For the second time today, I had to endure the laughter of my family and friends. Goaded, I opened my big mouth when I should have kept it shut.

"I'll have you know Reba says I'm doing fine and that all it takes is practice."

"Practice makes perfect or so I've heard. I'd better buy another couple of extinguishers," Max joked.

"Smartass. Just for that, I'll prove it to you. Come over tomorrow night, and I'll cook you a real dinner. What do you want?"

"Pot roast," he shot back. "Pot roast with onions, carrots, potatoes, and gravy."

"I'll even throw in a salad."

"How about apple pie for dessert—homemade apple pie?"

"I haven't as yet entered the pastry phase of my culinary education. You'll have to take store-bought."

"I wish I could be there to see this," Steve said. "Why is it I have the feeling it's going to turn out like some kind of demented science project?"

"Are you kidding? I wanna sell tickets," my brother hooted.

"I'll take a ringside seat for this," Julie added with a wink.

"Bring on the antacids," Max declared. "I'll brave anything for the sake of science."

I listened to them banter back and forth. Oh crap! I didn't know how to make a pot roast. So far, I hadn't actually made a damned thing. All I'd done was watch while Reba and Ruth instructed.

I wanted to smack myself in the head. When would I ever learn?

Now what was I going to do?

## Chapter Sixteen

I peeked under the lid of the Dutch oven once again to savor the delicious aroma of a perfectly cooking pot roast. Of course, I still had to make the gravy, but Reba had left a detailed list of instructions with the comment that if I could read, I could do it. I kept my fingers crossed.

Today had been busy with both construction and the new direction my career had to travel.

The workmen had shown up for a rare Saturday session to finish my closet. The master bath awaited the arrival of the fixtures I'd ordered, and then it, too, would be done. The conversion on one of the bedrooms into another bath had begun. Max assured me it wouldn't take long.

Enthused, I'd removed myself from the noise and introduced Dudley to the pond where I discovered the silly mutt was not only terrified of the water, but loved to chase butterflies. I watched him amuse himself for a while before he fell asleep. I used the time to look through a couple of wallpaper books, marking patterns for a second glance later.

During lunch, I pondered a possibility for a new book that had come to me earlier this morning. Suppose I were to write about Hester's doomed love affair with her Yankee? It fit the time frame Genevieve had laid out, and research wouldn't be a problem. I could even incorporate some battle scenes from the Colonel's exploits—both real and ongoing. Would Hester consider it an intrusion? I sought Reba's advice.

"Ask her. You don't have to use everything that

happened. Take—what do they call it—literary license. You're a writer. Use your imagination."

It made sense to me, so I followed her advice the next time Hester popped in.

"You want to write about me and Jonathon? But why? He left, and I never heard from him again. Where's the romance in that?"

"It's the essence of romance. Man and woman meet, have conflict, lose each other, and then get a second chance to make things right. It's a formula, but it works."

"But we didn't get a second chance."

"You will in my book."

Hester stared, and then smiled. "Jonathon and I would live happily ever after?"

"It's demanded in romance writing," I assured her.

"I think it's lovely. What do you need from me?"

"Details about what he looked like, when and where you met, your trysts, things like that. I don't need anything now. Just think about them for a while. We'll get together later."

Not long after Hester left, the Colonel paid a visit. He seemed tickled to death, departing to fight more Yankees in a fact finding tour.

Since Genevieve worked seven days a week, I had no trouble getting in touch with her at the office. I told her the gist of my idea. She urged me to get it to her as soon as possible. I also called my agent who made the same suggestion.

Then, it was time to start dinner. I squared my shoulders and walked into the kitchen determined to make an impression—a positive impression that didn't involve fire extinguishers.

Reba instructed, making me do all the work. It didn't take long for Ruth, Hester, and Zoë to join in, each giving their own methods of doing things. After a while I had trouble telling who was saying what.

"I always browned the meat in lard. It adds a special flavor," Hester declared.

"I think lard is considered bad for you now, dear," Ruth remarked.

"I never cooked much. Jefferson insisted on employing someone to do it."

"No, no, put the salt and pepper in the pan, not on the meat."

"What difference would it make?"

"Make sure the potatoes are done. There's nothing worse than undercooked potatoes."

"The gravy will be the tricky part."

I tried to weed out the bickering, ghostly voices to concentrate on Reba's directions. The barrage of advice stretched my nerves until Reba took pity on me and shooed the others away.

"I know you all want to make this dinner a success, but to coin an old phrase, too many cooks spoil the broth. Cybil needs to concentrate. Let me do this. You can watch, but keep still."

"Oh dear, I guess we are making things difficult, aren't we?" Ruth said. "I apologize. Come on, girls. Let's go find something else to do."

"Thank you, Reba," I said when they'd gone. "I love them dearly, but I was getting confused."

"I know. Now, let's continue, shall we? The most important thing to remember is if the recipe says two tablespoons of something, don't use three. Follow the recipe."

Then Reba took off and left me on my own.

I peeked under the lid again and added more water. It had something to do with moistness.

I had an hour before Max arrived and scooted upstairs to shower and change into something nice.

Forty-five minutes later, I returned to the kitchen, added more water, and then tried to relax in the drawing room, an impossible endeavor. Finally, I heard the crunch of tires on the gravel outside. Max had arrived. I opened the door before he had a chance to knock.

Max looked better than the dinner I'd planned. He wore tan dress slacks and a white long-sleeved shirt, the sleeves rolled up almost to his elbows. Through the vee of the open collar, I saw a few stray chest hairs. Real shoes, not work boots, adorned his feet. His dark hair was neatly combed, and when he smiled those wickedly sexy eyes seemed to say, *Take me, I'm yours.*

I wanted to, but the thought of the cooking meat and the necessity of fire extinguishers flitted through my mind. Later. I'd deal with sexy later.

He thrust a bouquet of mixed flowers at me. It was the second time in two days a man had given me flowers. God, I love Southern men. Their mamas taught them all the right things to win a girl. What do women in the rest of the world do?

"Max, how lovely. Thank you. Come in. Would you make us a drink while I put these in water?"

"Of course. What would you like?" he asked, heading for the drawing room and the liquor cabinet.

"A little red wine will do. I'll be right back."

I rushed into the kitchen and put the flowers in a vase, then set them in the middle of the dining room table. Without wallpaper the room looked bleak, and they added a nice touch of color.

I returned to the kitchen and peeked under the lid.

"Something smells wonderful," Max said from the doorway.

"Shoo. You're not supposed to be in here," I protested.

He set my wine glass on the counter, grasped the back of my head, kissing me hard. Heat shot through me, and I couldn't deny the rush of desire surging in my blood. Maybe I could turn the burner down. Uh, the one on the stove.

Much to my disappointment, he released me. When my eyes refocused, I noticed he, too, had a glass of wine.

"I have beer in the fridge."

His slow smile sent tendrils of flame licking out from my tummy. I felt like the Wicked Witch of the West melting.

"I like wine. Besides, it's sexier."

If this continued I'd never get around to making gravy—and I had the instructions memorized.

He took a sip, and then asked, "Do you feel better about dinner the other night now?"

"Much. You were right. I overreacted, but I can't understand how such goofy things happen to me. Did you explain to your mother that I'm not usually a klutz?"

"She thought nothing of it. She was kind of mad at my father for the martinis. She wanted to serve wine, but Dad wanted to make an impression on a city girl and show us rural Mississippians had some class."

I laughed. "Oh, no! How funny. I called your mother to thank her again and invited her for tea next week. Why don't you and your father come, too?"

"I'm not sure about the tea part, but I do know they're both curious about the house—Dad for technical reasons and Mom for aesthetic."

The timer buzzed and Gravy 101 was about to begin.

"Okay, I can't do this with you watching, so go into the dining room and wait to be served like a good guest."

Max laughed, kissed me again, and then did as I asked.

I painstakingly followed the recipe. Ten minutes later, I served up my very first pot roast. I waited with bated breath as Max cut and then ate.

"H-m. Tender, juicy, well-seasoned, and..."

I held my breath.

"...perfect gravy. Cybil, I'm impressed. Guess I'll have to return the two fire extinguishers out in the truck."

I relaxed and punched him lightly on the arm, laughing. "I'm glad you like it. I followed everything Reba told me. I wouldn't let her make a thing. I did it all."

I couldn't keep the pride out of my voice. Maybe there was culinary hope for me after all. My confidence soared. Then I thought about the ex-wife. Had she been a good cook? And why did she keep popping up in my mind at crucial moments that should have been reserved for me and Max?

"Well, you did a good job and Reba is to be commended for her diligence."

"Reba is a jewel. I am so glad you found her."

"Actually, she found me."

"What do you mean? I thought you knew her."

I sampled the meat. My taste buds exploded. God, it was good. Tender with a slight crunchiness on the bottom—just the way I liked it. Had I really made this? I watched as Max spooned more gravy over his potatoes.

"I've seen her around town before, but never met her. She was at the end of the driveway when I came to work that day asking if this was Shady Oaks. When I said yes, she made a comment about you needing a cook, so we introduced ourselves. I figured you'd found someone on your own or she'd come recommended by a friend."

"No. I assumed you knew her. I thought you'd picked her up from home."

"I have no idea where she lives."

"I wonder how she knew I needed a cook."

"Maybe Lavinia or Carjetta said something."

Carjetta could have told someone, but there was

no way Lavinia would open her mouth about what had happened. I wondered if she had ventured out of her house yet.

"I'll ask Reba tomorrow how she learned about me. Whoever aimed her in my direction deserves a huge thank you."

I sneaked glances at Max while he ate. Not only did I enjoy looking at him, but I was anxious to see how he attacked my dinner. Did he take a second helping of everything? If so, did he do it out of politeness? Were the seconds smaller? Did he like the gravy or just pour it on to mask any taste defects? Was the meat tender enough?

"Will you stop staring at every bite I take? The food is delicious, the wine excellent, and my dining companion beautiful."

Heat flooded my face from both the compliments and the fact I'd been caught watching.

"Thank you. I'm nervous. Are you taking seconds to avoid hurting my feelings?"

"Cybil, I may eat something once to be nice, but I eat seconds—and thirds"—he reached for another helping of meat—"because I like it."

I relaxed. "Okay. Point made. Maybe next week I'll try fried chicken all by myself."

"Am I invited?"

"Of course. Reba says my next lesson will be biscuits."

"I'd like to look in when she gets to bacon."

He tossed me a teasing look, sending the pet butterflies residing in my stomach fluttering. I took a deep breath.

"How about dessert. It's apple pie."

"Homemade?"

"No. I told you. I haven't graduated to that yet. A mountain climber doesn't tackle Everest first."

On that note I picked up our dinner plates, escaped to the kitchen, and returned a few minutes later with the pie. Store-bought or not, he ate every crumb of two pieces, and then helped me clear the table.

Since I'd used Grandmother Austin's china that meant I had to hand wash it. Max filled the dishwasher with the rest of the stuff.

With soapsuds up to my elbows, a pair of strong arms slipped around my waist and pulled me back against a broad chest. His nose nuzzled my hair away from the side of my head, and lips to die for slid down the sensitive tendon. They halted and gently sucked at the pulse point above my collarbone.

My insides turned to slush, and then liquefied like a glacier impacted by a fireball. Heartbeats drummed in a frantic rhythm. My breath stopped somewhere between lungs and nose. I experienced Jell-O knees. If he didn't quit, I'd end up a puddle of goo at his feet.

My body quivered and shook, but my hands continued to wash, rinse, and set the plates in the drain board.

Max nibbled on my ear, and one of his hands strayed north to cover my breast. His erection pressed against the small of my back. I grasped the edge of the sink and, leaning my head back on his shoulder, moaned. His thumb rasped across my nipple.

I pulled the plug in the sink. The hell with the dishes. I whipped around and clasped my soapy arms around his neck. His lips covered mine and our tongues danced and dueled. He tasted of apple pie and wine with a hint of gravy. I was hungry as hell, but not for food. I attacked him, running my hands through his hair.

Max's hands slipped under my rear end to support my weight. I wrapped both legs around his waist and we went at each other like demented tigers. I tore at his shirt. The buttons flew like confetti. Then I transferred my lips to that hair covered chest. His muscles bulged, and I now understood the term *six-pack*.

We careened around the kitchen, bouncing off the counters, the stove, and the fridge before backing into the table where he deposited me like a sack of groceries. He ripped my top over my head and with sure fingers, unfastened my bra, pulled it off, and threw it on the floor.

I fell back, dragging him with me. During this neither one of us had said a word. I don't think I could have articulated anything sensible anyway. When his lips covered my nipple, I proved my point. I made sounds, not words, and squirmed in sensual delight.

In the deep recesses of my mind, I heard a tiny little *pop*, and then a voice. "Oh, Cybil, I'm sorry."

My eyes jerked open. I gazed at Antoine over Max's shoulder. Naturally, I reacted before thinking of the consequences.

"Not now! Get out!"

Antoine gulped and promptly disappeared.

Max froze. "What?"

"Uh, not you."

He looked over his shoulder. "Who the hell else if not me?" he demanded.

"Uh, it—it..." He looked at me with a strange expression. I didn't blame him. This was the second time I'd goofed in his presence. I had to think of an explanation—fast. "The dog! It was Dudley. I don't like being watched."

Max straightened and stared at the hallway, then back at me with a guarded expression. "The dog's nowhere in sight."

"Well, of course not. He left."

Antoine's appearance had shattered the mood. I sat up, wiggled off the table, and picked up my discarded clothing. I wanted to cry. I would have to establish some ground rules between my housemates and me.

"What are you doing?"

"Getting dressed. I'm sorry, Max. I guess the timing isn't right."

"What do you mean the timing isn't right? I'm willing to take another crack at it if you are."

Frustration throbbed in his voice. Once again, I couldn't blame him. After all, I'd stuck my tongue down his throat first, leading him to higher expectations.

I apologized again. "I'm sorry. Really, I am. It's been a long time since I've...well, since anything like this has come up. I want the atmosphere to be perfect before I take the plunge. My kitchen table isn't it."

"So, we'll move. Honey, I'm not asking you to jump into the deep end with any type of permanent relationship. I thought we could explore the possibilities beyond a goodnight kiss. You know, get your feet wet with something more intimate."

Wait a minute. I'm waiting for the right moment, going all gooshy inside thinking about soft beds and candlelight, and he's suggesting something along the lines of a slap and tickle? I cooked him a damned fine dinner and in appreciation of him eating it, I'm supposed to get my feet wet? And how long after that will my name and number be published on the men's room wall at Rourke's?

Okay, maybe I was over-reacting again, but his casual let's-have-sex attitude pissed me off. Perhaps, I should thank Antoine for popping in.

"Get my feet wet? Well, excuse me! What makes you think I'm ready to take a cruise on the SS *Maitland*?"

Max glared, tucking the tattered remains of his shirt back into his slacks.

"I'm sorry I brought the subject up, but I'd like to remind you that *you* were the one trying to give me an instant tonsillectomy!"

There's nothing like having my actions tossed in my face to make me defensive. Even though I was looking for permanent, I didn't want him to know it—at least not yet.

"Why would you suppose I was looking for a permanent relationship? I dated lots of men in Memphis."

Uh-oh. Stupid thing to say since I'd just confessed to the exact opposite.

His brows drew together in a frown. "I'm not without a few women snapping at my heels either. I don't need to be led on, and then rejected by a snooty city girl. I can go home right now and call a very willing lady."

"If she's that willing, she's no lady!" I conveniently forgot how willing I'd been a few minutes ago.

Max headed for the door. "I don't need this. From now on our relationship is strictly business. I'll be here at seven o'clock on Monday morning. Don't talk to me unless it's about construction. Oh, I forgot—you can't talk about those subjects unless it's to change your mind."

"No wonder you have an *ex*-wife!"

"Never getting married again was the best decision I ever made. I don't need pot roast that bad!"

I wanted to throw something. "Fine with me. You have no sensitivity at all. I have three words of advice for you: read a romance! You need it."

He stomped down the hall and out the front door, slamming it shut behind him.

Ready to cry, I walked into the drawing room and plopped on the sofa. As though sensing my mood, Dudley jumped up next to me, his doggy tongue drenching my face.

"Thanks, Dudley. I needed that. At least you love me tonight."

He leaped down, stretched out, then rolled over, staring at me with big, limpid brown eyes. His tail thumped. I melted and bent to scratch his belly.

"As usual, I made a mess of things. I was hurt Max didn't see what we were about to do as a stepping stone to something serious. Just because I'm crazy in love with the guy doesn't mean he feels the same about me. Maybe it's just physical. Maybe I *was* being too sensitive. Maybe I *should* have gotten my feet wet, but I can't help it if the mood disappeared. And just bouncing up the steps to the bedroom didn't sound romantic either. What do you think, boy?"

Dudley didn't answer. He thumped his tail, went limp, then closed his eyes and snored.

"Thanks. You've been a great help."

****

I hung up the dishtowel, and then made tomorrow morning's coffee. Rather than feel sorry for myself, I decided to keep busy. I'd refilled the sink, finished the dishes, and scrubbed the already clean countertops cleaner. If I had thought it would occupy my mind, I was dead wrong. I kept wondering where Max had gone, what he was doing. Had he gone home to stew and pace? Was he reconsidering his attitude toward marriage? Was he discovering I meant more to him than he thought? Or had he found solace with the brunette? The last made me gnash my teeth. I was still disgruntled with Max, myself, and Antoine—which reminded me, I needed to have a talk with all of them concerning privacy.

I sat at the table and said, "I need to talk with you guys. It's important."

I waited a few seconds. Hester and Zoë popped

in followed by the others. Antoine showed up last, an embarrassed look on his face.

"What's wrong, Cybil? Didn't the dinner go well?" Ruth asked. Her kind face showed concern.

"The dinner was wonderful. But I need to talk to all of you about my privacy. There will be times when I simply do not want any of you just popping in. Can you float around invisible to me?"

"Yes," Hester admitted.

"We remain unseen until you want to see us or one of us wishes to be seen. Then we materialize."

Ruth's explanation was a little confusing, but I got the gist of it. They could see me at any time, but I could only see them if they materialized. It kind of creeped me out.

"What happened, Cybil? Did one of us show up at an awkward time?" Zoë asked.

"I'm afraid so. Max and I were busy...that is we were..."

"They were kissing, and I popped into view," Antoine finished for me.

"You interrupted a romantic moment?" Hester said in an outraged voice. "If you weren't already dead, I'd have killed you."

"Bad form, Antoine," the Colonel grumbled.

"I just didn't think. I had a question I wanted to ask and popped in. I'm sorry, Cybil." Antoine looked contrite.

"What question did you want to ask Cybil that caused you to lose all your common sense?" Hester asked.

"I—I was watching how courtship is done nowadays and I—well, what they were doing was—I mean, I'd never..."

I took pity on him. "What Antoine saw was a very intimate moment—the kind that should never be interrupted." I told them what had occurred.

Four pairs of ghostly eyes stared at Antoine who

squirmed and shuffled his feet.

"Bad form, bad form," the Colonel repeated. He seemed almost as embarrassed as Antoine. Maybe it was the subject matter.

"I'm afraid I agree with the Colonel," Zoë told him.

"I've already told you what I'd do. I think Cybil showed remarkable restraint not to ban you from the house."

"Now, Hester, everybody, let's not be too hard on Antoine. He made a mistake, that's all. I suppose we should set some ground rules about things like this," Ruth said.

"Without a doubt. I think the first should be that when I am entertaining a gentleman, nobody drifts into the room, especially the bedroom."

Zoë was the only one of the five who didn't look shocked at the prospect of me making love with a man not my husband. I'd spoken before I thought about the diversity of eras represented.

"Sometime soon we'll have a chat about how things are done in the twenty-first century, but not tonight. It's time for bed. I'm sure Zoë would like to go back to sleep, and Colonel, I think I interrupted a good battle. Good night everyone."

"I'm really sorry, Cybil," Antoine repeated.

"That's all right. I'll see you all tomorrow."

Five distinct pops marked their departures as I left the room.

****

Someone pounding on the front door startled me out of my sleep. All one hundred and eighty pounds of Dudley sprang from his pillow and charged down the stairs with menacing barks. I put on my robe to follow him.

I flew down the steps and across the foyer, flipping on lights as I went. Who would be hammering with such persistence at one o'clock in the morning?

I switched on the porch light and flung open the door. I figured if someone wanted to do me harm they were idiots. Dudley's snarls would have sent any intruder with an ounce of brains high-tailing it down the drive. If they didn't have an ounce of brains, then they got what they deserved.

It wasn't an intruder. It was Max. He barged his way in past me. Dudley quit barking and sat down, tail thumping. I slammed the door.

He tossed a duffle bag at the foot of the stairs, then turned to me and grasped my shoulders in a firm grip.

"I went home, had several drinks, and still couldn't sleep. I don't care if you are a little eccentric, there's something about you I can't resist. Damn it! I want you."

He brought his mouth down on mine. I forgot about being mad. I even forgot—almost—about the brunette. I suppose I should have been a bit more dignified, but leaped into his arms. Without a by-your-leave, he carried me upstairs. We were Scarlett O'Hara and Rhett Butler. His lips never left mine and his hands supported my derriere kneading my flesh like dough.

We floated up the steps to my bedroom. Stopping at the edge of the bed, I finally loosened my death grip from his waist and stood on shaking legs while he pulled off his T-shirt. I shivered, reaching out to touch the muscles of that fabulous chest. It was like stroking a warm statue.

My heart pounded in my ears, and I wondered when I would draw my next breath. God Almighty, I had never wanted anyone as badly as I wanted Max. Our silly argument of earlier faded into a distant memory. The brunette disappeared, too. My fantasies of the last weeks were about to come true.

I honestly do not remember taking off my

clothes until my robe and nightgown hit the floor. Frustrated I was the only one naked, my trembling hands groped for his belt buckle. He allowed my fumbling fingers to release it, unfasten the button, and slide the zipper down. Without hesitation, I pushed his slacks and briefs down his legs where he stepped out of them.

Oh, my God! He really was a statue—all muscle and sinew. His erection rose from a patch of dark hair like a long, powerful saber and my breath caught. I forgot about any other man in my previous life. He held me close for a moment and then laid me on the bed, covering my body with his. My insides quaked.

Max moved his hands and lips over my skin. My blood raced, while the fire inside raged. It gnawed and consumed, turning anything solid into a pool of boiling liquid. I no longer controlled the trembling. In the depths of my soul, I knew Max Maitland was the only man I'd ever love.

I'd always hinted at an affair between Lord Edgeware and Lady Katrina. I wrote about passionate kisses and thumping hearts. I had no idea what I had been writing about—not a clue. I had never experienced real gut-wrenching passion or desire until now.

Max's lips slid from my collarbone to my breast and when they fastened over an incredibly sensitive nipple, the rocket inside of me exploded. I saw stars, flames, and patterns of swirling light all mixed in with searing heat along with incoherent mutterings I assumed came from my mouth. I forgot about Lord Edgeware and Lady Katrina. There was only Max.

His hand found that slick, wet core of heat between my legs, stroking and massaging. I cried out and lifted my hips only to settle them back on the bed writhing. I moaned and whimpered, begging for release.

"Sh-h-h, darlin'," Max murmured in a thick voice. "We're almost there."

He continued to caress, then inched his way back up my quivering body. I felt the hot steel of his erection lying on my belly. Reaching down, I encircled it with my hand slowly moving my fingers up and down. It throbbed and the veins bulged. Max groaned.

His lips played havoc with the pulse point on my neck and his hand still caressed the junction of my thighs. I couldn't take much more.

"Please, Max. Do it. Do it now," I whispered brokenly.

In response, he once again moved his lips to my breast where he took the hard, erect center into the moist heat of his mouth and sucked hard.

I screamed his name, my hips undulating with frantic movement. I don't think I said anything sensible, but then I didn't have to. My actions spoke for me and Max understood I was close to the point of no return.

Maybe he was, too, for he suddenly groaned and fumbled in the pocket of his pants lying on the floor next to the bed. He tore open the foil packet, sheathed himself, and then nestled between my outspread knees. His dark eyes burned with a savage glow.

Then, with a powerful thrust, Max entered me. I screamed again, locking my legs around his waist. We parried and lunged like competing warriors on the battlefield. I held on for dear life.

The world outside ceased to exist. My world centered on the fire, the rockets, the climb to the highest peak—and Max. I strained, wanting to reach the summit, yet at the same time, I didn't want it to end. I wanted this magnificent build-up to continue forever.

Then, I shattered into a thousand shards. I

bucked, I screamed, and I sobbed as spasm after spasm racked my body from head to toe. Dimly, I was aware of Max shouting my name and making his final lunge.

I tightened my legs and rode the last of my orgasm, wringing that final sharp jolt from my satiated body before going limp.

My heart beat like a frantic drum and my breath rasped in and out of tortured lungs. Both of us trembled.

Max was still hard inside me. Shocked, I wanted more. With a sinuous stir of my hips, Max groaned and locked his lips on mine, then began to move.

Much later, we lay side by side holding hands. I squeezed his fingers. He squeezed back. The woman in me had to ask the question that usually sends a man running. I was taking a chance, but asked anyway, "Where do you see yourself five years from now?"

He answered in a drowsy voice. "Never thought about it."

"What do you want out of life? You said you're not interested in marriage, but that sounds shortsighted."

He released my hand and sighed. "Cybil, do we have to analyze things?"

"I'm not analyzing, just curious." I held my breath.

"Professionally, I want to be the best. I want my name known from Biloxi to Memphis and have clients clamoring at the door."

I exhaled. "And personally?"

"Why do women always make this so tough? I told you. Men are simple. Give us meat, potatoes, and a beer. We're happy. Women are like a seven course meal. Complex and hard to understand." He rolled onto his side facing me. "I was married. I expected to stay married. I didn't. I failed at the most important thing in life."

"Things just didn't work out."

"I failed."

"Doesn't mean it'll happen again."

"I'm terrified of failing a second time. It hurt too much watching my marriage disintegrate. I can't go through that again. The pain would kill me."

"So, you'll go on alone forever?"

"I haven't thought that far ahead. What about you? What do you see in five years?"

"I see me in this house with a husband and children. Shady Oaks is made for a family."

"No fears?"

"Everybody has fears about relationships. Love and trust are the keys."

"It's been a long time since I loved—or trusted." He propped himself up on an elbow and ran a finger down my cheek making my insides quiver. "What do you see in your professional future?"

"I'll probably die at the age of a hundred and one writing a sexy love scene."

He laughed and rolled onto his back again. The laughter died. "I hope I'm around to see it."

"So do I," I said softly.

His voice told me I may have gotten through.

Chapter Seventeen

I smiled, my gaze liquid and eyes dewy with emotion. "Max, I love you."

I paused and inhaled a deep breath. "All right. Not too bad. Direct and honest," I said to my reflection in the bathroom mirror, but the writer in me found it a trifle abrupt. I tried again with a different expression.

"Max, surely it has come to your attention that I find you attractive, and over the last few months our relationship has blossomed into more than friendship. I've fallen in love."

Crap. Now I sounded like Lady Katrina. There had to be a happy middle ground somewhere, but I would have to find it later. I heard the workmen arriving downstairs and hurried to finish dressing.

Sunday had passed in a blur. Max never left. We only came out of the bedroom to eat and tend to Dudley's needs. The duffle bag he'd so carelessly tossed at the foot of the stairs on Saturday night contained toiletries and extra clothing.

"Just in case I actually need clothes," he'd said with a twinkle in his eyes. "This way, on Monday morning, my men will assume I arrived early."

I came downstairs to an empty kitchen. We'd already had our coffee klatsch, and Max had safely stowed the telltale bag in his truck. He'd also given me one of those toe-curling, muscle-melting kisses.

Pouring another cup of coffee, I practiced my confession on Dudley. He grinned, panted, thumped his tail, and encouraged me by cocking his head.

"Okay, boy. How's this? 'Max, I don't know how

to say this, but honesty is the best policy. I love you.' Think that'll work?"

Dudley quit panting and wagged his tail half-heartedly.

"Yeah, you're right. I sound like a breathless half-wit." From the look in his eyes, I saw Dudley agreed. Maybe I should try the shy, modest approach. "Let me try this again. 'Max, I can't help myself. I love you.' Is that better?"

This time the tail stopped wagging. I didn't blame him. A vision of a simpering, third-rate Southern belle popped into my mind. Damn it! I'm a writer. I'm supposed to find the words. I do it all the time in my books. So, why did I find it so difficult in real life?

I sat sipping my coffee and mulling over my problem when a ball rolled across the kitchen floor. One of his favorite toys, Dudley leaped up, gave chase, then ran to the empty doorway where he dropped it and sat with an expectant look in his eyes. The ball rose about two feet into the air before bouncing across the room again. One of my housemates obviously wanted to play.

My little discussion regarding privacy had paid off. I hadn't seen or heard any ghosts all Sunday. I felt guilty at ignoring my new friends, although in all honesty, I'd forgotten about them what with Max and all. For all I know, they could have been invisible and hovering over the bed for the past thirty-six hours, but somehow, I thought they respected me enough not to do that.

"Whoever's there, you can materialize."

Zoë popped into view. "Hello, Cybil. I just wanted to play with Dudley. Am I disturbing you?"

"No, of course not."

"How was your weekend?" she asked, tossing the ball again. Dudley scrambled, trying to find traction on the floor.

"It was wonderful."

Zoë smiled the kind of smile Julie would have given me. In fact, Zoë reminded me of Julie in a lot of ways. Physically, with the exception of hair color, they were similar, and I had the feeling Zoë could be counted on when the chips were down. From the few conversations I'd had with her, I had gleaned intelligence and an ability to cut to the heart of any matter.

"Ruth said Max woke her up Saturday night pounding on the door. I'm glad he came back. We weren't spying, honest," she hastened to add.

"I'm sure you weren't. I'm glad he came back, too. He didn't leave for a long while."

"I guessed as much."

She tossed the ball, laughing as Dudley skidded after it.

I hesitated before answering. I wanted to talk about Max. I needed advice and since Julie wasn't available, I wondered if Zoë would mind giving me help. The thought of asking for advice from a ghost didn't seem at all strange.

"Zoë, I have a problem. It's about Max," I began.

"Max is very handsome. How that's a problem?"

I caught the teasing element in her voice and laughed. "It's not a problem at all. No, the problem lies in the fact I've fallen in love with him, and I just don't know how to say it. Isn't it ironic? I make my living with words, but when it comes to the most important words I could ever say to a man, I can't seem to come up with the right ones."

"It certainly is a big step. Don't try so hard. Just let it happen. If you try to match the right time to the right place, you'll never tell him."

I pondered her advice. It made sense. Maybe I was taking a simple declaration and turning it into *War and Peace*.

"I don't want to scare him away. He has a thing

about marriage and being financially independent."

"All men think that way. Subconsciously, they use it as an excuse. Believe me, when they fall in love—real love—it doesn't seem nearly as important."

"There's an ex-wife who took him to the cleaners during the divorce in the mix."

Zoë shrugged. "So what? She's gone. You're here. And you're the one he spent the weekend with."

"Yeah, but he also thinks I'm a little crazy. Saturday night, when Antoine accidentally popped in, I spoke without thinking. What I said made no sense and Max left in a huff after I tried to lie my way out of the situation."

"Antoine feels badly about that. He's been in hiding all weekend. Hester read him the riot act." Zoë paused for a moment, and then said, "Have you considered telling him about us? You told your brother and his friends."

"Tell Max! Are you kidding? I don't think he'd believe me for starters, and it would confirm his opinion about my eccentricity."

"I don't know. You can't tell. Our presence would explain a lot of the strange happenings. It's up to you."

I shivered imagining Max's reaction to such news. He'd definitely consider me rest home material.

"I'd sooner tell my mother."

"Ah, now there's a subject. What is it with your family? Your brother seems normal, but the rest really are nuts."

I sighed and drained the last of my coffee. "In case you didn't notice, it's all about my mother. Everything revolves around her."

"Oh, I noticed all right. She's controlling as hell. So was mine. That's how I ended up married to Jefferson LaForge. My mother was a former belle who couldn't take competition from her own daughter."

God, had my mother been jealous of her daughters all this time? I'd never considered the possibility. Mother was good-looking and stayed in shape. She had a thing about aging and worked like a dog to appear younger than her sixty-one years. Could she be resentful of her life? Even though her tastes weren't mine, she really did have a flair for decorating and cooking. Maybe she honestly thought she should have been Martha Stewart.

"Your sisters fell into the trap of always trying to please her, just like I did with Mama," Zoë continued.

"I know. I still don't understand how Daryl and I managed to escape."

"The more children, the harder it is to control. I was an only child." She placed the ball on the countertop. "Enough playtime, Dudley. You're panting and drooling on the floor. Go lie down and we'll toss the ball later."

"Zoë, do you mind if I ask you a question?"

"No, not at all."

"What's your story? How did you come to be a LaForge and why do you stay?"

Zoë sat down with a smile. "I was wondering when you'd ask. I'm afraid I'm a very boring entity."

"No way can a ghost's story ever be boring."

Cupping her chin in her hand, she began. "I was born in 1900 to Elizabeth and Harrison Prentiss. My mother was only eighteen at the time, and I guess having a child so soon after her marriage the year before confused her. Maternal is a word I've never connected with her. She left me in the care of servants while she and Daddy flitted about the state visiting friends.

"As I said, Mama was a former belle. According to her, she had beaus strung out in a never-ending line until Daddy swept her off her feet. I think she always saw herself in that role. Daddy was proud of her beauty, and loved to show her off in social settings. He was almost fifteen years older and crazy about her."

"Nowadays, we refer to that as having a trophy wife. Was he successful? What did he do?"

"Daddy was a planter over Clarksdale way. Mama came from Sampsonville. Her father owned the local feed store. Catching Daddy was quite a feather in her cap. Suddenly, she had money. While she loved my father, she also loved the prestige and privilege the money bought."

"Was she always controlling?" I wondered how she had managed to control via long distance.

"I saw very little of them for the first eight years of my life. Then Daddy got sick, severely curtailing their social life. He died two years later and the whole house of cards tumbled down."

"What happened?"

"Belle Glade, the plantation, had been mortgaged to the hilt to pay for everything. The creditors came banging on the front door two days after the funeral. With no money, all her old friends abandoned her. Even by selling off her jewelry and family heirlooms, she couldn't come close to covering the debts. Before the year was out, the bank got the farm. Mama and I had moved back to Sampsonville. We lived with my grandparents in what Mama scornfully called genteel poverty. That's when the controlling began."

"Maybe she feared losing you, too."

Zoë snorted. "No way. She saw me as her meal ticket back to a life of luxury. Suddenly, my playmates weren't good enough. She scrimped and saved for things like piano and voice lessons, both of which I hated."

"But you did what she wanted."

This I understood. I'd been subjected to the same. Mother finally gave up when my piano and ballet teachers all told her to save her money. I had zero talent.

"Of course. I was ten and wanted to please. By the time I turned fifteen, I was itching to get out from under her thumb. We had some battles, but in the end I usually gave in."

Oh, brother, did I ever relate to this. I remembered numerous arguments with my mother that had both of us in tears—mine real, Mother's faked.

"Two years later she met Jefferson Davis LaForge. The United States had just entered the Great War, and he came to our house soliciting war bonds. Totally charming, he flirted with Mama, and she bought bonds we couldn't afford. Then I walked into the room."

"Let me guess. He liked what he saw."

"Instantly, and not being a fool, Mama saw the possibilities. She had the richest man in the county standing in her living room ogling her daughter. She pushed us together at every opportunity. After her first visit to Shady Oaks, she bluntly told me she had to live here and to marry him. I didn't want to marry him. Oh, he was charming, dashing, and debonair, but he was also twelve years older with a reputation as a rake."

"Was he handsome?"

"Of course. That's how he got to be charming, dashing, and debonair with the reputation of a rake." She paused and shrugged. "In the end, Mother wore me down with guilt. All I heard was how *she* had sacrificed, how *she'd* scrimped and saved for everything I had, and how she deserved to see me marry well. I finally gave in and became Mrs. Jefferson Davis LaForge."

"Did you love him at all?"

"I tried, but it didn't take long for me to realize his evening 'business meetings' took place in the back room of Sissy Labelle's House of Pleasure over in Senatobia. And his philandering didn't stop there. He had women from right here in Cherokee all the way to Memphis."

"I'm sorry, Zoë. That must have hurt like hell."

"It did, at first. I tried talking to my mother. She told me to grow up. She blamed me for not pushing Jefferson and his gorgon of a mother into allowing her to move into Shady Oaks."

"Your mother-in-law was a bad one, huh?"

"She hated my guts. I overheard her refer to me as an upstart and not worthy of the LaForge name to one of her friends."

There didn't seem to be anything to say to that. Zoë could have used a Julie—or even a Cybil—in her life.

"You look to have died very young."

"I was twenty-eight. Jefferson for all his faults wasn't stingy. He even gave Mama a monthly allowance, which kept her in a nice house and allowed a few luxuries. I always had plenty of money and enjoyed spending it on nonsense just to irritate his mother.

"One of my favorite gifts from him was a Duesenberg. God, that car was fabulous. I loved jamming my foot down on the accelerator and flying down the road to forget my problems.

"Funny, I remember like it was yesterday. I'd been shopping in Senatobia and was driving back when a summer thunderstorm cropped up. Before I knew it, the rain poured down in sheets. I lost control. The Duesie skidded and fishtailed down the highway, then smashed head-on into a tree. I died instantly."

"How awful! At least you didn't suffer, although I can't think of dying as a pleasant alternative to anything. Why did you stay at Shady Oaks if your life here was so wretched?"

"Simple. In spite of the LaForges, I loved the place. It took a while to understand I had died, but not passed over. By the time I did, Ruth and her husband lived here. From what I've been told, my mother-in-law died shortly after me. The Depression almost cleaned out the LaForge bank account. In 1930, Jefferson ended it all with a bullet in his brain."

"Good heavens! And what about your mother?"

"She finally found a man in Jackson who had money and married him. I suppose she lived happily ever after. I don't know. Once she moved, I lost all contact."

Zoë had told me a sad, rather pitiful story. I felt sorry for her and understood why she always seemed to prefer sleep to materializing. Ruth had said something about Zoë not wanting to be a ghost, but not wanting to leave either.

She patted her lips, yawned, staring at me over her hand. "Do you know you're the first living person I've talked to about this? I wish you had lived in my time. I could have used a friend."

"Well, I'm here now. I liked talking to you, too."

I was so wrapped up in finding a new friend I missed hearing the *pop* of another housemate arriving.

"Hello, Antoine," Zoë said, gazing over my shoulder.

I twisted in my chair to see Antoine hovering up near the ceiling.

"What on earth are you doing up there?" I asked.

"I wasn't sure you would want to see me."

"Why not?"

"On account of the other night. I'm really sorry I interrupted," he said in a contrite tone.

"Oh, good heavens, don't worry about it. I was

never angry with you—just startled," I replied. I took pity on him. "Come on down and join us. Zoë was just telling me about her life—and death."

Antoine drifted down to settle in a chair opposite me. "Thank you, Cybil. For not being angry, I mean. Hester's been scolding me ever since Saturday night."

"I'll talk to her," Zoë said. "But first, I have to take a nap." She yawned again. "I'll see you later, Cybil. Tell Dudley I'll be back." She faded from view.

"Zoë's tired. She never pops in and out when she's tired. For some reason, materializing has always been hard on her. I know she looks lazy, but she isn't, not really," he explained.

"I never thought she was. Anyone who can think up the things to scare off the workmen and my family is not lazy. What a shame she never seemed to enjoy life."

"Ah, she told you her story, did she?"

"Yes."

I sat back and stared. He was a good-looking young man with delicate, almost feminine features and soft curly hair. Of all my entities, he often had the most confused expression in his eyes. I had instantly wanted to mother him. His clothing spoke of an era similar to the Colonel's, and I wondered if they'd known each other. His was also the only story I didn't know.

"What about you, Antoine? How do you fit into the equation here at Shady Oaks? I know you were born a LaForge, but how did you die and why do you continue to stay?"

"It's kind of complicated, even for the South, but I'll try to explain. I was born in 1856. My parents were both cousins of Gideon LaForge. My father owned a large plantation just outside of Vicksburg and my mother took great pride in being a descendent of one of founders of that city. When they married, they represented a large portion of the financial and social elements of the area. From what I've heard, hubris ran deep."

"How closely related were your parents?"

It wasn't unusual in those days for even first cousins to marry. It explained a lot of the jokes about the South and Southerners today. Unfortunately, some of the jokes were based in fact and at one time the South did have its fair share of inbreeding.

"It was just distant enough to not be a concern. A couple of times removed, I think."

"So, you must have visited Shady Oaks often."

"Never saw it until 1870. When the war broke out, my father formed a Mississippi regiment appointing himself Brigadier General and marched off to deliver the South from the Yankee invaders." He smiled and tried to laugh. "He didn't succeed. For some reason, his regiment was never assigned to defend Mississippi and the powers that be shipped him off to join Lee and the Army of Northern Virginia."

"Your mother must have had her hands full with a young child and a plantation to run," I murmured.

"She was, but in those days women often ran things while the men played at being gentlemen. I don't remember too much about those early war years. My first memories are of the siege of Vicksburg. At seven, it made a powerful impression. I think the Yankees overran the plantation and that's how we ended up with my grandparents in the city."

"What happened after Vicksburg fell?"

"The house had been damaged in the bombardment and like a lot of people we went underground to live in the caves. When it was all over, we fixed the house up as best we could and survived.

"My father was wounded at Gettysburg, but continued to fight until the end of the war. By the time he returned home both his body and his spirit had broken. The plantation was gone, his money was gone, and he had to live like a refugee. He died in 1868."

"I'm so sorry, Antoine. You must have missed him something dreadful."

He shrugged. "Father was gone for much of my life and when he returned was too sick to do the usual father-son things."

"How did you end up at Shady Oaks?"

"My grandmother passed in 1866. I don't know how grandfather supported mother and me, but when he died in 1870, we ended up in Cherokee. Being kin, Luther LaForge, Hester's father, had to take us in."

I understood that. It had happened all over the South after the war. Those who had a roof over their heads rarely turned a homeless relative away.

"So, you knew Hester when you were alive."

"She was older, of course, but used to give me sugar cookies so I wouldn't get under her feet. I made a pest out of myself for those cookies."

I laughed. "I'll bet. How did your mother and Hester get along?" I tried to imagine Hester sharing her house with another woman. It didn't compute.

"If my mother hadn't died when she had, Hester probably would have killed her. Mother never could get over losing everything and having to depend on the charity and kindness of others."

I wondered if he realized he had used a partial quote from *A Streetcar Named Desire,* and then remembered he didn't know Tennessee Williams from a hole in the ground.

"When did you lose your mother?"

"In 1872. Hester and Luther didn't mind me staying. I had the run of the house and the farm."

Sadness tinged his voice.

"You weren't happy?"

"I never felt like I fit in anywhere. I had playmates, but would rather read than hunt or fish, much to Luther's disgust. I was unhappy and never knew why."

"You died young like Zoë, didn't you? How did it happen?"

"I carried around pain I didn't understand—not physical pain, but pain inside—here." He tapped his chest. "To alleviate the pain, I drank. By my twenty-fifth birthday, I was drunk more often than sober.

"One night in early autumn, I had been in the Hitching Post Saloon in town all day. I always rode like a madman when I drank. That evening was no different. I cut across country on the way home and almost made it back to Shady Oaks. Only one fence remained between me and the property. My horse refused the jump. I flew over his head and crushed my skull on a rock."

"Why are you still here?"

"To tell you the truth, I don't know. Maybe because whatever happiness I'd known in life, I'd found here."

"What about the Colonel? Did you know him, too?"

"Very briefly. We'd only been here a few months when he died. His was the first familiar face I saw when I, ah, returned."

They were a strange bunch, these LaForges. With the exception of Ruth, unhappiness in the earthly realm seemed to have been a common thread. In death, they remained together, bickering and snapping, but still family. And the one great constant in their lives had been Shady Oaks. In a way, I suppose the house itself had given them the love and affection they'd sought.

"Good morning, Antoine," Reba's voice sounded

from the doorway.

Antoine rose, bowing slightly. "Good morning, Reba."

"Don't let me interrupt you," she said, placing her purse on the counter and gathering the used coffee cups from this morning.

"You're not. I was just going. I'm glad we had a chance to talk, Cybil. I'll see you later." Antoine popped out of sight.

As I watched a germ of an idea formed in my mind.

"So, how did Max enjoy his dinner?" she asked.

"Huh? Oh, dinner. It was fine." I answered absently.

"How's your headache?"

"What headache? Oh, my headache! Much better, thank you."

I'd called Reba on Sunday morning, telling her a little white lie about having a headache and not to bother coming out to fix dinner. I probably hadn't fooled her one iota. I had the feeling she knew what had gone on here.

"Well, if you have no objections, I think I'll rearrange the furniture in the back parlor, and then give it a good cleaning."

"That's fine, go ahead." The germ had grown.

Reba left the room. I mulled over what the ghosts had told me concerning their lives. Then I chewed on Genevieve's instructions as to my future with Lion Press. The more I thought the more reasonable the whole thing sounded.

"Oh, my God. Why couldn't it work? It's the answer to my career problem," I said out loud.

What if I wrote about not just Hester's life, but about *all* the lives of my ghosts? I could base new stories on their experiences. Talk about conflict! Good Lord! I had five books living under my roof. And who's to say how many more I could write? The

Colonel alone could give me several Civil War era novels. He'd be my technical advisor. Hester and Zoë could give me the lowdown on damn near everyone in the county. And I could use Antoine's recollections of the siege of Vicksburg as an ongoing series as seen through the eyes of the heroine.

I jumped to my feet and danced around the kitchen, then laughed. I'd have real ghostwriters!

## Chapter Eighteen

Still enthused about the idea of mining my ghosts for story lines, I sat in the drawing room after lunch with a pad of paper and a pencil jotting down possible plots. I flipped over another page, writing as the thoughts flowed. Not even the sound of workmen doing their thing disturbed me. I'd learned to tune it out.

Max came in for lunch and I told him about my publishing woes. He didn't understand the urgency of the situation, but I gave him points for trying. After a few discreet but heart-stopping kisses, he left for an appointment.

*It's just as well.* I needed to concentrate on the matter at hand and Max's presence was not conducive to concentration.

Five popping noises told me I was no longer alone. Now, I welcomed the interruption. I wanted to tell them about my idea, and then crossed my mental fingers hoping they'd agree.

Ruth drifted over to the sofa. "Cybil, dear, I hope we're not disturbing you, but we have a few questions we'd like to ask."

"Actually, I'm glad you're here. I have a few questions of my own."

Needing to ease into this, I told them the story of my publishing house and the changes due to take place in the near future. Zoë caught on first.

"So, the books you write are no longer going to be published, and if you don't change what you write, you may be out of a job?"

"Sort of."

"Aren't there other publishing houses?" Hester asked.

"Yes, but earlier this morning, I got online and checked out several publishers of historical fiction. They've either dropped the line or severely curtailed it. I have to find something else."

Zoë and Hester joined Ruth on the sofa while Antoine lounged in a chair. The Colonel stood straight as a ramrod in front of the fireplace, his hands clasped behind his back.

"I don't understand what online means, but have you come up with something new?" Ruth asked with a smile.

"I think so, but it involves all of you, and I need your cooperation. I've already spoken to Hester and the Colonel, and I'd like to expand on what I said."

I told them my idea and waited with bated breath for the reactions. If they said no, I'd have to convince them. The reactions were immediate.

Ruth looked pleased as punch, clapping her hands like an excited child. Hester had a smile on her face, and I swore I could see the gears meshing in her mind. She probably had more plot ideas already.

The Colonel harrumphed and looked embarrassed, but I could tell the thought of giving me technical details of battles filled him with pride. It showed in his eyes. They glowed with excitement.

Antoine had an eager expression on his face. But Zoë's reaction surprised me the most. She looked astonished.

"You can't be serious," she blurted. "About using my life, I mean. I just told you this morning how boring it had been."

"Zoë, no. On the contrary, you're life may be one of the first ones I do. I may move the time period up to pre-World War One. My heroine would not be under anyone's thumb and if she is, I'll have her grow into a strong and independent person—a woman coming of age or something."

I swear if a ghost could cry Zoë was close to doing so. I wanted to cry with her. I'd been talking about myself as much as Zoë.

"Well, I think it's a wonderful idea," Ruth declared. The others agreed with her.

"How soon can we get started?" Hester demanded. "I have a couple more things you can use. Henrietta once had two beaus prepared to fight a duel over her."

"First, I have to finish what I'm working on, and then consult my editor. She may want me to begin with a specific era."

Patience would not be one of Hester's strong points. On the other hand, an author friend of mine frequently declared that patience was for sissies. In the publishing world, nothing comes to those who wait.

"How long does it take to write a book?" Antoine inquired.

"I can usually produce two a year—three if I'm truly inspired. But with you guys helping me, I could do more. My God, I may have years of novels in the offing."

I didn't add that with them giving me historical data, my research time would be slashed to almost nothing. I wanted to dance a jig and pop the cork on a bottle of champagne. My ghosts had agreed. I foresaw a very happy author, editor, and agent in my future.

"Thanks everyone. What is it you wanted to ask me?"

The Colonel hadn't said much, but now he cleared his throat. "We were curious. Are all women in your time like you?"

"How do you mean?"

"Well, you—that is—you're not married and—"

Ruth interrupted him. "What the Colonel is trying to say is, you're not married, you have a job—I think you refer to it as a career, and your relationship with Max is, if you'll excuse me, certainly not platonic. In my day, such liaisons were frowned upon by society."

"I get it. You want to know about the modern world, is that it?"

Ruth beamed. "Precisely."

"I can handle that. Today, lots of men and women live together without benefit of marriage. They even have children out of wedlock, but it's no longer considered a sin unless you're very religious."

I tried to explain about the climbing divorce rates and how society in general had become more permissive than in their times.

"It sounds to me like the old Roman Empire right before its collapse," Antoine replied.

"Some people do see it that way," I conceded.

Zoë leaned forward. "Well, I have a question. What is that thing you write on? It kind of looks like a typewriter, but you don't use any paper or ribbons."

Explaining PCs was a little more challenging. I didn't understand how they worked either. I could solve simple problems, but whatever control-alt-delete didn't fix had me calling a twenty-four hour technical hotline.

"Does everyone use one of these things?" the Colonel asked.

"Most people do. Businesses today can't compete without them."

"What about the military?"

"You mean, how do they fight the Yankees?" He blushed and nodded. "The Yankees and the Confederates are all friends now, but the military is where computers come in the handiest."

I was no better at explaining about guided

missiles, smart bombs, and lasers than I was at the complexities of computers. I told him I'd Google and let him know. Then I had to tell them I'd explain the Internet at a later date. To tell the truth, I didn't think they were ready for that.

The questions came fast and furious. Zoë wanted to know about cars. I told her how safety measures were now built into automobiles. Considering her death, I thought she might appreciate it.

"I can't imagine something popping out of the steering wheel like a balloon or a car talking to me. On the other hand, if I'd had it and one of those belt things, I might have outlived Jefferson."

"I guess we shouldn't be surprised at innovations and improvements," Ruth said. "What kind of car do you drive, dear?"

"A Toyota Camry."

"I'm not familiar with that make. My husband and I drove a Hudson."

"Toyota is a Japanese company."

"Japanese! But we fought and soundly licked them in World War Two," she protested.

We swung into a discussion on post-war recovery and economics with the Colonel, Antoine and Hester comparing it to the post-war years of the War Between the States. I wasn't sure how much more information I could impart. They were a smart bunch, but some things remained beyond their scope of understanding, and I couldn't describe it in a way that made sense.

"I have another question," Ruth said. "What is that thing you and Max talk into? I assume it's some kind of telephone, but where is the cord?"

"It's called a cell phone. They're very convenient and most people can't live without them."

I'd barely get one explanation out of my mouth when another question would be fired at me. We covered radio, television, and kitchen appliances.

Ruth was especially impressed with the microwave.

"You mean you can cook things in a fraction of the time? Oh, that would have been so nice to have on the holidays."

Antoine asked about books. That led to everyone defending their favorite authors.

"I liked fantasy," Zoë said. "Jules Verne had the most outrageous stories."

"All he wrote was nonsense," Hester replied. "I liked reading about people's lives—biographies."

Ah, finally, my area of expertise. "Actually, much of what Jules Verne wrote wasn't far off. *Twenty Thousand Leagues Under the Sea* is a reality with nuclear submarines, as is his rocket to the moon."

I'd ripped open a Pandora's space box that began with rockets, moved on to Neil Armstrong and the lunar landing, and eventually spilled over into terrorists and global politics.

The computer, however, seemed to fascinate Zoë. She asked several more questions, most of which I couldn't answer.

"Zoë, you really need to ask my brother about this. He works out of his home as a graphic artist. His computer is very high tech, and he could explain things a lot better than I."

"There is a subject I'd like to talk about," Ruth said. Her knitting, absent for the last few weeks, had reappeared and the needles bobbed up and down as her fingers flew.

"What? High tech computers?" I asked, somewhat surprised.

"No, dear, your brother. He's such a handsome lad. Is he married?"

"Well, sort of."

"What do you mean, 'sort of'?" Hester demanded. "Either you are or you aren't."

"Hester, maybe he does that living together

thing," Zoë replied. "Is that it? Is he living with someone?"

"Uh, yes, he has a partner."

"That lovely young lady we saw with him last week?" Ruth inquired.

"Actually, no. Julie's happily married and has three children."

I hesitated to tell them about Daryl's lifestyle. It was up to Daryl to disclose that. Then, I had second thoughts. I wasn't ashamed of my brother, and his sexual orientation wasn't a secret.

"To tell the truth, Daryl is gay." There I'd said it.

"Oh, he certainly is," Ruth bubbled as she knitted. "So gay, and charming, and very good looking in the bargain. I may be old-fashioned, but I hope he marries his girlfriend soon."

I laughed at my stupidity. Of course, that's how she'd interpret the word.

"No, Ruth, you don't understand. Daryl doesn't live with a woman. He lives with Steve, the other gentleman who visited. Today, the word gay means homosexual."

That did it. Ruth, with a shocked look on her face, stopped knitting, her mouth hanging open. Hester's eyes popped wide, and she drew in a gasping breath. The Colonel seemed to be working on the word *homosexual,* then understood it, harrumphing. Zoë merely raised her eyebrows. If I remembered correctly, homosexuality was no big deal in the twenties. Antoine stared with a blank expression on his face, but curiosity in his eyes.

Ruth fumbled with her knitting. "Let's see, knit one, purl two...oh, dear, I've lost count. But your brother is so handsome! He could get any girl he wanted," she wailed.

"But he doesn't want a *girl*," Zoë reminded her.

Hester patted her Gibson girl hairdo. "It just seems like such a waste," she muttered.

"You mean they live together openly?" Antoine demanded. "In my day, someone like that would have been stoned or shot or something."

"Today's society is more accepting, although there are some people who like to target gays and lesbians with name-calling and violence."

"Fear makes people do strange things. Once again, in my time no one would have even admitted to something like that," he said.

"Some gays still don't want it known. Others admit how they feel. It's called coming out of the closet."

I glanced at the Colonel. He stared at Antoine and seemed embarrassed by the whole discussion. I understood. In his era, men might talk about such things privately, but never in mixed company. I decided to shelve the conversation for now.

"Look, you've all met Daryl and Steve. They're nice guys. Please don't judge them. I accept his choice and admire him. Being gay isn't easy."

"Must have been hell on your parents," the Colonel muttered.

"Daryl didn't announce anything until after Daddy died. Mother and my sisters aren't so understanding."

I looked at my watch. We'd been at it for almost three hours and I was exhausted. I'd have never made it as a teacher. From the kitchen, pots and pans clanged indicating Reba had started dinner.

"Before we wind this up, I'd like to ask you all one last question. What do you each miss the most about living?"

Ruth placed the knitting needles in her lap and sighed. "Food. I miss the wonderful ability to taste."

"A sense of time," Antoine answered. "I've been dead for well over a hundred years, yet sometimes when I wake up from what I think is a brief nap, I find five or six years have gone by."

"I miss the wind in my hair and the sunshine on my face as I drove my convertible down the road. It blew away my stifling life and gave me hope," Zoë said softly.

The Colonel had a faraway look in his eyes. "I miss the serenity of the years before the war."

"It's not so much what I miss as what I regret. I regret allowing my anger at my father over Jonathon to rule my life. Every parent wants their child to be happy, but my actions made him feel guilty. I wish I could ask his forgiveness and tell him how sorry I am." Hester shook her head.

"He knows," Reba said from the doorway.

Her sudden appearance startled me.

"How do you know," Hester demanded.

"It's the way of things. Forgiveness comes when we stand before God. I've always believed that," she replied calmly before asking me, "Have you heard from Max? Will he be joining you for dinner? Is there something special I can make?"

"No, not tonight. Why don't you take the night off? I'll drive into Senatobia and get something. I kinda feel like getting out."

"I think it's time for us to go," Zoë said with a smile. "Thank you for answering our questions, Cybil."

They drifted out of the room. What a strange afternoon. But at least I had a plan for several future novels and answered questions I'd have asked had our positions been reversed.

I picked up my pad to jot down a few more notes. Not only did I have ghosts as collaborators, but five close friends as well.

****

Since Max was busy interviewing another client, and Reba had the night off, I decided to go to that cute little restaurant in Senatobia and splurge. Go early, get home early, and spend the rest of the evening curled up with Nora Roberts or Heather Graham. I had several books from both authors in my to-be-read pile.

To my surprise, the restaurant was busy even at the obscenely early hour of six-fifteen. Still, I was shown to a table for two in a back corner.

"You sure are busy," I commented to the waitress after giving her my wine order.

"Early bird specials. Come in between five and six and if you're over fifty years old, the drinks are half price along with selected entrees."

After she left, I gazed around the room. Sure enough, most of the patrons were older. A few of the women wore Sunday go-to-meeting clothes and jewelry signifying a special occasion.

From my seat, I had a good view of the large foyer of the Victorian home. The front door opened and a gorgeous, statuesque redhead walked in, closely followed by none other than Max. I was all set to wave when the woman twined her arm through his, hugging it to her side. Max smiled at her. Suspicion and jealousy stabbed at me.

The hostess greeted the newcomers and escorted them upstairs. I remembered Max saying the upper floors had smaller, more intimate, dining areas.

*Okay, get a grip. He said he was seeing a client. She could be a client.* I closed my eyes trying to remember his words from earlier.

*I have a couple of meetings with prospective clients and an appointment tonight.*

My eyes snapped open. An appointment. Just an appointment. He didn't specify an appointment with a client. And the redhead's little black dress sure as hell didn't look like business attire.

My wine arrived and I took a generous gulp. My appetite had fled, but not wanting to screw the waitress out of a decent tip, ordered a chicken Caesar salad anyway. It would take no more than ten minutes to make. The sooner I was served, the sooner I could leave.

A half an hour later, I walked out the front door to my car. I got in and scanned the parking lot, but Max's pickup was no where to be seen. Curiosity, not to mention jealousy, burned a hole in my chest. Instead of leaving, I sat back and waited. My patience was rewarded an hour later when Max and the redhead emerged. Both were laughing.

I glowered through the windshield when the woman threw her arms around Max's neck. He hugged her, and then leaned down to give her a quick kiss on each cheek before leading her to a black Mercedes. She got in while Max slid behind the wheel.

*I get a pickup truck. She gets a Mercedes.*

They left and without a moment's hesitation, I followed them. The drive didn't take long. Max pulled into the Senatobia Guest House, parked, and went inside with her.

My heart plummeted to my toes. I couldn't believe it. After all the heart stopping kisses he'd given me, after a weekend of making incredible love with me, he was now at the no-tell motel with another woman. And what about the brunette? How did she fit into this?

*What am I? The blonde in the triumvirate?*

I peeled away, angry and disappointed. At home, I poured a large glass of wine, settled onto a sofa in the drawing room, and cried. Dudley sat in front of me, his head resting on my knee.

"Never trust a man," I told him.

\*\*\*\*

I had a lousy night's sleep. Not even killing a bottle of wine helped. My anger and jealousy simmered for hours. I finally rose, determined to be productive in spite of my inner turmoil. Dudley sprawled at my feet while I curled up on the sofa writing a rough outline for my first new endeavor. I thought Hester's story would make the best start.

Max's truck swept up the drive and on toward the back. I tensed when the back door slammed. Footsteps sounded through the kitchen and down the hallway. His cheerful whistling made my blood boil. *Must have been a damned fine night at the Senatobia Guest House.*

Max breezed into the drawing room, a grin on his face. "There you are. What are you doing?"

Dudley leaped off the sofa and wagging his tail trotted up to Max who scratched behind his ears.

"My job," I answered in a tight voice.

"You sound pissed. Have a bad night?"

"Certainly not as good as yours."

I knew I should shut up, but couldn't control my mouth.

He frowned. "What the hell are you talking about?"

"You should know. Who were those women?"

"What women?" His voice and expression clearly showed confusion.

An inner voice kept saying, *Don't do this. Don't go there.* I did anyway.

"Don't play dumb with me. You know what women. I saw you and some little brunette in the flashy sports car come out of the café a week or so ago. And what about the sexy redhead you had dinner with at the Senatobia Inn last night? You apparently have more women than a Sultan."

*Cybil, knock it off. You're screwing yourself.* I was unable to follow that sage advice.

"Have you been following me?" Max demanded, his eyebrows drawing together in a scowl.

I jumped from my seat, tossing the pad of paper and pencil onto the floor. I was ready for a fight.

"Only as far as the no-tell motel! And in a Mercedes, no less. I was only good enough for a pickup."

"What the hell is your problem?"

"Don't try to make me the villain here. I saw you go into the Senatobia Guest House with her."

"And you immediately assumed I was sleeping with the lady, is that it?" He fisted his hands on his hips and glared.

"What else! No wonder you're not interested in marriage. Your little black book must weigh a ton! A few smiles, a couple of kisses, and a long weekend in bed suits you to a T, doesn't it? How many more women are waiting in the wings?"

His scowl deepened and a flush spread from his neck to his forehead. "Is that what you think of me?"

"What else am I supposed to think?"

The green-eyed monster festering in my soul had spilled out against my better judgment. I was screeching like a banshee, and hated the sound. I hated those other women. I hated Max. But most of all I hated myself.

"It's none of your business, and I don't know why I'm explaining myself, but the brunette was my ex-wife. She and I were having lunch celebrating her engagement. Come November, I am officially off the alimony hook. And the redhead was my sister, Samantha."

"Your sister? At a motel? How dumb do you think I am?"

"Pretty damned dumb. She didn't want our folks to know she was in the area. She's getting married, too. Her fiancé is an older man with three kids. She wanted my advice before springing the news on Mom and Dad. And the car was hers. I drove because she'd had too much wine."

He raked a hand through is hair and glared. "I can't believe you're accusing me of being a womanizer. When did I ever lead you to suspect that? Do you honestly believe I could make love to you all weekend, and then waltz off to a motel with another woman? Do you really think I'm that shallow? Talk about a lack of trust! All you had to do was ask, 'Who was that woman I saw you with the other night,' or better yet, why not just come up and say hello? But oh no, not you! You had to jump to conclusions.

"Why the hell any man would want to get married is beyond me, especially the second time around. This just confirms it. Plus, you have problems, lady—real problems. You talk to thin air!"

He whirled and strode toward the foyer leaving me gasping.

Oh, crap! His ex-wife? His sister? My anger drained away like someone had pulled the plug. A hollow feeling spread throughout my body. God Almighty. What had I done? He was absolutely right. I'd been jealous and had jumped to conclusions when a simple, straightforward question would have solved the problem. I felt like a heel and took off after him.

"Max! Wait! I'm sorry!"

He jerked open the door, turned, and grasping the doorknob with one hand and the jamb with the other, glared a hole right through me.

"Cybil, your lack of trust hurts. I thought we had something special. I was falling for you. I was beginning to envision a...a...future with you in it. You once lectured me on romance and relationships. Seems to me, you're the one who needs a lecture. I have only three words to say: read a romance!"

He walked out, slamming the door behind him.

*Cybil Austin, you are too stupid to live.* Not only did I once again make myself look like an idiot, but had also managed to reinforce his beliefs about marrying again. And from his perspective, I *did* talk to thin air. Oh, damn.

I sat with a thump on the lower step of the

staircase and burst into tears. Dudley thrust his nose under my arm in an attempt to comfort. But not even my faithful companion could help this time. I had just lost the love of my life. I hiccupped and swallowed the last of my tears, then used the hem of my T-shirt to wipe my eyes. Dudley lay at my feet, not moving, but simply looking at me with a worried expression. I patted his head and rose from the step.

Work. I needed to work. If I thought about what an ass I'd been, I'd stay here all day crying. I had no idea how to make amends. Maybe it would come to me through Lord Edgeware and Lady Katrina. Perhaps it was time for the lovers to have one hell of an argument.

****

I typed *The End* and sat back, rubbing my neck and flexing my fingers. Dudley snored at my feet. I envied him. It was two o'clock in the morning and I was exhausted—exhausted, but finished. The words had flowed. I'd banged out the last three chapters in record time with Lady Katrina rescuing Lord Edgeware from the evil duke and his corrupt duchess. They married, had ten children, and lived happily ever after. Somebody should.

I vaguely remember eating lunch and dinner, and talking with Reba, but couldn't recall a damned word I'd said. I yawned. The workmen would arrive in a few hours and I needed to sleep.

I walked through the downstairs turning off lights trying not to think of Max.

Yawning again, I entered the drawing room. My hand reached for the switch when I casually glanced at Henrietta's portrait over the fireplace. Puzzled, I cocked my head to the side. It looked different. Then, my mouth dropped open in astonishment.

The rose held in her hand had turned a very pale, delicate shade of pink.

## Chapter Nineteen

I rose early the next morning to catch Max in the kitchen so we could talk things out, but he never showed. When in doubt—work. I spent the day editing what I'd written the night before. Genevieve claimed I wrote clean and after a few minor changes, I e-mailed the manuscript to her. Max didn't put in an appearance *this* morning either. One of the workmen said something about him being at another site today. I called his cell, getting voice mail, left a message, and hung up heaving a heavy sigh. He was avoiding me. At the moment, I couldn't do much about it.

I spent the morning forcing myself to organize the notes on Hester's story only stopping for a quick sandwich and iced tea at noon. I needed three coherent, tight chapters, and a synopsis for the proposal.

The words and ideas flowed. My pen flew across the pages of my notebook as though possessed. Already I visualized how the chapters would set up. I had whole scenes complete with dialogue spinning in my head. I wrote as if there was no tomorrow, alternating between outlining and scribbling down the basics of those scenes.

I finally ceased, giving my cramped fingers a rest while I read what I'd written. The first chapter had Hester meeting Jonathon. Their first kiss occurred in the third. The conflict between her and her father in the second would give the reader a hint of things to come. It wasn't bad, but now I needed more information.

"Yoo-hoo, Hester. Are you available?"

I waited a few seconds, and then tried again.

"Hester? Please come here for a few minutes. I need to talk to you." I paused. "Hester? Hester, where are you?"

A loud *pop* from in front of the fireplace signaled her appearance. "For pity's sake, give me a few moments. I can't just leap out of sleep and be at your beck and call in an instant. I didn't do that when I was alive and see no reason to start now. What do you want?" she asked, her face set in a frown.

Her pursed lips made me want to grin. I guess even dead people could be cantankerous. Why not, I decided? It was all part of the personality and if nothing else, my ghosts had personalities.

"I'm sorry to interrupt your sleep, but I need some more details about Jonathon. I'm going to do your story first and I—"

"You are? Really? In that case I'll be only too happy to supply anything you want to know." The petulance left her voice and she beamed.

Another loud *pop* signaled the Colonel's arrival.

"Why do Hester first? I have a wonderful war plot."

"Maybe because *my* story is more interesting than you waving a sword around."

"I'll have you know I was involved in very heavy fighting. The battles were packed with action and adventure."

Hester snorted. "My story is that of unresolved love. Cybil writes romance, not adventure, you old fool. Besides, you helped my father send Jonathon away."

"And after you died I told you how sorry I was about that—even though he was a Yankee."

"Ah, look you two, could we get back to—" They ignored me.

Hester's voice rose. "The war had ended and

Jonathon was an honorable man. It was none of your business."

"Excuse me," I said, trying again.

"Of course it was. Your father was afraid you'd be taken in by a smooth-talking soldier."

"Jonathon was not a smooth-talker! He was a gentleman and he loved me!"

"Excuse me!" The argument ceased, and they both jerked their heads toward me. "Thank you. I will need information from each of you. I plan to set the book during the war and just after Lee's surrender. Colonel, I'm sure you can give me valuable details concerning battles. After all, didn't Grant's army come through here on the way to Vicksburg?"

"Yes. He was the worst scoundrel of them all," the Colonel said.

"Well, we'll get to that later. Now Hester, how did you and Jonathon meet?"

She smiled, a dreamy look on her face. "In town. It was the spring of 1866 and I had several errands to run. Money was short, and I had scrimped for weeks in order to buy material for new clothing. The bundle was bulky and hard to handle. I almost dropped it in the muddy street when a voice asked if he could help. I turned around and looked into the handsomest face I'd ever seen. I fell in love with him on the spot."

I wrote as fast as I could while Hester told me more details about Jonathon Ritchie. She supplied a physical description not far off what I'd envisioned.

Hester took a break. I gave the Colonel his turn at the plate with battle scenes.

My mind teemed with romance set amid the drama of war, and while I didn't think I'd give Margaret Mitchell and *Gone With the Wind* any serious competition, I did have expectations of something above average.

During all of this I'd heard several more pops and now all my housemates stood or sat in the drawing room. Each had their own ideas regarding plots.

"When you write about me, make me heroic," Antoine begged. "I've never been heroic. I used to read about great heroes and wished I could have done something similar."

"I don't care what you write about me," Zoë said. "Just make sure I have a handsome lover and pots of money."

"I can't imagine what you'd find about me to put in a book," Ruth commented. "My husband and I lived very ordinary lives and had very boring deaths."

I had to laugh at the enthusiasm. "Don't worry, I'll get around to all of you sooner or later, but for now…"

Reba appeared in the doorway. "Cybil, I'm sorry to interrupt, but your mother has arrived up with a friend."

Damn. I swear my mother has a sixth sense about interrupting me. I was certain she'd come again to browbeat me into returning home. Naturally, I had no intention of doing so.

I heard five distinct pops as I left the room and threw open the door before her hand could lift the knocker.

"Hello, Mother. This is a surprise."

"Hello, Cybil," she replied, leaning forward to brush my cheek with her lips. "How are you, dear?"

The show of affection surprised me. An alarm bell jingled. She seemed much too controlled.

"I'm fine, but I wish you'd called first. I'm very busy today, and really don't have any time to spare."

"But you should take time to relax and smell the roses. Are you going to invite us in?"

I looked over her shoulder at her companion. He

was tall and incredibly slender with thinning brown hair and dark eyes. I knew most of her friends, but had never seen this guy before.

"Yes, of course. Please." I stepped aside. "What brings you down to Shady Oaks?"

"Cybil, this is Julian Brooks, a friend of mine."

"How do you do, Mr. Brooks?"

"A pleasure, Miss Austin," he acknowledged in a deep baritone.

He clutched my hand and his sharp gaze inspected my face giving me an intense once-over. Dropping my eyes, I disengaged my hand from his grasp and led them into the drawing room.

"Would you like some tea?"

I'd be the perfect hostess if it killed me. I'd allow thirty minutes of tea and conversation, then get them the hell out. I had novels to write.

"Yes, tea would be nice," Mother said, sitting gingerly on the edge of the sofa while Mr. Brooks took a seat in a chair.

Reba appeared once again in the doorway. "Reba, would you mind getting us some tea?" She nodded and left.

I looked from one guest to the other. Something was up. Mother fidgeted with her rings, refusing to look me in the eye while her friend sat and stared. Good grief! Could this guy be a *boy*friend? I shot him a quick glance. Awfully scary looking for my discerning mother. He resembled a not-so-friendly scarecrow.

"Mother, why are you here?"

"Can't I just drop by to see my daughter?"

The alarm bell rang louder. Now, I was suspicious. She spoke the words in a much too casual tone, sounding stiff and forced.

"Mother, every time you just drop by it's usually with an ulterior motive—shopping, a party, or something you know I don't like to do. So, what's up?"

"Well, really, Cybil. I'm a little hurt you'd think something like that."

Whoop, whoop! Red alert! Now, she was evasive.

I turned to the man. "Mr. Brooks, have you known my mother long?"

"Actually, we just—"

"We've known each other for several months, dear," Mother cut in smoothly.

"And what is it you do?"

Mr. Brooks cleared his throat, but before he could answer Mother once again interrupted.

"He's a doctor."

Oh, God Almighty! Had she brought him here to meet *me*? A closer look told me he was on the wrong side of fifty. She must be really desperate to marry me off if this was the best she could produce.

"Look, Mother—"

"Cybil, I want you to come home. Now. Today," she blurted.

"We've been through this. I am not leaving my home. I love this house and intend to live here. It inspires me. I've gotten several interesting plots from it already."

"That's interesting, Miss Austin." Dr. Brooks had finally been able to speak a whole sentence without interruption. "Do you feel as though the house is alive? Do you see it as a living entity?"

Was he nuts or something? "No, of course not, although it did seem to talk to me when I first saw it. You know what I mean? It was just a feeling I had that the house and I belonged together."

"H-m-m," he uttered, stroking his chin. "Do you ever feel a sense of overwhelming loneliness or isolation living here? Do you sometimes feel as if you can't cope?"

Who *was* this guy? He personified gloom and doom, reminding me of that old cartoon character my grandfather had loved. I couldn't remember the name, but he'd gone around with a perpetual rain cloud hanging over his head.

"I'm coping just fine, thank you."

Reba chose that moment to bring in the tea. I poured, feeling a bit like Alice at the Mad Hatter's. This was the strangest conversation I'd ever had, including those with the ghosts. I drank quickly. The sooner this ended the better.

"This is very good tea, dear. Cybil, I really am concerned about you. The last time I was here you seemed to be talking to thin air."

"Do you do that often?" Mr. Brooks asked. "Did you have imaginary friends as a child?"

"Uh, yes, I did."

"I see. Usually, as we mature they go away. Do you still have them?"

I'd had it. This guy was creeping me out. I wanted both of them gone. When in doubt, tell the truth.

"They aren't imaginary at all. The house is haunted. I talk to the ghosts."

Mother set her cup down with a clatter. "Oh, no! There, you see? I told you she was delusional," she wailed.

"Miss Austin, your mother is very concerned about you. I understand you're an author. I've written several books and can appreciate the stress of deadlines. Add to it the tension involved with a major move, and the mind can play tricks on you."

Nobody has ever accused me of being quick on the uptake, but now the nickel dropped.

"You're a psychiatrist!" I leaped to my feet. "Mother, how could you? I am perfectly sane. If anyone in this room needs a shrink, it's you!"

"Now, Cybil, calm down. Dr. Brooks runs a lovely little retreat where guests can relax for a while and let their lives return to calmer waters."

Never had Mother's voice sounded so convincing. Luckily, I was furious.

"Out! Out right now!"

Mother wasn't done yet. She reached into her purse and pulled out some papers.

"Cybil, I insist you sign this. You need a vacation and Dr. Brooks' retreat is perfect. You'll have rest, peace and quiet, excellent food, and I'm sure you can even write your little stories."

"Well, not for the first couple of weeks. If progress is made, I see no reason why she can't have access to a computer, but no Internet, I'm afraid," the doctor said.

"Yeah, I guess it would be too bad if I shot off an e-mail to my friends begging to be rescued from the loony bin," I spit out.

"Cybil, sign the papers," Mother demanded.

"Go to hell, and get out of my house!"

"Do not swear at me, young lady. I am your mother!"

The sound of heavy footsteps hurrying down the hall distracted all of us. Max appeared in the doorway closely followed by Reba.

"What's all the yelling about?"

"My mother and this man want to commit me to an asylum!"

"It's a retreat for those who are having mental problems, and it's none of your contractor's business."

"Honey, you're not crazy," Max said, throwing his arm around my shoulders hugging me close to his side.

I felt safe and secure in his presence, bringing my temper down a couple of notches. Thank God he'd shown up.

"We don't like to use the word *crazy*," Dr. Brooks said, also rising.

"Honey? You're contractor calls you 'honey'?

What's going on here? Are you involved with this man?" Mother demanded in a hard tone.

"Mother, I will not discuss my sex life with you or anyone else. Is that clear?"

"Sex? You're having sex with him? Oh, Cybil, how could you? He's not only stealing your money, but using sex to blind you to it. How could you be so stupid!"

Max's spine stiffened. "Mrs. Austin, this isn't the first time you've insinuated I'm a thief. I resent the implications. Your daughter may have a few eccentricities, but I happen to love her."

I swallowed hard and my heart thumped as a sweet gush of warmth swept over me. Oh, my God. Did he mean it or did he just want to shut Mother's mouth? Had he forgiven me for the horrible accusations I'd hurled at him? I didn't dare look at him, half-afraid I'd see the answer on his face.

"Cybil, if you believe this nonsense, then you really are crazy. Doctor, do something!"

"What do you suggest?"

"I demand you commit her. This man will tear her heart out and stomp on it. Then, she'll get depressed and lose the will to live. Not only is she delusional, but she'll end up suicidal as well."

The doctor sighed. "Mrs. Austin, you told me your daughter was having a breakdown and needed immediate care. In my professional opinion, she may have a few delusions, but she is most certainly not suicidal."

Mother screeched, "I said commit her!"

"I can't. She's not a danger to society. And neither can you. She's not a minor."

Mother whirled to face me. "Cybil, sign these papers now."

I snatched them from her hand and tore them into several pieces, then threw them on the floor.

"I think it's time you and the good doctor left,"

Max said firmly.

"I will be back with another, more sensible doctor. You *will* leave this house and you *will* return home."

"No, Mrs. Austin, I don't think so," Reba said quietly from the doorway.

"I beg your pardon? This is none of your business. You're a servant, and I would appreciate it if you and this contractor would leave us alone."

"No, this is my business. I like your daughter and after viewing your family, I'd have to say she's the most mentally stable of everyone," my cook said.

Mother gasped. "How dare you? What do you know about my family anyway?"

"I know enough to say that your daughter Francine is living on the edge. She has four children she can't control, and a disinterested husband who's contemplating leaving her. The pressure of trying to measure up to your standards and those of her older sister is building. Your only son is slipping farther away with every passing month, and Penelope's children are showing signs of psychological problems. Whether Cybil realizes it or not, moving into this house saved her sanity."

Mother stood silent and gaping.

"How do you know all of this?" I asked.

Reba shrugged. "I watch faces and what I saw at the dinner party gave me an enormous sense of sadness. Mrs. Austin, release your grip on your family and let them live their own lives. Doctor, if you talk to anyone, talk to Francine first. She's the closest to blowing."

The front door opened and Daryl's voice called out, "Is anybody home? Cybil?"

*Hail, hail, the gang's all here.* I wanted to giggle, but didn't. Dr. Brooks might think it irrational. God knows, I did.

Daryl and Steve appeared next to Reba. My jaw

dropped at the sight of my Aunt Rose.

"Rose, what are you doing here?" Mother asked.

"Hello, Lilith. I didn't expect to see you here so soon, but I can't say I'm surprised given our conversation last night."

"What conversation? Somebody please tell me what's going on," I said.

"Last night, Lilith told me what she had planned, and I'm afraid we had a rather heated argument. I won't go into the details now, but the upshot is I took a cab to Daryl's and spent the night there. This morning he and Steve very graciously agreed to drive me home where I packed my bags. Do you mind if I stay with you for a while, Cybil? I won't be a bother."

"Of course you can stay, Aunt Rose. Stay as long as you want."

"Well, I should have known you wouldn't show any gratitude for the things I've done for you these last ten years," Mother huffed.

"Done for me? All you've done is bully me and call me stupid."

"May I remind you that I was the only relative willing to take you in after your no-account husband ran off with his secretary? If it hadn't been for me, you'd have ended up pushing a shopping cart down the street."

"Lilith, did it ever occur to you that I might have preferred that? Now, Cybil dear, you haven't signed anything, have you?"

"No."

"Good," Daryl said with a grim expression. "Mother, how could you? You've done some low, manipulative things in your life, but this takes the prize."

"Ahem." Reba coughed gently. "Perhaps Steve and Max will help carry Mrs. Merriweather's bags upstairs while I make up the bed. That will give

Mrs. Austin time to talk privately with her children."

"Yeah, sure," Steve replied. "Come on, Max. The bags are in the car."

"No retreating, Cybil," Aunt Rose admonished.

Max's arm tightened, and he kissed my temple accelerating my heartbeat even further before leaving with the others. After they'd disappeared upstairs, I turned back to Mother.

"Mother, I'm not going to pretend I'm not hurt and furious with what you've done. I spent a lifetime trying to please you, and no matter what I do, it's never right."

"That's because you have an incredible talent for doing the wrong thing," she snapped back.

"No, Cybil has an incredible talent for doing what *she* wants to do. Why can't you be happy that she enjoys this house and being independent? Most mothers would," Daryl said.

"I am not most mothers. I only want what's best for my children and if my children can't find the best route through life, then it's my job to do so."

"Mrs. Austin, why do you feel such a need to control your children's lives?" Dr. Brooks asked.

"Doctor, may I remind you that I brought you here to talk to my daughter? This is not about me."

"Of course, it is, Mother," Daryl said. "It's always been about you."

Mother glared at him before turning on me again.

"Cybil, this is your last chance to give up this house and come home where you belong. In spite of what Dr. Brooks says, I know you have serious mental problems. This asinine insistence that you see ghosts is proof."

"Mrs. Austin, if everybody who claimed to see ghosts or aliens were put away there would be no room left in places like Sunnyvale. It is not necessarily a sign of mental problems," the good doctor theorized.

"Oh, shut up! I'll be back, and won't rest until you do as I want. Ow! Who pinched me," she yelped, whirling and grabbing her arm.

"Nobody pinched you." Daryl had a strange look on his face.

"They most certainly did!" Mother bent over to pick up her purse from the sofa when she stumbled and sat down heavily. "Stop that! Who pushed me?"

I knew. "Mother, maybe you and Dr. Brooks should leave now."

The sculpture on the coffee table levitated a couple of inches, and then skimmed the surface to settle on the opposite side.

I shot a glance at my brother who returned my look with wide eyes. He knew who was responsible, too.

Mother let loose a strangled gasp, her hand at her throat. Dr. Brooks lost his professional cool and gaped. Then he jumped and gasped.

"Someone—something just poked me in the ribs," he said. He looked around as though expecting to find someone hiding behind the sofa.

*So much for delusions.* The candlestick on the mantel danced through the air to land next to the sculpture. A pillow moved from the sofa to a chair.

Mother cried out and rose. She made a grab for the doctor's arm, but missed and stumbled again.

"Quit shoving me! Ow! They're poking me all over! Cybil, make them stop!"

"Okay, everybody, just hold it for a moment," I ordered my friends.

"Amazing," Dr. Brooks said in awed tones. "Miss Austin, do you mind if I bring some colleagues to the house? They're paranormal psychologists and must see this."

"I'm afraid not, Doctor. You'll just have to hope

they believe you."

"Amazing, my ass," Mother blurted, clearly frightened—not so much of the ghosts I suspected, but at not being in control of the situation. "There's nothing amazing about this. It's evil, that's what it is. Cybil, you cannot live in this environment. You'll lose your immortal soul or something. Tomorrow, I will return with an exorcist and clear these unsavory—things—out of this house."

Reba appeared in the doorway. "I wouldn't advise that."

"And why not?" Mother demanded. Her teeth chattered. The room had gone cold.

"It has been my experience with ghosts that they often transfer their energy someplace else. Not all go directly to the other side."

Mother sniffed. "And how would you know?"

"I've studied ghosts, Mrs. Austin, and it's never wise to anger them. In this case, the house belongs to Cybil, and she welcomes their presence. An exorcism wouldn't work in the usual way. No, I'm afraid they would be very angry indeed, and may even decide to move into your house as revenge."

A look of sheer horror crossed Mother's face. Grabbing the doctor's arm, she said, "I think it's time to leave. I'll talk to you later, Cybil. Goodbye, Daryl."

She and the doctor practically ran out the door. A few seconds later we heard them drive away at a fast clip.

Daryl and I looked at Reba, then each other, and began to laugh. I flopped down in a chair holding my sides. I looked at Henrietta's portrait.

My mirth ceased.

The lady gazed back, a flush on her cheeks and smiling with coral tinted lips. Her blue eyes held a hint of laughter, as though she'd enjoyed the past hour.

The rose in her hand was no longer pale, but a vivid red. The distant edges of her dress glowed ice-blue.

She winked.

Chapter Twenty

Daryl finally brought his laughter under control, saying, "I don't know about you, but I can use a drink." He headed for the liquor cabinet. "Do you want something?"

I couldn't tear my eyes away from the portrait.

"Hmm? Oh! No. No, thanks," I said, turning to look at him, and then back at the picture.

He poured a short scotch and also transferred his gaze to Henrietta.

"Nice portrait. Why is she only halfway colored?"

"Actually, that's recent." I gave him the lowdown.

"Nothing about this house surprises me. You've never felt unsafe, have you? You sure there aren't any nasty entities around?"

"My ghosts have been wonderful. Even when they tried to scare me away, they weren't nasty. They save that for people like Mother and Penelope."

He grinned, then sobered and said, "I can't believe the lengths to which Mother will go to get her own way. When Aunt Rose told us what she had planned, I almost exploded. I wanted to give you a heads-up last night, but it was after midnight when she showed up half hysterical. It took hours to calm her down. We didn't figure Mother would move so fast."

"Why is Mother the way she is?" I asked sadly. For better or worse, she was my mother and I loved her. But I never figured out if she loved us or simply had us—like trophies.

My brother shrugged and sipped his scotch. "I

don't know, but somewhere in her life, she must have felt enormous insecurities. She can't let go, afraid we won't love her if she does."

"Mother, insecure?" I tried to come to grips with it. My mother always had control.

"Sure. By controlling and keeping her kids close, she maintains the status quo."

"How do you know this?"

"Before I admitted I was gay, I had a lot of therapy," Daryl confessed, taking another sip of his drink.

"I never knew that."

I hadn't, but should have. He'd spent a lot of unhappy years before making his declaration.

"I didn't advertise it."

The rest of the crowd tromped back downstairs to join us. My eyes flew to Max's face, his gaze holding mine while his lips curled in a gentle smile.

"I take it they finally left," Steve said.

"Yeah," Daryl replied. "I don't think either Mother or the doctor will return any time soon."

"Well, thank goodness for small favors," Aunt Rose declared. "When I found out what she had up her sleeve, I couldn't take her shenanigans any longer. Do you know I actually called her a bitch? Daryl, honey, what is that you're drinking?"

"Scotch, Aunt Rose. Could I pour you a little sherry?"

"No, thank you, dear. A good stiff scotch will do just fine."

I still hadn't disconnected from Max's gaze. We hadn't spoken a word, but I had no trouble reading the message he sent. He had spoken the truth. He loved me.

"Perhaps I should make an early dinner," Reba said. "Why don't we all retire to the kitchen, so Max and Cybil can have a few minutes alone?"

"I think that's a wonderful idea," Daryl

murmured.

"Me, too," Steve answered, tossing me a grin.

My aunt was more practical. "Get me that scotch first."

They trooped out together leaving us alone.

I rose on trembling legs to face him. "Max, I'm so sorry for yesterday. I didn't mean it. You were right. I jumped to conclusions because I was so damned jealous I could barely stand it. The thought of you with another woman sent me off the deep end. Please forgive me."

"I have to admit, I was pretty sore. Took me all day to calm down. I borrowed a buddy's boat down on Sardis and fished. Kept telling myself you weren't worth the trouble. I tossed and turned all night, but couldn't get you out of my mind. This morning I finally realized you were worth everything."

I had to hear the words. "Did you mean it? Do you love me?"

"From the top of your head to the tips of those pink toenails. I was attracted the first day we met. I've never spent so much time on one single renovation in my life. I showed up every day just to see you." An anxious look crossed his face. "You do love me, too, don't you?"

I threw myself into his arms and held him close. "Of course, I do. You made my heart go pitty-pat that first day, too, and I admitted to myself how I felt after our first date. Your kiss sent me into another dimension—not to mention down the steps."

He laughed. "Like this?"

He tightened his arms and seared my lips with one of those incredible kisses. *Yep. Just like that.* I curled my leg around his.

If hearts could sing, mine did it, the heavy thudding keeping time to the music. His heart pounded against my chest.

When we came up for air, he rested his forehead

on mine, and whispered, "I love you, Cybil Austin. You're a little bit crazy, but that's part of your charm. I want to spend the rest of my life with you here at Shady Oaks raising our kids and being happy. Will you marry me?"

My breath stopped, my heart hammered, and my eyes filled with tears. He'd just spoken the words every woman wanted to hear—me included. I kissed the dimple in his chin.

"What about financial independence before taking on other responsibilities?" I took a chance here.

"A silly excuse. I spent the morning at my parents'. Mother knew how I felt when I brought you to dinner. She told me to quit putting up barriers. Said love, marriage, and family may be responsibilities, but they're the kind of responsibilities that bring joy with the right person. She never liked Clarissa. Told me up front the woman wasn't for me. She was right, too. A man should always listen to his mother. Hell, I even bought *The Lord and the Lady.*"

"You bought one of my books? Did you read it?"

"Cover to cover. I have to admit, the dueling and fight scenes were damned good. They talk funny and I'm still not sure about the romance, but give me time. I'm trainable."

"And the fear? About marriage again, I mean."

"You were right. Love and trust are the keystones of any relationship. I love you and I trust you. A part of me is still afraid of failing, but I can't live life based on fear. I'd rather face the fear head-on and conquer it."

His admission necessitated another sizzling kiss. By the time it ended, we both breathed heavily. I tried to think of a way to get upstairs without the other people in the house knowing.

"I also told Mother about our argument and she

said women in love often do stranger things than men in love. And as for the eccentricity, Mom pointed out you wouldn't be the first in our family. Her Uncle Harry lines his caps and hats with aluminum foil so aliens can't steal his thoughts, and my father has a cousin who insists she was the mistress of a pharaoh."

I laughed. "I've got a few of those, too."

"What well-bred Southern family doesn't? You know, you still haven't said yes."

I leaped into his arms again. "Yes, yes, yes!"

He twirled me around. "Thank goodness. I'd hate to have to return this." He set me back on the floor and pulled a small black velvet box from his pocket and handed it to me.

I opened it with trembling fingers and gazed upon the most gorgeous diamond solitaire I'd ever seen. Simple and elegant, I couldn't believe it belonged to me. My eyes welled, and then overflowed.

"Oh, Max, It's the most beautiful..." I couldn't finish.

He removed it from where it nestled and slipped it on my finger, sealing it in place with a kiss.

"After I left Mom's, I made a little stop at Cartland's Jewelry on Main Street. If it doesn't fit, we'll take it in later to get it sized."

"No need. It's perfect." Naturally, I had to thank him, so we kissed some more before until the need for oxygen called a halt.

I leaned my head on his shoulder and admired the way the light refracted off the diamond. I could hardly wait to be Mrs. Max Maitland. Then I remembered something from that first day.

"Max, can I ask you a personal question?"

"Anything."

"What does the 'C' stand for in your name?"

He stepped back and gave me an *oops, I'm*

*caught* look.

"I was named after one of my great-grandfathers. It was a ceremonial type of thing and nobody in the family ever used anything except Max."

I stared. "As your fiancée, don't I have a right to know the full name of the man I'm marrying?"

"All right. The 'C' stands for..." He hesitated, clearly not wanting to divulge the information, then blurted in a rush, "It stands for Cornelius."

I felt my lips twitch and tried not to laugh, but didn't succeed. After a couple of seconds, he laughed, too.

"Cornelius Maxwell Maitland? I'm sorry. I don't mean to make fun of your name. You know, it does sound distinguished. If you ever run for political office, it might not look bad on the ballot."

"I have no intention of running for anything, except maybe father of the year some day."

I laid my hand on his cheek and whispered, "That can be arranged."

"God, I love you. How did I get so lucky to find someone as beautiful as you?"

A gush of warmth spread out from the pit of my stomach. "I'm not beautiful. My nose is too big and my chin too pointed."

"And don't ever change them. I like them just the way they are."

In the throes of love and almost marriage, I decided now was the time to tell him about my housemates.

"Max, there's something I've been wanting to tell you."

"What's that?"

"Remember our practical joker?"

"Who could forget?"

"Well, it wasn't really a practical joker. I'm not alone in this house. I have several very active ghosts. That's why I seemed to talk to thin air every once in a while."

The smile left his face as he placed his hands on my shoulders.

"Ghosts? How do you figure that?"

"All those things that happened when we first started renovations were the ghosts trying to scare me off."

His hands tightened. "Cybil, honey, this is an old house. It creaks, it groans, and the wind finds every crack. Plus, you're a writer with a highly developed imagination. There's no such thing as ghosts."

"Oh, but there are! They were also responsible for what happened at my dinner party."

A look of concern crossed his face. "Sweetheart, it's been a rather long last couple of months for you. Moving, the mess, and the noise have been an awful strain. Add in our relationship and it's not surprising you imagine things. Why don't we go down to Biloxi or over to Pensacola and just vegetate on the beach for a week or so. Don't worry about Dudley. Mom and Dad will take care of him."

I pulled back a step. This was not the reaction I'd envisioned. "But, darling, it's true."

He started to pull me back into his arms when I heard five pops. Over his shoulder my ghosts stood in front of the fireplace.

"What was that?" Max asked.

Oh, my God. If he heard the pops, then that meant...

Max turned. His reaction fell somewhere between stunned and comical. He sucked in a huge breath, while his eyes bugged out and his jaw dropped.

"Uh, Max, honey, I'd like you to meet the past residents of Shady Oaks."

"Those—ghosts—good Lord..."

I guess for a man like Max, so practical and down to earth, seeing ghosts for the first time could rob him of speech. Inarticulate sounds were better than fainting, however.

"You'd better sit down, dear." I pushed him onto the sofa heading for the liquor cabinet where I poured a glass of scotch. I brought the bottle with me. He was going to need it. I returned to his side and grabbed his limp hand, screwing the glass into it. "There you go. Drink up."

He obeyed, slugging it down in a single swallow.

Taking the lead, Ruth stepped forward. "Hello, Max. My name is Ruth LaForge. Welcome to the family. I hope you don't mind, Cybil, but we eavesdropped on his proposal."

"No harm done. Wasn't it romantic?"

"Very romantic. I'm Zoë LaForge, Max."

Max handed me his glass. I refilled it. He gulped again, struggling to deal with what floated in front of him.

"They're—I mean—Good God, they're ghosts!" He stammered and drank. I took pity on him, filling it again.

"Yes, dear." I kissed his cheek.

"My God. I guess you don't need a vacation after all."

He still kind of babbled, but I understood.

"Let me finish the introductions. This gentleman is Colonel George Washington LaForge and this is Antoine LaForge. The lady on the end is Hester LaForge. I'll bring you up to date on when they lived and died later."

"Glad to see Cybil's going to have a man around the house," the Colonel said. "A woman needs a man. See you take good care of her."

"Ah, yeah. Sure. Good care. I promise."

He stared at the apparitions with a dazed expression, but whether from shock or the scotch I didn't know.

"My heartfelt congratulations," Antoine told us. "I know you're going to be very happy."

"Thank you. I'm sure we will." Max took another drink.

Hester stepped forward. "I'm blunt and speak my mind. If you ever cause Cybil to cry, you'll have to answer to me, young man. Is that clear?"

"Absolutely." The scotch helped him to a fast recovery. He shot a glance at me and smiled. "I promise never to make her cry, except with joy."

"Hear, hear," the Colonel replied.

"I think we should leave the two of them alone now," Ruth said. "I'm sure they need to discuss us."

My—soon to be our—housemates said goodbye and popped out of sight.

"I wasn't hallucinating, was I?"

I shook my head. "Nope."

"Holy shit. Who'd have believed it?"

"You didn't. You don't mind, do you? In time, you'll come to love them like I do. We have ground rules regarding when and where they can materialize."

"I should hope so." He chuckled. "That night after dinner when we were in the kitchen..."

I nodded. "Yep. It was Antoine. He was curious about courtship and just didn't think."

"I'm still not sure I believe what I saw. Who else knows about them?"

"Well, Daryl, Steve, and Julie found out last week. Reba knew before I did. And Dudley, of course. He and Zoë are great pals."

"Don't forget Dr. Brooks and your mother. They must suspect something."

"They don't count. There's more to tell, but I'll save it for later. Right now, I want to I want to shout it from the rooftop that I am going to be a bride!"

\*\*\*\*

The impromptu dinner and engagement party was in full swing. We'd sprung our news in the kitchen and instantly been smothered with hugs and good wishes. After eating, the celebration moved into the drawing room where the liquor flowed and the laughter continued nonstop. Daryl saw to that with constant anecdotes about my childhood escapades. I told Max not to laugh too hard. His time would come.

Reba joined us, which brought up a question that had been bugging me for a while. I cast a glance toward the sofa. Aunt Rose was wedged in a corner, snoring softly, out cold.

"Reba, how is it you know so much about us? And how come you can see...ah...everyone."

"I'm a psychic. A rather sensitive one, too. I often see the dead, and can sense when someone's in need of help. That's how I found you, Cybil. I was vacuuming one day when suddenly a voice in my head told me the new owner of Shady Oaks needed a cook and a friend. The next morning Reuben Hollister gave me a lift to the foot of the drive, and here I am."

"A voice in your head?" If she'd told me that two or three weeks ago, I'd have wondered about my cook's mental health. Now, it seemed like a natural occurrence.

"Yes. A male voice. On the elderly side. He said something about you needing help with more than just the house, and how he couldn't do it."

I gazed at Daryl. "Grandfather Austin," we said simultaneously.

"It's very possible," Reba replied. "The minute I saw your family, I knew what the voice meant. Reading them was really quite easy."

"No wonder my ghosts were scared of you."

"The ghosts were scared of Reba?" Max said.

"Oh, yes," she answered. "They'd never come up

against a person like me who could see their presence without them revealing themselves." Reba waved a hand. "But that's been resolved now. They understand I mean them no harm."

Max hugged me. "Maybe you don't need me after all."

"Oh, no, you don't, Max Maitland. You've proposed and I've accepted. You're stuck with me."

Daryl grinned. "Looks like you have no wiggle room, buddy."

Max laughed and kissed the top of my head. "With the ghosts and Reba, what's my job?"

"I'll come up with something," I replied.

"You won't be needing me," my cook said.

"Of course I will. You can't leave. I still don't know how to make chicken fricassee."

She smiled, and then laughed. "I'll be happy to stay for a while. But you're a new woman."

"Reba's right," Max said. "You're independent, and while you'll always compromise, you won't do so just to keep the peace. You'll do it on your terms. I think we'll have a lively marriage," Max said, giving me a kiss.

I sighed, happy beyond belief. Max loved me and I loved Max. Life was wonderful.

****

My ghosts had tactfully retired for the evening, and now only the living remained.

"Cybil, I'm tempted to come and live here. You throw the damnedest parties," Steve said.

"He's right, sis. I hope you've kept a journal of what's happened over the last couple of months, because it would make one hell of a book. Max, did she tell you about the Sunday dinner?"

"More or less. I take it the ghosts were responsible for what happened."

Daryl and Steve filled Max in on details of that day while I thought about what my brother had said.

318

No, I hadn't been keeping a journal, but would have no problem remembering all that had occurred. Every incident had been a prod in the rear end toward my goal of living my own life.

I wondered what would have happened if Julie and I had turned around earlier or farther on down the road. Would I have eventually caved in to Mother and become a miniature Lilith? Would I have simply found another house—one that may or may not have talked to me? Or had Shady Oaks and its otherworld inhabitants been unknowingly, but patiently, waiting all these years just for me?

I guess I'd never know if it had all been part of a grand design. I did know, however, that finding Shady Oaks had led me to Max. That was the best change of all. I'd fallen deeply in love and had no trouble visualizing the future.

A small scene flitted through my mind in which I saw family, friends, and children cavorting on the side lawn beneath those magnificent live oaks. Max barbequed over a huge open pit. Laughter and conversation echoed in the air. The fact we were all dressed in mid-nineteenth century clothing didn't faze me at all. For a brief moment I wondered if, perhaps, I was remembering. Now wouldn't *that* be a kick in the pants?

A rather loud hiccup brought my thoughts back into the room. Aunt Rose opened her eyes, and then blinked like an owl.

"'Scuse me," she muttered.

"Maybe we should all call it a night," Daryl suggested.

Everyone echoed the sentiment. He and Steve helped a wobbly Aunt Rose upstairs, while Max and I took the glasses out to the kitchen.

I had just dumped them in the sink when a sexy voice growled in my ear. "Come here, woman."

Max then proceeded to lay one of those out-of-this-world kisses on me. Finished turning my insides into mush and my knees into rubber, he held me close. We laughed at the craziness of our relationship. I confessed as to why I had fallen over a roll of roofing material and why I had been so absent-minded concerning the bacon.

"You must have thought me an awful klutz."

He chuckled. "Not at all. I thought you looked kind of cute lying on the ground. It was the first time I admitted I wanted to ask you out. And as for the fire, well, I had a hard time keeping my eyes off your foam-covered boobs in that skimpy tank top."

I kissed him and passion rose taking on serious let's-make-love overtones.

We walked hand in hand through the house, turning off lights as we went. I paused for a moment in the drawing room and drew a deep breath.

"You know, I love this house almost as much as I love you. I feel like a LaForge."

Max held me in his arms. "Just remember, soon you'll become a Maitland."

"I can hardly wait."

I reached for the switch on the lamp and glanced up at Henrietta. She smiled, her eyes as blue as a summer sky.

The portrait bloomed with vibrant, living colors.

Epilogue

It's amazing how fast time can slip away. Antoine once told me he missed the sense of time the most. I understand now. The last three years have flown by.

We married under the oak trees, the only possible place to hold the ceremony. If I do say so myself, I looked gorgeous. My dress was a simple strapless white sheath with little adornment. I wore no veil, but twined spring flowers in my upswept hair and carried a huge bouquet of red roses. I'm sure Henrietta approved. I looked like a bride and felt like a princess.

Mother attended. She had to; my sisters were in the wedding party. Julie stood next to me as matron of honor. Most of the guests saw three attendants walk down the aisle, but those of us in the know also watched Ruth, Hester, and Zoë march between the living. The Colonel and Antoine hovered near Max.

At one point in the ceremony, Julie turned to wink at Zoë standing next to her. Unfortunately, the organist thought it was meant for him and winked back. Oh, well. She'd learn.

It was during the reception that Antoine dropped his bomb on us. I found him deep in conversation with Daryl and Steve in the drawing room.

"Who are you hiding from? Mother?"

Daryl laughed, and then sobered. "No, but Antoine has something to tell you."

I sipped my champagne. "Oh? What?"

He smiled, cast a glance at my brother and

Steve, and then plunged in.

"Cybil, do you remember me telling you how I never felt like I belonged? Well, I've figured out why. I'm like Daryl and Steve. I'm—what do you call it—gay."

I stopped in mid-sip. "What?"

"It's true. I just never realized it before, but after seeing and talking to them, I finally understood." He paused and inhaled a deep breath. "So, when they leave for Memphis, I'm going with them. I want to experience the life I should have led."

I tossed the champagne down my throat in one giant gulp. "I didn't know ghosts could be gay."

Steve laughed. "We didn't either, but I guess anything's possible. Doesn't it just figure you'd have a gay ghost?"

I had to laugh with him. "All right, but promise me you'll come to Sunday dinner once a month. I want to hear all about this. And if the two of you don't write a screenplay about two gay men living with a gay ghost in the heart of the South, I will!"

When we returned from our honeymoon, I was one ghost short.

Mother has mellowed. She hasn't done an about-face, but accepts Max and is trying to accept me as my own person.

"She's even made overtures to Steve and me," Daryl said at one of those Sunday dinners.

"Actually invited both of us to dinner a couple of weeks ago," Steve added. "I'll give her this, she tried."

"She comes down here occasionally, but keeps her eyes open and her opinions to herself. Never know when those pesky ghosts will appear," I told them with a laugh.

Daryl looked around the dining room. "Max, I've got to say, the house and grounds look spectacular.

You did one helluva job."

Max grinned and forked more pot roast onto his plate. "Thanks. According to the Colonel and Hester, it looks like it did in their lifetimes. I'm glad I could make them feel at home."

"We love the place. It's a happy house." I sipped from my wine glass. "It took a while, but I finally figured out the correlation between our housemates and my life before Shady Oaks. Ruth represents the mother I wish I'd had. She listens, gives good advice, and never criticizes.

"The Colonel reminds me so much of Grandfather Austin, I sometimes wonder if it really is him. And whenever I'm tempted to give in to others, Hester is there telling me to stay strong. And then there's Zoë. She's as close to me as Julie. Did I tell you Julie organized a trip to the Wolf Chase Mall for the three of us?"

Steve and Daryl both broke into laughter.

"You're kidding. What was the reaction," my brother asked.

"It boggled her mind at first, but then she got right into the swing of things. Drained all her energy, so we commandeered a wheelchair and wheeled her to the car."

"I can just see the two of you pushing an empty wheelchair through the mall and into the parking lot," Steve said, chuckling.

"It was a sight to behold."

It's a shame Zoë is dead, because she's embraced the modern era with enthusiasm. She loves the computer and I set up her, the Colonel, and Hester with e-mail and accounts on a social networking site. They spend the nighttime hours online with the living that haven't a clue about certain technicalities. Even the Colonel dabbles in chat rooms with war buffs. I think he misses Antoine.

A few weeks ago I carried three items into the

kitchen where they argued over the computer.

"And I tell you I must be in my chat room. I'm supposed to discuss the Battle of Atlanta with Alwaysarebel at midnight," the Colonel declared.

"And Zoë and I are set to discuss fashion through the years with Fashionista and someone calling herself Knickersinaknot. You were babbling about Chickamauga for hours last night," Hester retorted.

"Am I interrupting?" I asked as I entered.

"Not at all," Zoë answered. "As you can see, we're just agreeing to disagree."

"Well, maybe this will help." I set the items on the table. "Zoë, the red one is yours. Hester, you take the purple, and Colonel, you get the blue."

"What are they?" he asked.

"The newest in technology. It's a mini-computer called a Netbook. Now each of you can surf the Web and chat at the same time. They're all set up and ready to go. Have fun."

I left with their thanks ringing in my ears.

Reba is still with us, but not on a daily basis. I can cook now, but as a joke, whenever I slap bacon in a pan, Max casually sits a fire extinguisher on the counter—just in case. I pretend to get mad. That way he has to kiss me in apology.

A few months ago, I initiated a search of old army records in the hopes of discovering what had happened to Hester's Jonathon. Still a work in progress, I'm convinced the answers will come to light.

As for my career, it's going great. The last Lord Edgeware book was nominated for a Rita—the highest award possible for published authors from The Romance Writers of America. It didn't win, but Hester's story did the following year. My latest novel, based on Zoë's life with a *happy* ending, will hit the bookstores just in time for Christmas.

Max turned out to be very trainable. He now reads romance, especially the historicals with sword fights and duels, and westerns with manly-type cowboys. He also reads my novels, giving great constructive criticism. And I'm not ashamed to say my husband has even suggested a few interesting plot lines for potential books.

Aunt Rose still lives with us. The ghosts finally appeared for her, and I was surprised at how easily she accepted the whole thing. She and Ruth have become close friends. They knit and sit chattering like magpies for hours on end. Lately, they've been busy knitting baby clothes. Well, Aunt Rose knits baby clothes. Yes, Max and I are expecting our first child in March. Max is so excited he's ready to burst.

Even Mother went into full grandmother mode when she heard the news.

"Now Cybil, don't do a thing. I'll handle it all for you. Let's see, we'll need a baby shower. I'll rent that darling little B & B in town. Have you planned a theme for the nursery yet? Oh no, of course you haven't. Well, don't worry, I'll come down soon and do it."

I was polite and listened, but Aunt Rose, Ruth, Hester, and Zoë have it covered. The living and the dead insist on doing all the work.

I never thought I could be this happy. Max is not perfect, thank God, and even a simple argument gets resolved in the most satisfying way—if you get my drift.

The other night I sat curled up on his lap. "I have this terrific new idea for a book. Here's my pitch. It's all about this author who in order to escape a domineering mother, buys and renovates a dilapidated old house, which just happens to be haunted by a covey of friendly ghosts, all the while falling in love with her contractor."

Max grinned and kissed my nose. "Sounds like a

winner to me."
    But then again, I don't know.
    Maybe it sounds too far-fetched.
    You think?

## A word about the author...

Suzanne was born and raised in Indiana but has had the pleasure of living in several states during her adult life. She attended Ball State University where she majored in History, and confesses to being the only student in the dorm who actually enjoyed writing term papers. She has two grown sons and is blessed with five grandchildren, three boys and two girls.

Currently, Suzanne and her husband live in Ft. Lauderdale, Florida, taking advantage of year-round warm weather, the beach, and sailing. She's a member of Mystery Writers of America, Romance Writers of America, River City Romance Writers, and Florida Romance Writers, where she sat on the board and co-chaired the 2007 Fun in the Sun Conference. Suzanne loves to read almost as much as she loves writing and can't wait to share her fantasies with readers.